T0144698

Kate Bonnet

Kate Bonnet

The Romance of a Pirate's Daughter

Frank R. Stockton

MINT EDITIONS

Kate Bonnet: The Romance of a Pirate's Daughter was first published in 1902.

This edition published by Mint Editions 2021.

ISBN 9781513277578 | E-ISBN 9781513277981

Published by Mint Editions®

MINT
EDITIONS

minteditionbooks.com

Publishing Director: Jennifer Newens
Design & Production: Rachel Lopez Metzger
Project Manager: Micaela Clark
Typesetting: Westchester Publishing Services

Contents

I

Two Young People, a Ship, and a Fish

The month was September and the place was in the neighbourhood
of Bridgetown, in the island of Barbadoes. The seventeenth century
was not seventeen years old, but the girl who walked slowly down to the
river bank was three years its senior. She carried a fishing-rod and line,
and her name was Kate Bonnet. She was a bright-faced, quick-moving
young person, and apparently did not expect to catch many fish, for she
had no basket in which to carry away her finny prizes. Nor, apparently,
did she have any bait, except that which was upon her hook and which
had been affixed there by one of the servants at her home, not far away. In
fact, Mistress Kate was too nicely dressed and her gloves were too clean
to have much to do with fish or bait, but she seated herself on a little rock
in a shady spot not far from the water and threw forth her line. Then she
gazed about her; a little up the river and a good deal down the river.

It was truly a pleasant scene which lay before her eyes. Not half a
mile away was the bridge which gave this English settlement its name,
and beyond the river were woods and cultivated fields, with here and
there a little bit of smoke, for it was growing late in the afternoon,
when smoke meant supper. Beyond all this the land rose from the lower
ground near the river and the sea, in terrace after terrace, until the upper
stretches of its woodlands showed clear against the evening sky.

But Mistress Kate Bonnet now gazed steadily down the stream,
beyond the town and the bridge, and paid no more attention to the
scenery than the scenery did to her, although one was quite as beautiful
as the other.

There was a bunch of white flowers in the hat of the young girl; not
a very large one, and not a very small one, but of such a size as might be
easily seen from the bridge, had any one happened to be crossing about
that time. And, in fact, as the wearer of the hat and the white flowers
still continued to gaze at the bridge, she saw some one come out upon it
with a quick, buoyant step, and then she saw him stop and gaze steadily
up the river. At this she turned her head, and her eyes went out over
the beautiful landscape and the wide terraces rising above each other
towards the sky.

It is astonishing how soon after this a young man, dressed in a brown suit, and very pleasant to look upon, came rapidly walking along the river bank. This was Master Martin Newcombe, a young Englishman, not two years from his native land, and now a prosperous farmer on the other side of the river.

It often happened that Master Newcombe, at the close of his agricultural labours, would put on a good suit of clothes and ride over the bridge to the town, to attend to business or to social duties, as the case might be. But, sometimes, not willing to encumber himself with a horse, he walked over the bridge and strolled or hurried along the river bank. This was one of the times in which he hurried. He had been caught by the vision of the bunch of white flowers in the hat of the girl who was seated on the rock in the shade.

As Master Newcombe stepped near, his spirits rose, as they had not always risen, as he approached Mistress Kate, for he perceived that, although she held the handle of her rod in her hand, the other end of it was lying on the ground, not very far away from the bait and the hook which, it was very plain, had not been in the water at all. She must have been thinking of something else besides fishing, he thought. But he did not dare to go on with that sort of thinking in the way he would have liked to do it. He had not too great a belief in himself, though he was very much in love with Kate Bonnet.

"Is this the best time of day for fishing, Master Newcombe?" she said, without rising or offering him her hand. "For my part, I don't believe it is."

He smiled as he threw his hat upon the ground. "Let me put your line a little farther out." And so saying, he took the rod from her hand and stepped between her and the bait, which must have been now quite hot from lying so long in a bit of sunshine. He rearranged the bait and threw the line far out into the river. Then he gave her the rod again. He seated himself on the ground near-by.

"This is the second time I have been over the bridge to-day," he said, "and this morning, very early, I saw, for the first time, your father's ship, which was lying below the town. It is a fine vessel, so far as I can judge, being a landsman."

"Yes," said she, "and I have been on board of her and have gone all over her, and have seen many things which are queer and strange to me. But the strangest thing about her, to my mind, being a landswoman, is, that she should belong to my father. There are many things which he has not, which it would be easy to believe he would like to have, but that a ship, with sails and anchors and hatchways, should be one of these things, it is hard to imagine."

Young Newcombe thought it was impossible to imagine, but he expressed himself discreetly.

"It must be that he is going to engage in trade," he said; "has he not told you of his intentions?"

"Not much," said she. "He says he is going to cruise about among the islands, and when I asked him if he would take me, he laughed, and answered that he might do so, but that I must never say a word of it to Madam Bonnet, for if she heard of it she might change his plans."

The wicked young man found himself almost wishing that the somewhat bad-tempered Madam Bonnet might hear of and change any plan which might take her husband's daughter from this town, especially in a vessel; for vessels were always terribly tardy when any one was waiting for their return. And, besides, it often happened that vessels never came back at all.

"I shall take a little trip with him even if we don't go far; it would be ridiculous for my father to own a ship, and for me never to sail in her."

"That would not be so bad," said Master Martin, feeling that a short absence might be endured. Moreover, if a little pleasure trip were to be made, it was reasonable enough to suppose that other people, not belonging to the Bonnet family, might be asked to sail as guests.

"What my father expects to trade in," said she contemplatively gazing before her, "I am sure I do not know. It cannot be horses or cattle, for he has not enough of them to make such a venture profitable. And as to sugar-cane, or anything from his farm, I am sure he has a good enough market here for all he has to sell. Certainly he does not produce enough to make it necessary for him to buy a ship in order to carry them away."

"It is opined," said Martin, "by the people of the town, that Major Bonnet intends to become a commercial man, and to carry away to the other islands, and perhaps to the old country itself, the goods of other people."

"Now that would be fine!" said Mistress Kate, her eyes sparkling, "for I should then surely go with him, and would see the world, and perhaps London." And her face flushed with the prospect.

Martin's face did not flush. "But if your father's ship sailed on a long voyage," he said, with a suspicion of apprehension, "he would not sail with her; he would send her under the charge of others."

The girl shook her head. "When she sails," said she, "he sails in her. If you had heard him talking as I have heard him, you would not doubt that. And if he sails, I sail."

Martin's soul grew quite sad. There were very good reasons to believe that this dear girl might sail away from Bridgetown, and from him. She might come back to the town, but she might not come back to him.

"Mistress Kate," said he, looking very earnestly at her, "do you know that such speech as this makes my heart sink? You know I love you, I have told you so before. If you were to sail away, I care not to what port, this world would be a black place for me."

"That is like a lover," she exclaimed a little pertly; "it is like them all, every man of them. They must have what they want, and they must have it, no matter who else may suffer."

He rose and stood by her.

"But I don't want you to suffer," he said. "Do you think it would be suffering to live with one who loved you, who would spend his whole life in making you happy, who would look upon you as the chief thing in the world, and have no other ambition than to make himself worthy of you?"

She looked up at him with a little smile.

"That would, doubtless, be all very pleasant for you," she said, "and in order that you might be pleased, you would have her give up so much. That is the way with men! Now, here am I, born in the very end of the last century, and having had, consequently, no good out of that, and with but seventeen years in this century, and most of it passed in girlhood and in school; and now, when the world might open before me for a little, here you come along and tell me all that you would like to have, and that you would like me to give up."

"But you should not think," said he, and that was all he said, for at that moment Kate Bonnet felt a little jerk at the end of her line, and then a good strong pull.

"I have a fish!" she cried, and sprang to her feet. Then, with a swoop, she threw into the midst of the weeds and wild flowers a struggling fish which Martin hastened to take from the hook.

"A fine fellow!" he cried, "and he has arrived just in time to make a dainty dish for your supper."

"Ah, no!" she said, winding the line about her rod; "if I were to take that fish to the house, it would surely disturb Madam Bonnet. She would object to my catching it; she would object to having it prepared for the table; she would object to having it eaten, when she had arranged that we should eat something else. No, I will give it to you, Master Newcombe; I suppose in your house you can cook and eat what you please."

"Yes," said he; "but how delightful it would be if we could eat it together."

"Meaning," said she, "that I should never eat other fish than those from this river. No, sir; that may not be. I have a notion that the first foreign fish I shall eat will be found in the island of Jamaica, for my father said, that possibly he might first take a trip there, where lives my mother's brother, whom we have not seen for a long time. But, as I told you before, nobody must know this. And now I must go to my supper, and you must take yours home with you."

"And I am sure it will be the sweetest fish," he said, "that was ever caught in all these waters. But I beg, before you go, you will promise me one thing."

"Promise you!" said she, quite loftily.

"Yes," he answered; "tell me that, no matter where you go, you will not leave Bridgetown without letting me know of it?"

"I will not, indeed," said she; "and if it is to Jamaica we go, perhaps my father—but no, I don't believe he will do that. He will be too much wrapped up in his ship to want for company to whom he must attend and talk."

"Ah! there would be no need of that!" said Newcombe, with a lover's smile.

She smiled back at him.

"Good-night!" she said, "and see to it that you eat your fish to-night while it is so fresh." Then she ran up the winding path to her home.

He stood and looked after her until she had disappeared among the shrubbery, after which he walked away.

"I should have said more than I did," he reflected; "seldom have I had so good a chance to speak and urge my case. It was that confounded ship. Her mind is all for that and not for me."

II

A Fruit-basket and a Friend

Major Stede Bonnet, the father of Kate, whose mother had died when the child was but a year old, was a middle-aged Englishman of a fair estate, in the island of Barbadoes. He had been an officer in the army, was well educated and intelligent, and now, in vigorous middle life, had become a confirmed country gentleman. His herds and his crops were, to him, the principal things on earth, with the exception of his daughter; for, although he had married for the second time, there were a good many things which he valued more than his wife. And it had therefore occasioned a good deal of surprise, and more or less small talk among his neighbours, that Major Bonnet should want to buy a ship. But he had been a soldier in his youth, and soldiers are very apt to change their manner of living, and so, if Major Bonnet had grown tired of his farm and had determined to go into commercial enterprises, it was not, perhaps, a very amazing thing that a military man who had turned planter should now turn to be something else.

Madam Bonnet had heard of the ship, although she had not been told anything about her step-daughter taking a trip in her, and if she had heard she might not have objected. She had regarded, in an apparently careless manner, her husband's desire to navigate the sea; for, no matter to what point he might happen to sail, his ship would take him away from Barbadoes, and that would very well suit her. She was getting tired of Major Bonnet. She did not believe he had ever been a very good soldier; she was positively sure that he was not a good farmer; and she had the strongest kind of doubt as to his ability as a commercial man. But as this new business would free her from him, at least for a time, she was well content; and, although she should feel herself somewhat handicapped by the presence of Kate, she did not intend to allow that young lady to interfere with her plans and purposes during the absence of the head of the house. So she went her way, saying nothing derisive about the nautical life, except what she considered it necessary for her to do, in order to maintain her superior position in the household.

Major Bonnet was now very much engaged and a good deal disturbed, for he found that projected sailing, even in one's own craft, is not always smooth sailing. He was putting his vessel in excellent order, and was fitting her out generously in the way of stores and all manner of nautical needfuls, not forgetting the guns necessary for defence in these somewhat disordered times, and his latest endeavours were towards the shipping of a suitable crew. Seafaring men were not scarce in the port of Bridgetown, but Major Bonnet, now entitled to be called "Captain," was very particular about his crew, and it took him a long time to collect suitable men.

As he was most truly a landsman, knowing nothing about the sea or the various intricate methods of navigating a vessel thereupon, he was compelled to secure a real captain—one who would be able to take charge of the vessel and crew, and who would do, and have done, in a thoroughly seamanlike manner, what his nominal skipper should desire and ordain.

This absolutely necessary personage had been secured almost as soon as the vessel had been purchased, before any of the rest of the crew had signed ship's articles; and it was under his general supervision that the storing and equipment had been carried on. His name was Sam Loftus. He was a big man with a great readiness of speech. There were, perhaps, some things he could not do, but there seemed to be nothing that he was not able to talk about. As has been said, the rest of the crew came in slowly, but they did come, and Major Bonnet told his daughter that when he had secured four more men, it was his intention to leave port.

"And sail for Jamaica?" she exclaimed.

"Oh, yes," he said, with an affectionate smile, "and I will leave you with your Uncle Delaplaine, where you can stay while I make some little cruises here and there."

"And so I am really to go?" she exclaimed, her eyes sparkling.

"Really to go," said he.

"And what may I pack up?" she asked, thinking of her step-mother.

"Not much," he said, "not much. We will be able to find at Spanish Town something braver in the way of apparel than anything you now possess. It will be some days before we sail, and I shall have quietly conveyed on board such belongings as you need."

She was very happy, and she laughed.

"Yours will be an easily laden ship," said she, "for you take in with you no great store of goods for traffic. But I suppose you design to pick up your cargo among the islands where you cruise, and at a less cost, perchance, than it could be procured here?"

"Yes, yes," he said; "you have hit it fairly, my little girl, you have hit it fairly."

New annoyances now began to beset Major Bonnet. What his daughter had remarked in pleasantry, the people of the town began to talk about unpleasantly. Here was a good-sized craft about to set sail, with little or no cargo, but with a crew apparently much larger than her requirements, but not yet large enough for the desires of her owner. To be sure, as Major Bonnet did not know anything about ships, he was bound to do something odd when he bought one and set forth to sail upon her, but there were some odd things which ought to be looked into; and there were people who advised that the attention of the colonial authorities should be drawn to this ship of their farmer townsman. Major Bonnet had such a high reputation as a good citizen, that there were few people who thought it worth while to trouble themselves about his new business venture, but a good many disagreeable things came to the ears of Sam Loftus, who reported them to his employer, and it was agreed between them that it would be wise for them to sail as soon as they could, even if they did not wait for the few men they had considered to be needed.

Early upon a cloudy afternoon, Major Bonnet and his daughter went out in a small boat to look at his vessel, the Sarah Williams, which was then lying a short distance below the town.

"Now, Kate," said the good Major Bonnet, when they were on board, "I have fitted up a little room for you below, which I think you will find comfortable enough during the voyage to Jamaica. I will take you with me when I return to the house, and then you can make up a little package of clothes which it will be easy to convey to the river bank when the time shall come for you to depart. I cannot now say just when that time will arrive; it may be in the daytime or it may be at night, but it will be soon, and I will give you good notice, and I will come up the river for you in a boat. But now I am very busy, and I will leave you to become acquainted with the Sarah Williams, which, for a few days, will be your home. I shall be obliged to row over to the town for, perhaps, half an hour, but Ben Greenway will be here to attend to anything you need until I return."

Ben Greenway was a Scotchman, who had for a long time been Major Bonnet's most trusted servant. He was a good farmer, was apt at carpenter work, and knew a good deal about masonry. A few months ago, any one living in that region would have been likely to say, if the subject had been brought up, that without Ben Greenway Major Bonnet could not get along at all, not even for a day, for he depended upon him in so many ways. And yet, now the master of the estate was about to depart, for nobody knew how long, and leave his faithful servant behind. The reason he gave was, that Ben could not be spared from the farm; but people in general, and Ben in particular, thought this very poor reasoning. Any sort of business which made it necessary for Major Bonnet to separate himself from Ben Greenway was a very poor business, and should not be entered upon.

The deck of the Sarah Williams presented a lively scene as Kate stood upon the little quarter-deck and gazed forward. The sailors were walking about and sitting about, smoking, talking, or coiling things away. There were people from the shore with baskets containing fruit and other wares for sale, and all stirring and new and very interesting to Miss Kate as she stood, with her ribbons flying in the river breeze.

"Who is that young fellow?" she said to Ben Greenway, who was standing by her, "the one with the big basket? It seems to me I have seen him before."

"Oh, ay!" said Ben, "he has been on the farm. That is Dickory Charter, whose father was drowned out fishing a few years ago. He is a good lad, an' boards all ships comin' in or goin' out to sell his wares, for his mither leans on him now, having no ither."

The youth, who seemed to feel that he was being talked about, now walked aft, and held up his basket. He was a handsome youngster, lightly clad and barefooted; and, although not yet full grown, of a strong and active build. Kate beckoned to him, and bought an orange.

"An' how is your mither, Dickory?" said Ben.

"Right well, I thank you," said he, and gazed at Kate, who was biting a hole in her orange.

Then, as he turned and went away, having no reason to expect to sell anything more, Kate remarked to Ben: "That is truly a fine-looking young fellow. He walks with such strength and ease, like a deer or a cat."

"That comes from no' wearin' shoes," said Ben; "but as for me, I would like better to wear shoes an' walk mair stiffly."

Now there came aft a sailor, who touched his cap and told Ben Greenway that he was wanted below to superintend the stowing some cases of the captain's liquors. So Kate, left to herself, began to think about what she should pack into her little bundle. She would make it very small, for the fewer things she took with her the more she would buy at Spanish Town. But the contents of her package did not require much thought, and she soon became a little tired staying there by herself, and therefore she was glad to see young Dickory, with his orange-basket, walking aft.

"I don't want any more oranges," she said, when he was near enough, "but perhaps you may have other fruit?"

He came up to her and put down his basket. "I have bananas, but perhaps you don't like them?"

"Oh, yes, I do!" she answered.

But, without offering to show her the fruit, Dickory continued: "There's one thing I don't like, and that's the men on board your ship."

"What do you mean?" she asked, amazed.

"Speak lower," he said; and, as he spoke, he bethought himself that it might be well to hold out towards her a couple of bananas.

"They're a bad, hard lot of men," he said. "I heard that from more than one person. You ought not to stay on this ship."

"And what do you know about it, Mr. Impudence?" she asked, with brows uplifted. "I suppose my father knows what is good for me."

"But he is not here," said Dickory.

Kate looked steadfastly at him. He did not seem as ruddy as he had been. And then she looked out upon the forward deck, and the thought came to her that when she had first noticed these men it had seemed to her that they were, indeed, a rough, hard lot. Kate Bonnet was a brave girl, but without knowing why she felt a little frightened.

"Your name is Dickory, isn't it?" she said.

He looked up quickly, for it pleased him to hear her use his name. "Indeed it is," he answered.

"Well, Dickory," said she, "I wish you would go and find Ben Greenway. I should like to have him with me until my father comes back."

He turned, and then stopped for an instant. He said in a clear voice: "I will go and get the shilling changed." And then he hurried away.

He was gone a long time, and Kate could not understand it. Surely the Sarah Williams was not so big a ship that it would take all this time to look for Ben Greenway. But he did come back, and his face seemed even less ruddy than when she had last seen it. He came up close to her, and began handling his fruit.

"I don't want to frighten you," he said, "but I must tell you about things. I could not find Ben Greenway, and I asked one of the men about him, feigning that he owed me for some fruit, and the man looked at another man and laughed, and said that he had been sent for in a hurry, and had gone ashore in a boat."

"I cannot believe that," said Kate; "he would not go away and leave me."

Dickory could not believe it either, and could offer no explanation.

Kate now looked anxiously over the water towards the town, but no father was to be seen.

"Now let me tell you what I found out," said Dickory, "you must know it. These men are wicked robbers. I slipped quietly among them to find out something, with my shilling in my hand, ready to ask somebody to change, if I was noticed."

"Well, what next?" laying her hand on his arm.

"Oh, don't do that!" he said quickly; "better take hold of a banana. I spied that Big Sam, who is sailing-master, and a black-headed fellow taking their ease behind some boxes, smoking, and I listened with all sharpness. And Sam, he said to the other one—not in these words, but in language not fit for you to hear—what he would like to do would be to get off on the next tide. And when the other fellow asked him why he didn't go then and leave the fool—meaning your father—to go back to his farm, Big Sam answered, with a good many curses, that if he could do it he would drop down the river that very minute and wait at the bar until the water was high enough to cross, but that it was impossible because they must not sail until your father had brought his cash-box on board. It would be stupid to sail without that cash-box."

"Dickory," said she, "I am frightened; I want to go on shore, and I want to see my father and tell him all these things."

"But there is no boat," said Dickory; "every boat has left the ship."

"But you have one," said she, looking over the side.

"It is a poor little canoe," he answered, "and I am afraid they would not let me take you away, I having no orders to do so."

Kate was about to open her mouth to make an indignant reply, when he exclaimed, "But here comes a boat from the town; perhaps it is your father!"

She sprang to the rail. "No, it is not," she exclaimed; "it holds but one man, who rows."

She stood, without a word, watching the approaching boat, Dickory doing the same, but keeping himself out of the general view. The boat came alongside and the oarsman handed up a note, which was presently brought to Kate by Big Sam, young Dickory Charter having in the meantime slipped below with his basket.

"A note from your father, Mistress Bonnet," said the sailing-master. And as she read it he stood and looked upon her.

"My father tells me," said Kate, speaking decidedly but quietly, "that he will come on board very soon, but I do not wish to wait for him. I will go back to the town. I have affairs which make it necessary for me to return immediately. Tell the man who brought the note that I will go back with him."

Big Sam raised his eyebrows and his face assumed a look of trouble.

"It grieves me greatly, Mistress Bonnet," he said, "but the man has gone. He was ordered not to wait here."

"Shout after him!" cried Kate; "call him back!"

Sam stepped to the rail and looked over the water. "He is too far away," he said, "but I will try." And then he shouted, but the man paid no attention, and kept on rowing to shore.

"I thought it was too far," he said, "but your father will be back soon; he sent that message to me. And now, fair mistress, what can we do for you? Shall it be that we send you some supper? Or, as your cabin is ready, would you prefer to step down to it and wait there for your father?"

"No," said she, "I will wait here for my father. I want nothing."

So, with a bow he strode away, and presently Dickory came back. She drew near to him and whispered. "Dickory," she said, "what shall I do? Shall I scream and wave my handkerchief? Perhaps they may see and hear me from the town."

"No," said Dickory, "I would not do that. The night is coming on, and the sky is cloudy. And besides, if you make a noise, those fellows might do something."

"Oh, Dickory, what shall I do?"

"You must wait for your father," he said; "he must be here soon, and the moment you see him, call to him and make him take you to shore. You should both of you get away from this vessel as soon as you can."

For a moment the girl reflected. "Dickory," said she, "I wish you would take a message for me to Master Martin Newcombe. He may be able to get here to me even before my father arrives."

Dickory Charter knew Mr. Newcombe, and he had heard what many people had talked about, that he was courting Major Bonnet's daughter. The day before Dickory would not have cared who the young planter was courting, but this evening, even to his own surprise, he cared very much. He was intensely interested in Kate, and he did not desire to help Martin Newcombe to take an interest in her. Besides, he spoke honestly as he said: "And who would there be to take care of you? No, indeed, I will not leave you."

"Then row to the town," said she, "and have a boat sent for me."

He shook his head. "No," he said, "I will not leave you."

Her eyes flashed. "You should do what you are commanded to do!" and in her excitement she almost forgot to whisper.

He shook his head and left her.

III

The Two Clocks

It was already beginning to grow dark. She sat, and she sat; she waited, and she waited; and at last she wept, but very quietly. Her father did not come; Ben Greenway was not there; and even that Charter boy had gone. A man came aft to her; a mild-faced, elderly man, with further offers of refreshment and an invitation to go below out of the night air. But she would have nothing; and as she sadly waited and gently wept, it began to grow truly dark. Presently, as she sat, one arm leaning on the rail, she heard a voice close to her ear, and she gave a great start.

"It is only Dickory," whispered the voice.

Then she put her head near him and was glad enough to have put her arms around his neck.

"I have heard a great deal more," whispered Dickory; "these men are dreadful. They do not know what keeps your father, although they have suspicions which I could not make out; but if he does not come on board by ten o'clock they will sail without him, and without his cash-box."

"And what of me?" she almost cried, "what of me?"

"They will take you with them," said he; "that's the only thing for them to do. But don't be frightened, don't tremble. You must leave this vessel."

"But how?" she said.

"Oh! I will attend to that," he answered, "if you will listen to me and do everything I tell you. We can't go until it is dark, but while it is light enough for you to see things I will show you what you must do. Now, look down over the side of the vessel."

She leaned over and looked down. He was apparently clinging to the side with his head barely reaching the top of the rail.

"Do you see this bit of ledge I am standing on?" he asked. "Could you get out and stand on this, holding to this piece of rope as I do?"

"Yes," said she, "I could do that."

"Then, still holding to the rope, could you lower yourself down from the ledge and hang to it with your hands?"

"And drop into your boat?" said she. "Yes, I could do that."

"No," said he, "not drop into my boat. It would kill you if you fell into the boat. You must drop into the water."

She shuddered, and felt like screaming.

"But it will be easy to drop into the water; you can't hurt yourself, and I shall be there. My boat will be anchored close by, and we can easily reach it."

"Drop into the water!" said poor Kate.

"But I will be there, you know," said Dickory.

She looked down upon the ledge, and then she looked below it to the water, which was idly flapping against the side of the vessel.

"Is it the only way?" said she.

"It is the only way," he answered, speaking very earnestly. "You must not wait for your father; from what I hear, I fear he has been detained against his will. By nine o'clock it will be dark enough."

"And what must I do?" she said, feeling cold as she spoke.

"Listen to every word," he answered. "This is what you must do. You know the sound of the bell in the tower of the new church?"

"Oh, yes," said she, "I hear it often."

"And you will not confound it with the bell in the old church?"

"Oh, no!" said she; "it is very different, and generally they strike far apart."

"Yes," said he, "the old one strikes first; and when you hear it, it will be quite dark, and you can slip over the rail and stand on this ledge, as I am doing; then keep fast hold of this rope and you can slip farther down and sit on the ledge and wait until the clock of the new church begins to strike nine. Then you must get off the ledge and hang by your two hands. When you hear the last stroke of nine, you must let go and drop. I shall be there."

"But if you shouldn't be there, Dickory? Couldn't you whistle, couldn't you call gently?"

"No," said Dickory; "if I did that, their sharp ears would hear and lanterns would be flashed on us, and perhaps things would be cast down upon us. That would be the quickest way of getting rid of you."

"But, Dickory," she said, after a moment's silence, "it is terrible about my father and Ben Greenway. Why don't they come back? What's the matter with them?"

He hesitated a little before answering.

"From what I heard, I think there is some trouble on shore, and that's the reason why your father has not come for you as soon as he expected.

But he thinks you safe with Ben Greenway. Now what we have to do is to get away from this vessel; and then if she sails and leaves your father and Ben Greenway, it will be a good thing. These fellows are rascals, and no honest person should have to do with them. But now I must get out of sight, or somebody will come and spoil everything."

Big Sam did come aft and told Kate he thought she would come to injury sitting out in the night air. But she would not listen to him, and only asked him what time of night it was. He told her that it was not far from nine, and that she would see her father very soon, and then he left her.

"It would have been a terrible thing if he had come at nine," she said to herself. Then she sat very still waiting for the sound of the old clock.

Dickory Charter had not told Miss Kate Bonnet all that he had heard when he was stealthily wandering about the ship. He had slipped down into the chains near a port-hole, on the other side of which Big Sam and the black-haired man were taking supper, and he heard a great deal of talk. Among other things he heard a bit of conversation which, when expurgated of its oaths and unpleasant expressions, was like this:

"You are sure you can trust the men?" said Black-hair.

"Oh, yes!" replied the other, "they're all right."

"Then why don't you go now? At any time officers may be rowing out here to search the vessel."

"And well they might. For what needs an old farmer with an empty vessel, a crew of seventy men, and ten guns? He is in trouble, you may wager your life on that, or he would be coming to see about his girl."

"And what will you do about her?"

"Oh, she'll not be in the way," answered Big Sam with a laugh. "If he doesn't take her off before I sail, that's his business. If I am obliged to leave port without his cash-box, I will marry his daughter and become his son-in-law—I don't doubt we can find a parson among all the rascals on board—then, perhaps, he will think it his duty to send me drafts to the different ports I touch at."

At this good joke, both of them laughed.

"But I don't want to go without his cash-box," continued Big Sam, "and I will wait until high-tide, which will be about ten o'clock. It would be unsafe to miss that, for I must not be here to-morrow morning. But the long-boat will be here soon. I told Roger to wait until half-past nine, and then to come aboard with old Bonnet or without him, if he didn't show himself by that time."

"But, after all," said the black-haired man, "the main thing is, will the men stand by you?"

"You needn't fear them," said the other with an aggravated oath, "I know every rascal of them."

"Now, then," said Dickory Charter to himself as he slipped out of the chains, "she goes overboard, if I have to pitch her over."

Nothing had he heard about Ben Greenway. He did not believe that the Scotchman had deserted his young mistress; even had he been sent for to go on shore in haste, would he leave without speaking to her. More than that, he would most likely have taken her with him.

But Dickory could not afford to give much thought to Ben Greenway. Although a good friend to both himself and his mother, he was not to be considered when the safety of Mistress Kate Bonnet was in question.

The minutes moved slowly, very slowly indeed, as Kate sat, listening for the sound of the old clock, and at the same time listening for the sound of approaching footsteps.

It was now so dark that she could not have seen anybody without a light, but she could hear as if she had possessed the ears of a cat.

She had ceased to expect her father. She was sure he had been detained on shore; how, she knew not. But she did know he was not coming.

Presently the old clock struck, one, two—In a moment she was climbing over the rail. In the darkness she missed the heavy bit of rope which Dickory had showed her, but feeling about she clutched it and let herself down to the ledge below. Her nerves were quite firm now. It was necessary to be so very particular to follow Dickory's directions to the letter, that her nerves were obliged to be firm. She slipped still farther down and sat sideways upon the narrow ledge. So narrow that if the vessel had rolled she could not have remained upon it.

There she waited.

Then there came, sharper and clearer out of the darkness in the direction of the town, the first stroke of nine o'clock from the tower of the new church. Before the second stroke had sounded she was hanging by her two hands from the ledge. She hung at her full length; she put her feet together; she hoped that she would go down smoothly and make no splash. Three—four—five—six—seven—eight—nine—and she let her fingers slip from the ledge. Down she went, into the darkness and into the water, not knowing where one ended and the other began. Her eyes were closed, but they might as well have been open; there was nothing for her to see in all that blackness. Down she went, as if it were to the very bottom of black air and black water. And then, suddenly she felt an arm around her.

Dickory was there!

She felt herself rising, and Dickory was rising, still with his arm around her. In a moment her head was in the air, and she could breathe. Now she felt that he was swimming, with one arm and both legs. Instinctively she tried to help him, for she had learned to swim. They went on a dozen strokes or more, with much labour, until they touched something hard.

"My boat," said Dickory, in the lowest of whispers; "take hold of it."

Kate did so, and he moved from her. She knew that he was clambering into the boat, although she could not see or hear him. Soon he took hold of her under her arms, and he lifted with the strength of a young lion, yet so slowly, so warily, that not a drop of water could be heard dripping from her garments. And when she was drawn up high enough to help herself, he pulled her in, still warily and slowly. Then he slipped to the bow and cast off the rope with which the canoe had been anchored. It was his only rope, but he could not risk the danger of pulling up the bit of rock to which the other end of it was fastened. Then, with a paddle, worked as silently as if it had been handled by an Indian, the canoe moved away, farther and farther, into the darkness.

"Is all well with you?" said Dickory, thinking he might now safely murmur a few words.

"All well," she murmured back, "except that this is the most uncomfortable boat I ever sat in!"

"I expect you are on my orange basket," he said; "perhaps you can move it a little."

Now he paddled more strongly, and then he stopped.

"Where shall I take you, Mistress Bonnet?" he asked, a little louder than he had dared to speak before.

Kate heaved a sigh before she answered; she had been saying her prayers.

"I don't know, you brave Dickory," she answered, "but it seems to me that you can't see to take me anywhere. Everything is just as black as pitch, one way or another."

"But I know the river," he said, "with light or without it. I have gone home on nights as black as this. Will you go to the town?"

"I would not know where to go to there," she answered, "and in such a plight."

"Then to your home," said he. "But that will be a long row, and you must be very cold."

She shuddered, but not with cold. If her father had been at home it would have been all right, but her step-mother would be there, and that would not be all right. She would not know what to say to her.

"Oh, Dickory," she said, "I don't know where to go."

"I know where you can go," he said, beginning to paddle vigorously, "I will take you to my mother. She will take care of you to-night and give you dry clothes, and to-morrow you may go where you will."

IV

On the Quarter-deck

As the time approached when Big Sam intended to take the Sarah Williams out of port, it seemed really necessary that Mistress Kate Bonnet should descend from the exposed quarterdeck and seek shelter from the night air in the captain's cabin or in her own room; and, as she had treated him so curtly at his last interview with her, he sent the elderly man with the mild countenance to tell her that she really must go below, for that he, Big Sam, felt answerable to her father for her health and comfort. But when the elderly man and his lantern reached the quarter-deck, there was no Mistress Kate there, and, during the rapid search which ensued, there was no Mistress Kate to be found on the vessel.

Big Sam was very much disturbed; she must have jumped overboard. But what a wild young woman to do that upon such little provocation, for how should she know that he was about to run away with her father's vessel!

"This is a bad business," he said to the black-haired man, "and who would have thought it?"

"I see not that," said Black Paul, "nor why you should trouble yourself about her. She is gone, and you are well rid of her. Had she stayed aboard with us, every ship in the colony might have been cruising after us before to-morrow's sun had gone down."

But this did not quiet the cowardly soul of Big Sam.

"Now I shall tell you," said he, "exactly what happened. A little before dark she went ashore in a boat which was then leaving the ship. I allowed her to do this because she was very much in earnest about it, and talked sharply, and also because I thought the town was the best place for her, since it was growing late and her father did not seem to be coming. Now, if the old man comes on board, that's what happened; but if he does not come on board, the devil and the fishes know what happened, and they may talk about it if they like. But if any man says anything to old Bonnet except as I have ordered, then the fishes shall have another feast."

"And now, what I have to say to you," said Black Paul, "is, that you should get away from here without waiting for the tide. If one of these rascals drops overboard and swims ashore, he may get a good reward for news of the murder committed on this vessel, and there isn't any reason to think, so far as I know, that the Sarah Williams can sail any faster than two or three other vessels now in the harbour."

"There's sense in all that," said Big Sam as he walked forward. But he suddenly stopped, hearing, not very far away, the sound of oars.

Now began the body and soul of Big Sam to tremble. If the officers of the law, having disposed of Captain Bonnet, had now come to the ship, he had no sufficient tale to tell them about the disappearance of Mistress Kate Bonnet; nor could he resist. For why should the crew obey his orders? They had not yet agreed to receive him as their captain, and, so far, they had done nothing to set themselves against the authorities. It was a bad case for Big Sam.

But now the ship was hailed, and the voice which hailed it was that of Captain Bonnet. And the soul of Big Sam upheaved itself.

In a few minutes Bonnet was on board, with a big box and the crew of the long-boat. Speaking rapidly, he explained to Big Sam the situation of affairs. The authorities of the port had indeed sadly interfered with him. They had heard reports about the unladen vessel and the big crew; and, although they felt loath to detain and to examine a fellow-townsman, hitherto of good report, they did detain him and they did examine him, and they would have gone immediately to the ship had it not been so dark.

But under the circumstances they contented themselves with the assurance of the respectable Mr. Bonnet that he would appear before them the next morning and give them every opportunity of examining his most respectable ship. Having done this, they retired to their beds, and the respectable Bonnet immediately boarded his vessel.

"Now," cried Captain Bonnet, "where is my daughter? I hope that Ben Greenway has caused her to retire to shelter?"

"Your daughter!" exclaimed Big Sam, before any one else could speak, "she is not here. It was still early twilight when she told me she would wait no longer, and desired to be sent ashore in a boat. This request, of course, I immediately granted, feeling bound thereto, as she was your daughter, and that I was, in a measure, under her orders."

Captain Bonnet stood, knitting his brows.

"Well, well!" he presently cried, with an air of relief, "it is better so. Her home is the best place for her, as matters have turned out. And now," said he, turning to Big Sam, "call the men together and set them to quick work. Pull up your anchors and do whatever else is necessary to free the ship; then let us away. We must be far out of sight of this island before to-morrow's sunrise."

As Big Sam passed Black Paul he winked and whispered: "The old fool is doing exactly what I would have done if he hadn't come aboard. This suits my plan as if he were trying his best to please me."

In a very short time the cable was slipped, for Big Sam had no notion of betraying the departure of the vessel by the creaking of a capstan; and, with the hoisting of a few sails and no light aboard except the shaded lamp at the binnacle, the Sarah Williams moved down the river and out upon the sea.

"And when are you going to take the command in your hands?" asked Black Paul of Big Sam.

"To-morrow, some time," was the answer, "but I must first go around among the men and let them know what's coming."

"And how about Ben Greenway? Has the old man asked for him yet?"

"No," said the other; "he thinks, of course, that the Scotchman has gone ashore with the young woman. What else could he do, being a faithful servant? To-morrow I shall set Greenway free and let him tell his own tale to his master. But I shall tell my tale first, and then he can speak or not speak, as he chooses; it will make no difference one way or another."

Soon after dawn the next morning Captain Bonnet was out of his hammock and upon deck. He looked about him and saw nothing but sea, sea, sea.

Big Sam approached him. "I forgot to tell you," said he, "that yesterday I shut up that Scotchman of yours, for, from his conduct, I thought that he had some particular reason for wanting to go on shore; and, fearing that if he did so he would talk about this vessel, and so make worse the trouble I was sure you were in, I shut him up as a matter of precaution and forgot to mention him to you last night."

"You stupid blockhead!" roared Mr. Bonnet, "how like an ass you have acted! Not for a bag of gold would I have taken Ben Greenway on this cruise; and not for a dozen bags would I have deprived my family of his care and service. You ought to be thrown into the sea! Ben Greenway here! Of all men in the world, Ben Greenway here!"

"I only thought to do you a service," said Big Sam.

"Service!" shouted the angry Bonnet. But as it was of no use to say anything more upon this subject, he ordered the sailing-master to send to him, first, Ben Greenway, and then to summon to him, no matter where they might be or what they might be doing, the whole crew.

The other, surprised at this order, objected that all of the men could not leave their posts, but Bonnet overruled him.

"Send me the whole of them, every man jack. The fellow at the wheel will remain here and steer. As for the rest, the ship will take care of itself for a space."

"What can that old fool of a farmer intend to do?" said Big Sam, as he went away; "he is like a child with a toy, and wants to see his crew in a bunch."

Presently came Ben Greenway in a smothered rage.

"An' I suppose, sir," said he without salutation, "that ye have gi'en orders about the care o' the cows and the lot o' poultry that I engaged to send to the town to-day?"

"Don't mention cows or poultry to me!" cried Bonnet. "I am a more angry man than you are, Ben Greenway, and as soon as I have time to attend to it, I shall look into this matter of your shutting up, and shall come down upon the wrongdoers like sheeted lightning."

"What a fearful rage ye're in, Master Bonnet," said Ben. "I never saw the like o' it. If ye're really angrier than I am, I willna revile; leavin' it to ye to do the revilin' wha are so much better qualified. An' so it wasna accident that I was shut up in the ship's pantry, leavin' Mistress Kate to gang hame by hersel', an' to come out this mornin' findin' the ship at sea an' ye in command?"

"Say no more, Ben," cried Bonnet. "I am more sorry to see you here than if you were any other man I know in this world. But I cannot put you off now, nor can I talk further about it, being very much pressed with other matters. Now here comes my crew."

Ben Greenway retired a little, leaning against the rail.

"An' this is his crew?" he muttered; "a lot o' unkempt wild beasts, it strikes me. Mayhap he has gathered them togither to convert their souls, an' he is about to preach his first sermon to them."

Now all the mariners of the Sarah Williams were assembled aft and Captain Bonnet was standing on his quarter-deck, looking out upon them. He was dressed in a naval uniform, to which was added a broad red sash. In his belt were two pairs of big pistols, and a stout sword hung by his side. He folded his arms; he knitted his brows, and he gazed fiercely about to see if any one were absent, although if any one had been absent he would not have known it. His eyes flashed, his cheeks were flushed, and it was plain enough to all that he had something important to say.

"My men," he cried, in a stalwart voice which no one there had ever heard him use before, "my men, look upon me and you will not see what you expect to see! Here is no planter, no dealer in horses and fat cattle, no grower of sugar-cane! Instead of that," he yelled, drawing his sword and flourishing it above his head, "instead of that I am pirate Bonnet, the new terror of the sea! You, my men, my brave men, you are not the crew of the good merchantman, the Sarah Williams, you are pirates all. You are the pirate crew of the pirate ship Revenge. That is now the name of this vessel on which you sail, and you are all pirates, who henceforth shall sail her.

"Now look aloft, every man of you, and you will see a skull and bones, under which you sail, under which you fight, under which you gain great riches in coins, in golden bars, and in fine goods fit for kings and queens!"

As he spoke, every rascal raised his eyes aloft, and there, sure enough, floated the black flag with the skull and bones—the terrible "Jolly Roger" of the Spanish Main, and which Bonnet himself had hoisted before he called together his crew.

For the most part the men were astounded, and looked blankly the one upon the other. They knew they had been shipped to sail upon some illegal cruise, and that they were to be paid high wages by the wealthy Bonnet; but that this worthy farmer should be their pirate captain had never entered their minds, they naturally supposing that their future commander would not care to show himself at Barbadoes, and that he would be taken on board at some other port.

As for Big Sam, he was more than astounded—he was stupefied. He had well known the character of the ship from the time that Bonnet had taken him into his service, and he it was who had mainly managed the fitting-up of the vessel and the shipping of her crew. He did not know whom Bonnet intended to command the ship, but from the very beginning he had intended to command her himself. But he had been too late. He had not gone among the men as he had expected to do soon after setting sail, and here this country bumpkin had taken the wind out of his sails and had boldly announced that he himself was the captain of the pirate ship Revenge.

The men now began to talk among themselves; and as Bonnet still stood, his sword clutched in his hand and his chest heaving with the excitement of his own speech, there arose from the crew a cheer. Some of them had known a little about Stede Bonnet and some of them scarcely anything at all, except that he was able to pay them good wages. Now he had told them that he was a pirate captain, and each of them knew that he himself was a pirate, or was waiting for the chance to become one.

And so they cheered, and their captain's chest heaved higher, and the soul of the luckless Big Sam collapsed, for he knew that after that cheer there was no chance for him; at least, not now.

"Now go, my boys," shouted Bonnet, "back to your places, every one of you, and fall to your duty; and in honour of that black flag which floats above you, each one of you shall drink a glass of grog."

With another shout the crew hurried forward, and Stede Bonnet stood upon the quarter-deck, the pirate captain of the pirate ship Revenge.

And now stepped up to his master that good Presbyterian, Ben Greenway.

"An' ye call yoursel' a pirate, sir?" said he, "an' ye go forth upon the sea to murder an' to rob an' to prepare your soul for hell?"

Mr. Bonnet winked a little.

"You speak strongly, Ben," said he, "but that might have been expected from a man of your fashion of thinking. But let me tell you again, my good Ben Greenway, that I was no party to your being on this vessel. Even now, when my soul swells within me with the pride of knowing that I am a sovereign of the seas and that I owe no allegiance to any man or any government and that my will is my law and is the law of every man upon this vessel—even now, Ben Greenway, it grieves me to know that you are here with me. But the first chance I get I shall set you ashore and have you sent home. Thou art not cut out for a pirate, and as no other canst thou sail with me."

Ben Greenway looked at him steadfastly.

"Master Stede Bonnet," said he, "ye are no more fit to be a bloody pirate than I am. Ye oversee your plantation weel, although I hae often been persuaded that ye knew no' as much as ye think ye do. Ye provide weel for your family, although ye tak' no' the pleasure therein ye might hae ta'en had ye been content wi' ane wife, as the Holy Scriptures tell us is enough for ony mon, an' ye hae sufficient judgment to tak' the advice o' a judgmatical mon about your lands an' your herds; but when it comes to your ca'in' yoursel' a pirate captain, it is enough to make a deceased person chuckle by the absurdity o' it."

"Ben Greenway," exclaimed Major Bonnet, "I don't like your manner of speech."

"O' course ye don't," cried Ben; "an' I didna expect ye to like it; but it is the solemn truth for a' that."

"I don't want any of your solemn truths," said Bonnet, "and as soon as I get a chance I am going to send you home to your barnyard and your cows."

"No' so fast, Master Bonnet, no' so fast," answered Ben. "I hae ta'en care o' ye for mony years; I hae kept ye out o' mony a bad scrape both in buyin' an' sellin', an' I am sure ye never wanted takin' care o' mair than ye do now; an' I'm just here to tell ye that I am no' goin' back to Barbadoes till ye do, an' that I am goin' to stand by ye through your bad luck and through your good luck, in your sin an' in your repentance."

"Ben Greenway," cried Captain Bonnet, as he waved his sword in the air, "if you talk to me like that I will cut you down where you stand! You forget that you are not talking to a country gentleman, but to a pirate, a pirate of the seas!"

Ben grinned, but seeing the temper his master was in, thought it wise to retire.

FRANK R. STOCKTON

V

An Unsuccessful Errand

For what seemed a very long time to Kate Bonnet, Dickory Charter paddled bravely through the darkness. She was relieved of the terror and the uncertainty which had fallen upon her during the past few hours, and she was grateful to the brave young fellow who had delivered her from the danger of sailing out upon the sea with a crew of wicked scoundrels who were about to steal her father's ship, and her heart should have beaten high with gratitude and joy, but it did not. She was very cold, and she knew not whither young Dickory was taking her. She did not believe that in all that darkness he could possibly know where he was going; at any moment that dreadful ship might loom up before them, and lights might be flashed down upon them. But all of a sudden the canoe scraped, grounded, and stopped.

"What is that?" she cried.

"It is our beach," said Dickory, and almost at that moment there came a call from the darkness beyond.

"Dickory!" cried a woman's voice, "is that you?"

"It is my mother," said the boy; "she has heard the scraping of my keel."

Then he shouted back, "It is Dickory; please show me a light, mother!"

Jumping out, Dickory pulled the canoe high up the shelving shore, and then he helped Kate to get out. It was not an easy job, for she could see nothing and floundered terribly; but he seemed to like it, and half led, half carried her over a considerable space of uneven ground, until he came to the door of a small house, where stood an elderly woman with a lantern.

"Dickory! Dickory!" shouted the woman, "what is that you are bringing home? Is it a great fish?"

"It is a young woman," said the boy, "but she is as wet as a fish."

"Woman!" cried good Dame Charter. "What mean you, Dickory, is she dead?"

"Not dead, Mother Charter," said Kate, who now stood, unassisted, in the light of the lantern, "but in woeful case, and more like to startle you than if I were the biggest fish. I am Mistress Kate Bonnet, just out of the river between here and the town. No, I will not enter your house, I am not fit; I will stand here and tell my tale."

"Dickory!" shouted Dame Charter, "take the lantern and run to the kitchen cabin, where ye'll make a fire quickly."

Away ran Dickory, and standing in the darkness, Kate Bonnet told her tale. It was not a very satisfactory tale, for there was a great part of it which Kate herself did not understand, but it sufficed at present for the good dame, who had known the girl when she was small, and who was soon busily engaged in warming her by her fire, refreshing her with food, and in fortifying her against the effects of her cold bath by a generous glass of rum, made, the good woman earnestly asserted, from sugar-cane grown on Master Bonnet's plantation.

Early the next morning came Dickory from the kitchen, where he had made a fire (before that he had been catching some fish), and on a rude bench by the house door he saw Kate Bonnet. When he perceived her he laughed; but as she also laughed, it was plain she was not offended.

This pretty girl was dressed in a large blue gown, belonging to the stout Dame Charter, and which was quite as much of a gown as she had any possible need for. Her head was bare, for she had lost her hat, and she wore neither shoes nor stockings, those articles of apparel having been so shrunken by immersion as to make it impossible for her to get them on.

"Thy mother is a good woman," said Kate, "and I am so glad you did not take me to the town. I don't wonder you gaze at me; I must look like a fright."

Dickory made no answer, but by the way in which he regarded her, she knew that he saw nothing frightful in her face.

"You have been very good to me," said she, rising and making a step towards him, but suddenly stopping on account of her bare feet, "and I wish I could tell you how thankful I am to you. You are truly a brave boy, Dickory; the bravest I have ever known."

His brows contracted. "Why do you call me a boy?" he interrupted. "I am nineteen years old, and you are not much more than that."

She laughed, and her white teeth made him ready to fall down and worship her.

"You have done as much," said she, "as any man could do, and more." Then she held out her hand, and he came and took it.

FRANK R. STOCKTON

"Truly you are a man," she said, and looking steadfastly into his face, she added, "how very, very much I owe you!"

He didn't say anything at all, this Dickory; just stood and looked at her. As many a one has been before, he was more grateful for the danger out of which he had plucked the fair young woman than she was thankful for the deliverance.

Just then Dame Charter called them to breakfast. When they were at the table, they talked of what was to be done next; and as, above everything else, Miss Kate desired to know where her father was and why he hadn't come aboard the Sarah Williams, Dickory offered to go to the town for news.

"I hate to ask too much, after all you have done," said the girl, "but after you have seen my father and told him everything, for he must be in sore trouble, would you mind rowing to our house and bringing me some clothes? Madam Bonnet will understand what I need; and she too will want to know what has become of me."

"Of course I will do that," cried Dickory, grateful for the chance to do her service.

"And if you happen to see Mr. Newcombe in the town, will you tell him where I am?"

Now Dickory gave no signs of gratitude for a chance to do her service, but his mother spoke quickly enough.

"Of course he will tell Master Newcombe," said she, "and anybody else you wish should know."

In ten minutes Dickory was in his canoe, paddling to the town. When he was out of the little inlet, on the shore of which lay his mother's cottage, he looked far up and down the broad river, but he could see nothing of the good ship Sarah Williams.

"I am glad they have gone," said Dickory to himself, "and may they never come back again. It is a pity that Major Bonnet should lose his ship, but as things have turned out, it is better for him to lose it than to have it."

When he had fastened his canoe to a little pier in the town with a rope which he borrowed, having now none of his own, Dickory soon heard strange news. The man who owned the rope told him that Major Bonnet had gone off in his vessel, which had sailed out of the harbour in the night, showing no light. And, although many people had talked of this strange proceeding, nobody knew whether he had gone of his own free will or against it.

"Of course it was against his will," cried Dickory. "The ship was stolen, and they have stolen him with it. The wretches! The beasts!" And then he went up into the town.

Some men were talking at the door of a baker's shop, and the baker himself, a stout young man, came out.

"Oh, yes," said he, "we know now what it means. The good Major Bonnet has gone off pirating; he thinks he can make more money that way than by attending to his plantation. The townspeople suspected him last night, and now they know what he is."

At this moment Master Dickory jumped upon the baker, and both went down. When Dickory got up, the baker remained where he was, and it was plain enough to everybody that the nerves and muscles of even a vigorous young man were greatly weakened by the confined occupation of a baker.

Dickory now went further to ask more, and he soon heard enough. The respectable Major Bonnet had gone away in his own ship with a savage crew, far beyond the needs of the vessel, and if he had not gone pirating, what had he gone for? And to this question Dickory replied every time: "He went because he was taken away." He would not give up his faith in Kate Bonnet's father.

"And Greenway," the people said. "Why should they take him? He is of no good on a ship."

On this, Dickory's heart fell further. He had been troubled about the Scotchman, but had tried not to think of him.

"The scoundrels have stolen them both, with the vessel," he said; and as he spoke his soul rose upward at the thought of what he had done for Kate; and as that had been done, what mattered it after all what had happened to other people?

Five minutes afterward a man came running through the town with the news that old Bonnet's daughter, Miss Kate, had also gone away in the ship. She was not at home; she was not in the town.

"That settles it!" said some people. "The black-hearted rascal! He has gone of his own accord, and he has taken Greenway and his fair young daughter with him."

"And what do you think of that!" said some to the doubter Dickory.

"I don't believe a word of it!" said he; and not wishing on his own responsibility to tell what he knew of Mistress Kate Bonnet, he rowed up the river towards the Bonnet plantation to carry her message. On his way, whom should he see, hurrying along the road by the river bank coming towards the town and looking hot and worried, but Mr. Martin Newcombe. At the sight of the boat he stopped.

"Ho! young man," he cried, "you are from the town; has anything fresh been heard about Major Bonnet and his daughter?"

Now here was the best and easiest opportunity of doing the third thing which Kate had asked him to do; but his heart did not bound to do it. He sat and looked at the man on the river bank.

"Don't you hear me?" cried Newcombe. "Has anybody heard further from the Bonnets?"

Dickory still sat motionless, gazing at Newcombe. He didn't want to tell this man anything. He didn't want to have anything to do with him. He hesitated, but he could not forget the third thing he had been asked to do, and who had asked him to do it. Whatever happened, he must be loyal to her and her wishes, and so he said, with but little animation in his voice, "Major Bonnet's daughter did not go with him."

Instantly came a great cry from the shore. "Where is she? Where is she? Come closer to land and tell me everything!"

This was too much! Dickory did not like the tone of the man on shore, who had no right to command him in that fashion.

"I have no time to stop now," said he; "I am carrying a message to Madam Bonnet."

And so he paddled away, somewhat nearer the middle of the river.

Martin Newcombe was wild; he ran and he bounded on his way to the Bonnet house; he called and he shouted to Dickory, but apparently that young person was too far away to hear him. When the canoe touched the shore, almost at the spot where the fair Kate had been fishing with a hook lying in the sun, Newcombe was already there.

"Tell me," he cried, "tell me about Miss Kate Bonnet! What has befallen her? If she did not go with her father, where is she now?"

"I have come," said Dickory sturdily, as he fastened his boat with the borrowed rope, "with a message for Madam Bonnet, and I cannot talk with anybody until I have delivered it."

Madam Bonnet saw the two persons hurrying towards her house, and she came out in a fine fury to meet them.

"Have you heard from my runaway husband," she cried, "and from his daughter? I am ashamed to hear news of them, but I suppose I am in duty bound to listen."

Dickory did not hesitate now to tell what he knew, or at least part of it.

"Your daughter—" said he.

"She is not my daughter," cried the lady; "thank Heaven I am spared that disgrace. And from what hiding-place does she and her sire send me a message?"

Dickory's face flushed.

"I bring no message from a hiding-place," he said, "nor any from your husband. He went to sea in his ship, but Mistress Kate Bonnet left the vessel before it sailed, and her clothes having been injured by water, she sent me for what a young lady in her station might need, supposing rightly that you would know what that might be."

"Indeed I do!" cried Madam Bonnet. "What she needs are the clouts of a fish-girl, and a stick to her back besides."

"Madam!" cried Newcombe, but she heeded him not; she was growing more angry.

"A fine creature she is," exclaimed the lady, "to run away from my house in this fashion, and treat me with such contumely, and then to order me to send her her fine clothes to deck herself for the eyes of strangers!"

"But, young man," cried Newcombe, "where is she? Tell that without further delay. Where is she?"

"I don't care where she is!" interrupted Madam Bonnet. "It matters not to me whether she is in the town, or sitting waiting for her finery on the bridge. If she didn't go with her father (cowardly sneak that he is), that gives her less reason to stay away all night from her home, and send her orders to me in the morning. No, I will have none of that! If my husband's daughter wants anything of me, let her come here and ask for it, first giving me the reason of her shameful conduct."

"Madam!" cried Newcombe, "I cannot listen to such speech, such—"

"Then stop your ears with your thumbs," she exclaimed, "and you will not hear it."

Then turning to Dickory: "Now, go you, and tell the young woman who sent you here she must come in sackcloth and ashes, if she can get them, and she must tell me her tale and her father's tale, without a lie mixed up in them; and when she has done this, and has humbly asked my pardon for the foul affront she has put upon me, then it will be time enough to talk of fine clothes and fripperies."

Newcombe now expostulated with much temper, but Dickory gave him little chance to speak.

FRANK R. STOCKTON

"I carry no such message as that," he said. "Do you truly mean that you deny the young lady the apparel she needs, and that I am to tell her that?"

"Get away from here!" cried Madam Bonnet, with her face in a blaze. "I send her no message at all; and if she comes here on her knees, I shall spurn her, if it suit me."

If Dickory had waited a little he might have heard more, but he did not wait; he quickly turned, and away he went in his boat. And away went Martin Newcombe after him. But as the younger man was barefooted, the other one could not keep up with him, and the canoe was pushed off before he reached the water's edge.

"Stop, you young rascal!" cried Newcombe. "Where is Kate Bonnet? Stop! and tell me where she is!"

Troubled as he was at the tale he was going to tell, Dickory laughed aloud, and he paddled down the river as few in that region had ever paddled before.

Madam Bonnet went into her house, and if she had met a maid-servant, it might have been bad for that poor woman. She was not troubled about Kate. She knew the young man to be Dickory Charter, and she was quite sure that her step-daughter was in his mother's cottage. Why she happened to be there, and what had become of the recreant Bonnet, the equally recreant young woman could come and tell her whenever she saw fit.

VI

A Pair of Shoes and Stockings

The tide was running down, and Dickory made a swift passage to the town. Seeing on the pier the man from whom he had borrowed the rope, he stopped to return him his property, and thinking that the good people of the town should know that, no matter what had befallen Major Bonnet, his daughter had not gone with him and was safe among friends, he mentioned these facts to the man, but with very few details, being in a hurry to return with his message.

Before he turned into the inlet, Dickory was called from the shore, and to his surprise he saw his mother standing on the bank in front of a mass of bushes, which concealed her from her house.

"Come here, Dickory," she said, "and tell me what you have heard?"

Her son told his doleful tale.

"I fear me, mother," he said, "that Major Bonnet's ship has gone on some secret and bad business, and that he is mixed up in it. Else why did he desert his daughter? And if he intended to take her with him, that was worse."

"I don't know, Dickory," said good Dame Charter reflectively; "we must not be too quick to believe harm of our fellow-beings. It does look bad, as the townspeople thought, that Major Bonnet should own such a ship with such a strange crew, but he is a man who knows his own business, and may have had good reason for what he has done. He might have been sailing out to some foreign part to bring back a rich cargo, and needed stout men to defend it from the pirates that he might meet with on the seas."

"But his daughter, mother," said Dickory; "how could he have left her as he did? That was shameful, and even you must admit it."

"Not so fast, Dickory," said she; "there are other ways of looking at things than the way in which we look at them. He had intended to take Mistress Kate on a little trip; she told me that herself. And most likely, having changed his mind on account of the suspicions in the town, he sent word to her to return to her home, which message she did not get."

Dickory considered.

"Yes, mother," he said, "it might have been that way, but I don't believe that he went of his own accord, and I don't believe that he would take Ben Greenway with him. I think, mother, that they were both stolen with the ship."

"That might be," said his mother, "but we have no right to take such a view of it, and to impart it to his daughter. If he went away of his own accord, everything will doubtless be made right, and we shall know his reasons for what he has done. It is not for us to make up our minds that Major Bonnet and good Ben Greenway have been carried off by wicked men, for this would be sad indeed for that fair girl to believe. So remember, Dickory, that it is our duty always to think the best of everything. And now I will go through the underbrush to the house, and when you get there yourself you must tell your story as if you had not told it to me."

Before Dickory had reached his mother's cottage Mistress Kate Bonnet came running to meet him, and she did not seem to be the same girl he had left that morning. Her clothes had been dried and smoothed; even her hat, which had been found in the boat, had been made shapely and wearable, and its ribbons floated in the breeze. Dickory glanced at her feet, and as he did so, a thrill of strange delight ran through him. He saw his own Sunday shoes, with silver buckles, and he caught a glimpse of a pair of brown stockings, which he knew went always with those shoes.

"I am quite myself again," she said, noticing his wide eyes, "and your mother has been good enough to lend me a pair of your shoes and stockings. Mine are so utterly ruined, and I could not walk barefooted."

Dickory was so filled with pride that this fair being could wear his shoes, and that she was wearing them, that he could only mumble some stupid words about being so glad to serve her. And she, wise girl, said nothing about the quantities of soft cotton-wool which Dame Charter had been obliged to stuff into the toes before they would stay upon the small feet they covered.

"But my father," cried Kate, "what of him? Where is he?"

Now Dame Charter was with them, her eyes hard fixed upon her son.

Dickory, mindful of those eyes, told her what he had to tell, saying as little as possible about Major Bonnet—because, of course, all that he knew about him was mere hearsay—but dilating with much vigour upon the shameful conduct of Madam Bonnet; for the young lady ought surely to know what sort of a woman her father's wife really was, and what she might expect if she should return to her house. He could have said even more about the interview with the angry woman, but his mother's eyes were upon him.

Kate heard everything without a word, and then she burst into tears.

"My father," she sobbed, "carried away, or gone away, and one is as bad as the other!"

"Dickory," said Dame Charter, "go cut some wood; there is none ready for the kitchen."

Dickory went away, not sorry, for he did not know how to deport himself with a young lady whose heart was so sorely tried. He might have discovered a way, if he had been allowed to do so; but that would not have been possible with his mother present. But, in spite of her sorrow, his heart sang to him that she was wearing his shoes and stockings! Then he cheerfully brought down his axe upon the wood for the dinner's cooking.

Dame Charter led the weeping girl to the bench, and they talked long together. There was no optimist in all the British colonies, nor for that matter in those belonging to France or Spain, or even to the Dutch, who was a more conscientious follower of her creed than Dame Charter. She sat by Kate and she talked to her until the girl stopped sobbing and began to see for herself that her father knew his own business, and that he had most certainly sent her a message to go on shore, which had not been delivered.

As to poor Ben Greenway, the good woman was greatly relieved that her son had not mentioned him, and she took care not to do it herself. She did not wish to strain her optimism. Kate, having so much else upon her mind, never thought of this good man.

When Dickory came back, he first looked to see if Kate still wore his shoes and stockings, and then he began to ask what there was that he might now do. He would go again to the town if he might be of use. But Kate had no errand for him there. Dickory had told her how he had been with Mr. Newcombe at her home, and therefore there was no need of her sending him another message.

"I don't know where to go or where to send," she said simply; "I am lost, and that is all of it."

"Oh, no," cried Dame Charter, "not that! You are with good friends, and here you can stay just as long as you like."

"Indeed she can!" said Dickory, as if he were making a response in church.

His mother looked at him and said nothing. And then she took Kate out into a little grove behind the house to see if she could find some ripe oranges.

It was a fair property, although not large, which belonged to the Widow Charter. Her husband had been a thriving man, although a little inclined to speculations in trade which were entirely out of his line, and when he met his death in the sea he left her nothing but her home and some inconsiderable land about it. Dickory had been going to a grammar-school in the town, and was considered a fair scholar, but with his father's death all that stopped, and the boy was obliged to go to work to do what he could for his mother. And ever since he had been doing what he could, without regard to appearances, thinking only of the money.

But on Sunday, when he rowed his mother to church, he wore good clothes, being especially proud of his buckled shoes and his long brown hose, which were always of good quality.

They were eating dinner when oars were heard on the river, and in a moment a boat swung around into the inlet. In the stern sat Master Martin Newcombe, and two men were rowing.

Now Dickory Charter swore in his heart, although he was not accustomed to any sort of blasphemy; and as Miss Kate gazed eagerly through the open window, our young friend narrowly scrutinized her face to see if she were glad or not. She was glad, that was plain enough, and he went out sullenly to receive the arriving interloper.

When they were all standing on the shore, Kate did not think it worth while to ask Master Newcombe how he happened to know where she was. But the young man waited for no questions; he went on to tell his story. When he related that it was a man fishing on a pier who had told him that young Mistress Kate Bonnet was stopping with Dame Charter, Kate wondered greatly, for as Dickory had met Master Newcombe, what need had there been for the latter to ask questions about her of a stranger? But she said nothing. And Dickory growled in his soul that he had ever spoken to the man on the pier, except to thank him for the rope he had borrowed.

Martin Newcombe's story went on, and he told that, having been extremely angered by the conduct and words of Madam Bonnet, he had gone into the town and made inquiries, hoping to hear something of the whereabouts of Mistress Kate. And, having done so, by means of the very obliging person on the pier, he had determined that the daughter of Major Bonnet should have her rights; and he had gone to his own lawyer, who assured him that being a person of recognised respectability, possessing property, he was fully authorized, knowing the wishes of Mistress Kate Bonnet, to go to her step-mother and demand that those wishes be complied with; and if this very reasonable request should be denied, then the lawyer would take up the matter himself, and would see to it that reasonable raiment and the necessities of a young lady should not be withheld from her.

With these instructions, Newcombe had gone to Madam Bonnet and had found that much disturbed lady in a state of partial collapse, which had followed her passion of the morning, and who had declared that nothing in the world would please her better than to get rid of her husband's daughter and never see her again. And if the creature needed clothes or anything else which belonged to her, a maid should pack them up, and anybody who pleased might take them to any place, provided she heard no more about them or their owner.

In all this she spoke most truthfully, for she hated her step-daughter, both because she was a fine young woman and much regarded by her father, and because she had certain rights to the estate of said father, which his present wife did not wish to recognise, or even to think about. So Martin Newcombe was perfectly welcome to take away such things as would render it unnecessary for the girl to now return to the home in which she had been born. Martin had brought the box, and here he was.

It was not long before Newcombe and the lady of his love were walking away through the little plantation, in order that they might speak by themselves. Dickory looked after them and frowned, but he bravely comforted himself by thinking that he had been the one into whose arms she had dropped, through the blackness of the night and the blackness of the water, knowing in her heart that he would be there ready for her, and also by the thought that it was his shoes and stockings that she wore. Dame Charter saw this frown on her son's face, but she did not guess the thoughts which were in his mind.

VII

KATE PLANS

It was nearly an hour before Kate and Mr. Newcombe returned, and when they came back they did not look happy. Dickory observed their sad visages, but the sight did not make him sad. Kate took Dame Charter by the hand and led her to the bench.

"You have been so kind to me," she said, "that I have almost come to look upon you as a mother, even though I have known you such a little while, and I want to tell you what I have been talking about, and what I think I am going to do."

Mr. Newcombe now stood by, and Dickory also. His mother was not quite sure that this was the right place for him, but as he had already done so much for the young lady, there was, perhaps, no reason why he should be debarred from hearing what she had to say.

"This gentleman," said Kate, indicating Martin Newcombe, "sympathizes with me very greatly in my present unfortunate position: having no home to which I can go, and having no relative belonging to this island but my father, who is sailing upon the seas, I know not where; and therefore, in his great kindness, has offered to marry me and to take me to his home, which thereafter would be my home, and in which I should have all comforts and rights."

Now Dickory's face was like the sky before a shower. His mother saw it out of the corner of her eye, but the others did not look at him.

"This was very kind and very good," continued Kate.

"Not at all, not at all," interrupted Master Newcombe, "except that it was kind and good to myself; for there is nothing in this world which you need and want as much as I need and want you."

At this Dickory's brow grew darker.

"I believe all you say," said Kate, "for I am sure you are an honest and a true man, but, as I told you, I cannot marry you; for, even had I made up my mind on the subject, which I have not, I could not marry any one at such a time as this, not knowing my father's will upon the subject or where he is."

The sun broke out on Dickory's countenance without a shower; his mother noticed the change.

"But as I must do something," Kate went on, "a plan came to me while Mr. Newcombe was talking to me, and I have been thinking of it ever since, and now, as I speak, I am becoming fully determined in regard to it; that is, if I can carry it out. It often happens," she said, with a faint smile, "that when people ask advice they become more and more strengthened in their own opinion. My opinion, and I may say my plan, is this: When my father told me he was going away in his ship, he agreed to take me with him on a little voyage, leaving me with my mother's brother at the island of Jamaica, not far from Spanish Town. In purposing this he thought, no doubt, that it would be far better for me to be with my own blood, if his voyage should be long, rather than to live with one who is no relative of mine, and does not wish to act like one. This, then, being my father's intention, which he was prevented, by reasons which I know not of, from carrying out, I shall carry it out myself with all possible dispatch, and go to my uncle in Jamaica by the earliest vessel which sails from this port. Not only as this is my natural refuge in my trouble, but as my father intended to go there when he thought of having me with him, it may be a part of his plan to go there any way, even though I be not with him; and so I may see him, and all may be well."

Clouds now settled heavily on the faces of each of the young men, and even the ordinarily bright sky of Dame Charter became somewhat overcast; although, in her heart, she did not believe that anybody in this world could have devised a better plan, under the circumstances, than this forsaken Mistress Kate Bonnet.

"Now there is my plan," said Kate, with something of cheerfulness in her voice, "if it so be I can carry it out. Do either of you know," glancing at the young men impartially, but apparently not noticing the bad weather, "if in a reasonable time a vessel will leave here for Jamaica?"

Dickory knew well, but he would not answer; Kate had no right to put such a thing upon him. Newcombe, however, did not hesitate. "It is very hard for me to say," he made reply, "but there is a merchantman, the King and Queen, which sails from here in three days for Jamaica. I know this, for I send some goods; and I wish, Mistress Bonnet, that I could say something against your sailing in her, but I cannot; for, since you will not let me take care of you, your uncle is surely the best one in the world to do it; and as to the vessel, I know she is a safe one."

"But you could not go sailing away in any vessel by yourself," cried Dame Charter, "no matter how safe she may be."

FRANK R. STOCKTON

"Oh, no!" cried Kate; "and the more we talk about our plan the more fully it reveals itself to me in all its various parts. I am going to ask you to go with me, my dear Dame Charter," and as she spoke she seized both of the hands of the other. "I have funds of my own which are invested in the town, and I can afford the expense. Surely, my good friend, you will not let me go forth alone, and all unused to travel? Leaving me safely with my uncle, you could return when the ship came back to Bridgetown."

Dame Charter turned upon the girl a look of kind compassion, but at the same time she knit her brows.

"Right glad would I be to do that for you," she said, "but I cannot go away and leave my son, who has only me."

"Take him with you," cried Kate. "Two women travelling to unknown shores might readily need a protector, and if not, there are so many things which he might do. Think of it, my dear Dame Charter; to my uncle's home in Jamaica is the only place to which I can go, and if you do not go with me, how can I go there?"

Dame Charter now shed tears, but they were the tears of one good woman feeling for the misfortunes of another.

"I will go with you, my dear young lady," she said, "and I will not leave you until you are in your uncle's care. And, as to my boy here—"

Now Dickory spoke from out of the blazing noontide of his countenance.

"Oh, I will go!" he cried. "I do so greatly want to see Jamaica."

Without being noticed, his mother took him by the hand; she did not know what he might be tempted to say next.

Mr. Newcombe stood very doleful. And well he might; for if his lady-love went away in this fashion, there was good reason to suppose that he might never see her again. But Kate said no word to comfort him—for how could she in this company?—and began to talk rapidly about her preparations.

"I suppose until the ship shall sail I may stay with you?" addressing Dame Charter.

"Stay here?" exclaimed the good dame. "Of course you can stay here. We are like one family now, and we will all go on board ship together."

Kate walked to the boat with Mr. Newcombe, he having offered to undertake her business in town and at her father's house, and to see the owners of the King and Queen in regard to passage.

Dickory stood radiant, speaking to no one. Master Martin Newcombe was the lover of Mistress Kate Bonnet, but he, Dickory, was going with her to Jamaica!

The following days fled rapidly. Long-visaged Martin Newcombe, whose labours in behalf of his lady were truly labours of love, as their object was to help her to go where his eyes could no longer feast upon her, and from which place her voice would no longer reach him, went, with a bitter taste in his mouth, to visit Madam Bonnet, to endeavour to persuade her to deliver to her step-daughter such further belongings as that young lady was in need of.

That forsaken person was found to be only too glad to comply with this request, hoping earnestly that neither the property nor its owner should ever again be seen by her. She was in high spirits, believing that she was a much better manager of the plantation than her eccentric husband had ever been, and she had already engaged a man to take the place of Ben Greenway, who had been a sore trouble to her these many years. She was buoyed up and cheered by the belief that the changes she was making would be permanent, and that she would live and die the owner of the plantation. She alone, in all Bridgetown and vicinity, had no doubts whatever in regard to her husband's sailing from Barbadoes in his own ship, and with a redundancy of rascality below its decks. The respectability and good reputation of Major Bonnet did not blind her eyes. She had heard him talk about the humdrum life on shore and the reckless glories of the brave buccaneers, but she had never replied to these remarks, fearing that she might feel obliged to object to them, and she did not tell him how, in late years, she had heard him talk in his sleep about standing, with brandished sword, on the deck of a pirate ship. It was her dream, that his dreams might all come true.

So Kate's baggage was put on board the King and Queen, a very humble vessel considering her sounding name, and Dame Charter's few belongings were conveyed to the vessel in Dickory's canoe, the cottage being left in charge of a poor and well-pleased neighbour.

When the day came for sailing, our friends, with not a few of the townspeople, were gathered upon the deck, where Kate at first looked about for Dickory, not recognising at the moment the well-dressed young fellow who had taken his place. His Sunday costume became him well, and he was so bravely decked out in the matter of shoes and stockings that Kate did not recognise him.

　　　　　　　　　　　　　　　　FRANK R. STOCKTON

To every one Mistress Kate Bonnet made clear that she was going to her uncle's house in Jamaica, where she expected to meet her father; and many were the good wishes bestowed upon her. When the time drew near when the anchor should be heaved, Kate withdrew to one side with Mr. Newcombe. "You must believe," said she kindly, "that everything between us is just as it was when we used to sit on the shady bank and look out over the ripples of the river. There will be waves instead of ripples for us to look over now, but there will be no change either the one way or the other."

Then they shook hands fervently; more than that would have been unwarrantable.

The King and Queen dropped down the stream, and Master Newcombe stood sadly on the pier, while Kate Bonnet waved her handkerchief to him and to her friends. Dame Charter sat and smiled at the town she was leaving and at the long stretches of the river before her. She knew not to what future she was going, but her heart was uplifted at the thought that a new life was opening before her son. In her little cottage and in her little fields there was no future for him, and now to what future might he not be sailing!

As for Dickory, he knew no more of his future than the sea-birds knew what was going to happen to them; he cared no more for his future than the clouds cared whether they were moving east or west. His life was like the sparkling air in which he moved and breathed. He stood upon the deck of the vessel, with the wind filling the sails above, while at a little distance stood Kate Bonnet, her ribbons floating in the breeze. He would have been glad to sing aloud, but he knew that that would not be proper in the presence of the ladies and the captain. And so he let his heart do his singing, which was not heard, except by himself.

VIII

Ben Greenway is Convinced that Bonnet is a Pirate

B ut how in the name o' common sense did ye ever think o' becomin' a pirate, Master Bonnet?" said Ben Greenway as they stood together. "Ye're so little fitted for a wicked life."

"Out upon you, Ben Greenway!" exclaimed the captain, beginning to stride up and down the little quarter-deck. "I will let you know, that when the time comes for it, I can be as wicked as anybody."

"I doubt that," said Ben sturdily. "Would ye cut down an' murder the innocent? Would ye drive them upon an unsteady plank an' make them walk into the sea? Could ye raise thy great sword upon the widow an' the orphan?"

"No more of this disloyal speech," shouted Bonnet, "or I will put you upon a wavering plank and make you walk into the sea."

Now Greenway laughed.

"An' if ye did," he said, "ye would next jump upon the plank yoursel' an' slide swiftly into the waves, that ye might save your old friend an' servant, knowin' he canna swim."

"Ben Greenway," said Bonnet, folding his arms and knitting his brows, "I will not suffer such speech from you. I would sooner have on board a Presbyterian parson."

"An' a happier fate couldna befall ye," said Ben, "for ye need a parson mair than ony mon I know."

Bonnet looked at him for a moment.

"You think so?" said he.

"Indeed I do," said Ben, with unction.

"There now," cried Bonnet, "I told you, Ben, that I could be wicked upon occasion, and now you have acknowledged it. Upon my word, I can be wickeder than common, as you shall see when good fortune helps us to overhaul a prize."

The Revenge had been at sea for about a week and all had gone well, except she had taken no prizes. The crew had been obedient and fairly orderly, and if they made fun of their farmer-captain behind his back, they showed no disrespect when his eyes were upon them. The fact was

FRANK R. STOCKTON

that the most of them had a very great respect for him as the capitalist of the ship's company.

Big Sam had early begun to sound the temper of the men, but they had not cared to listen to him. Good fare they had and generous treatment, and the less they thought of Bonnet as a navigator and commander, the more they thought of his promises of rich spoils to be fairly divided with them when they should capture a Spanish galleon or any well-laden merchantman bound for the marts of Europe. In fact, when such good luck should befall them, they would greatly prefer to find themselves serving under Bonnet than under Big Sam. The latter was known as a greedy scoundrel, who would take much and give little, being inclined, moreover, to cheat his shipmates out of even that little if the chance came to him. Even Black Paul, who was an old comrade of Big Sam—the two having done much wickedness together—paid no heed to his present treasons.

"Let the old fool alone," he said; "we fare well, and our lives are easy, having three men to do the work of one. So say I, let us sail on and make merry with his good rum; his money-chest is heavy yet."

"That's what I'm thinking of," said the sailing-master. "Why should I be coursing about here looking for prizes with that chest within reach of my very arm whenever I choose it?"

Black Paul grinned and said to himself: "It is your arm, old Sam, that I am afraid of." Then aloud: "No, let him go. Let us profit by our good treatment as long as it lasts, and then we will talk about the money-box."

Thus Big Sam found that his time had not arrived, and he swore in his soul that his old shipmate would some day rue that he had not earlier stood by him in his treacherous schemes.

So all went on without open discontent, and Bonnet, having sailed northward for some days, set his course to the southeast, with some hundred and fifty eyes wide open for the sight of a heavy-sailing merchantman.

One morning they sighted a brig sailing southward, but as she was of no great size and not going in the right direction to make it probable that she carried a cargo worth their while, they turned westward and ran towards Cuba. Had Captain Bonnet known that his daughter was on the brig which he thus disdained, his mind would have been far different; but as it was, not knowing anything more than he could see, and not understanding much of that, he kept his westerly course, and on the next day the lookout sighted a good-sized merchantman bearing eastward.

Now bounded every heart upon the swiftly coursing vessel of the planter-pirate. There were men there who had shared in the taking of many a prize; who had shared in the blood and the cruelty and the booty; and their brawny forms trembled with the old excitement, of the sea-chase; but no man's blood ran more swiftly, no man's eyes glared more fiercely, than those of Captain Bonnet as he strapped on his pistols and felt of his sword-hilt.

"Ah, ye needna glare so!" said Ben Greenway, close at his side. "Ye are no pirate, an' ye canna make yoursel' believe ye are ane, an' that ye shall see when the guns begin to roar an' the sword-blades flash. Better get below an' let ane o' these hairy scoundrels descend into hell in your place."

Captain Bonnet turned with rage upon Ben Greenway, but the latter, having spoken his mind and given his advice, had retired.

Now came Big Sam. "'Tis an English brig," he said, "most likely from Jamaica, homeward bound; she should be a good prize."

Bonnet winced a little at this. He would have preferred to begin his career of piracy by capturing some foreign vessel, leaving English prizes for the future, when he should have become better used to his new employment. But sensitiveness does not do for pirates, and in a moment he had recovered himself and was as bold and bloody-minded as he had been when he first saw the now rapidly approaching vessel. All nations were alike to him now, and he belonged to none.

"Fire some guns at her," he shouted to Big Sam, "and run up the Jolly Roger; let the rascals see what we are."

The rascals saw. Down came their flag, and presently their vessel was steered into the wind and lay to.

"Shall we board her?" cried Big Sam.

"Ay, board her!" shouted back the infuriated Bonnet. "Run the Revenge alongside, get out your grappling-irons, and let every man with sword and pistols bound upon her deck."

The merchantman now lay without headway, gently rolling on the sea. Down came the sails of the Revenge, while her motion grew slower and slower as she approached her victim. Had Captain Bonnet been truly sailing the Revenge, he would have run by with sails all set, for not a thought had he for the management of his own vessel, so intent he was upon the capture of the other. But fortunately Big Sam knew what was necessary to be done in a nautical manoeuvre of this kind, and his men did not all stand ready with their swords in their hands to bound upon the deck of the merchantman. But there were enough of Pirate Bonnet's crew crowded alongside the rail of the vessel to inspire terror in any peaceable merchantman. And this one, although it had several carronades and other guns upon her deck, showed no disposition to use them, the odds against her being far too great.

At the very head of the long line of ruffians upon the deck of the Revenge stood Ben Greenway; and, although he held no sword and wore no pistol, his eyes flashed as brightly as any glimmering blade in the whole ship's company.

The two vessels were now drawing very near to each other. Men with grappling-irons stood ready to throw them, and the bow of the well-steered pirate had almost touched the side of the merchantman, when, with a bound, of which no one would have considered him capable, the good Ben Greenway jumped upon the rail and sprang down upon the deck of the other vessel. This was a hazardous feat, and if the Scotchman had known more about nautical matters he would not have essayed it before the two vessels had been fastened together. Ignorance made him fearless, and he alighted in safety on the deck of the merchantman at the very instant when the two vessels, having touched, separated themselves from each other for the space of a yard or two.

There was a general shout from the deck of the pirate at this performance of Ben Greenway. Nobody could understand it. Captain Bonnet stood and yelled.

"What are you about, Ben Greenway? Have you gone mad? Without sword or pistol, you'll be—"

The astonished Bonnet did not finish his sentence, for his power of speech left him when he saw Ben Greenway hurry up to the captain of the merchantman, who was standing unarmed, with his crew about him, and warmly shake that dumfounded skipper by the hand. In their surprise at what they beheld the pirates had not thrown their grapnels at the proper moment, and now the two vessels had drifted still farther apart.

Presently Ben Greenway came hurrying to the side of the merchantman, dragging its captain by the hand.

"Master Bonnet! Master Bonnet!" he cried; "this is your old friend, Abner Marchand, o' our town; an' this is his good ship the Amanda. I knew her when I first caught sight o' her figure-head, havin' seen it so often at her pier at Bridgetown. An' so, now that ye know wha it is that ye hae inadvertently captured, ye may ca' off your men an' bid them sheathe their frightful cutlasses."

At this, a roar arose from the pirates, who, having thrown some of their grappling-irons over the gunwale of the merchantman, were now pulling hard upon them to bring the two vessels together, and Captain Bonnet shouted back at Ben: "What are you talking about, you drivelling idiot; haven't you told Mr. Marchand that I am a pirate?"

"Indeed I hae no'," cried Ben, "for I don't believe ye are are; at least, no' to your friends an' neebours."

To this Bonnet made a violent reply, but it was not heard. The two vessels had now touched and the crowd of yelling pirates had leaped upon the deck of the Amanda. Bonnet was not far behind his men, and, sword in hand, he rushed towards the spot where stood the merchant captain with his crew hustling together behind him. As there was no resistance, there was so far no fighting, and the pirates were tumbling over each other in their haste to get below and find out what sort of a cargo was carried by this easy prize.

Captain Marchand held out his hand. "Good-day to you, friend Bonnet," he said. "I had hoped that you would be one of the first friends I should meet when I reached port at Bridgetown, but I little thought to meet you before I got there."

Bonnet was a little embarrassed by the peculiarity of the situation, but his heart was true to his new career.

"Friend Marchand," he said, "I see that you do not understand the state of affairs, and Ben Greenway there should have told you the moment he met you. I am no longer a planter of Barbadoes; I am a pirate of the sea, and the Jolly Roger floats above my ship. I belong to no nation; my hand is against all the world. You and your ship have been captured by me and my men, and your cargo is my prize. Now, what have you got on board, where do you hail from, and whither are you bound?"

Captain Marchand looked at him fixedly.

"I sailed from London with a cargo of domestic goods for Kingston; thence, having disposed of most of my cargo, I am on my way to Bridgetown, where I hope to sell the remainder."

"Your goods will never reach Bridgetown," cried Bonnet; "they belong now to my men and me."

"What!" cried Ben Greenway, "ye speak wi'out sense or reason. Hae ye forgotten that this is Mr. Abner Marchand, your fellow-vestryman an' your senior warden? An' to him do ye talk o' takin' awa' his goods an' legal chattels?"

Bonnet looked at Greenway with indignation and contempt.

"Now listen to me," he yelled. "To the devil with the vestry and da—" the Scotchman's eyes and mouth were so rounded with horror that Bonnet stopped and changed his form of expression—"confound the senior warden. I am the pirate Bonnet, and regard not the Church of England."

"Nor your friends?" interpolated Ben.

"Nor friends nor any man," shouted Bonnet.

"Abner Marchand, I am sorry that your vessel should be the first one to fall into my power, but that has happened, and there is no help for it. My men are below ransacking your hold for the goods and treasure it may contain. When your cargo, or what we want of it, is safe upon my ship, I shall burn your vessel, and you and your men must walk the plank."

At this dreadful statement, Ben Greenway staggered backward in speechless dismay.

"Yes," cried Bonnet, "that shall I do, for there is naught else I can do. And then you shall see, you doubting Greenway, whether I am a pirate or no."

To all this Captain Marchand said not a word. But at this moment a woman's scream was heard from below, and then there was another scream from another woman. Captain Marchand started.

"Your men have wandered into my cabin," he exclaimed, "and they have frightened my passengers. Shall I go and bring them up, Major Bonnet? They will be better here."

"Ay, ay!" cried the pirate captain, surprised that there should be female passengers on board, and Marchand, followed by Ben Greenway, disappeared below.

"Confound women passengers," said Bonnet to himself; "that is truly a bit of bad luck."

In a few minutes Marchand was back, bringing with him a middle-aged and somewhat pudgy woman, very pale; a younger woman of exceeding plainness, and sobbing steadfastly; and also an elderly man, evidently an invalid, and wearing a long dressing-gown.

"These," said Captain Marchand, "are Master and Madam Ballinger and daughter, of York in England, who have been sojourning in Jamaica for the health of the gentleman, but are now sailing with me to

Barbadoes, hoping the air of our good island may be more salubrious for the lungs."

Captain Bonnet had never been in the habit of speaking loudly before ladies, but he now felt that he must stand by his character.

"You cannot have heard," he almost shouted, "that I am the pirate Bonnet, and that your vessel is now my prize."

At this the two ladies began to scream vigorously, and the form of the gentleman trembled to such a degree that his cane beat a tattoo upon the deck.

"Yes," continued Bonnet, "when my men have stripped this ship of its valuables I shall burn her to the water's edge, and, having removed you to my vessel, I shall shortly make you walk the plank."

Here the younger lady began to stiffen herself out as if she were about to faint in the arms of Captain Marchand, who had suddenly seized her; but her great curiosity to hear more kept her still conscious. Mrs. Ballinger grew very red in the face.

"That cannot be," she cried; "you may do what you please with our belongings and with Captain Marchand's ship, but my husband is too sick a man to walk a plank. You have not noticed, perchance, that his legs are so feeble that he could scarce mount from the cabin to the deck. It would be impossible for him to walk a plank; and as for my daughter and myself, we know nothing about such a thing, and could not, out of sheer ignorance."

For a moment a shadow of perplexity fell upon Captain Bonnet's face. He could readily perceive that the infirm Mr. Ballinger could not walk a plank, or even mount one, unless some one went with him to assist him, and as to his wife, she was evidently a termagant; and, having sailed his ship and floated his Jolly Roger in order to get rid of one termagant, he was greatly annoyed at being brought thus, face to face, with another. He stood for a moment silent. The old gentleman looked as if he would like to go down to his cabin and cover up his head with his blanket until all this commotion should be over; the daughter sobbed as she gazed about her, taking in every point of this most novel situation; and the mother, with dilated nostrils, still glared.

In the midst of all this varying disturbance Captain Marchand stood quiet and unmoved, apparently paying no attention to any one except his old neighbour and fellow-vestryman, Stede Bonnet, upon whose face his eyes were steadily fixed.

Ben Greenway now approached the pirate captain and led him aside.

"Let your men make awa' wi' the cargo as they please—I doubt if it be more than odds an' ends, for such are the goods they bring to Bridgetown—an' let them cast off an' go their way, an' ye an' I will return to Bridgetown in the Amanda an' a' may yet be weel, this bit o' folly bein' forgotten."

It might have been supposed that Bonnet would have retaliated upon the Scotchman for thus advising him, in the very moment of triumph, to give up his piratical career and to go home quietly to his plantation, but, instead of that, he paused for a moment's reflection.

"Ben Greenway," said he, "there is good sense in what you say. In truth, I cannot bring myself to put to death my old friend and neighbour and his helpless passengers. As for the ship, it will do me no more good burned than unburned. And there is another thing, Ben Greenway, which I would fain do, and it just came into my mind. I will write a letter to my wife and one to my daughter Kate. There is much which I wish them to know and which I have not yet been able to communicate. I will allow the Amanda to go on her way and I will send these two letters by her captain. They shall be ready presently, and you, Ben, stand by these people and see that no harm comes to them."

At this moment there were loud shouts and laughter from below, and Captain Marchand came forward.

"Friend Bonnet," he said, "your men have discovered my store of spirits; in a short time they will be drunk, and it will then be unsafe for these, my passengers. Bid them, I pray you, to convey the liquors aboard your ship."

"Well said!" cried Bonnet. "I would not lose those spirits." And, stepping forward, he spoke to Big Sam, who had just appeared on deck, and ordered the casks to be conveyed on board the Revenge.

The latter laughed, but said: "Ay, ay, sir!"

Returning to Captain Marchand, Bonnet said: "I will now step on board my ship and write some letters, which I shall ask you to take to Bridgetown with you. I shall be ready by the time the rest of your cargo is removed."

"Oh, don't do that!" cried Ben; "there is surely pen an' paper here, close to your hand. Go down to Captain Marchand's cabin an' write your letters."

"No, no," cried Bonnet, "I have my own conveniences." And with that he leaped on board the Revenge.

"That's a chance gone," said Ben Greenway to Captain Marchand, "a good chance gone. If we could hae kept him on board here an' down in your cabin, I might hae passed the word to that big miscreant, the sailing-master, to cast off an' get awa' wi' that wretched crowd. The scoundrels will be glad to steal the ship, an' it will be the salvation o' Master Bonnet if they do it."

"If that's the case," said Captain Marchand, "why should we resort to trickery? If his men want his ship and don't want him, why can't we seize him when he comes on board with his letters, and then let his men know that they are free to go to the devil in any way they please? Then we can convey Major Bonnet to his home, to repentance, perhaps, and a better life."

"That's good," said Ben, "but no' to punishment. Ye an' I could testify that his head is turned, but that, when kindness to a neebour is concerned, his heart is all right."

"Ay, ay," said the captain, "I could swear to that. And now we must act together. When I put my hand on him, you do the same, and give him no chance to use his sword or pistols."

The captain of the pirates sat down in his well-furnished little room to write his letters, and the noise and confusion on deck, the swearing and the singing and the shouting to be heard everywhere, did not seem to disturb him in the least. He was a man whose mind could thoroughly engage itself with but one thing at a time, and the fact that his men were at work sacking the merchantman did not in the least divert his thoughts from his pen and paper.

So he quietly wrote to his wife that he had embraced a pirate's life, that he never expected to become a planter again, and that he left to her the enjoyment and management of his estate in Barbadoes. He hoped that, his absence having now relieved her of her principal reason for discontent with her lot, she would become happy and satisfied, and would allow those about her to be the same. He expected to send Ben Greenway back to her to help take care of her affairs, but if she should need further advice he advised her to speak to Master Newcombe.

The letter to his daughter was different; it was very affectionate. He assured her of his sorrow at not being able to take her with him and to leave her at Jamaica, and he urged her at the earliest possible moment to go to her uncle and to remain there until she heard from him or saw him—the latter being probable, as he intended to visit Jamaica as soon as he could, even in disguise if this method were necessary. He alluded to the glorious career upon which he was entering, and in which he expected some day to make a great name for himself, of which he hoped she would be proud.

When these letters were finished Bonnet hurried to the side of the vessel and looked upon the deck of the Amanda.

Captain Marchand and Greenway had been waiting in anxious expectation for the return of Bonnet, and wondering how in the world a man could bring his mind to write letters at such a time as this.

"Take these letters, Ben," he said, leaning over the rail, "and give them to Captain Marchand."

Ben Greenway at first declined to take the letters which Bonnet held out to him, but the latter now threw them at his feet on the deck, and, running forward, he soon found himself in a violent and disorderly crowd, who did not seem to regard him at all; booty and drink were all they cared for. Presently came Big Sam, giving orders and thrusting the men before him. He had not been drinking, and was in full possession of his crafty senses.

"Throw off the grapnels," exclaimed Big Sam, "and get up the foresel!" And then he perceived Bonnet. With a scowl upon his face Big Sam muttered: "I thought you were on the merchantman, but no matter. Shove her off, I say, or I'll break your heads."

The grapnels were loosened; the few men who were on duty shoved desperately; the foresail went up, and the two vessels began to separate. But they were not a foot apart when, with a great rush and scramble, Ben Greenway left the merchantman and tumbled himself on board the Revenge.

Bonnet rushed up to him. "You scoundrel! You rascal, Ben Greenway, what do you mean? I intended you to go back to Bridgetown on that brig. Can I never get rid of you?"

"No' till ye give up piratin'," said Ben with a grin. "Ye may split open my head, an' throw overboard my corpse, but my live body stays here as long as ye do."

With a savage growl Bonnet turned away from his faithful adherent. Things were getting very serious now and he could waste no time on personal quarrels. Great holes and splits had been discovered in the heads of the barrels of spirits, and the precious liquor was running over the decks. This was the work of the sagacious Big Sam, who had the strongest desire to get away from the Amanda before the pirate crew became so drunk that they could not manage the vessel. He was a deep man, that Big Sam, and at this moment, although he said nothing about it, he considered himself the captain of the pirate ship which he sailed.

For a time Bonnet hurried about, not knowing what to do. Some of the men were quarrelling about the booty; others trying to catch the rum as it flowed from the barrels; others howling out of pure devilishness, and no one paying him any respect whatever. Big Sam was giving orders; a few sober men were obeying him, and Captain Stede Bonnet, with his faithful servant, Ben Greenway, seemed to be entirely out of place amid this horrible tumult.

"I told ye," said Ben, "ye had better stayed on board that merchantman an' gone back like a Christian to your ain hame an' family. It will be no safe place for ye, or for me neither, when that black-hearted scoundrel o' a Big Sam gets time to attend to ye."

"Black-hearted?" inquired Bonnet, but without any surprise in his voice.

"Ay," said Ben, "if there's onything blacker than his heart, only Satan himsel' ever looked at it. It was to be sailin' this ship on his own account that he's had in his villainous soul ever since he came on board; an' I can tell ye, Master Bonnet, that it won't be long now before he's doin' it. I had me eye on him when he was on board the Amanda, an' I saw that the scoundrel was goin' to separate the ships."

"That was my will," said Bonnet, "although I did not order it."

Ben gave a little grunt. "Ay," said he, "hopin' to leave me behind just as he was hopin' to leave ye behind. But neither o' ye got your wills, an' it'll be the de'il that'll have a hand in the next leavin' behind that's likely to be done."

Bonnet made no reply to these remarks, having suddenly spied Black Paul.

"Look here," said he, stepping up to that sombre-hued personage, "can you sail a ship?"

The other looked at Bonnet in astonishment. "I should say so," said he. "I have commanded vessels before now."

"Here then," said Bonnet, "I want a sailing-master. I am not satisfied with this Big Sam. I am no navigator myself, but I want a better man than that fellow to sail my ship for me."

Black Paul looked hard at him but made no answer.

"He thinks he is sailing the ship for himself," said Bonnet, "and it would be a bad day for you men if he did."

"That indeed would it," said Black Paul; "a close-fisted scoundrel, as I know him to be."

"Quick then," said Bonnet; "now you're my sailing-master; and after this, when we divide the prizes, you take the same share that I do. As to these goods from the Amanda, I will have no part at all; I give them all to you and the rest, divided according to rule.

"Go you now among the men, and speak first to such as have taken the least liquor; let them know that it was Big Sam that broke in the hogsheads, which, but for that, would have been sold and divided. Go quickly and get about you a half-dozen good fellows."

"Ye're gettin' wickeder and wickeder," said Ben when Black Paul had hurried away; "the de'il himsel' couldna hae taught ye a craftier trick than that. Weel ye kenned that that black fellow would fain serve under a free-handed fool than a stingy knave. Ay, sir, your education's progressin'!"

At this moment Big Sam came hurrying by. Not wishing to excite suspicion, Bonnet addressed him a question, but instead of answering the burly pirate swore at him. "I'll attend to your business," said he, "as soon as I have my sails set; then I'll give you two leather-headed landsmen all the hoisting and lowering you'll ever ask for." Then with another explosion of oaths he passed on.

Bonnet and Ben stood waiting with much impatience and anxiety, but presently came Black Paul with a party of brawny pirates following him.

"Come now," said Bonnet, walking boldly aft towards Big Sam, who was still cursing and swearing right and left. Bonnet stepped up to him and touched him on the arm. "Look ye," said he, "you're no longer sailing-master on this ship; I don't like your ways or your fashions. Step forward, then, and go to the fo'castle where you belong; this good mariner," pointing to Black Paul, "will take your place and sail the Revenge."

Big Sam turned and stood astounded, staring at Bonnet. He spoke no word, but his face grew dark and his great eyebrows were drawn together. His mouth was half open, as if he were about to yell or swear. Then suddenly his right hand fell upon the hilt of his cutlass, and the great blade flashed in the air. He gave one bound towards Bonnet, and in the same second the cutlass came down like a stroke of lightning. But Bonnet had been a soldier and had learned how to use his sword; the cutlass was caught on his quick blade and turned aside. At this moment

Black Paul sprung at Big Sam and seized him by the sword arm, while another fellow, taking his cue, grabbed him by the shoulder.

"Now some of you fellows," shouted Bonnet, "seize him by the legs and heave him overboard!"

This order was obeyed almost as soon as it was given; four burly pirates rushed Big Sam to the bulwarks, and with a great heave sent him headforemost over the rail. In the next instant he had disappeared—gone, passed out of human sight or knowledge.

"Now then, Mr. Paul—not knowing your other name—"

"Which it is Bittern," said the other.

"You are now sailing-master of this ship; and when things are straightened out a bit you can come below and sign articles with me."

"Ay, ay, sir," said Black Paul, and calling to the men he gave orders that they go on with the setting of the main-topsail.

"Now, truly," said Ben, "I believe that ye're a pirate."

Bonnet looked at him much pleased. "I told you so, my good Ben. I knew that the time would come when you would acknowledge that I am a true pirate; after this, you cannot doubt it any more."

"Never again, Master Bonnet," said Ben Greenway, gravely shaking his head, "never again!"

The brig Amanda, with full sails and an empty hold, bent her course eastward to the island of Barbadoes, and the next morning, when the drunken sailors on board the Revenge were able to look about them and consider things, they found their vessel speeding towards the coast of Cuba, and sailed by Black Paul Bittern.

IX

Dickory Sets Forth

M r. Felix Delaplaine, merchant and planter of Spanish Town, the capital of Jamaica, occupied a commodious house in the suburbs of the town, twelve miles up the river from Kingston, the seaport, which establishment was somewhat remarkable from the fact that there were no women in the family. Madam Delaplaine had been dead for several years, and as her husband's fortune had steadily thriven, he now found himself possessor of a home in which he could be as independent and as comfortable as if he had been the president and sole member of a club.

Being of a genial disposition and disposed to look most favourably upon his possessions and surrounding conditions, Mr. Delaplaine had come to be of the opinion that his lot in life was one in which improvement was not to be expected and scarcely to be desired. He had been perfectly happy with his wife, and had no desire to marry another, who could not possibly equal her; and, having no children, he continually thanked his happy stars that he was free from the troubles and anxieties which were so often brought upon fathers by their sons and their daughters.

Into this quiet and self-satisfied life came, one morning, a great surprise in the shape of a beautiful young woman, who entered his office in Spanish Town, and who stated to him that she was the daughter of his only sister, and that she had come to live with him. There was an elderly dame and a young man in company with the beautiful visitor, but Mr. Delaplaine took no note of them. With his niece's hands in his own, gazing into the face so like that young face in whose company he had grown from childhood to manhood, Mr. Delaplaine saw in a flash, that since the death of his wife until that moment he had never had the least reason to be content with the world or to be satisfied with his lot. This was his sister's child come to live with him!

When Mr. Delaplaine sufficiently recovered his ordinary good sense to understand that there were other things in this world besides the lovely niece who had so suddenly appeared before him, he remembered that she had a father, and many questions were asked and answered; and he was told who Dame Charter was, and why her son came with her. Then the uncle and the niece walked into the garden, and there talked of Major Bonnet. Little did Kate know upon this subject, and nothing could her uncle tell her; but in many and tender words she was assured that this was her home as long as she chose to live in it, and that it was the most fortunate thing in the world that Dame Charter had come with her and could stay with her. Had this not been so, where could he have found such a guardian angel, such a chaperon, for this tender niece? As for the young man, it was such rare good luck that he had been able to accompany the two ladies and give them his protection. He was just the person, Mr. Delaplaine believed, who would be invaluable to him either on the plantation or in his counting-house. In any case, here was their home; and here, too, was the home of his brother-in-law, Bonnet, whenever he chose to give up his strange fancy for the sea. It was not now to be thought of that Kate or her father, or either one of them, should go back to Barbadoes to live with the impossible Madam Bonnet.

If her father's vessel were in the harbour and he were here with them, or even if she had had good tidings from him, Kate Bonnet would have been a very happy girl, for her present abode was vastly different from any home she had ever known. Her uncle's house on the highlands beyond the town lay in a region of cooler breezes and more bracing air than that of Barbadoes. Books and music and the general air of refinement recalled her early life with her mother, and with the exception of the anxiety about her father, there were no clouds in the bright blue skies of Kate Bonnet. But this anxiety was a cloud, and it was spreading.

WHEN THE AMANDA MOVED AWAY from the side of the pirate vessel Revenge she hoisted all sail, and got away over the sea as fast as the prevailing wind could take her. When she passed the bar below Bridgetown and came to anchor, Captain Marchand immediately lowered a boat and was rowed up the river to the recent residence of Major Stede Bonnet, and there he delivered two letters—one to the wife of that gentleman, and the other for his daughter. Then the captain rowed back and went into the town, where he annoyed and nearly distracted the citizens by giving them the most cautious and expurgated account of the considerate and friendly manner in which the Amanda had been relieved of her cargo by his old friend and fellow-vestryman, Major Bonnet.

Captain Marchand had been greatly impressed by the many things which Ben Greenway had said about his master's present most astounding freak, and hoping in his heart that repentance and a suitable reparation might soon give this hitherto estimable man an opportunity to return to his former place in society, he said as little as he could against the name and fame of this once respected fellow-citizen. When he communicated with the English owners of his now departed cargo, he would know what to say to them, but here, safe in harbour with his vessel and his passengers, he preferred to wait for a time before entirely blackening the character of the man who had allowed him to come here. Like the faithful Ben Greenway, he did not yet believe in Stede Bonnet's piracy.

Madam Bonnet read her letter and did not like it. In fact, she thought it shameful. Then she opened and read the letter to her step-daughter. This she did not like either, and she put it away in a drawer; she would have nothing to do with the transmission of such an epistle as this. Most abominable when contrasted with the scurrilous screed he had written to her.

DAY AFTER DAY PASSED ON, and Kate Bonnet arose each morning feeling less happy than on the day before. But at last a letter came, brought by a French vessel which had touched at Barbadoes. This letter was to Kate from Martin Newcombe. It was a love-letter, a very earnest, ardent love-letter, but it did not make the young girl happy, for it told her very little about her father. The heart of the lover was so tender that he would say nothing to his lady which might give her needless pain. He had heard what Captain Marchand had told and he had not understood it, and could only half believe it. Kate must know far more about all this painful business than he did, for her father's letter would tell her all he wished her to know. Therefore, why should he discuss that most distressing and perplexing subject, which he knew so little about and which she knew all about. So he merely touched upon Major Bonnet and his vessel, and hoped that she might soon write to him and tell him what she cared for him to know, what she cared for him to tell to the people of Bridgetown, and what she wished to repose confidentially to his honour. But whatever she chose to say to him or not to say to him, he would have her remember that his heart belonged to her, and ever would belong, no matter what might happen or what might be said for good or for bad, on the sea or the land, by friends or enemies.

This was a rarely good love-letter, but it plunged Kate into the deepest woe, and Dickory saw this first of all. He had brought the letter, and for the second time he saw tears in her eyes. The absence of news of Major Bonnet was soon known to the rest of the family, and then there were other tears. It was perfectly plain, even to Dame Charter, that things had been said in Bridgetown which Mr. Newcombe had not cared to write.

"No, Dame Charter," said Kate, "I cannot talk to you about it. My uncle has already spoken words of comfort, but neither you nor he know more than I do, and I must now think a little for myself, if I can."

So saying, she walked out into the grounds to a spot at a little distance where Dickory stood, reflectively gazing out over the landscape.

"Dickory," said the girl, "my mind is filled with horrible doubts. I have heard of the talk in Bridgetown before we left, and now here is this letter from Mr. Newcombe from which I cannot fail to see that there must have been other talk that he considerately refrains from telling me."

"He should not have written such a letter," exclaimed Dickory hotly; "he might have known it would have set you to suspecting things."

"You don't know what you are talking about, you foolish boy," said she; "it is a very proper letter about things you don't understand."

She stepped a little closer to him as if she feared some one might hear her. "Dickory," said she, "he did not put that thing into my mind; it was there already. That was a dreadful ship, Dickory, and it was filled with dreadful men. If he had not intended to go with them he would not have put himself into their power, and if he had not intended to be long away he would not have planned to leave me here with my uncle."

"You ought not to think such a thing as that for one minute," cried Dickory. "I would not think so about my mother, no matter what happened!"

She smiled slightly as she answered. "I would my father were a mother, and then I need not think such things. But, Dickory, if he had but written to me! And in all this time he might have written, knowing how I must feel."

Dickory stood silent, his bosom heaving. Suddenly he turned sharply towards her. "Of course he has written," said he, "but how could his letter come to you? We know not where he has sailed, and besides, who could have told him you had already gone to your uncle? But the people at Bridgetown must know things. I believe that he has written there."

"Why do you believe that?" she asked eagerly, with one hand on his arm.

"I think it," said Dickory, his cheeks a little ruddier in their brownness, "because there is more known there than Master Newcombe chose to put into his letter. If he has not written, how should they know more?"

She now looked straight into his eyes, and as he returned the gaze he could see in her pupils his head and his straw hat, with the clear sky beyond.

"Dickory," she said, "if he wrote to anybody he also wrote to me, and that letter is still there."

"That is what I believe," said he, "and I have been believing it."

"Then why didn't you say so to me, you wretched boy?" cried Kate. "You ought to have known how that would have comforted me. If I could only think he has surely written, my heart would bound, no matter what his letter told; but to be utterly dropped, that I cannot bear."

"You have not been dropped," he exclaimed, "and you shall know it. Kate, I am going—"

"Nay, nay," she exclaimed, "you must not call me that!"

"But you call me Dickory," he said.

"True, but you are so much younger."

"Younger!" he exclaimed in a tone of contempt, not for the speaker but for the word she had spoken. "Eleven months!"

She laughed a little laugh; her nature was so full of it that even now she could not keep it back.

"You must have been making careful computation," she said, "but it does not matter; you must not call me Kate, and I shall keep on calling you Dickory; I could not help it. Now, where is it you were about to say you were going?"

"If you think me old enough," said he, "I am going to Barbadoes in the King and Queen. She sails to-morrow. I shall find out about everything, and I shall get your letter, then I shall come back and bring it to you."

"Dickory!" she exclaimed, and her eyes glowed.

There was silence for some moments, and then he spoke, for it was necessary for him to say something, although he would have been perfectly content to stand there speechless, so long as her eyes still glowed.

"If I don't go," said he, "it may be long before you hear from him; having written, he will wait for an answer."

She thought of no difficulties, no delays, no dangers. "How happy you have made me, Dickory!" she said. "It is this dreadful ignorance, these fearful doubts of which I ought to be ashamed. But if I get his letter, if I know he has not deserted me!"

"You shall get it," he cried, "and you shall know."

"Dickory," said she, "you said that exactly as you spoke when you told me that if I let myself drop into the darkness, you would be there."

"And you shall find me there now," said he; "always, if you need me, you shall find me there!"

Dame Charter had been standing and watching this interview, her foolish motherly heart filled with the brightest, most unreasonable dreams. And why should she not dream, even if she knew her dreams would never come true? In a few short weeks that Dickory boy had grown to be a man, and what should not be dreamed about a man!

As Kate ran by the open door towards her uncle's apartments, Dame Charter rose up, surprised.

"What have you been saying to her, Dickory?" she exclaimed. "Do you know something we have not heard? Have you been giving her news of her father?"

"No," said the son, who had so lately been a boy, "I have no news to give her, but I am going to get news for her."

She looked at him in amazement; then she exclaimed: "You!"

"Yes," he said, "there is no one else. And besides I would not want any one else to do it. I am going to Bridgetown in the brig which brought us here; it is a little sail, and when I get there I will find out everything. No matter what has happened, it will break her heart to think that her father deserted her without a word. I don't believe he did it, and I shall go and find out."

"But, Dickory," she said, with anxious, upraised face, "how can you get back? Do you know of any vessel that will be sailing this way?"

He laughed.

"Get back? If I go alone, dear mother, you may be sure I shall soon get back. Craft of all kinds sail one way or another, and there are many ways in which I can get back not thought of in ordinary passage. When any kind of a vessel sails from Jamaica, I can get on board of her, whether she takes passengers or not. I can sleep on a bale of goods or on the bare deck; I can work with the crew, if need be. Oh! you need not doubt that I shall speedily come back."

They talked long together, this mother and this son, and it was her golden dreams for him that made her invoke Heaven's blessings upon him and tell him to go. She knew, too, that it was wise for her to tell him to go and to bless him, for it would have been impossible to withstand him, so set was he in his purpose.

"I tell you, Dame Charter," said Mr. Delaplaine an hour later, "this son of yours should be a great credit and pride to you, and he will be, I stake my word upon it."

"He is now," said the good woman quietly.

"I have been pondering in my brain," said he, "what I should do to relieve my niece of this burden of anxiety which is weighing upon her. I could see no way, for letters would be of no use, not knowing where to send them, and it would be dreary, indeed, to sit and wait and sigh and dream bad dreams until chance throws some light upon this grievous business, and here steps up this young fellow and settles the whole matter. When he comes back, Dame Charter, I shall do well for him; I shall put him in my counting-house, for, although doubtless he would fain live his young life in the fields and under the open sky, he will find the counting-house lies on the road to fortune, and good fortune he deserves."

If that loving mother could have composed this speech for Master Delaplaine to make she could not have suited it better to her desires.

When the King and Queen was nearly ready to sail, Dickory Charter, having been detained by Mr. Delaplaine, who wished the young man to travel as one of importance and plentiful resources, hurried to the house to take his final instructions from Mistress Kate Bonnet, in whose service he was now setting forth. It might have been supposed by some that no further instructions were necessary, but how could Dickory know that? He was right. Kate met him before he reached the house.

"I am so glad to see you again before you sail," she said. "One thing was forgotten: You may see my father; his cruise may be over and he may be, even now, preparing for me to come back to Bridgetown. If this be so, urge him rather to come here. I had not thought of your seeing him, Dickory, and I did not write to him, but you will know what to say. You have heard that woman talk of me, and you well know I cannot go back to my old home."

"Oh, I will say all that!" he exclaimed. "It will be the same thing as if you had written him a long letter. And now I must run back, for the boat is ready to take me down the river to the port."

"Dickory," said she, and she put out her hand—he had never held that hand before—"you are so true, Dickory, you are so noble; you are going—" it was in her mind to say "you are going as my knight-errant," but she deemed that unsuitable, and she changed it to—"you are going to do so much for me."

She stopped for a moment, and then she said: "You know I told you you should not call me Kate, being so much younger; but, as you are so much younger, you may kiss me if you like."

"Like!"

X

CAPTAIN CHRISTOPHER VINCE

It was truly surprising to see the change which came over the spirits of our young Kate Bonnet when she heard that the King and Queen had sailed from Kingston port. She was gay, she was talkative, she sang songs, she skipped in the paths of the garden. One might have supposed she was so happy to get rid of the young man on the brig which had sailed away. And yet, the news she might hear when that young man came back was likely to be far worse than any misgivings which had entered her mind. Kate's high spirits delighted her uncle. This child of his sister had grown more lovely than even her mother had ever been.

Now came days of delight which Kate had never dreamed of. She had not known that there were such shops in Spanish Town, which, although a youngish town, had already drawn to itself the fashion and the needs of fashion of that prosperous colony. With Dame Charter, and often also with her uncle in company, this bright young girl hovered over fair fabrics which were spread before her; circled about jewels, gems, and feathers, and revelled in tender colours as would a butterfly among the blossoms, dipping and tasting as she flew.

There were some fine folk in Spanish Town, and with this pleasant society of the capital Mr. Delaplaine renewed his previous intercourse and Kate soon learned the pleasures of a colonial social circle, whose attractions, brought from afar, had been warmed into a more cheerful glow in this bright West Indian atmosphere.

To add to the brilliancy of the new life into which Kate now entered, there came into the port an English corvette—the Badger—for refitting. From this welcome man-of-war there flitted up the river to Spanish Town gallant officers, young and older; and in their flitting they flitted into the drawing-room of the rich merchant Delaplaine, and there were some of them who soon found that there were no drawing-rooms in all the town where they could talk with, walk with, and perchance dance with such a fine girl as Mistress Kate Bonnet.

Kate greatly fancied gallant partners, whether for walking or talking or dancing, and among such, those which came from the corvette in the harbour pleased her most.

Those were not bright days for Dame Charter. Do what she would, her optimism was growing dim, and what helped to dim it was Kate's gaiety. It did not comfort her at all when Kate told her that she was so light-hearted because she knew that Dickory would bring her good news.

"Truly, too many fine young men here," thought Dame Charter, "while Dickory is away, and all of them together are not worth a curl on his head."

But, although her dreams were dimmed, she did not cease dreaming. A stout-hearted woman was Dickory's mother.

But it was not long before there were other people thereabout who began to feel that their prospects for present enjoyment were beginning to look a little dim, for Captain Christopher Vince, having met Mistress Kate Bonnet at an entertainment at the Governor's house, was greatly struck by this young lady. Each officer of the Badger who saw their captain in company with the fair one to whom their gallant attentions had been so freely offered, now felt that in love as well as in accordance with the regulations of the service, he must give place to his captain. Moreover, when that captain took upon himself, the very next day, to call at the residence of Mr. Delaplaine, and repeated the visit upon the next day and the following, the crestfallen young fellows were compelled to acknowledge that there were other houses in the town where it might be better worth their while to spend their leisure hours.

Captain Vince was not a man to be lightly interfered with, whether he happened to be engaged in the affairs of Mars or Cupid. He was of a resolute mind, and of a person more than usually agreeable to the female eye. He was about forty years of age, of an excellent English family, and with good expectations. He considered himself an admirable judge of women, but he had never met one who so thoroughly satisfied his aesthetic taste as this fair niece of the merchant Delaplaine. She had beauty, she had wit, she had culture, and the fair fabrics of Spanish Town shops gave to her attractions a setting which would have amazed and entranced Master Newcombe or our good Dickory. The soul of Captain Vince was fired, and each time he met Kate and talked with her the fire grew brighter.

He had never considered himself a marrying man, but that was because he had never met any one he had cared to marry. Now things were changed. Here was a girl he had known but for a few days, and already, in his imagination, he had placed her in the drawing-rooms of the English home he hoped soon to inherit, more beautiful and even more like a princess than any noble dame who was likely to frequent those rooms. In fancy he had seen her by his side, walking through the shaded alleys of his grand old gardens; he had looked proudly upon her as she stood by him in the assemblages of the great; in fact, he had fallen suddenly and absolutely in love with her. When he was away from her he could not quite understand this condition of things, but when he was with her again he understood it all. He loved her because it was absolutely impossible for him to do anything else.

Naturally, Captain Vince was very agreeable to Mistress Kate, for she had never seen such a handsome man, taking into consideration his uniform and his bearing, and had never talked with one who knew so well what to say and how to say it. Comparing him with the young officers who had been so fond of making their way to her uncle's house, she was glad that they had ceased to be such frequent visitors.

The soul of Mr. Delaplaine was agitated by the admiration of his niece which Captain Vince took no trouble to conceal. The worthy merchant would gladly have kept Kate with him for years and years if she would have been content to stay, but this could not be expected; and if she married, from what other quarter could come such a brilliant match as this? What his brother-in-law might think about it he did not care; if Kate should choose to wed the captain, such an eccentric and untrustworthy person should not be permitted to interfere with the destiny that now appeared to open before his daughter. These thoughts were not so idle as might have been supposed, for the captain had already said things to the merchant, in which the circumstances of the former were made plain and his hopes foreshadowed. If the captain were not prepared to leave the service, this rich merchant thought, why should not he make it possible for him to do so, for the sake of his dear niece?

With these high ambitions in his mind, the happily agitated Mr. Delaplaine did not hesitate to say some playful words to Kate concerning the captain of the Badger; and these having been received quietly, he was emboldened to go on and say some other words more serious.

Then Kate looked at him very steadfastly and remarked: "But, uncle, you have forgotten Master Newcombe."

The good Delaplaine made no answer, for his emotions made it impossible for him to do so, but, rising, he went out, and at a little distance from the house he damned Master Newcombe.

Days passed on and the captain's attentions did not wane. Mr. Delaplaine, who was a man of honour expecting it in others, made up his mind that something decisive must soon be said; while Kate began greatly to fear that something decisive might soon be said. She was in a difficult position. She was not engaged to Martin Newcombe, but had believed she might be. The whole affair involved a question which she did not want to consider. And still the captain came every day, generally in the afternoon or evening.

But one morning he made his appearance, coming to the house quite abruptly.

"I am glad to find you by yourself," said he, "for I have some awkward news."

Kate looked at him surprised.

"I have just been ordered on duty," he continued, "and the order is most unwelcome. A brig came in last night and brought letters, and the Governor sent for me this morning. I have just left him. The cruise I am about to take may not be a long one, but I cannot leave port without coming here to you and speaking to you of something which is nearer to my heart than any thought of service, or in fact of anything else."

"Speaking to my uncle, you mean," said Kate, now much disturbed, for she saw in the captain's eyes what he wished to talk of.

"Away with uncles!" he exclaimed; "we can speak with them by-and-bye; now my words are for you. You may think me hasty, but we gentlemen serving the king cannot afford to wait; and so, without other pause, I say, sweet Mistress Kate, I love you, better than I have ever loved woman; better than I can ever love another. Nay, do not answer; I must tell you everything before you reply." And to the pale girl he spoke of his family, his prospects, and his hopes. In the warmest colours he laid before her the life and love he would give her. Then he went quickly on: "This is but a little matter which is given to my charge, and it may not engage me long; I am going out in search of a pirate, and I shall make short work of him. The shorter, having such good reason to get quickly back.

"In fact, he is not a real pirate anyway, being but a country gentleman tiring of his rural life and liking better to rob, burn, and murder on the high seas. He has already done so much damage, that if his evil career be not soon put an end to good people will be afraid to voyage in these waters. So I am to sail in haste after this fellow Bonnet; but before—"

FRANK R. STOCKTON

Kate's face had grown so white that it seemed to recede from her great eyes. "He is my father," said she, "but I had not heard until now that he is a pirate!"

The captain started from his chair. "What!" he cried, "your father? Yes, I see. It did not strike me until this instant that the names are the same."

Kate rose, and as she spoke her voice was not full and clear as it was wont to be. "He is my father," she said, "but he sailed away without telling me his errand; but now that I know everything, I must—" If she had intended to say she must go, she changed her mind, and even came closer to the still astounded captain. "You say that you will make short work of his vessel; do you mean that you will destroy it, and will you kill him?"

CAPTAIN VINCE LOOKED DOWN UPON her, his face filled with the liveliest emotions. "My dear young lady," he said, and then he stopped as if not knowing what words to use. But as he looked into her eyes fixed upon his own and waiting for his answer, his love for her took possession of him and banished all else. "Kill him," he exclaimed, "never! He shall be as safe in my hands as if he were walking in his own fields. Kill your father, dearest? Loving you as I do, that would be impossible. I may take the rascals who are with him, I may string them up to the yard-arm, or I may sink their pirate ship with all of them in it, but your father shall be safe. Trust me for that; he shall come to no harm from me."

She stepped a little way from him, and some of her colour came back. For some moments she looked at him without speaking, as if she did not exactly comprehend what he had said.

"Yes, my dear," he continued, "I must crush out that piratical crew, for such is my duty as well as my wish, but your father I shall take under my protection; so have no fear about him, I beg you. With his ship and his gang of scoundrels taken away from him, he can no longer be a pirate, and you and I will determine what we shall do with him."

"You mean," said Kate, speaking slowly, "that for my sake you will shield my father from the punishment which will be dealt out to his companions?"

He smiled, and his face beamed upon her. "What blessed words," he exclaimed. "Yes, for your sake, for your sweet, dear sake I will do anything; and as for this matter, I assure you there are so many ways—"

"You mean," she interrupted, "that for my sake you will break your oath of office, that you will be a traitor to your service and your king? That for my sake you will favour the fortunes of a pirate whom you are sent out to destroy? Mean it if you please, but you will not do it. I love my father, and would fain do anything to save him and myself from this great calamity, but I tell you, sir, that for my sake no man shall do himself dishonour!"

Without power to say another word, nor to keep back for another second the anguish which raged within her, she fled like a bird and was gone.

The captain stretched out his arms as if he would seize her; he rushed to the door through which she had passed, but she was gone. He followed her, shouting to the startled servants who came; he swore, and demanded to see their mistress; he rushed through rooms and corridors, and even made as if he would mount the stairs. Presently a woman came to him, and told him that under no circumstances could Mistress Bonnet now be seen.

But he would not leave the house. He called for writing materials, but in an instant threw down the pen. Again he called a servant and sent a message, which was of no avail. Dame Charter would have gone down to him, but Kate was in her arms. For several minutes the furious officer stood by the chair in which Kate had been sitting; he could not comprehend the fact that this girl had discarded and had scorned him. And yet her scorn had not in the least dampened the violence of his love. As she stood and spoke her last bitter words, the grandeur of her beauty had made him speechless to defend himself.

He seized his hat and rushed from the house; hot, and with blazing eyes, he appeared in the counting-room of Mr. Delaplaine, and there, to that astounded merchant, he told, with brutal cruelty, of his orders to destroy the pirate Bonnet, his niece's father; and then he related the details of his interview with that niece herself.

Mr. Delaplaine's countenance, at first shocked and pained, grew gradually sterner and colder. Presently he spoke. "I will hear no more such words, Captain Vince," he said, "regarding the members of my family. You say my niece knows not what fortune she trifles with; I think she does. And when she told you she would not accept the offer of your dishonour, I commend her every word."

Captain Vince frowned black as night, and clapped his hand to his sword-hilt; but the pale merchant made no movement of defence, and the captain, striking his clinched fist against the table, dashed from the room. Before he reached his ship he had sworn a solemn oath: he vowed that he would follow that pirate ship; he would kill, burn, destroy, annihilate, but out of the storm and the fire he would pick unharmed the father of the girl who had entranced him and had spurned him. He laughed savagely as he thought of it. With that dolt of a father in his hands, a man wearing always around his neck the hangman's noose, he would hold the card which would give him the game. What Mistress Kate Bonnet might say or do; what she might like or might not like; what her ideas about honour might be or might not be, it would be a very different thing when he, her imperious lover, should hold the end of that noose in his hand. She might weep, she might rave, but come what would, she was the man's daughter, and she would be Lady Vince.

So he went on board the Badger, and he cursed and he commanded and he raged; and his officers and his men, when the hurried violence of his commands gave them a chance to speak to each other, muttered that they pitied that pirate and his crew when the Badger came up with them.

Clouds settled down upon the home of Mr. Delaplaine. There were no visitors, there was no music, there seemed to be no sunshine. The beautiful fabrics, the jewels, and the feathers were seen no more. It was Kate of the broken heart who wandered under the trees and among the blossoms, and knew not that there existed such things as cooling shade and sweet fragrance. She could not be comforted, for, although her uncle told her that he had had information that her father's ship had sailed northward, and that it was, therefore, likely that the corvette would not overtake him, she could not forget that, whatever of good or evil befell that father, he was a pirate, and he had deserted her.

So they said but little, the uncle and the niece, who sorrowed quietly.

Dame Charter was in a strange state of mind. During the frequent visits of Captain Vince she had been apprehensive and troubled, and her only comfort was that the Badger had merely touched at this port to refit, and that she must soon sail away and take with her her captain. The good woman had begun to expect and to hope for the return of Dickory, but later she had blessed her stars that he was not there. He was a fiery boy, her brave son, but it would have been a terrible thing for him to become involved with an officer in the navy, a man with a long, keen sword.

Now that the captain had raged himself away from the Delaplaine house her spirits rose, and her great fear was that the corvette might not leave port before the brig came in. If Dickory should hear of the things that captain had said—but she banished such thoughts from her mind, she could not bear them.

After some days the corvette sailed, and the Governor spoke well of the diligence and ardour which had urged Captain Vince to so quickly set out upon his path of duty.

"When Dickory comes back," said Dame Charter to Kate, "he may bring some news to cheer your poor heart, things get so twisted in the telling."

Kate shook her head. "Dickory cannot tell me anything now," she said, "that I care to know, knowing so much. My father is a pirate, and a king's ship has gone out to destroy him, and what could Dickory tell me that would cheer me?"

But Dame Charter's optimism was beginning to take heart again and to spread its wings.

"Ah, my dear, you don't know what good things do in this life continually crop up. A letter from your father, possibly withheld by that wicked Madam Bonnet—which is what Dickory and I both think—or some good words from the town that your father has sold his ship, and is on his way home. Nobody knows what good news that Dickory may bring with him."

The poor girl actually smiled. She was young, and in the heart of youth there is always room for some good news, or for the hope of them.

But the smile vanished altogether when she went to her room and wrote a letter to Martin Newcombe. In this letter, which was a long one, she told her lover how troubled she had been. That she had nothing now to ask him about the bad news he had, in his kindness, forborne to tell her, and that when he saw Dickory Charter he might say to him from her that there was no need to make any further inquiries about her father; she knew enough, and far too much—more, most likely, than any one in Bridgetown knew. Then she told him of Captain Vince and the dreadful errand of the corvette Badger.

Having done this, Kate became as brave as any captain of a British man-of-war, and she told her lover that he must think no more of her; it was not for him to pay court to the daughter of a pirate. And so, she blessed him and bade him farewell.

When she had signed and sealed this letter she felt as if she had torn out a chapter of her young life and thrown it upon the fire.

XI

BAD WEATHER

When Dickory Charter sailed away from the island of Jamaica, his reason, had it been called upon, would have told him that he had a good stout brig under him on which there were people and ropes and sails and something to eat and drink. But in those moments of paradise he did not trouble his reason very much, and lived in an atmosphere of joy which he did not attempt to analyze, but was content to breathe as if it had been the common air about him. He was going away from every one he loved, and yet never before had he been so happy in going to any one he loved. He cared to talk to no one on board, but in company with his joy he stood and gazed westward out over the sea.

He was but little younger than she was, and yet that difference, so slight, had lifted him from things of earth and had placed him in that paradise where he now dwelt.

So passed on the hours, so rolled the waves, and so moved the King and Queen before the favouring breeze.

It was on the second day out that the breeze began to be less favouring, and there were signs of a storm; and, in spite of his preoccupied condition, Dickory was obliged to notice the hurried talk of the officers about him, he occupying a point of vantage on the quarter-deck. Presently he turned and asked of some one if there was likelihood of bad weather. The mate, to whom he had spoken, said somewhat unpleasantly, "Bad weather enough, I take it, as we may all soon know; but it is not wind or rain. There is bad weather for you! Do you see that?"

Dickory looked, and saw far away, but still distinct, a vessel under full sail with a little black spot floating high above it.

He turned to the man for explanation. "And what is that?" he said.

"It is a pirate ship," said the other, his face hardening as he spoke, "and it will soon be firing at us to heave to."

At that moment there was a flash at the bow of the approaching vessel, a little smoke, and then the report of a cannon came over the water.

Without further delay, the captain and crew of the King and Queen went to work and hove to their brig.

Young Dickory Charter also hove to. He did not know exactly why, but his dream stopped sailing over a sea of delight. They stood motionless, their sails flapping in the wind.

"Pirates!" he thought to himself, cold shivers running through him, "is this brig to be taken? Am I to be taken? Am I not to go to Barbadoes, to Bridgetown, her home? Am I not to take her back the good news which will make her happy? Are these things possible?"

He stared over the water, he saw the swiftly approaching vessel, he could distinguish the skull and bones upon the black flag which flew above her.

These things were possible, and his heart fell; but it was not with fear. Dickory Charter was as bold a fellow as ever stood on the deck in a sea fight, but his heart fell at the thought that he might not be going to her old home, and that he might not sail back with good news to her.

As the swift-sailing pirate ship sped on, Ben Greenway came aft to Captain Bonnet, and a grievous grin was on the Scotchman's face.

"Good greetin's to ye, Master Bonnet," said he, "ye're truly good to your old friends an' neebours an' pass them not by, even when your pockets are burstin' wi' Spanish gold."

A minute before this Captain Stede Bonnet had been in a very pleasant state of mind. It was only two days ago that he had captured a Spanish ship, from which he got great gain, including considerable stores of gold. Everything of value had been secured, the tall galleon had been burned, and its crew had been marooned on a barren spot on the coast of San Domingo. The spoils had been divided, at least every man knew what his share was to be, and the officers and the crew of the Revenge were in a well-contented state of mind. In fact, Captain Bonnet would not have sailed after a little brig, certainly unsuited to carry costly cargo, had it not been that his piratical principle made it appear to him a point of conscience to prey upon all mercantile craft, little or big, which might come in his way. Thus it was, that he was sailing merrily after the King and Queen, when Ben Greenway came to him with his disturbing words.

"What mean you?" cried Bonnet. "Know you that vessel?"

"Ay, weel," said Ben, "it is the King and Queen, bound, doubtless, for Bridgetown. I tell ye, Master Bonnet, that it was a great deal o' trouble an' expense ye put yersel' to when ye went into your present line o' business on this ship. Ye could have stayed at hame, where she is owned, an' wi' these fine fellows that ye have gathered thegither, ye might have robbed your neebours right an' left wi'out the trouble o' goin' to sea."

"Ben Greenway," roared the captain, "I will have no more of this. Is it not enough for me to be annoyed and worried by these everlasting ships of Bridgetown, which keep sailing across my bows, no matter in what direction I go, without hearing your jeers and sneers regarding the matter? I tell you, Ben Greenway, I will not have it. I will not suffer these paltry vessels, filled, perhaps, with the grocers and cloth dealers from my own town, to interfere thus with the bold career that I have chosen. I tell you, Ben Greenway, I'll make an example of this one. I am a pirate, and I will let them know it—these fellows in their floating shops. It will be a fair and easy thing to sink this tub without more ado. I'd rather meet three Spanish ships, even had they naught aboard, than one of these righteous craft commanded by my most respectable friends and neighbours."

Black Paul, the sailing-master, had approached and had heard the greater part of these remarks.

"Better board her and see what she carries," said he, "before we sink her. The men have been talking about her and, many of them, favour not the trouble of marooning those on board of her. So, say most of us, let's get what we can from her, and then quickly rid ourselves of her one way or another."

"'Tis well!" cried Bonnet, "we can riddle her hull and sink her."

"Wi' the neebours on board?" asked Greenway.

Captain Bonnet scowled blackly.

"Ben Greenway," he shouted, "it would serve you right if I tied you hand and foot and bundled you on board that brig, after we have stripped her, if haply she have anything on board we care for."

"An' then sink her?" asked the Scotchman.

"Ay, sink her!" replied Bonnet. "Thus would I rid myself of a man who vexes me every moment that I lay my eyes on him, and, moreover, it would please you; for you would die in the midst of those friends and neighbours you have such a high regard for. That would put an end to your cackle, and there would be no gossip in the town about it."

The sailing-master now came aft. The vessel had been put about and was slowly approaching the brig. "Shall we make fast?" asked Black Paul. "If we do we shall have to be quick about it; the sea is rising, and that clumsy hulk may do us damage."

For a moment Captain Bonnet hesitated, he was beginning to learn something of the risks and dangers of a nautical life, and here was real danger if the two vessels ran nearer each other. Suddenly he turned and glared at Greenway. "Make fast!" he cried savagely, "make fast! if it be only for a minute."

"Do ye think in your heart," asked the Scotchman grimly, "that ye're pirate enough for that?"

XII

FACE TO FACE

With her head to the wind the pirate vessel Revenge bore down slowly upon the King and Queen, now lying to and awaiting her. The stiff breeze was growing stiffer and the sea was rising. The experienced eye of Paul Bittern, the sailing-master of the pirate, now told him that it would be dangerous to approach the brig near enough to make fast to her, even for the minute which Captain Bonnet craved—the minute which would have been long enough for a couple of sturdy fellows to toss on board the prize that exasperating human indictment, Ben Greenway.

"We cannot do it," shouted Black Paul to Bonnet, "we shall run too near her as it is. Shall we let fly at short range and riddle her hull?"

Captain Bonnet did not immediately answer; the situation puzzled him. He wanted very much to put the Scotchman on board the brig, and after that he did not care what happened. But before he could speak, there appeared on the rail of the King and Queen, holding fast to a shroud, the figure of a young man, who put his hand to his mouth and hailed:

"Throw me a line! Throw me a line!"

Such an extraordinary request at such a time naturally amazed the pirates, and they stood staring, as they crowded along the side of their vessel.

"If you are not going to board her," shouted Dickory again, "throw me a line!"

Filled with curiosity to know what this strange proceeding meant, Black Paul ordered that a line be thrown, and, in a moment, a tall fellow seized a coil of light rope and hurled it through the air in the direction of the brig; but the rope fell short, and the outer end of it disappeared beneath the water. Now the spirit of Black Paul was up. If the fellow on the brig wanted a line he wanted to come aboard, and if he wanted to come aboard, he should do so. So he seized a heavier coil and, swinging it around his head, sent it, with tremendous force, towards Dickory, who made a wild grab at it and caught it.

Although a comparatively light line, it was a long one, and the slack of it was now in the water, so that Dickory had to pull hard upon it before he could grasp enough of it to pass around his body. He had scarcely done this, and had made a knot in it, before a lurch of the brig brought a strain on the rope, and he was incontinently jerked overboard.

The crew of the merchantman, who had not had time to comprehend what the young fellow was about to do, would have grasped him had he remained on the rail a moment longer, but now he was gone into the sea, and, working vigorously with his legs and arms, was endeavouring to keep his head above water while the pirates at the other end of the rope pulled him swiftly towards their vessel.

Great was the excitement on board the Revenge. Why should a man from a merchantman endeavour, alone, to board a vessel which flew the Jolly Roger? Did he wish to join the crew? Had they been ill-treating him on board the brig? Was he a criminal endeavouring to escape from the officers of the law? It was impossible to answer any of these questions, and so the swarthy rascals pulled so hard and so steadily upon the line that the knot in it, which Dickory had not tied properly, became a slipknot, and the poor fellow's breath was nearly squeezed out of him as he was hauled over the rough water. When he reached the vessel's side there was something said about lowering a ladder, but the men who were hauling on the line were in a hurry to satisfy their curiosity, so up came Dickory straight from the water to the rail, and that proceeding so increased the squeezing that the poor fellow fell upon the deck scarcely able to gasp. When the rope was loosened the half-drowned and almost breathless Dickory raised himself and gave two or three deep breaths, but he could not speak, despite the fact that a dozen rough voices were asking him who he was and what he wanted.

With the water pouring from him in streams, and his breath coming from him in puffs, he looked about him with great earnestness.

Suddenly a man rushed through the crowd of pirates and stooped to look at the person who had so strangely come aboard. Then he gave a shout. "It is Dickory Charter," he cried, "Dickory Charter, the son o' old Dame Charter! Ye Dickory! an' how in the name o' all that's blessed did ye come here? Master Bonnet! Master Bonnet!" he shouted to the captain, who now stood by, "it is young Dickory Charter, of Bridgetown. He was on board this vessel before we sailed, wi' Mistress Kate an' me. The last time I saw her he was wi' her."

"What!" exclaimed Bonnet, "with my daughter?"

"Ay, ay!" said Greenway, "it must have been a little before she went on shore."

"Young man!" cried Bonnet, stooping towards Dickory, "when did you last see my daughter? Do you know anything of her?"

The young man opened his mouth, but he could not yet do much in the way of speaking, but he managed to gasp, "I come from her, I am bringing you a message."

"A message from Kate!" shouted Bonnet, now in a state of wild excitement. "Here you, Greenway, lift up the other arm, and we will take him to my cabin. Quick, man! Quick, man! he must have some spirits and dry clothes. Make haste now! A message from my daughter!"

"If that's so," said Greenway, as he and Bonnet hurried the young man aft, "ye'd better no' be in too great haste to get his message out o' him or ye'll kill him wi' pure recklessness."

Bonnet took the advice, and before many minutes Dickory was in dry clothes and feeling the inspiriting influence of a glass of good old rum. Now came Black Paul, wanting to know if he should sink the brig and be done with her, for they couldn't lie by in such weather.

"Don't you fire on that ship!" yelled Bonnet, "don't you dare it! For all I know, my daughter may be on board of her."

At this Dickory shook his head. "No," said he, "she is not on board."

"Then let her go," cried Bonnet, "I have no time to fool with the beggarly hulk. Let her go! I have other business here. And now, sir," addressing Dickory, "what of my daughter? You have got your breath now, tell me quickly! What is your message from her? When did you sail from Bridgetown? Did she expect me to overhaul that brig? How in the name of all the devils could she expect that?"

"Come, come now, Master Bonnet!" exclaimed the Scotchman, "ye are talkin' o' your daughter, the good an' beautiful Mistress Kate, an' no matter whether ye are a pirate or no, ye must keep a guard on your tongue. An' if ye think she knew where to find ye, ye must consider her an angel an' no' to be spoken o' in the same breath as de'ils."

"I didn't sail from Bridgetown," said Dickory, "and your daughter is not there. I come from Jamaica, where she now is, and was bound to Bridgetown to seek news of you, hoping that you had returned there."

"Which, if he had," said Ben, who found it very difficult to keep quiet, "ye would hae been under the necessity o' givin' your message to his bones hangin' in chains."

Bonnet looked savagely at Ben, but he had no time even to curse.

"Jamaica!" he cried, "how did she get there? Tell me quickly, sir—tell me quickly! Do you hear?"

Dickory was now quite recovered and he told his story, not too quickly, and with much attention to details. Even the account of the unusual manner in which he and Kate had disembarked from the pirate vessel was given without curtailment, nor with any attention to the approving grunts of Ben Greenway. When he came to speak of the letter which Mr. Newcombe had written her, and which had thrown her into such despair on account of its shortcomings, Captain Bonnet burst into a fury of execration.

"And she never got my letter?" he cried, "and knew not what had happened to me. It is that wife of mine, that cruel wild-cat! I sent the letter to my house, thinking, of course, it would find my daughter there. For where else should she be?"

"An' a maist extraordinary wise mon ye were to do that," said Ben Greenway, "for ye might hae known, if ye had ever thought o' it at all, that the place where your wife was, was the place where your daughter couldna be, an' ye no' wi' her. If ye had spoke to me about it, it would hae gone to Mr. Newcombe, an' then ye'd hae known that she'd be sure to get it."

At this a slight cloud passed over Dickory's face, and, in spite of the misfortunes which had followed upon the non-delivery of her father's letter, he could not help congratulating himself that it had not been sent to the care of that man Newcombe. He had not had time to formulate the reasons why this proceeding would have been so distasteful to him, but he wanted Martin Newcombe to have nothing to do with the good or bad fortune of Mistress Kate, whose champion he had become and whose father he had found, and to whom he was now talking, face to face.

The three talked for a long time, during which Black Paul had put the vessel about upon her former course, and was sailing swiftly to the north. As Dickory went on, Bonnet ceased to curse, but, over and over, blessed his brother-in-law, as a good man and one of the few worthy to take into his charge the good and beautiful. Stede Bonnet had always been very fond of his daughter, and, now, as it became known to him into what desperate and direful condition his reckless conduct had thrown her, he loved her more and more, and grieved greatly for the troubles he had brought upon her.

"But it'll be all right now," he cried, "she's with her good uncle, who will show her the most gracious kindness, both for her mother's sake and for her own; and I will see to it that she be not too heavy a charge upon him."

"As for ye, Dickory," exclaimed Greenway, "ye're a brave boy an' will yet come to be an' honour to yer mither's declining years an' to the memory o' your father. But how did ye ever come to think o' boardin' this nest o' sea-de'ils, an' at such risk to your life?"

"I did it," said Dickory simply, "because Mistress Kate's father was here, and I was bound to come to him wherever I should find him, for that was my main errand. They told me on the brig that it was Captain Bonnet's ship that was overhauling us, and I vowed that as soon as she boarded us I would seek him out and give him her message; and when I heard that the sea was getting too heavy for you to board us, I determined to come on board if I could get hold of a line."

"Young man," cried Bonnet, rising to his full height and swelling his chest, "I bestow upon you a father's blessing. More than that"—and as he spoke he pulled open a drawer of a small locker—"here's a bag of gold pieces, and when you take my answer you shall have another like it."

But Dickory did not reach out his hand for the money, nor did he say a word.

"Don't be afraid," cried Bonnet. "If you have any religious scruples, I will tell you that this gold I did not get by piracy. It is part of my private fortune, and came as honestly to me as I now give it to you."

But Dickory did not reach out his hand.

Now up spoke Ben Greenway: "Look ye, boy," said he, "as long as there's a chance left o' gettin' honest gold on board this vessel, I pray ye, seize it, an' if ye're afraid o' this gold, thinkin' it may be smeared wi' the blood o' fathers an' the tears o' mithers, I'll tell ye ane thing, an' that is, that Master Bonnet hasna got to be so much o' a pirate that he willna tell the truth. So I'll tak' the money for ye, Dickory, an' I'll keep it till ye're ready to tak' it to your mither; an' I hope that will be soon."

XIII

Captain Bonnet Goes to Church

The pirate vessel Revenge was now bound to the coast of the Carolinas and Virginia, and perhaps even farther north, if her wicked fortune should favour her. The growing commerce of the colonies offered great prizes in those days to the piratical cruisers which swarmed up and down the Atlantic coast. To lie over for a time off the coast of Charles Town was Captain Bonnet's immediate object, and to get there as soon as possible was almost a necessity.

The crew of desperate scoundrels whom he had gathered together had discovered that their captain knew nothing of navigation or the management of a ship, and there were many of them who believed that if Black Paul had chosen to turn the vessel's bows to the coast of South America, Bonnet would not have known that they were not sailing northward. Thus they had lost all respect for him, and their conduct was kept within bounds only by the cruel punishments which he inflicted for disobedience or general bad conduct, and which were rendered possible by the dissensions and bad feelings among the men themselves; one clique or faction being always ready to help punish another. Consequently, the landsman pirate would speedily have been tossed overboard and the command given to another, had it not been that the men were not at all united in their opinions as to who that other should be.

There was also another very good reason for Bonnet's continuance in authority; he was a good divider, and, so far, had been a good provider. If he should continue to take prizes, and to give each man under him his fair share of the plunder, the men were likely to stand by him until some good reason came for their changing their minds. So with floggings and irons, on deck and below, and with fair winds filling the sails above, the Revenge kept on her way; and, in spite of the curses and quarrels and threats which polluted the air through which the stout ship sailed, there was always good-natured companionship wherever the captain, Dickory, and Ben Greenway found themselves together. There seemed to be no end to the questions which Bonnet asked about his daughter, and when he had asked them all he began over again, and Dickory made answer, as he had done before.

The young fellow was growing very anxious at this northern voyage, and when he asked questions they always related to the probability of his getting back to Jamaica with news from the father of Mistress Kate Bonnet. The captain encouraged the hopes of an early return, and vowed to Dickory that he would send him to Spanish Town with a letter to his daughter just as soon as an opportunity should show itself.

When the Revenge reached the mouth of Charles Town harbour she stationed herself there, and in four days captured three well-laden merchantmen; two bound outward, and one going in from England.

Thus all went well, and with willing hands to man her yards and a proudly strutting captain on her quarter-deck, the pirate ship renewed her northward course, and spread terror and made prizes even as far as the New England coast; and if Dickory had had any doubts that the late reputable planter of Bridgetown had now become a veritable pirate he had many opportunities of setting himself right. Bonnet seemed to be growing proud of his newly acquired taste for rapacity and cruelty. Merchantmen were recklessly robbed and burned, their crews and passengers, even babes and women, being set on shore in some desolate spot, to perish or survive, the pirate cared not which, and if resistance were offered, bloody massacres or heartless drownings were almost sure to follow, and, as his men coveted spoils and delighted in cruelty, he satisfied them to their heart's content.

"I tell you, Dickory Charter," said he, one day, "when you see my daughter I want you to make her understand that I am a real pirate, and not playing at the business. She's a brave girl, my daughter Kate, and what I do, she would have me do well and not half-heartedly, to make her ashamed of me. And then, there is my brother-in-law, Delaplaine. I don't believe that he had a very high opinion of me when I was a plain farmer and planter, and I want him to think better of me now. A bold, fearless pirate cannot be looked upon with disrespect."

Dickory groaned in his heart that this man was the father of Kate.

Turning southward, rounding the cape of Delaware, the Revenge ran up the bay, seeking some spot where she might take in water, casting anchor before a little town on the coast of New Jersey. Here, while some of the men were taking in water, others of the crew were allowed to go on shore, their captain swearing to them that if they were guilty of any disorder they should suffer for it. "On my vessel," he swore, "I am a pirate, but when I go on shore I am a gentleman, and every one in my service shall behave himself as a gentleman. I beg of you to remember that."

Agreeable to this principle, Captain Bonnet arrayed himself in a fine suit of clothes, and without arms, excepting a genteel sword, and carrying a cane, he landed with Ben Greenway and Dickory, and proceeded to indulge himself in a promenade up the main street of the town.

The citizens of the place, terrified and amazed at this bold conduct of a vessel fearlessly flying a black flag with the skull and bones, could do nothing but await their fate. The women and children, and many of the men, hid themselves in garrets and cellars, and those of the people who were obliged to remain visible trembled and prayed, but Captain Stede Bonnet walked boldly up the right-hand side of the main street waving his cane in the air as he spoke to the people, assuring them that he and his men came on an errand of business, seeking nothing but some fresh water and an opportunity to stretch their legs on solid ground.

"If you have meat and drink," he cried, "bestow it freely upon my men, tired of the unsavoury food on shipboard, and if they transgress the laws of hospitality then I, their captain, shall be your avenger; we want none of your goods or money, having enough in our well-laden vessel to satisfy all your necessities, if ye have them, and to feel it not."

The men strolled along the street, swarmed into the two little taverns, soon making away with their small stores of ale and spirits, and accepting everything eatable offered them by the shivering citizens; but as to violence there was none, for every man of the rascally crew bore enmity against most of the others, and held himself ready for a chance to report a shipmate or to break his head.

Black Paul was a powerful aid in the preservation of order among the disorderly. Conflicts between factions of the crew were greatly feared by him, for the schemes which happy chance had caused to now revolve themselves in his master mind would have been sadly interfered with by want of concord among the men of the Revenge.

Captain Bonnet, followed at a short distance by Dickory and Ben, was interested in everything he saw. A man of intelligence and considerable reading, it pleased him to note the peculiarities of the people of a country which he had never visited. The houses, the shops, and even the attire of the citizens, were novel and well worthy of his observation. He looked over garden walls, he gazed out upon the fields which were visible from the upper end of the street, and when he saw a man who was able to command his speech he asked him questions.

There was a little church, standing back from the thoroughfare, its door wide open, and this was an instant attraction to the pirate captain, who opened the gate of the yard and walked up to it.

"That I should ever again see Master Stede Bonnet goin' into a church was something I didna dream o', Dickory," said Ben Greenway, "it will be a meeracle, an' I doubt if he dares to pass the door wi' his sins an' his plunders on his head."

But Captain Bonnet did pass the door, reverentially removing his hat, if not his crimes, as he entered. In but few ways it resembled the houses of worship to which he had been accustomed in his earlier days, and he gazed eagerly from side to side as he slowly walked up the central aisle. Dickory was about to follow him, but he was suddenly jerked back by the Scotchman, who forcibly drew him away from the door.

"Look ye," whispered Ben, speaking quickly, under great excitement, "look ye, Dickory, Heaven has sent us our chance. He's in there safe an' sound, an' the good angels will keep his mind occupied. I'll quietly close the door an' turn the key, then I'll slip around to the back, an' if there be anither door there, I'll stop it some way, if it be not already locked. Now, Dickory boy, make your heels fly! I noticed, before we got here, that some o' the men were makin' their way to the boats; dash ye amang them, Dickory, an' tell them that the day they've been longin' for, ever since they set foot on the vessel, has now come. Their captain is a prisoner, an' they are free to hurry on board their vessel an' carry awa wi' them a' their vile plunder."

"What!" exclaimed Dickory, speaking so earnestly that the Scotchman pulled him farther away from the church, "do you mean that you would leave Captain Bonnet here by himself, in a foreign town?"

"No' a bit o' it," said Ben, "I'll stay wi' him an' so will you. Now run, Dickory!"

"Ben!" exclaimed the other, "you don't know what you are talking about! Captain Bonnet would be seized and tried as a pirate. His blood would be on your head, Ben!"

"I canna talk about that now," said Ben impatiently, "ye think too much o' the man's body, Dickory, an' I am considerin' his soul."

"And I am considering his daughter," said Dickory fearlessly; "do you suppose I am going to help to have her father hanged?" and with these words he made a movement towards the door.

The eager Scotchman seized him. "Dickory, bethink yoursel'," said he. "I don't want to hang him, I want to save him, body an' soul. We will get him awa' from here after the ship has gone, he will be helpless then, he canna be a pirate a minute longer, an' he will give up an' do what I tell him. We can leave before there is ony talk o' trial or hangin'. Run, Dickory, run! Ye're sinfully losin' time. Think o' his soul, Dickory; it's his only chance!"

With a great jerk Dickory freed himself from the grasp of the Scotchman.

"It is Kate Bonnet I am thinking of!" he exclaimed, and with that he bolted into the church.

The captain was examining the little pulpit. "Haste ye! haste ye!" cried Dickory, "your men are all hurrying to the boats, they will leave you behind if they can; that's what they are after."

BONNET TURNED QUICKLY. HE TOOK in the situation in a second. With a few bounds he was out of the church, nearly overturning Ben Greenway as he passed him. Without a word he ran down the street, his cane thrown away, and his drawn sword in his hand.

Dickory's warning had not come a minute too soon; one boat full of men was pulling towards the ship, and others were hurrying in the direction of an empty boat which awaited them at the pier. Bonnet, with Dickory close at his heels, ran with a most amazing rapidity, while Greenway followed at a little distance, scarcely able to maintain the speed.

"What means this?" cried Bonnet, now no longer a gentleman, but a savage pirate, and as he spoke he thrust aside two of the men who were about to get into the boat, and jumped in himself. "What means this?" he thundered.

Black Paul answered quietly: "I was getting the men on board," he said, "so as to save time, and I was coming back for you."

Bonnet glared at his sailing-master, but he did not swear at him, he was too useful a man, but in his heart he vowed that he would never trust Paul Bittern again, and that as soon as he could he would get rid of him.

But when he reached the ship, three men out of each boat's crew, selected at random to represent the rest, were tied up and flogged, the blows being well laid on by scoundrels very eager to be brutal, even to their own shipmates.

"Ah! Dickory, Dickory," cried Ben Greenway, as they were sailing down the bay, "ye have loaded your soul wi' sin this day; I fear ye'll never rise from under it. Whatever vile deeds that Major Bonnet may henceforth be guilty o' ye'll be responsible for them a', Dickory, for every ane o' them."

"He's bad enough, Ben," said the other, "and it's many a wicked deed he may do yet, but I am going to carry news of him to his daughter if I can; and what's more, I am not going to stay behind and be hanged, even if it is in such good company as Major Bonnet and you, Ben Greenway."

Whatever should happen on the rest of that voyage; whether the well-intentioned treachery of Ben Greenway, or the secret villainies of the crew, should prevail; whether disaster or success should come to the planter pirate, Dickory Charter resolved in his soul that a message from her father should go to Kate Bonnet, and that he should carry it.

THE SPIRITS OF DICKORY ROSE very much as the bow of the Revenge was pointed southward. Every mile that the pirate vessel sailed brought him nearer to the delivery of his message—a message which, while it told of her father's wicked career, still told her of his safety and of his steadfast affection for her. Indirectly, the bringing of such a message, and the story of how the bearer brought it, might have another effect, which, although he had no right to expect, was never absent from Dickory's soul. This ardent young lover did not believe in Master Martin Newcombe. He had no good reason for not believing in him, but his want of faith did not depend upon reason. If lovers reasoned too much, it would be a sad world for many of them.

When the Revenge stopped in her progress towards the heavenly Island of Jamaica, or at least that island which was the abode of an angel, and anchored off Charles Town harbour, South Carolina, Dickory fumed and talked impatiently to his friend Ben Greenway. Why a man, even though he were a pirate, and therefore of an avaricious nature, should want more booty, when his vessel was already crowded with valuable goods, he could not imagine.

But Ben Greenway could very easily imagine. "When the spirit o' sin is upon ye," said the Scotchman, "the more an' more wicked ye're likely to be; an' ye must no' forget, Dickory, that every new crime he commits, an' a' the property he steals, an' a' the unfortunate people he maroons, will hae to be answered for by ye, Dickory, when the time comes for ye to stand up an' say what ye hae got to say about your ain sins. If ye had stood by me an' helped to cut him short in his nefarious career, he might now be beginnin' a new life in some small coastin' vessel bound for Barbadoes."

Dickory gave an impatient kick at the mast near which he was standing. "It would have been more likely," said he, "that before this he would have begun a new life on the gallows with you and me alongside of him, and how do you suppose you would have got rid of the sin on your soul when you thought of his orphan daughter in Jamaica?"

"Your thoughts are too much on that daughter," snapped Greenway, "an' no' enough on her father's soul."

"I am tired of her father's soul," said Dickory. "I wonder what new piece of mischief they are going to do here; there are no ships to be robbed?"

Dickory did not know very much, or care very much about the sea and its commerce, and some ships to be robbed soon made their appearance. One was a large merchantman, with a full cargo, and the other was a bark, northward bound, in ballast. The acquisition of the latter vessel put a new idea into Captain Bonnet's head. The Revenge was already overloaded, and he determined to take the bark as a tender to relieve him of a portion of his cargo and to make herself useful in the business of marooning and such troublesome duties.

Being now commander of two vessels, which might in time increase to a little fleet, Captain Bonnet's ideas of his own importance as a terror of the sea increased rapidly. On the Revenge he was more despotic and severe than ever before, while the villain who had been chosen to command the tender, because he had a fair knowledge of navigation, was informed that if he kept the bark more than a mile from the flagship, he would be sunk with the vessel and all on board. The loss of the bark and some men would be nothing compared to the maintenance of discipline, quoth the planter pirate.

Bonnet's ambition rose still higher and higher. He was not content with being a relentless pirate, bloody if need be, but he longed for recognition, for a position among his fellow-terrors of the sea, which should be worthy of a truly wicked reputation. A pirate bold, he would consort with pirates bold. So he set sail for the Gulf of Honduras, then a great rendezvous for piratical craft of many nations. If the father of Kate Bonnet had captured and burned a dozen ships, and had forced every sailor and passenger thereupon to walk a plank, he would not have sinned more deeply in the eyes, of Dickory Charter than he did by thus ruthlessly, inhumanly, hard-heartedly, and altogether shamefully ignoring and pitilessly passing by that island on which dwelt an angel, his own daughter.

But Bonnet declared to the young man that it would now be dangerous for him and his ship to approach the harbour of Kingston, generally the resort of British men-of-war, but in the waters of Honduras he could not fail to find some quiet merchant ship by which he could send a message to his daughter. Ay! and in which—and the pirate's eye glistened with parental joy as this thought came into his mind—he might, disguised as a plain gentleman, make a visit to Mistress Kate and to his good brother-in-law, Delaplaine.

So Dickory was now to be satisfied, and even to admit that there might be some good common sense in these remarks of that most uncommon pirate, Captain Bonnet.

So the Revenge, with her tender, sailed southward, through the fair West-Indian waters and by the fair West-Indian isles, to join herself to the piratical fleet generally to be found in the waters of Honduras.

XIV

A Girl to the Front

The days were getting very long at Spanish Town, although there were no more hours of sunlight than was usual at the season; and even the optimism of Dame Charter was scarcely able to brighten her own soul, much less that of Kate Bonnet, who had almost forgotten what it was to be optimistic. Poor Mr. Delaplaine, whose life had begun to cheer up wonderfully since the arrival of his niece and her triumphant entry into the society of the town, became more gloomy than he had been since the months which followed the death of his wife. Over and over did he wish that his brother-in-law Bonnet had long since been shut up in some place where his eccentricities could do no harm to his fellow-creatures, especially to his most lovely daughter.

Mistress Kate Bonnet was not a girl to sit quietly under the tremendous strain which bore upon her after the departure of the Badger. How could she be contented or even quiet at any moment, when at that moment that heartless Captain Vince might have his sword raised above the head of her unfortunate father?

"Uncle," she said, "I cannot bear it any longer, I must do something."

"But, my dear," he asked, looking down upon her with infinite affection, "what can you do? We are here upon an immovable island, and your father and Captain Vince are sailing upon the sea, nobody knows where."

"I thought about it all last night," said Kate, "and this is what I will do. I will go to the Governor; I will tell him all about my father. I do not think it will be wrong even to tell him why I think his mind has become unsettled, for if that woman in Bridgetown has behaved wickedly, her wickedness should be known. Then I will ask him to give me written authority to take my father wherever I may find him, and to bring him here, where it shall be decided what shall be done with him; and I am sure the decision will be that he must be treated as a man whose mind is not right, and who should be put somewhere where he can have nothing to do with ships."

This was all quite childish to Mr. Delaplaine, but for Kate's dear sake he treated her scheme seriously.

"But tell me, my dear," said he, "how are you going to find your father, and in what way can you bring him back here with you?"

"The first thing to do," said Kate, "is to hire a ship; I know that my little property will yield me money enough for that. As for bringing him back, that's for me to do. With my arms around his neck he cannot be a pirate captain. And think of it, uncle! If my arms are not soon around his neck, it may be the hangman's rope which will be there. That is, if he is not killed by that revengeful Captain Vince."

Mr. Delaplaine was troubled far more than he had yet been. His sorrowing niece believed that there was something which might be done for her father, but he, her practical uncle, did not believe that anything could be done. And, even if this were possible, he did not wish to do it. If, by some unheard-of miracle, his niece should be enabled to carry out her scheme, she could not go alone, and thoughts of sailing upon the sea, and the dangers from pirates, storms, and wrecks, were very terrible to the quiet merchant. He could not encourage this night-born scheme of his niece.

"But there is one thing I can do," cried Kate, "and I must do it this very day. I must go to the Governor's house, and I pray you, uncle, that you will go with me. I must tell him about my father. I must make him do something which shall keep that Captain Vince from sailing after him and killing him. How I wish I had thought of all this before. But it did not come to me."

It was not half an hour after that when Kate and her uncle entered the grounds of the Governor's mansion.

XV

THE GOVERNOR OF JAMAICA

The Governor of Jamaica was much interested in the visit of Kate Bonnet, whom he saw alone in a room adjoining the public apartments. He had met her two or three times before, and had been forced to admit that the young girls of Barbadoes must be pretty and piquant in an extraordinary degree, and he had not wondered that his friend, Captain Vince, should have spoken of her in such an enthusiastic manner.

But now she was different. Her sorrow had given her dignity and had added to her beauty. She quickly told her tale, and he started upright in his chair as he heard it.

"Do you mean," he exclaimed, "that that pirate, after whom I sent the Badger, is your father? It amazes me! The similarity of names did not strike me; I never imagined any connection between you and the captain of that pirate ship."

"That's what Captain Vince said when I last saw him," remarked Kate.

"It must have astounded him to know it," exclaimed the Governor, "and I wonder, knowing it, that he consented to obey my orders; and had I been in his place I would have preferred to be dismissed from the service rather than to sail after your father and to destroy him. If I had known what I know now, my orders to Captain Vince would have been very different from what they were. I would have told him to capture your father, and to bring him here to me. It cannot be that he is in his right mind!"

Now Kate was weeping; the terrible words "destroy him," and the assurance that if she had thought sooner of appealing to the Governor, much misery, or at least the thought of misery, might have been spared her, so affected her that she could not control herself.

The Governor did not attempt to console her. Her sorrow was natural, and it was her right.

When she looked up again she spoke about what she had come to ask him for; the authority to bring back her father wherever she might find him, and to defend him from the attacks of all persons, whoever they might be, until she reached Jamaica. And then she told him how she would seek for her father on every sea.

The Governor sat and pondered. The father of such a girl should be saved from the terrible fate awaiting him, if the thing could possibly be done. And yet, what a difficult, almost hopeless thing it was to do. To find a pirate, a fierce and bloody pirate, and bring him back unharmed to his daughter's arms and to reasonable restraint.

He spoke earnestly. "What you propose," he said, "you cannot do. It would be impossible for you to find your father; and if you did, no matter who might be with you, and no matter how successful you might be with him, his crew would not let him go. But there is one thing which might be done. The Badger will report at different stations, and her course and present cruising ground might be discovered. Thus I might send a despatch to Captain Vince, ordering him not to harm your father, but to take him prisoner, and to bring him here to be dealt with."

Kate sprang to her feet.

"An order to Captain Vince!" she exclaimed, "an order to withhold his hand from my father? Ah, sir, your goodness is great, this is far more than I had dared to expect! When I last saw Captain Vince he left me in a great rage, but, knowing that he would respect your order, I would dare his rage. If his revengeful hand should be withheld from my father I would fear nothing."

"I beg you to be seated," said the Governor, "and let me assure you, that in offering to send this order to Captain Vince I do not in the least expect you to take it. But there is one thing I do not understand. Why should the captain have left you in a great rage? Perhaps I have not a right to ask this, but it seems to me to have some bearing upon his alacrity in setting forth in pursuit of the Revenge."

"I fear," said Kate, "that this may be true; I do not deem it improper for me to say to you, sir, that Captain Vince made me an offer of marriage, and that in order to induce me to accept it he offered, should he come up with the Revenge, to spare my father and to let him go free, visiting the punishment he was sent to inflict upon the rest of the people in the ship."

"I am surprised," said the Governor, "to hear you say that; such an action would have been direct disobedience to his orders. It would have been disloyalty, which not even the possession of your fair hand could justify. And you refused his offer?"

"That did I," said Kate, her face flushing at the recollection of the unpleasant interview with the captain; "I cared not for him, and even had I, I would not have consented to wed a man who offered me his dishonour as a bribe for doing so. Not even for my father's life would I become the bride of such a one!"

"Well spoken, Mistress Bonnet," exclaimed the Governor, "your heart, though a tender, is a stout one. But this you tell me of Captain Vince is very bad; he is a vindictive man and will have what he wants, even without regard to the means by which he may get it. I am glad to know what you have told me, Mistress Bonnet, and if I had known it betimes I would not have sent, in pursuit of your father, a man whose anger had been excited against his daughter. But now I shall despatch orders to Captain Vince which shall be very exact and peremptory. After he has received them he will not dare to harm your father, and would cause him to be brought here as I command."

"From my heart I thank you, sir," cried Kate, "give me the orders and I will take them, or I will—"

"Nay, nay," said the Governor, "such offices are not for you, but I will give the matter my present attention. On any day a vessel may enter the port with news of the Badger, and on any day a vessel may clear from Kingston, possibly for Bridgetown, where I imagine the Badger will first touch. Rely upon me, my dear young lady, my order shall go to Captain Vince by the very earliest opportunity."

Kate rose and thanked him warmly. "This is much to do, your Excellency, for one poor girl," she said.

"It is but little to do," said the Governor, "and that girl be yourself."

With that he rose, offered Kate his arm, and conducted her to her uncle.

When Mr. Delaplaine was made acquainted with the result of the interview, both his gratitude and surprise were great. He comprehended far better than Kate could the extent of the favour which the Governor had offered to bestow. It was, indeed, extraordinary to commute what was really a sentence of death against a notorious and dangerous pirate for the sake of a beautiful and pleading woman. An ambitious idea shot through the merchant's brain. The Governor was a widower; he had met Kate before. Was there any other lady on the island better fitted to preside over the gubernatorial household? But, although a man of high position could not wed the daughter of a pirate, a pirate, evidently of an unsound mind, could be adjudged demented, as he truly was, and thus the shadow of his crime be lifted from him. This was a great deal to think in a very short time, but the good merchant did it, and the fervour of his thankfulness was greatly increased by his rapid reflections.

As they were on their way home Kate's eyes were bright, and her step lighter than it had been of late. "Now, uncle," said she, "you know we shall not wait for any chance ship which may take the Governor's despatch. We shall engage a swift vessel ourselves, by which the orders may be carried. And, uncle, when that ship sails I must go in her."

"You!" cried Mr. Delaplaine, "you go in search of the Badger and Captain Vince? That can never—"

"But remember, uncle," cried Kate, "it is just as likely that I shall meet my father's ship as any other, and then we can snap our fingers at all orders and all captains. My father shall be brought here and the good Governor will make him safe, and free him, as he best knows how, from the terrible straits into which his disturbed reason has led him."

Her uncle would not darken Kate's bright hopes, ill-founded though he thought them. To look into those sparkling eyes again was a joy of which he would not deprive himself, if he could help it.

"Suppose he should capture our vessel," she exclaimed; "what a grand thing it would be for him, all unknowing, to spring upon our deck and instantly be captured by me. After that, there would be no more pirate's life for him!"

When Dame Charter heard what had happened at the Governor's house and had listened to the recital of Kate's glowing schemes, her eyes did not immediately glisten with joy.

"If you go, Mistress Kate," said she, "in search of your father or that wicked Captain Vince, I go with you, but I cannot go without my Dickory. It is full time to expect his return, although, as he was to depend upon so many chances before he could come back, his absence may, with good reason, continue longer, and I could not have him come back and find his mother gone, no man knows where. For in such a quest, what man could know?"

"Oh, Dickory will be here soon!" cried Kate; "any ship which comes sailing towards the harbour may bring him."

The Governor of Jamaica was a man of great experience, and with a fairly clear insight into the ways of the wicked. When Kate and her uncle had left him and he paced the floor, with the memory of the beautiful eyes of the pirate's daughter as they had been uplifted to his own, he felt assured that he could see rightly into the designs of the unscrupulous Captain Vince. Of what avail would it be for him to kill the father of the girl who had rejected him? It would be an atrocious but temporary triumph scarcely to be considered. But to capture that father; to disregard the laws of the service and the orders of his superiors, which he had already proposed to do; to communicate with Kate and to hold up before her terror-stricken eyes the life of her father, to be ended in horror or enjoyed in peace as she might decide—that would be Vince, as the Governor knew him.

The Governor knew well his man, and those were the designs and intentions of Captain Christopher Vince of his Majesty's corvette the Badger.

XVI

A QUESTION OF ETIQUETTE

Proudly sailed the Revenge and her attendant bark into the waters of Honduras Gulf, and proudly stood Captain Stede Bonnet upon his quarter-deck, dressed in a handsome uniform which might have been that of a captain or admiral in the royal navy; one hand caressed his ornate sword-hilt, while the other was thrust into the bosom of his gilt-embroidered coat. A newly fashioned Jolly Roger, in which the background was very black and the skull and cross-bones ghastly white, flew from his masthead.

As night came on there could be seen, twinkling far away upon the horizon, a beacon light, which in those days was kept burning for the benefit of the piratical craft which made a rendezvous of the waters off Belize, then the commercial centre for the vessels of the "free companions." Having supposed, in his unnautical mind, that his entrance into the Gulf of Honduras meant the end of his present voyage, and not wishing to lower his own feeling of importance by asking too many questions of his inferiors, Captain Bonnet had bedecked himself a day too soon, and there were some jeers and sneers among his crew when he descended to his cabin to take off his fine clothes. But his self-complacency was well armoured, and he did not hear the jokes of which he was the subject, especially by the little clique of which Black Paul was the centre. But the sailing-master knew his business, and the Revenge was safely, though slowly, sailed among the coral-reefs and islands until she dropped anchor off Belize. Early in the morning the now dignified and pompous Captain Bonnet, of that terror of the seas, the pirate craft Revenge, again arrayed himself in a manner befitting his position, and stationed himself on the quarter-deck, where he might be seen by the eyes of all the crews of the other pirate vessels anchored about them and by the glasses of their officers.

Apart from a general desire to show himself in the ranks of his fellow-pirates and to receive from them the respect which was due to a man of his capabilities and general merits, Stede Bonnet had a particular reason for his visit to this port and for surrounding himself with all the pomp and circumstance of high piratical rank. He had been informed that a great man, a hero and chief among his fellows—in fact, the dean of the piratical faculty, and known as "Blackbeard," the most desperate and reckless of all the pirates of the day—was now here.

To meet this most important sea-robber and to receive from him the hand of fellowship had been Bonnet's desire and ambition since he had heard that it was possible.

The morning was advanced and the Revenge was rolling easily at her anchorage, but Bonnet was somewhat uncertain as to the next step he ought to take. He wanted to see Blackbeard as soon as possible, but it would certainly be a breach of etiquette entirely inconsistent with his present position for him to go to see him. He was the latest comer, and thought it was the part of Blackbeard to make the first visit.

Paul Bittern now came aft. "The men are getting very restless," he said; "they want to go on shore. They'd all go if I'd let 'em."

Captain Bonnet gave his sailing-master a lofty glare.

"If I should let them, you mean, sir. I am sorry I cannot break you of the habit of forgetting that I command this ship. Well, sir, you may tell them that they cannot go. I am expecting a visit from the renowned Blackbeard, now in this port, and I wish to welcome him with all respect and a full crew."

Black Paul smiled disagreeably. "I will tell you, sir, that you cannot keep these men on board much longer with the town of Belize within a row of half a mile. They've been at sea too long for that. There'll be a mutiny, sir, if I go forward with that message of yours. It will be prudent to let some of them go ashore now and others later in the day. I will go in the first boat and see to it that the men come back with me. And, by the way, it would not be a bad thing if I touch at Blackbeard's vessel and inform him that you are here; I don't suppose he knows the Revenge, nor her captain neither."

"I doubt that, Bittern," said Bonnet, "I doubt it very much. I assure you that I am known from one end of this coast to the other, and Captain Blackbeard is not an ignorant man. So you can go ashore and take some of the men, stopping at Blackbeard's ship. And, by the way, I want you to go by that bark of ours and give her the old black Roger I used to fly. I forgot to send it to her, and a man might as well not own and command two vessels if he get not the credit of it."

When Black Paul had gone to execute his orders, Ben Greenway heaved a heavy sigh. "Now I begin to fear, Master Bonnet, that the day o' your salvation has really gone by. When ye not only murder an' rob upon the high seas, but keep consort with other murderers an' robbers, then I fear ye are indeed lost. But I shall stand by ye, Master Bonnet, I shall stand by ye; an' if, ever I find there is the least bit o' ye to be snatched from the flames, I'll snatch it!"

"I don't like that sort of talk, Ben Greenway," cried Bonnet, "especially at this time when my soul swells with content at the success which has crowned my undertakings. This Blackbeard is a valiant man and a great one, but it is my belief that when we have sat down to compare our notes, it will be found that I have captured as many cargoes, burned as many ships, and marooned as many people in my last cruise as he has."

"So I suppose," said Ben, "that ye think ye hae achieved the right to sink deeper into hell than he can ever hope to do?"

Bonnet made no answer, but turned away. The Scotchman was becoming more and more odious to him every day, but he would not quarrel on this most auspicious morning. He must keep his mind unruffled and his head high. He had his own plans about Greenway: he was not far from Barbadoes, and when he left the harbour of Belize it would be of advantage to his peace of mind as well as to the comfort of a faithful old servant if he should anchor for a little while in the river below the town and put Ben Greenway on shore.

Ben gave no further reason for quarrelling. He was greatly dejected, but he had sworn to himself to stand by his old master, no matter what might happen, and when he took an oath he meant what he swore.

Dickory Charter was in much worse case than Ben Greenway. He was not much of a geographical scholar, but he knew that the Gulf of Honduras was not really very far from the Island of Jamaica, where dwelt, waited, and watched Mistress Kate Bonnet and his mother. If he had known that during the voyage down from the Atlantic coast the Revenge had sailed through the Windward Passage, running in some of her long tacks within less than a day's sail of Jamaica, he would have chafed, fumed, and fretted even more than he did now.

"Captain Bonnet," he cried, "if you could but let me go on shore, I might surely find some vessel bound to Kingston, or to any place upon the Island of Jamaica, from which spot I could make my way on foot, even if it were on the opposite end. Thus I could take messages and letters from you to your daughter and Mr. Delaplaine, and ease the minds both of them and my mother, all of whom must now be in most doleful plight, not knowing anything about you or hearing anything from me, and this for so long a time; then you could remain here with no feelings of haste until you had disposed of your cargoes and had finished your business."

Captain Bonnet stood loftily with a smile of benignity upon his face. "It is a clever plan," said he, "and you are a good fellow, Dickory, but your scheme, though well intentioned, is unsound. I have too much regard for you to trust you in any vessel sailing from Belize to Kingston, where there are often naval vessels. Going from this port, you would be as likely to be strung up to the yard-arm as to be allowed to go ashore. Be patient then, my good fellow; when my affairs are settled here, the Revenge may run up to the coast of Jamaica, where you may be put off at some quiet spot, and all may happen as you have planned, my good Dickory. Even now I am writing a letter, hoping for some such opportunity of sending it to my daughter."

Dickory sighed in despair. It might take a month or more before Kate's father could settle his affairs, and how long, how long it had been since his soul had been reaching itself out towards Kate and his mother!

When the sailing-master set out in the long-boat, crowded with men, he stopped at the bark but did not go too near for fear that some of the crew might jump into his already overloaded boat.

"You are to run up this rag," cried Black Paul to Clip, the fellow in command; and so saying, he handed up the old Jolly Roger on the blade of an oar. "Our noble admiral fears that if you do not that you may be captured by some of these good vessels lying hereabout."

Clip roared out with a laugh: "I will attend to the capture as soon as I get out of reach of his guns, which he will not dare to use here, I take it. But I want you to know and him to know that we're not goin' to stay on board and in sight of the town. If you go ashore, so go we."

"Stay where ye are till orders come to ye," shouted Black Paul, "if ye want to keep the cat off your backs!" And as he rowed away the men on the bark gave him a cheer and proceeded to lower two boats.

From nearly every pirate ship in the anchorage the proceedings of the newly arrived vessels had been watched. No one wanted to board them or in any way to interfere with them until it was found out what they intended to do. The Revenge was a stranger in that harbour, although her fame was known on not a few pirate decks; but if she came to Belize to fraternize with the other pirate vessels there gathered together, why didn't she do it? No idea of importance and dignity, which his position imposed upon Captain Stede Bonnet, entered their piratical minds. When the long-boat put forth from the Revenge, a good deal of interest was excited in the anchored vessels. The great Blackbeard himself stood high upon his deck and surveyed the strangers through a glass.

The men in the sailing-master's boat rowed steadily towards Blackbeard's vessel. Bittern knew it well, for he had seen it before, and had even had the honour, so to speak, of having served for a short time under the master pirate of that day.

As soon as the boat was near enough Blackbeard hailed it in a tremendous voice and ordered the stranger to pull up and make fast. This being done, a rope ladder was lowered and Bittern mounted to the deck, being assisted in his passage over the side by a tremendous pull given by Blackbeard.

The great pirate seemed to be in high good spirits, and very glad to see his visitor. Blackbeard was a large man, wide and heavy, and the first impression conveyed by his personality was that of hair and swarthiness. An untrimmed black beard lay upon his chest, and his long hair hung in masses from under his slouched hat; his eyes were dark and sparkling, and gleamed like beacon lights from out a midnight sky; the sleeves of his shirt were rolled up, and his arms seemed almost as hairy as his head; two pairs of pistols were stuck into his belt, and a great cutlass was conveniently tucked up by his side.

"Ho, ho!" he cried, "Black Paul! And where do you come from, and what are you doing here? And what is the name of that vessel with the brand-new Roger? Has she just gone into the business, that she decks herself out so fine? Come now, sit here and have some brandy and tell me what is the meaning of these two vessels coming into the harbour, and what you have to do with them."

Bittern was delighted to know that his old commander remembered him, and was ready enough to talk with him, for that was the errand he had come upon.

"But, captain," said he, "I am afraid to wander away from the gunwale, for if I have not my eye upon them, my men will be rowing to the town before I know it. They are mad to be on shore."

Blackbeard made no answer; he stepped to the side of the vessel and looked over. "Let go!" he shouted to the man who held the boat's rope, "and you rascals row out a dozen strokes from my vessel and keep your boat there; and if you move an oar towards the town I will sink you!" With that he ordered two small guns to be trained upon the boat.

The boat's crew did not hesitate one second in obeying these orders. They knew by whom they were given, and there was no man in the great body of free companions who would disobey an order given by Blackbeard. They rowed to the position assigned them and sat quietly looking into the mouths of the two cannon which were pointed towards them.

"Now then," said Blackbeard, turning to Bittern, "I think they'll stay there till they get some other order."

Between frequent sips at the cup of brandy Bittern told the story of the Revenge, and Blackbeard listened with many an oath and many a pound upon his massive knee by his mighty fist.

"Oh, I have heard of him," he cried, "I have heard of him! He has played the devil along the Atlantic coast. He must he a great fellow this—what did you say his name was?"

"Bonnet," said the other.

Blackbeard laughed. "That suits him well; he must have clapped his name over the eyes of many a merchant captain! Where did he sail before he hoisted the Jolly Roger?"

At this Bittern laughed. "He never sailed anywhere, he is no seaman; and if he were not rich enough to pay others to do his navigatin' for him he would have run his vessel upon the first sand-bar on his way from Bridgetown to the sea. But he pays some good mariner to sail his Revenge, and he now pays me. I am, in fact, the captain of his vessel."

"You mean," cried Blackbeard, "that he knows nothing of navigation?"

"Not a whit," replied the other; "he doesn't know the backstays from the taffrail. It was only yesterday that he thought he was already in the port of Belize, and dressed himself up like a fighting-cock to meet you."

"To meet me?" roared Blackbeard; "what does he want to meet me for, and why don't he come and do it instead of sending you?"

"Not he," said Bittern. "He is a great man, if not a sailor; he knows what is politeness on shipboard, and as he is the last comer you must be the first caller. He is all dressed up now, hoping that you will row over to the Revenge as soon as you know that he is its commander."

The hairy pirate leaned back and laughed in loud explosions.

"He is a rare man, truly," he exclaimed, "this Captain Nightcap of yours—"

"Bonnet," interrupted Bittern.

"Well, one is as good as the other," cried Blackbeard, "and he be well clothed if it be of the right colour. And you started out with him to sail his ship, you rascal? That's a piece of impudence almost as great as his own."

Bittern did not much like this speech, and wanted to explain that since he had served under Blackbeard he had commanded vessels himself, but he restrained himself and told how Sam Loftus had been tumbled overboard for running afoul his captain, and how he had been appointed to his place.

Now Blackbeard laughed again, with a great pound upon his knee. "He is a man after my own heart," he shouted, "be he sailor or no sailor, this nightcap commander of yours. I know I shall love him!" And springing to his feet and uttering a resounding oath, he swore that he would visit his new brother that afternoon.

"Now, away with you!" cried Blackbeard, "and tell Sir Nightcap—"

"Bonnet," interrupted Bittern.

"Well, Bonnet, or Cap, it matters not to me. Row straight back to your ship, and let him know that I shall be there and shall expect to be received with admiral's honours."

Bittern looked somewhat embarrassed. "But, captain," he said, "my men are on their way to the town, and I fear me they will rebel if I tell them they cannot now go there."

In saying this the sailing-master spoke not only for his men, but for himself. He was very anxious to go ashore; he had business there; he wanted to see who were in the place, and what was going on before Bonnet should go to the town.

"What!" cried Blackbeard, putting his head down like a charging bull. "I order you to row back to your vessel and take my message; and if you do it not I will sink you all in a bunch! Into your boat, sir, and waste not another minute. If you are not able to command your men, I will keep you here and give them a coxswain who can."

Without another word, Bittern scuffled over the side, and, his boat being brought up, he dropped into it.

"Now, men," he said, "I have a message from Captain Blackbeard to the Revenge; bend to it as I steer that way."

"Give my pious regards to your Sir Nightcap," shouted Blackbeard. And then, in a still higher tone, he yelled to them that if they disobeyed their coxswain and turned their bow shoreward he would sink them all to the unsounded depths of Hades. Without a protest the men pulled vigorously towards the Revenge, while Black Paul, considering it a new affront to be called "coxswain" when he was in reality captain, earnestly sent Blackbeard to the same regions to which he had just referred.

XVII

An Ornamented Beard

It was about the middle of the afternoon when a large boat, well filled, was seen approaching the Revenge from Blackbeard's vessel. As soon as it had become known that this chief of all pirates of that day, this Edward Thatch of England, was really coming on board the Revenge, not one word was uttered among the crew on the subject of going ashore, although they had been long at sea. The shore could wait when Blackbeard was coming. Even to look upon this doughty desperado would be an honour and a joy to the brawny scoundrels who made up the crew of the Revenge.

It might have been supposed that everything upon Captain Bonnet's vessel had been made ready for the expected advent of Blackbeard, but nothing seemed good enough, nothing seemed as effectively placed and arranged as it might have been; and with execrations and commands, Bonnet hurried here and there, making everything, if possible, more ship-shape than it had been before.

"Stay you two in the background," he said to Ben Greenway and Dickory; "you are both landsmen, and you don't count in a ceremony such as this is going to be. Station your men as I told you, Bittern, and man the yards when it is time."

Captain Bonnet, in his brave uniform and wearing a cocked hat with a feather, his hand upon his sword-hilt, stood up tall and stately. When the boat was made fast and the great pirate's head appeared above the rail, six cannon roared a welcome and Bonnet stepped forward, hand extended and hat uplifted.

The instant Blackbeard's feet touched the deck he drew from their holsters a pair of pistols and fired them in the air.

"Now then," he shouted, "we are even, salute for salute, for my pistols are more than equal to the cannon of any other man. How goes it with you, Sir Nightcap—Bonnet, I mean?" And with that he clasped the hand reached out to him in a bone-crushing grasp.

His fingers aching and his brain astonished, Bonnet could not comprehend what sort of a man it was who stood before him. With hair purposely dishevelled; with his hat more slouched than usual;

with his beard divided into tails, each tied with a different-coloured ribbon; with half a dozen pistols strung across his breast; with other pistols and a knife or two stuck into his belt; with his great sword by his side, and his eyes gleaming brighter than ever and a general expression, both in face and figure, of an aggressive impudence, Blackbeard stood on his stout legs, clothed in rough red stockings, and gazed about him. But the captain of the Revenge did not forget his manners. He welcomed Blackbeard with all courtesy and besought him to enter his poor cabin.

Blackbeard laughed. "Poor cabin, say you? But I'll tell you this one thing, my valiant Captain Cap; you have not a poor vessel, not a poor vessel, I swear that to you, my brave captain, I swear that!"

Then, with no attention to Bonnet's invitation, Captain Blackbeard strolled about the deck, examining everything, cursing this and praising that, and followed by Captain Bonnet, Black Paul, and a crowd of admiring pirates.

Ben Greenway bowed his head and groaned. "I doubt if Master Bonnet will ever go to the de'il as I feared he would, for now has the de'il come to him. Oh, Dickory, Dickory! this master o' mine was a worthy mon an' a good ane when I first came to him, an' a' that I hae I owe to him, for I was in sad case, Dickory, very sad case; but now that he has Apollyon for his teacher, he'll cease to know righteousness altogither."

Dickory was angry and out of spirits. "He is a vile poltroon, this master of yours," said he, "consorting with these bloody pirates and leaving his daughter to pine away her days and nights within a little sail of him, while he struts about at the heel of a dirty freebooter dressed like a monkey! He doesn't deserve the daughter he possesses. Oh, that I could find a ship that would take me back to Jamaica! And I would take you too, Ben Greenway, for it is a foul shame that a good man should spend his days in such vile company."

Ben shook his head. "I'll stand by Master Bonnet," he said, "until the day comes when I shall bid him farweel at the door o' hell. I can go no farther than that, Dickory, no farther than that!"

From forecastle to quarter-deck, from bowsprit to taffrail, Blackbeard scrutinized the Revenge.

"What mean you, dog?" he said to Bittern, Bonnet being at a little distance; "you tell me he is no mariner. This is a brave ship and well appointed."

"Ay, ay," said the sailing-master, "it has the neatness of his kitchen or his storehouses; but if his cables were coiled on his yard-arms or his anchor hung up to dry upon the main shrouds, he would not know that anything was wrong. It was Big Sam Loftus who fitted out the Revenge, and I myself have kept everything in good order and ship-shape ever since I took command."

"Command!" growled Blackbeard. "For a charge of powder I would knock in the side of your head for speaking with such disrespect of the brave Sir Nightcap."

The supper in the cabin of the Revenge was a better meal than the voracious Blackbeard had partaken of for many a year, if indeed he had ever sat down to such a sumptuous repast. Before him was food and drink fit for a stout and hungry sea-faring man, and there were wines and dainties which would have had fit place upon the table of a gentleman.

Blackbeard was in high spirits and tossed off cup after cup and glass after glass of the choicest wine and the most fiery spirits. He clapped his well-mannered host upon the back as he shouted some fragment of a wild sea-song.

"And who is this?" he cried, as they rose from the table and he first caught sight of Ben Greenway. "Is this your chaplain? He looks as sanctimonious as an empty rum cask. And that baby boy there, what do you keep him for? Are they for sale? I would like to buy the boy and let him keep my accounts. I warrant he has enough arithmetic in his head to divide the prize-moneys among the men."

"He is no slave," said Bonnet; "he came to this vessel to bring me a message from my daughter, but he is an ill-bred stripling, and can neither read nor write."

"Then let's kill him!" cried Blackbeard, and drawing his pistol he sent a bullet about two inches above Dickory's head.

At this the men who had gathered themselves at every available point set up a cheer. Never before had they beheld such a magnificent and reckless miscreant.

Dickory did not start or move, but he turned very pale, and then he reddened and his eyes flashed. Blackbeard swore at him a great approbative oath. "A brave boy!" he cried, "and fit to carry messages if for nothing else. And what is this nonsense about a daughter?" said he to Bonnet. "We abide no such creatures in the ranks of the free companions; we drown them like kittens before we hoist the Jolly Roger."

FRANK R. STOCKTON

When Blackbeard's boat left the ship's side the departing chieftain fired his pistols in the air as long as their charges lasted, while the motley desperadoes of the Revenge gave him many a parting yell. Then all the boats of the Revenge were lowered, and every man who could crowd into them left their ship for the shore. Black Paul tried to restrain them, for he feared to leave the Revenge too weakly manned, she having such a valuable cargo; but his orders and shouts were of no avail, and despairing of stopping them the sailing-master went with them; and as they pulled wildly towards the town the men of one boat shouted to another, and that one to another, "Hurrah for our captain, the brave Sir Nightcap! Hurrah! Hurrah! Hurrah!"

"The dirty Satan!" exclaimed Dickory, as he gazed after Blackbeard's boat. "I would kill him if I could."

"Say not so, Dickory," said Captain Bonnet, speaking gravely. "That great pirate is not a man of breeding, and he speaks with disesteem alike of friend and enemy, but he is the famous Blackbeard, and we must treat him with honour although he pays us none."

"I had deemed," said Greenway calmly, "that ye were goin' to be the maist unholy sinner that ever blackened this fair earth; but not only did ye tell a pious lie for the sake o' good Dickory, but, compared wi' that monstrosity, ye are a saint graved in marble, Master Bonnet, a white and shapely saint."

BLACKBEARD'S BOAT WAS NOT ROWED to his vessel, but his men pulled steadily shoreward.

With the wild crew of the Revenge, fresh from sea and their appetites whetted for jovial riot, and with Blackbeard, his war-paint on, to lead them into every turbulent excess, there were wild times in the town of Belize that night.

XVIII

I have no Right; I am a Pirate

As has been made plain, Captain Bonnet of the Revenge was a punctilious man when the rules of society were concerned, be that society official, high-toned, or piratical. Thus it was a positive duty, in his mind, to return Blackbeard's visit on the next day, but until afternoon he was not able to do so on account of the difficulty of getting a sober and decently behaved boat's crew who should row him over.

Black Paul, the sailing-master, had returned to his vessel early in the morning, feeling the necessity of keeping watch over the cargo, but most of the men came over much later, while some of them did not come at all.

Bonnet was greatly inclined to punish with an unwonted severity this breach of rules, but Black Paul assured him that it was always the custom for the crew of a newly arrived vessel to go ashore and have a good time, and that if they were denied this privilege they would be sure to mutiny, and he might be left without any crew at all. Bonnet grumbled and swore, but, as he was aware there were several things concerning a nautical life with which he was not familiar, he determined to let pass this trespass.

Dressed in his finest clothes, and even better than the day before, he was followed into the boat by Ben Greenway, who vowed his captain should never travel without his chaplain, who, if his words were considered, would be the most valuable officer on the vessel.

"Come, then, Greenway," said Bonnet; "you have troubled me so much on my own vessel that now, perchance, you may be able to do me some service on that of another. Anyway, I should like to have at least one decent person in my train, who, an you come not, will be wholly missing. And Dickory may come too, if he like it."

But Dickory did not like it. He hated the big black pirate, and cared not if he should never see him again, so he stayed behind.

When Bonnet mounted to the deck of Blackbeard's vessel he found there a very different pirate captain from the one who had called upon him the day before. There were no tails to the great black beard, there were few pistols visible, and Captain Bonnet's host received him with a certain salt-soaked, sun-browned, hairy, and brawny hospitality which did not sit badly upon him. There was meat, there was drink, and then the two captains and Greenway walked gravely over the vessel, followed by a hundred eyes, and before long by many a coarse and jeering laugh which Bonnet supposed were directed at sturdy Ben Greenway, deeming it quite natural, though improper, that the derision of these rough fellows should be excited by the appearance among them of a prim and sedate Scotch Presbyterian.

But that crew of miscreants had all heard of the derisive title which had been given to Bonnet, and now they saw without the slightest difficulty how little he knew of the various nautical points to which Blackbeard continually called his attention.

The vessel was dirty, it was ill-appointed; there was an air of reckless disorder which showed itself everywhere; but, apart from his evident distaste for dirt and griminess, the captain of the Revenge seemed to be very well satisfied with everything he saw. When he passed a small gun pointed across the deck, and with a nightcap hung upon a capstan bar thrust into its muzzle, there was such a great laugh that Bonnet looked around to see what the imprudent Greenway might be doing.

Many were the nautical points to which Blackbeard called his guest's attention and many the questions the grim pirate asked, but in almost all cases of the kind the tall gentleman with the cocked hat replied that he generally left those things to his sailing-master, being so much occupied with matters of more import.

Although he found no fault and made no criticisms, Bonnet was very much disgusted. Such a disorderly vessel, such an apparently lawless crew, excited his most severe mental strictures; and, although the great Blackbeard was to-day a very well-behaved person, Bonnet could not understand how a famous and successful captain should permit his vessel and his crew to get into such an unseamanlike and disgraceful condition. On board the Revenge, as his sailing-master had remarked, there was the neatness of his kitchen and his store-houses; and, although he did not always know what to do with the nautical appliances which surrounded him, he knew how to make them look in good order. But he made few remarks, favourable or otherwise, and held himself loftier than before, with an air as if he might have been an admiral entire instead of resembling one only in clothes, and with ceremonious and even condescending politeness followed his host wherever he was led, above decks or below.

Ben Greenway had gone with his master about the ship with much of the air of one who accompanies a good friend to the place of execution. Regardless of gibes or insults, whether they were directed at Bonnet or himself, he turned his face neither to the right nor to the left, and apparently regarded nothing that he heard. But while endeavouring to listen as little as possible to what was going on around him, he heard a great deal; but, strange to say, the railing and scurrility of the pirates did not appear to have a depressing influence upon his mind. In fact, he seemed in somewhat better spirits than when he came on board.

"Whatever he may do, whatever he may say, an' whatever he may swear," said the Scotchman to himself, "he is no' like ane of these. Try as he may, he canna descend so low into the blackness o' evil as these sons o' perdition. Although he has done evil beyond a poor mortal's computation, he walks like a king amang them. Even that Blackbeard, striving to be decent for an hour or two, knows a superior when he meets him."

When they had finished the tour of the vessel, Blackbeard conducted his guest to his own cabin and invited him to be seated by a little table. Bonnet sat down, placing his high-plumed cocked hat upon the bench beside him. He did not want anything more to eat or to drink, and he was, in fact, quite ready to take his leave. The vessel had not pleased him and had given him an idea of the true pirate's life which he had never had before. On the Revenge he mingled little with the crew, scarcely ever below decks, and his own quarters were as neat and commodious as if they were on a fine vessel carrying distinguished passengers. Dirt and disorder, if they existed, were at least not visible to him.

But, although he had no desire ever to make another visit to the ship of the great Blackbeard, he would remember his position and be polite and considerate now that he was here. Moreover, the savage desperado of the day before, dressed like a monkey and howling like an Indian, seemed now to be endeavouring to soften himself a little and to lay aside some of his savage eccentricities in honour of the captain of that fine ship, the Revenge. So, clothed in a calm dignity, Bonnet waited to hear what his host had further to say.

Blackbeard seated himself on the other side of the table, on which he rested his massive arms. Behind him Ben Greenway stood in the doorway. For a few moments Blackbeard sat and gazed at Bonnet, and then he said: "Look ye, Stede Bonnet, do you know you are now as much out of place as a red herring would be at the top of the mainmast?"

Bonnet flushed. "I fear, Captain Blackbeard," he said, "I very much fear me that you are right; this is no place for me. I have paid my respects to you, and now, if you please, I will take my leave. I have not been gratified by the conduct of your crew, but I did not expect that their captain would address me in such discourteous words." And with this he reached out his hand for his hat.

Blackbeard brought down his hand heavily upon the table.

"Sit where you are!" he exclaimed. "I have that to say to you which you shall hear whether you like my vessel, my crew, or me. You are no sailor, Stede Bonnet of Bridgetown, and you don't belong to the free companions, who are all good men and true and can sail the ships they command. You are a defrauder and a cheat; you are nothing but a landsman, a plough-tail sugar-planter!"

At this insult Bonnet rose to his feet and his hand went to his sword.

"Sit down!" roared Blackbeard; "an you do not listen to me, I'll cut off this parley and your head together. Sit down, sir."

Bonnet sat down, pale now and trembling with rage. He was not a coward, but on board this ship he must give heed to the words of the desperado who commanded it.

"You have no right," continued Blackbeard, "to strut about on the quarter-deck of that fine vessel, the Revenge; you have no right to hoist above you the Jolly Roger, and you have no right to lie right and left and tell people you are a pirate. A pirate, forsooth! you are no pirate. A pirate is a sailor, and you are no sailor! You are no better than a blind man led by a dog: if the dog breaks away from him he is lost, and if the sailing-masters you pick up one after another break away from you, you are lost. It is a cursed shame, Stede Bonnet, and it shall be no longer. At this moment, by my own right and for the sake of every man who sails under the Jolly Roger, I take away from you the command of the Revenge."

Now Bonnet could not refrain from springing to his feet. "Take from me the Revenge!" he cried, "my own vessel, bought with my own money! And how say you I am not a pirate? From Massachusetts down the coast into these very waters I have preyed upon commerce, I have taken prizes, I have burned ships, I have made my name a terror."

Now his voice grew stronger and his tones more angry.

"Not a pirate!" he cried. "Go ask the galleons and the merchantmen I have stripped and burned; go ask their crews, now wandering in misery upon desert shores, if they be not already dead. And by what right, I ask, do you come to such an one as I am and declare that, having put me in the position of a prisoner on your ship, you will take away my own?"

Blackbeard gazed at him with half-closed eyes, a malicious smile upon his face.

"I have no right," he said; "I need no right; *I* am a pirate!"

At these words Bonnet's legs weakened under him, and he sank down upon the bench. As he did so he glanced at Ben Greenway as if he were the only person on earth to whom he could look for help, but to his amazement he saw before him a face almost jubilant, and beheld the Scotchman, his eyes uplifted and his hands clasped as if in thankful prayer.

XIX

The New First Lieutenant

When the boat of the Revenge was pulled back to that vessel Bonnet did not go in it; it was Blackbeard who sat in the stern and held the tiller, while one of his own men sat by him.

When Blackbeard stepped on deck he announced, much to the delight of the crew and the consternation of Paul Bittern, that the Revenge now belonged to him, and that all the crew who were fit to be kept on board such a fine vessel would be retained, and that he himself, for the present at least, would take command of the ship, would haul down that brand-new bit of woman's work at the masthead and fly in its place his own black, ragged Jolly Roger, dreaded wherever seen upon the sea. At this a shout went up from the crew; the heart of every scoundrel among them swelled with joy at the idea of sailing, fighting, and pillaging under the bloody Blackbeard.

But the sailing-master stood aghast. He had known very well what was going to happen; he had talked it all over in the town with Blackbeard; he had drunk in fiery brandy to the success of the scheme, and he had believed without a doubt that he was to command the Revenge when Bonnet should be deposed. And now where was he? Where did he stand?

Trembling a little, he approached Blackbeard. "And as for me," he asked; "am I to command your old vessel?"

"You!" roared Blackbeard, making as if he would jump upon him; "you! You may fall to and bend your back with the others in the forecastle, or you can jump overboard if you like. My quarter-master, Richards, now commands my old vessel. Presently I shall go over and settle things on that bark, but first I shall step down into the cabin and see what rare good things Sir Nightcap, the sugar-planter, has prepared for me."

With this he went below, followed by the man he had brought with him.

It was Dickory, half dazed by what he had heard, who now stepped up to Paul Bittern. The latter, his countenance blacker than it had ever been before, first scowled at him, but in a moment the ferocity left his glance.

"Oho!" he said, "here's a pretty pickle for me and you, as well as for Bonnet and the Scotchman!"

"Do you suppose," exclaimed Dickory, "that what he says is true? That he has stolen this ship from Captain Bonnet, and that he has taken it for his own?"

"Suppose!" sneered the other, "I know it. He has stolen from me as well as from Bonnet. I should have commanded this ship, and I had made all my plans to do it when I got here."

"Then you are as great a rascal," said Dickory, "as that vile pirate down below."

"Just as great," said Bittern, "the only difference being that he has won everything while I have lost everything."

"What are we to do!" asked Dickory. "I cannot stay here, and I am sure you will not want to. Now, while he is below, can we not slip overboard and swim ashore? I am sure I could do it."

Black Paul grinned grimly. "But where should we swim to?" he said. "On the coast of Honduras there is no safety for a man who flees from Blackbeard. But keep your tongue close; he is coming."

The moment Blackbeard put his foot upon the deck he began to roar out his general orders.

"I go over to the bark," he said, "and shall put my mate here in charge of her. After that I go to my own vessel, and when I have settled matters there I will return to this fine ship, where I shall strut about the quarter-deck and live like a prince at sea. Now look ye, youngster, what is your name?"

"Charter," replied Dickory grimly.

"Well then, Charter," the pirate continued, "I shall leave you in charge of this vessel until I come back, which will be before dark."

"Me!" exclaimed Dickory in amazement.

"Yes, you," said the pirate. "I am sure you don't know anything about a ship any more than your master did, but he got on very well, and so may you. And now, remember, your head shall pay for it if everything is not the same when I come back as it is now."

Thereupon this man of piratical business was rowed to the bark, quite satisfied that he left behind him no one who would have the power to tamper with his interests. He knew the crew, having bound most of them to him on the preceding night, and he trusted every one of them to obey the man he had set over them and no other. As Dickory would have no orders to give, there would be no need of obedience, and Black Paul would have no chance to interfere with anything.

FRANK R. STOCKTON

WHEN BONNET HAD BEEN LEFT by Blackbeard—who, having said all he had to say, hurried up the companion-way to attend to the rest of his plans—the stately naval officer who had so recently occupied the bench by the table shrunk into a frightened farmer, gazing blankly at Ben Greenway.

"Think you, Ben," he said in half a voice, "that this is one of that man's jokes! I have heard that he has a fearful taste for horrid jokes."

The Scotchman shook his head. "Joke! Master Bonnet," he exclaimed, "it is no joke. He has ta'en your ship from ye; he has ta'en from ye your sword, your pistols, an' your wicked black flag, an' he has made evil impossible to ye. He has ta'en from ye the shame an' the wretched wickedness o' bein' a pirate. Think o' that, Master Bonnet, ye are no longer a pirate. That most devilish o' all demons has presarved the rest o' your life from the dishonour an' the infamy which ye were labourin' to heap upon it. Ye are a poor mon now, Master Bonnet; that Beelzebub will strip from ye everything ye had, all your riches shall be his. Ye can no longer afford to be a pirate; ye will be compelled to be an honest mon. An' I tell ye that my soul lifteth itsel' in thanksgivin' an' my heart is happier than it has been since that fearsome day when ye went on board your vessel at Bridgetown."

"Ben," said Bonnet, "it is hard and it is cruel, that in this, the time of my great trouble, you turn upon me. I have been robbed; I have been ruined; my life is of no more use to me, and you, Ben Greenway, revile me while that I am prostrate."

"Revile!" said the Scotchman. "I glory, I rejoice! Ye hae been converted, ye hae been changed, ye hae been snatched from the jaws o' hell. Moreover, Master Bonnet, my soul was rejoiced even before that master de'il came to set ye free from your toils. To look upon ye an' see that, although ye called yoursel' a pirate, ye were no like ane o' these black-hearted cut-throats. Ye were never as wicked, Master Bonnet, as ye said ye were!"

"You are mistaken," groaned Bonnet; "I tell you, Ben Greenway, you are mistaken; I am just as wicked as I ever was. And I was very wicked, as you should admit, knowing what I have done. Oh, Ben, Ben! Is it true that I shall never go on board my good ship again?"

And with this he spread his arms upon the table and laid his head upon them. He felt as if his career was ended and his heart broken. Ben Greenway said no more to comfort him, but at that moment he himself was the happiest man on the Caribbean Sea. He seated himself in the little dirty cabin, and his soul saw visions. He saw his master, deprived of all his belongings, and with them of every taint of piracy, and put on shore, accompanied, of course, by his faithful servant. He saw a ship sail, perhaps soon, perhaps later, for Jamaica; he saw the blithe Mistress Kate, her soul no longer sorrowing for an erring father, come on board that vessel and sail with him for good old Bridgetown. He saw everything explained, everything forgotten. He saw before the dear old family a life of happiness—perhaps he saw the funeral of Madam Bonnet—and, better than all, he saw the pirate dead, the good man revived again.

To be sure, he did not see Dickory Charter returning to his old home with his mother, for he could not know what Blackbeard was going to do with that young fellow; but as Dickory had thought of him when he had escaped with Kate from the Revenge, so thought he now of Dickory. There were so many other important things which bore upon the situation that he was not able even to consider the young fellow.

It did not take very long for a man of practical devilishness, such as Blackbeard was, to finish the business which had called him away, and he soon reappeared in the cabin.

"Ho there! good Sir Nightcap—an I may freely call you that since now I own you, uniform, cocked hat, title, and everything else—don't cry yourself to sleep like a baby when its toys are taken away from it, but wake up. I have a bit of liking for you, and I believe that that is because you are clean. Not having that virtue myself, I admire it the more in others, and I thank you from my inmost soul—wherever that may be— for having provided such comely quarters and such fair accommodations for me while I shall please to sail the Revenge. But I shall not condemn you to idleness and cankering thoughts, my bold blusterer, my terror of the sea, my harrier of the coast, my flaunter of the Jolly Roger washed clean in the tub with soap; I shall give you work to do which shall better suit you than the troublesome trade you've been trying to learn. You write well and read, I know that, my good Sir Nightcap; and, moreover, you are a fair hand at figures. I have great work before me in landing and selling the fine cargoes you have brought me, and in counting and dividing the treasure you have locked in your iron-bound chests. And you shall attend to all that, my reformed cutthroat, my regenerated sea-robber. You shall have a room of your own, where you can take off that brave uniform and where you can do your work and keep your accounts

FRANK R. STOCKTON

and so shall be happier than you ever were before, feeling that you are in your right place."

To all this Stede Bonnet did not answer a word; he did not even raise his head.

"And now for you, my chaplain," said Blackbeard, suddenly turning toward Ben Greenway, "what would you like? Would it suit you better to go overboard or to conduct prayers for my pious crew?"

"I would stay wi' my master," said the Scotchman quietly.

The pirate looked steadily at Greenway. "Oho!" said he, "you are a sturdy fellow, and have a mind to speak from. Being so stiff yourself, you may be able to stiffen a little this rag of a master of yours and help him to understand the work he has to do, which he will bravely do, I ween, when he finds that to be my clerk is his career. Ha! ha! Sir Nightcap, the pirate of the pen and ink!"

Deeply sunk these words into Stede Bonnet's heart, but he made no sign.

When Blackbeard went back to the Revenge he took with him all of his own effects which he cared for, and he also took the ex-pirate's uniform, cocked hat, and sword. "I may have use for them," he said, "and my clerk can wear common clothes like common people."

When her new commander reached the Revenge, Dickory immediately approached him and earnestly besought him that he might be sent to join Captain Bonnet and Ben Greenway. "They are my friends," said Dickory, "and I have none here, and I have brought a message to Captain Bonnet from his daughter, and it is urgently necessary that I return with one from him to her. I must instantly endeavour to find a ship which is bound for Jamaica and sail upon her. I have nothing to do with this ship, having come on board of her simply to carry my message, and it behooves me that I return quickly to those who sent me, else injury may come of it."

"I like your speech, my boy, I like your speech!" cried Blackbeard, and he roared out a big laugh. "'Urgently necessary' you must do this, you must do that. It is so long since I have heard such words that they come to me like wine from a cool vault."

At this Dickory flushed hot, but he shut his mouth.

"You are a brave fellow," cried Blackbeard, "and above the common, you are above the common. There is that in your eye that could never be seen in the eye of a sugar-planter. You will make a good pirate."

"Pirate!" cried Dickory, losing all sense of prudence. "I would sooner be a wild beast in the forest than to be a pirate!"

Blackbeard laughed loudly. "A good fellow, a brave fellow!" he cried. "No man who has not the soul of a pirate within him could stand on his legs and speak those words to me. Sail to Jamaica to carry messages to girls? Never! You shall stay with me, you shall be a pirate. You shall be the head of all the pirates when I give up the business and take to sugar-planting. Ha! ha! When I take to sugar-planting and merrily make my own good rum!"

Dickory was dismayed. "But, Captain Blackbeard," he said, with more deference than before, "I cannot."

"Cannot!" shouted the pirate, "you lie, you can. Say not cannot to me; you can do anything I tell you, and do it you shall. And now I am going to put you in your place, and see that you hold it and fill it. An if you please me not, you carry no more messages in this world, nor receive them. Charter, I now make you the first officer of the Revenge under me. You cannot be mate because you know nothing of sailing a ship, and besides no mate nor any quarter-master is worthy to array himself as I shall array you. I make you first lieutenant, and you shall wear the uniform and the cocked hat which Sir Nightcap hath no further use for."

With that he went forward to speak to some of the men, leaving Dickory standing speechless, with the expression of an infuriated idiot. Black Paul stepped up to him.

"How now, youngster," said the ex-sailing-master, "first officer, eh? If you look sharp, you may find yourself in fine feather."

"No, I will not," answered Dickory. "I will have nothing to do with this black pirate; I will not serve under him, I will not take charge of anything for him. I am ashamed to talk with him, to be on the same ship with him. I serve good people, the best and noblest in the world, and I will not enter any service under him."

"Hold ye, hold ye!" said Black Paul, "you will not serve the good people you speak of by going overboard with a bullet in your head; think of that, youngster. It is a poor way of helping your friends by quitting the world and leaving them in the lurch."

At this moment Blackbeard returned, and when he saw Bittern he roared at him: "Out of that, you sea-cat, and if I see you again speaking to my lieutenant, I'll slash your ears for you. In the next boat which leaves this ship I shall send you to one of the others; I will have no sneaking schemer on board the Revenge. Get ye for'ad, get ye for'ad, or I shall help ye with my cutlass!"

FRANK R. STOCKTON

And the man who had safely brought two good ships, richly laden, into the harbour of Belize, and who had given Blackbeard the information which made him understand the character of Captain Bonnet and how easy it would be to take possession of his person and his vessels, and who had done everything in his power to enable the black-hearted pirate to secure to himself Bonnet's property and crews, and who had only asked in return an actual command where before he had commanded in fact though not in name, fled away from the false confederate to whom he had just given wealth and increased prestige.

The last words of the unfortunate Bittern sunk quickly and deeply into the heart of Dickory. If he should really go overboard with a bullet in his brain, farewell to Kate Bonnet, farewell to his mother! He was yet a very young man, and it had been but a little while since he had been wandering barefooted over the ships at Bridgetown, selling the fruit of his mother's little farm. Since that he had loved and lived so long that he could not calculate the period, and now he was a man and stood trembling at the point where he was to decide to begin life as a pirate or end everything. Before Blackbeard had turned his lowering visage from his retreating benefactor, Dickory had decided that, whatever might happen, he would not of his own free-will leave life and fair Kate Bonnet.

"And so you are to be my first lieutenant," said Blackbeard, his face relaxing. "I am glad of that. There was nothing needed on this ship but a decent man. I have put one on my old vessel, and if there were another to be found in the Gulf of Honduras, I'd clap him on that goodly bark. Now, sir, down to your berth, and don your naval finery. You're always to wear it; you're not fit to wear the clothes of a real sailor, and I have no landsman's toggery on this ship."

Dickory bowed—he could not speak—and went below. When next he appeared on deck he wore the ex-Captain Bonnet's uniform and the tall plumed hat.

"It is for Kate's sweet sake," he said to himself as he mounted the companion-way; "for her sake I'd wear anything, I'd do anything, if only I may see her again."

When the new first lieutenant showed himself upon the quarter-deck there was a general howl from the crew, and peal after peal of derisive laughter rent the air.

Then Blackbeard stepped quietly forward and ordered eight of the jeerers to be strung up and flogged.

"I would like you all to remember," said the master pirate, "that when I appoint an officer on this ship, there is to be no sneering at him nor any want of respect, and it strikes me that I shall not have to say anything more on the subject—to this precious crew, at any rate."

The next day lively times began on board the two rich prizes which the pirate Blackbeard had lately taken. There had been scarcely more hard work and excitement, cursing and swearing when the rich freight had been taken from the merchantmen which had originally carried it. Poor Bonnet's pen worked hard at lists and calculations, for Blackbeard was a practical man, and not disposed to loose and liberal dealings with either his men or the tradefolk ashore.

At times the troubled and harassed mind of the former captain of the Revenge would have given way under the strain had not Ben Greenway stayed bravely by him; who, although a slow accountant, was sure, and a great help to one who, in these times of hurry and flurry, was extremely rapid and equally uncertain. Blackbeard was everywhere, anxious to complete the unloading and disposal of his goods before the weather changed; but, wherever he went, he remembered that upon the quarter-deck of his fine new ship, the Revenge, there was one who, knowing nothing of nautical matters, was above all suspicion of nautical interferences, and who, although having no authority, represented the most powerful nautical commander in all those seas.

XX

ONE NORTH, ONE SOUTH

I f our dear Kate Bonnet had really imagined, in her inexperienced mind, that it would be a matter of days, and perhaps weeks, to procure a vessel in which she, with her uncle and good Dame Charter, could sail forth to save her father, she was wonderfully mistaken. Not a free-footed vessel of any class came into the harbour of Kingston. Sloops and barks and ships in general arrived and departed, but they were all bound by one contract or another, and were not free to sail away, here and there, for a short time or a long time, at the word of a maiden's will.

Mr. Delaplaine was a rich man, but he was a prudent one, and he had not the money to waste in wild rewards, even if there had been an opportunity for him to offer them. Kate was disconcerted, disappointed, and greatly cast down.

The vengeful Badger was scouring the seas in search of her father, commissioned to destroy him, and eager in his hot passion to do it; and here was she, with a respite for that father, if only she were able to carry it.

Day after day Kate waited for notice of a craft, not only one which might bring Dickory back but one which might carry her away.

The optimism of Dame Charter would not now bear her up, the load which had been put upon it was too big. Everything about her was melancholy and depressed, and Dickory had not come back. So many things had happened since he went away, and so many days had passed, and she had entirely exhausted her plentiful stock of very good reasons why her son had not been able to return to her.

The Governor was very kind; frequently he came to the Delaplaine mansion, and always he brought assurances that, although he had not heard anything from Captain Vince, there was every reason to suppose that before long he would find some way to send him his commands that Captain Bonnet should not be injured, but should be brought back safely to Jamaica.

And then Kate would say, with tears in her eyes: "But, your Excellency, we cannot wait for that; we must go, we must deliver ourselves your message to the captain of the Badger. Who else will do it? And we cannot trust to chance; while we are trusting and hoping, my father may die."

At such moments Mr. Delaplaine would sometimes say in his heart, not daring to breathe such thoughts aloud, "And what could be better than that he should die and be done with it? He is a thorn in the side of the young, the good, and the beautiful, and as long as he lives that thorn will rankle."

Moreover, not only did the good merchant harbour such a wicked thought, but Dame Charter thought something of the very same kind, though differently expressed. If he had never been born, she would say to herself, how much better it would have been; but then the thought would come crowding in, how bad that would have been for Dickory and for the plans she was making for him.

In the midst of all this uncertainty, this anxiety, this foreboding, almost this despair, there came a sunburst which lighted up the souls of these three good people, which made their eyes sparkle and their hearts swell with thankfulness. This happiness came in the shape of a letter from Martin Newcombe.

The letter was a long one and told many things. The first part of it Kate read to herself and kept to herself, for in burning words it assured her that he loved her and would always love her, and that no misfortune of her own nor wrongdoings of others could prevent him from offering her his most ardent and unchangeable affection. Moreover, he begged and implored her to accept that affection, to accept it now that it might belong to her forever. Happiness, he said, seemed opening before her; he implored her to allow him to share that happiness with her. The rest of the letter was read most jubilantly aloud. It told of news which had come to Newcombe from Honduras Gulf: great news, wonderful news, which would make the heart sing. Major Bonnet was at Belize. He had given up all connection with piracy and was now engaged in mercantile pursuits. This was positively true, for the person who had sent the news to Bridgetown had seen Major Bonnet and had talked to him, and had been informed by him that he had given up his ship and was now an accountant and commission agent doing business at that place.

The sender of this great news also stated that Ben Greenway was with Major Bonnet, working as his assistant—and here Dame Charter sat open-mouthed and her heart nearly stopped beating—young

Dickory Charter had also been in the port and had gone away, but was expected ere long to return.

Kate stood on her tip-toes and waved the letter over her head.

"To Belize, my dear uncle, to Belize! If we cannot get there any other way we must go in a boat with oars. We must fly, we must not wait. Perhaps he is seeking in disguise to escape the vengeance of the wicked Vince; but that matters not; we know where he is; we must fly, uncle, we must fly!"

The opportunities for figurative flying were not wanting. There were no vessels in the port which might be engaged for an indeterminate voyage in pursuit of a British man-of-war, but there was a goodly sloop about to sail in ballast for Belize. Before sunset three passages were engaged upon this sloop.

Kate sat long into the night, her letter in her hand. Here was a lover who loved her; a lover who had just sent to her not only love, but life; a lover who had no intention of leaving her because of her overshadowing sorrow, but who had lifted that sorrow and had come to her again. Ay more, she knew that if the sorrow had not been lifted he would have come to her again.

The Governor of Jamaica was a man of hearty sympathies, and these worked so strongly in him that when Kate and her uncle came to bring him the good news, he kissed her and vowed that he had not heard anything so cheering for many a year.

"I have been greatly afraid of that Vince," he said. "Although I did not mention it, I have been greatly afraid of him; he is a terrible fellow when he is crossed, and so hot-headed that it is easy to cross him. There were so many chances of his catching your father and so few chances of my orders catching him. But it is all right now; you will be able to reach your father before Vince can possibly get to him, even should he be able to do him injury in his present position. Your father, my dear, must have been as mad as a March hare to embark upon a career of a pirate when all the time his heart was really turned to ways of peace, to planting, to mercantile pursuits, to domestic joys."

Here, now, was to be a voyage of conquest. No matter what his plans were; no matter what he said; no matter what he might lose, or how he might suffer by being taken into captivity and being carried away, Major Stede Bonnet, late of Bridgetown and still later connected with some erratic voyages upon the high seas, was to be taken prisoner by his daughter and carried away to Spanish Town, where the actions of his disordered mind were to be condoned and where he would be safe from all vengeful Vinces and from all temptations of the flaunting skull and bones.

It was a bright morning when, with a fair wind upon her starboard bow, the sloop Belinda, bearing the jubilant three, sailed southward on her course to the coast of Honduras; and it was upon that same morning that the good ship Revenge, bearing the pirate Blackbeard and his handsomely uniformed lieutenant, sailed northward, the same fair wind upon her port bow.

XXI

A Projected Marriage

Strange as it may appear, Dickory Charter was not a very unhappy young fellow as he stood in his fine uniform on the quarter-deck of the Revenge, the fresh breeze ruffling his brown curls when he lifted his heavy cocked hat.

True, he was leaving behind him his friends, Captain Bonnet and Ben Greenway, with whom the wayward Blackbeard would allow no word of leave-taking; true, he was going, he knew not where, and in the power of a man noted the new world over for his savage eccentricities; and true, he might soon be sailing, hour by hour, farther and farther away from the island on which dwelt the angel Kate—that angel Kate and his mother. But none of these considerations could keep down the glad feeling that he was going, that he was moving. Moreover, in answer to one of his impassioned appeals to be set ashore at Jamaica, Blackbeard had said to him that if he should get tired of him he did not see, at that moment, any reason why he should not put him on board some convenient vessel and have him landed at Kingston.

Dickory did not believe very much in the black-bearded pirate, with his wild tricks and inhuman high spirits, but Jamaica lay to the east, and he was going eastward.

Incited, perhaps, by the possession of a fine ship, manned by a crew picked from his old vessel and from the men who had formed the crew of the Revenge, Blackbeard was in better spirits than was his wont, and so far as his nature would allow he treated Dickory with fair good-humour. But no matter what happened, his unrestrained imagination never failed him. Having taken the fancy to see Dickory always in full uniform, he allowed him to assume no other clothes; he was always in naval full-dress and cocked hat, and his duties were those of a private secretary.

"The only shrewd thing I ever knew your Sir Nightcap to do," he said, "was to tell me you could not read nor write. He spoke so glibly that I believed him. Had it not been so I should have sent you to the town to help with the shore end of my affairs, and then you would have been there still and I should have had no admiral to write my log and straighten my accounts."

Sometimes, in his quieter moods, when there was no provocation to send pistol-balls between two sailors quietly conversing, or to perform some other demoniac trick, Blackbeard would talk to Dickory and ask all manner of questions, some of which the young man answered, while some he tried not to answer. Thus it was that the pirate found out a great deal more about Dickory's life, hope, and sorrows than the young fellow imagined that he made known. He discovered that Dickory was greatly interested in Bonnet's daughter, and wished above all other things in this world to get to her and to be with her.

This was a little out of the common run of things among the brotherhood; it was their fashion to forget, so far as they were able, the family ties which already belonged to them, and to make no plans for any future ties of that sort which they might be able to make. Such a thing amused the generally rampant Blackbeard, but if this Dickory boy whom they had on board really did wish to marry some one, the idea came into the crafty mind of Blackbeard that he would like to attend to that marrying himself. It pleased him to have a finger in every pie, and now here was a pie in the fingering of which he might take a novel interest.

This renowned desperado, this bloody cutthroat, this merciless pirate possessed a home—a quiet little English home on the Cornwall coast, where the cheerful woods and fields stretched down almost in reach of the sullen sea. Here dwelt his wife, quiet Mistress Thatch, and here his brawny daughter. Seldom a word came to this rural home from the father, burning and robbing, sinking and slaying out upon the western seas. But from the stores of pelf which so often slipped so easily into his great arms, and which so often slipped just as easily out of them, came now and then something to help the brawn grow upon his daughter's bones and to ease the labours of his wife.

Eliza Thatch bore no resemblance to a houri; her hair was red, her face was freckled; she had enough teeth left to do good eating with when she had a chance, and her step shook the timbers of her little home.

Her father had heard from her a little while ago by a letter she had had conveyed to Belize. His parental feelings, notwithstanding he had told Bonnet he knew no such sentiments, were stirred. When he had finished her letter he would have been well pleased to burn a vessel and make a dozen passengers walk the plank as a memorial to his girl. But this not being convenient, it had come to him that he would marry the wench to the gaily bedecked young fellow he had captured, and it filled his reckless heart with a wild delight. He drew his cutlass, and with a great oath he drove the heavy blade into the top of the table, and he swore by this mark that his grand plan should be carried out.

He would sail over to England; this would be a happy chance, for his vessel was unladen and ready for any adventure. He would drop anchor in the quiet cove he knew of; he would go ashore by night; he would be at home again. To be at home again made him shout with profane laughter, the little home he remembered would be so ridiculous to him now. He would see again his poor little trembling wife—she must be gray by now—and he was sure that she would tremble more than ever she did when she heard the great sea oaths which he was accustomed to pour forth now. And his daughter, she must be a strapping wench by this time; he was sure she could stand a slap on the back which would kill her mother.

Yes, there should be a wedding, a fine wedding, and good old rum should water the earth. And he would detail a boat's crew of jolly good fellows from the Revenge to help make things uproarious. This Charter boy and Eliza should have a house of their own, with plenty of money—he had more funds in hand than ever in his life before—and his respectable son-in-law should go to London and deposit his fortune in a bank. It would be royal fun to think of him and Eliza highly respectable and with money in the bank. A quart of the best rum could scarcely have made Blackbeard more hilarious than did this glorious notion. He danced among his crew; he singed beards; he whacked with capstan bars; he pushed men down hatchways; he was in lordly spirits, and his crew expected some great adventure, some startling piece of deviltry.

Of course he did not keep his great design from Dickory—it was too glorious, too transcendent. He took his young admiral into his cabin and laid before him his dazzling future.

Dickory sat speechless, almost breathless. As he listened he could feel himself turn cold. Had any one else been talking to him in this strain he would have shouted with laughter, but people did not laugh at Blackbeard.

When the pirate had said all and was gazing triumphantly at poor Dickory, the young man gasped a word in answer; he could not accept this awful fate without as much as a wave of the hand in protest.

"But, sir," said he, "if—"

Blackbeard's face grew black; he bent his head and lowered upon the pale Dickory, then, with a tremendous blow, he brought down his fist upon the table.

"If Eliza will not have you," he roared; "if that girl will not take you when I offer you to her; if she or her mother as much as winks an eyelash in disobedience of my commands, I will take them by the hair of their heads and I will throw them into the sea. If she will not have you," he repeated, roaring as if he were shouting through a speaking trumpet in a storm, "if I thought that, youngster, I would burn the house with both of them in it, and the rum I had bought to make a jolly wedding should be poured on the timbers to make them blaze. Let no notions like that enter your mind, my boy. If she disobeys me, I will cook her and you shall eat her. Disobey me!" And he swore at such a rate that he panted for fresh air and mounted to the deck.

It was not a time for Dickory to make remarks indicating his disapproval of the proposed arrangement.

As the Revenge sailed on over sunny seas or under lowering clouds, Dickory was no stranger to the binnacle, and the compass always told him that they were sailing eastward. He had once asked Blackbeard where they now were by the chart, but that gracious gentleman of the midnight beard had given him oaths for answers, and had told him that if the captain knew where the ship was on any particular hour or minute nobody else on that ship need trouble his head about it. But at last the course of the Revenge was changed a little, and she sailed northward. Then Dickory spoke with one of the mildest of the mates upon the subject of their progress, and the man made known to him that they were now about half-way through the Windward passage. Dickory started back. He knew something of the geography of those seas.

"Why, then," he cried, "we have passed Jamaica!"

"Of course we have," said the man, and if it had not been for Dickory's uniform he would have sworn at him.

XXII

BLADE TO BLADE

When the corvette Badger sailed from Jamaica she moved among the islands of the Caribbean Sea as if she had been a modern vessel propelled by a steam-engine. That which represented a steam-engine in this case was the fiery brain of Captain Christopher Vince of his Majesty's navy. More than winds, more than currents, this brain made its power felt upon the course and progress of the vessel.

Calling at every port where information might possibly be gained, hailing every sloop or ship or fishing-smack which might have sighted the pirate ship Revenge, with a constant lookout for a black flag, Captain Vince kept his engine steadily at work.

But it was not in pursuit of a ship that the swift keel of the Badger cut through the sea, this way and that, now on a long course, now doubling back again, like a hound fancying he has got the scent of a hare, then raging wildly when he finds the scent is false; it was in pursuit of a woman that every sail was spread, that the lookout swept the sea, and that the hot brain of the captain worked steadily and hard. This English man-of-war was on a cruise to make Kate Bonnet the bride of its captain. The heart of this naval lover was very steady; it was fixed in its purpose, nothing could turn it aside. Vince's plans were well-digested; he knew what he wanted to do, he knew how he was going to do it.

In the first place he would capture the man Bonnet; all the details of the action were arranged to that end; then, with Kate's father as his prisoner, he would be master of the situation.

There was nothing noble about this craftily elaborated design; but, then, there was nothing noble about Captain Vince. He was a strong hater and a strong lover, and whether he hated or loved, nothing, good or bad, must stand in his way. With the life or death, the misery or the happiness of the father in his hands, he knew that he need but beckon to the daughter. She might come slowly, but she would come. She was a grand woman, but she was a woman; she might resist the warm plea of love, but she could not resist the cold commands of that cruel figure of death who stood behind the lover.

Captain Bonnet was returning from his visit to the New England coast, picking up bits of profit here and there as fortune befell him, when Captain Vince first heard that the Revenge had gone northward. The news was circumstantial and straightforward, and was not to be doubted. Vince raged upon his quarter-deck when he found out how he had been wasting time. Northward now was pointed the bow of the Badger, and the vengeful Vince felt as if his prey was already in his hands. If Bonnet had sailed up the Atlantic coast he was bound to sail down again. It might be a long cruise, there might be impatient waitings at the mouths of coves and rivers where the pirates were accustomed to take refuge or refit, but the light of the eyes of Kate Bonnet were worth the longest pursuit or the most impatient waiting.

So, steadily sailed the corvette Badger up the long Atlantic coast, and she passed the capes of the Delaware while Captain Bonnet was examining the queer pulpit in the little bay-side town where his ship had stopped to take in water.

At the various ports of the northern coast where the Revenge had sailed back and forth outside, the Badger boldly entered, and the tales she heard soon turned her back again to sail southward down the long Atlantic coast. But the heart of Christopher Vince never failed. The vision of Kate Bonnet as he had seen her, standing with glorious eyes denouncing him; as he should see her when, with bowed head and proffered hand, she came to him; as all should see her when, in her clear-cut beauty, she stood beside him in his ancestral home, never left him.

Off the port of Charles Town, South Carolina, the Badger lay and waited, and soon, from an outgoing bark, the news came to Captain Vince that several weeks before the pirate Bonnet of the Revenge had taken an English ship as she was entering port, and had then sailed southward. Southward now sailed the Badger, and, as there was but little wind, Captain Vince swore with an unremitting diligence.

It was a quiet morning and the Badger was nearing the straits of Florida when a sail was reported almost due south.

Up came Captain Vince with his glass, and after a long, long look, and another, and another, during which the two vessels came slowly nearer and nearer each other, the captain turned to his first officer and said quietly: "She flies the skull and bones. She's the first of those hellish pirates that we have yet met on this most unlucky cruise."

"If we could send her, with her crew on board, ten times to the bottom," said the other, "she would not pay us what her vile fraternity has cost us. But these pirate craft know well the difference between a Spanish galleon and a British man-of-war, and they will always give us a wide berth."

"But this one will not," said the captain.

Then again he looked long and earnestly through his glass. "Send aft the three men who know the Revenge," said he.

Presently the men came aft, and one by one they went aloft, and soon came the report, vouched for by each of them:

"The sail ahead is the pirate Revenge."

Now all redness left the face of Captain Vince. He was as pale as if he had been afraid that the pirate ship would capture him, but every man on his vessel knew that there was no fear in the soul or the body of the captain of the Badger. Quickly came his orders, clear and sharp; everything had been gone over before, but everything was gone over again. The corvette was to bear down upon the pirate, her cannon—great guns for those days, and which could soon have disabled, if they had not sunk, the smaller vessel—were muzzled and told to hold their peace. The man-of-war was to bear down upon the pirate and to capture her by boarding. There was to be no broadside, no timber-splitting cannon balls.

The wind was light and in favour of the corvette, and slowly the two vessels diminished the few miles between them; but there was enough wind to show the royal colours on the Badger.

"He is a bold fellow, that pirate," said some of the naval men, "and he will wait and fight us."

"He will wait and fight us," said some of the others, "because he cannot get away; in this wind he is at our mercy."

Captain Vince stood and gazed over the water, sometimes with his glass and sometimes without it. Here now was the end of his fuming, his raging, his long and untiring search. All the anxious weariness of long voyaging, all the impatience of watching, all the irritation of waiting had gone. The notorious vessel in which the father of Kate Bonnet had made himself a terror and a scourge was now almost within his reach. The beneficent vessel by which the father of Kate Bonnet should give to him his life's desire was so near to him that he could have sent a musket ball into her had he chosen to fire. It was so near to him that he could now, with his glass, read the word "Revenge" on her bow. His brows were knit, his jaws were set tight, his muscles hardened themselves with energy.

Again the orders were passed, that when the men of the corvette boarded the pirate they were to cut down the rascals without mercy, and not one of them was to draw sword or pistol against the pirate captain. He would be attended to by their commander.

Vince knew the story of Stede Bonnet; he knew that early in life he had been in the army, and that it was likely that he understood the handling of a sword. But he knew also that he himself was one of the best swordsmen in the royal navy. He yearned to cross blades with the man whose blood should not be shed, whose life should be preserved throughout the combat as if he were a friend and not a foe, who should surrender to him his sword and give to him his daughter.

"They're a brave lot, those bloody rascals," said one of the men of the Badger.

"They've a fool of a captain," said another; "he knows not the difference between a British man-of-war and a Spanish galleon, but we shall teach him that."

Slowly they came together, the Revenge and the Badger, the bow of one pointed east and the bow of the other to the west; from neither vessel there came a word; the low waves could be heard flapping against their sides. Suddenly there rang out from the man-of-war the order to make fast. The grapnels flew over the bulwarks of the pirate, and in a moment the two vessels were as one. Then, with a great shout, the men of the Badger leaped and hurled themselves upon the deck of the Revenge, and upon that deck and from behind bulwarks there rose, yelling and howling and roaring, the picked men of two pirate crews, quick, furious, and strong as tigers, the hate of man in their eyes and the love of blood in their hearts. Like a wave of massacre they threw themselves against the drilled masses of the Badger's crew, and with yells and oaths and curses and cries the battle raged.

With a sudden dash the captain of the man-of-war plunged through the ranks of the combatants and stood upon the middle of the deck; his quick eyes shot here and there; wherever he might be, he sought the captain of the pirate ship. In an instant a huge man bounded aft and made one long step towards him. Vast in chest and shoulder, and with mighty limbs, fiery-eyed, hairy, horribly fantastic, Blackbeard stood, with great head lowered for the charge.

"A sugar-planter?" was the swift thought of Vince.

"Are you the captain of this ship?" he shouted.

"I am!" cried the other, and with a curse like bursting thunder the pirate came on and his blade crossed that of Captain Vince.

Forward and amidships surged the general fight: men plunged, swords fell, blood flowed, feet slipped upon the deck, and roars of blasphemy and pain rose above the noise of battle. But farther aft the two captains, in a space by themselves, cut, thrust, and trampled, whirling around each other, dashing from this side and that, ever with keen eyes firmly fixed, ever with strong arms whirling down and upward; now one man felt the keen cut of steel and now the other. The blood ran upon rich uniform or stained rough cloth and leather. It was a fight as if between a lioness and a tigress, their dead cubs near-by.

As most men in the navy knew, Captain Vince was a most dangerous swordsman. In duel or in warfare, no man yet had been able to stand before him. With skilled arm and eye and with every muscle of his body trained, his sword sought a vital spot in his opponent. There was no thought now in the mind of Vince about disarming the pirate and taking him prisoner; this terrible wild beast, this hairy monster must be killed or he himself must die. Through the whirl and clash and hot breath of battle he had been amazed that Kate Bonnet's father should be a man like this.

The pirate, his eyes now shrunken into his head, where they glowed like coals, his breath steaming like a volcano, and his tremendous muscles supple and quick as those of a cat, met his antagonist at every point, and with every lunge and thrust and cut forced him to guard.

Now Vince shut himself in his armour of trained defence; this bounding lion must be killed, but the death-stroke must be cunningly delivered, and until, in his hot rage, the pirate should forget his guard Vince must shield himself.

Never had the great Blackbeard met so keen a swordsman; he howled with rage to see the English captain still vigorous, agile, warding every stroke. Blackbeard was now a wild beast of the sea: he fought to kill, for naught else, not even his own life. With a yell he threw himself upon Captain Vince, whose sword passed quick as lightning through the brawny masses of his left shoulder. With one quick step, the pirate pressed closer to Vince, thus holding the imprisoned blade, which stuck out behind his body, and with a tremendous blow of his right fist, in which he held the heavy brazen hilt of his sword, he dashed his enemy backward to the ground. The fall drew the blade from the shoulder of Blackbeard, whose great right arm went up, whose sword hissed in the air and then came down upon the prostrate Vince. Another stroke and the English captain lay insensible and still.

With the scream of a maddened Indian, Blackbeard sprung into the air, and when his feet touched the deck he danced. He would have hewn his victim into pieces, he would have scattered him over the decks, but there was no time for such recreations. Forward the battle raged with tremendous fury, and into the midst of it dashed Blackbeard.

From the companion-way leading to the captain's cabin there now appeared a pale young face. It was that of Dickory Charter, who had been ordered by Blackbeard, before the two vessels came together, to shut himself in the cabin and to keep out of the broil, swearing that if he made himself unfit to present to Eliza he would toss his disfigured body into the sea. Entirely unarmed and having no place in the fight, Dickory had obeyed, but the spirit of a young man which burned within him led him to behold the greater part of the conflict between Blackbeard and the English captain. Being a young man, he had shut his eyes at the end of it, but when the pirate had left he came forth quietly. The fight raged forward, and here he was alone with the fallen figure on the deck.

As Dickory stood gazing downward in awe—in all his life he had never seen a corpse—the man he had supposed dead opened his eyes for a moment and gazed with dull intelligence, and then he gasped for rum. Dickory was quickly beside him with a tumbler of spirits and water, which, raising the fallen man's head, he gave him. In a few moments the eyes of Captain Vince opened wider, and he stared at the young man in naval uniform who stood above him. "Who are you?" he said in a low voice, but distinct, "an English officer?"

"No," said Dickory, "I am no officer and no pirate; I am forced to wear these clothes."

And then, his natural and selfish instincts pushing themselves before anything else, Dickory went on: "Oh, sir, if your men conquer these pirates will you take me—" but as he spoke he saw that the wounded man was not listening to him; his half-closed eyes turned towards him and he whispered:

"More spirits!"

DICKORY DASHED INTO THE CABIN, half-filled a tumbler with rum and gave it to Vince. Presently his eyes recovered something of their natural glow, and with contracted brow he fixed them upon the stream of blood which was running from him over the deck.

Suddenly he spoke sharply: "Young fellow," he said, "some paper and a pen, a pencil, anything. Quick!"

Dickory looked at him in amazement for a moment and then he ran into the cabin, soon returning with a sheet of paper and an English pencil.

The eyes of Captain Vince were now very bright, and a nervous strength came into his body. He raised himself upon his elbow, he clutched at the paper, and clapping it upon the deck began to write. Quickly his pencil moved; already he was feeling that his rum-given strength was leaving him, but several pages he wrote, and then he signed his name. Folding the sheet he stopped for a moment, feeling that he could do no more; but, gathering together his strength in one convulsive motion, he addressed the letter.

"Take that," he feebly said, "and swear. . . that it shall be. . . delivered."

"I swear," said Dickory, as on his knees he took the blood-smeared letter. He hastily slipped it into the breast of his coat, and then he was barely able to move quick enough to keep the Englishman's head from striking the deck.

"How now!" sounded a harsh growl at his ear. "Get you into your cabin or you will be hurt. It is not time yet for the fleecing of corpses! I am choking for a glass of brandy. Get in and stay there!"

In another minute Blackbeard, refreshed, was running aft, the cut through his shoulder bleeding, but entirely forgotten.

There was no fighting now upon the deck of the Revenge; the conflict raged, but it had been transferred to the Badger. The sailors of the man-of-war had fought valiantly and stoutly, even impetuously, but their enemies—picked men from two pirate crews—had fought like wire-muscled devils. Ablaze with fury they had cut down the Badger's men, piling them upon their own fallen comrades; they had followed the brave fellows with oaths, cutlasses, and pistols as, little at a time and fighting all the while, they slowly clambered back into their own ship. The pirates had thrown their grapnels over the bulwarks of the man-of-war; they had followed, cut by cut, shot by shot, until they now stood upon the Badger, fighting with the same fury that they had just fought upon the blood-soaked Revenge. Blackbeard was not yet with them—whatever happened, Blackbeard must be refreshed—but now he sprang into the enemy's ship—that fine British man-of-war, the corvette Badger, which had so bravely sailed down upon his ship to capture her—and led the carnage.

They were tough men, those British seamen, tough in heart, tough in arms and body; they fought above decks and they fought below, and they laid many a pirate scoundrel dead; but they had met a foe which was too strong for them—a pack of brawny, hairy desperadoes, picked from two pirate crews. The first officer now commanding, panting, bleeding, and torn, groaned as he saw that his men could fight no longer, and he surrendered the Badger to the pirates.

The great Blackbeard yelled with delight. When had any other captain sailing under the Jolly Roger captured a British man-of-war, a first-class corvette of the royal navy? His frenzied joy was so intense that he was on the point of cutting down the officer who was offering him his sword, but he withheld his hand.

"Go, somebody, and fetch me a glass of his Majesty's rum," he cried, "and I will drink to his perdition!"

The door of a locker was smashed, the spirits were brought, and the great Blackbeard was again refreshed.

Standing on the quarter-deck where but an hour or two before Captain Christopher Vince had stood commanding his fine corvette as she sailed down upon her pirate enemy, Blackbeard had brought before him all the survivors of the Badger's crew.

"Well, you're a lot of damnable knaves," said he, "and you have cost me many a good man this day. But my crew will now be short-handed, and if any or all of you will turn pirate and ship with me, I will let bygones pass; but, if any of you choose not that, overboard you go. I will have no unwilling rascals in my crew."

All but one of the men of the Badger, downcast, wounded, panting with thirst and loving life, agreed to become pirates and to ship on board the Revenge.

The first mate would not break his oath of allegiance to the king, and he went overboard.

FRANK R. STOCKTON

XXIII

The Address of the Letter

There was hard and ghastly work that day when the Revenge was cleared after action, and there was lively and interesting work on board the Badger when Blackbeard and his officers went over the captured vessel to discover what new possessions they had won.

At first Blackbeard had thought to establish himself upon the corvette and abandon the Revenge. It would have been such a grand thing to scourge the seas in a British man-of-war with the Jolly Roger floating over her. But this would have been too dangerous; the combined naval force of England in American waters would have been united to put down such presumption. So the wary pirate curbed his ambition.

Everything portable and valuable was stripped from the Badger— her guns would have been taken had it been practicable to ship them to the Revenge in a rising sea—and then she was scuttled, fired, and cast off, and with her dead on board she passed out of commission in the royal navy.

During the turmoil, the horror and the bringing aboard of pillage, Dickory Charter had kept close below deck, his face in his hands and his heart almost broken. It is so easy for young hearts to almost break.

When he had seen the British ship come sailing down upon them, hope had sprung up brightly in his heart; now there was a chance of his escaping from this hell of the waves. When the Revenge should be taken he would rush to the British captain, or any one in authority, and tell his tale. It would be believed, he doubted not; even his uniform would help to prove he was no pirate; he would be taken away, he would reach Jamaica; he would see Kate; he would carry to her the great news of her father. After that his life could take care of itself.

But now the blackness of darkness was over everything. Those who were to have been his friends had vanished, the ship which was to have given him a new life had disappeared forever. He was on board the pirate ship, bound for the shores of England—horrible shores to him— bound to the shores of England and to Blackbeard's Eliza!

He was not a fool, this Dickory; he had no unwarrantable and romantic fears that in these enlightened days one man could say to another, "Go you, and marry the woman I have chosen for you." There was nothing silly or cowardly about him, but he knew Blackbeard.

Not one ray of hope thrust itself through his hands into his brain. Hope had gone, gone to the bottom, and he was on his storm-tossed way to the waters of another continent.

But in the midst of his despair Dickory never thought of freeing himself, by a sudden bound, of the world and his woes. So long as Kate should live he must live, even if it were to prove to himself, and to himself only, how faithful to her he could be.

It was dark when men came tumbling below, throwing themselves into hammocks and bunks, and Dickory prepared to turn in. If sleep should come and without dreams, it would be greater gain than bags of gold. As he took off his coat, the letter of the English captain dropped from his breast. Until then he had forgotten it, but now he remembered it as a sacred trust. The dull light of the lantern barely enabled him to discern objects about him, but he stuck the letter into a crack in the woodwork where in the morning he would see it and take proper care of it.

Soon sleep came, but not without dreams. He dreamed that he was rowing Kate on the river at Bridgetown, and that she told him in a low sweet voice, with a smile on her lips and her eyes tenderly upturned, that she would like to row thus with him forever.

Early in the morning, through an open port-hole, the light of the eastern sun stole into this abode of darkness and sin and threw itself upon the red-stained letter sticking in the crack of the woodwork. Presently Dickory opened his eyes, and the first thing they fell upon was that letter. On the side of the folded sheet he could see the superscription, boldly but irregularly written: "Miss Kate Bonnet, Kingston, Ja."

Dickory sat upright, his eyes hard-fixed and burning. How long he sat he knew not. How long his brain burned inwardly, as his eyes burned outwardly, he knew not. The noise of the watch going on deck roused him, and in a moment he had the letter in his hands.

All that day Dickory Charter was worth nothing to anybody. Blackbeard swore at him and pushed him aside. The young fellow could not even count the doubloons in a bag.

"Go to!" cried the pirate, blacker and more fantastically horrible than ever, for his bare left shoulder was bound with a scarf of silk and his great arm was streaked and bedabbled with his blood, "you are the most cursed coward I have met with in all my days at sea. So frightened out of your wits by a lively brush as that of yesterday! Too scared to count gold! Never saw I that before. One might be too scared to pray, but to count gold! Ha! ha!" and the bold pirate laughed a merry roar. He was in good spirits; he had captured and sunk an English man-of-war; sunk her with her English ensign floating above her. How it would have overjoyed him if all the ships, little and big, that plied the Spanish Main could have seen him sink that man-of-war. He was a merry man that morning, the great Blackbeard, triumphant in victory, glowing with the king's brandy, and with so little pain from that cut in his shoulder that he could waste no thought upon it.

"But Eliza will like it well," continued the merry pirate; "she will lead you with a string, be you bold or craven, and the less you pull at it the easier it will be for my brave girl. Ah! she will dance with joy when I tell her what a frightened rabbit of a husband it is that I give her. Now get away somewhere, and let your face rid itself of its paleness; and should you find a dead man lying where he has been overlooked, come and tell me and I will have him put aside. You must not be frightened any more or Eliza may find that you have not left even the spirit of a rabbit."

All day Dickory sat silent, his misery pinned into the breast of his coat. "Miss Kate Bonnet, Kingston, Ja."—and this on a letter written in the dying moments of an English captain, a high and mighty captain who must have loved as few men love, to write that letter, his life's blood running over the paper as he wrote. And could a man love thus if he were not loved? That was the terrible question.

Sometimes his mind became quiet enough for him to think coherently, then it was easy enough for him to understand everything. Kate had been a long time in Jamaica; she had met many people; she had met this man, this noble, handsome man. Dickory had watched him with glowing admiration as he stood up before Blackbeard, fighting like the champion of all good against the hairy monster who struck his blows for all that was base and wicked.

How Dickory's young heart had gone out in sympathy and fellowship towards the brave English captain! How he had hoped that the next of his quick, sharp lunges might slit the black heart of the pirate! How he had almost wept when the noble Englishman went down! And now it made him shudder to think his heart had stood side by side with the heart of Kate's lover! He had sworn to deliver the letter of that lover, and he would do it. More cruel than the bloodiest pirate was the fate that forced him thus to bear the death-warrant of his own young life.

XXIV

Belize

There were not many captains of merchantmen in the early part of the eighteenth century who cared to sail into the Gulf of Honduras, that body of water being such a favourite resort of pirates.

But no such fears troubled the mind of the skipper of the brig Belinda, which was now making the best of her way towards the port of Belize. She was a sturdy vessel and carried no prejudices. Sometimes she was laden with goods bought from the pirates and destined to be sold to honest people; and, again, she carried commodities purchased from those who were their legal owners and intended for the use of the bold rascals who sailed under the Jolly Roger. Then, as now, it was impossible for thieves to steal all the commodities they desired; some things must be bought. Thus, serving the pirates as well as honest traders, the sloop Belinda feared not to sail the Gulf of Honduras or to cast anchor by the town of Belize.

As the good ship approached her port Kate Bonnet kept steadfastly on deck during most of the daylight, her eyes searching the surface of the water for something which looked like her father's ship, the Revenge. True, Mr. Newcombe had written her that Major Bonnet had given up piracy and was now engaged in commercial business in the town, but still, if she should see the Revenge, the sight would be of absorbing interest to her. She was a girl of quick observation and good memory, but the town came in view and she had seen no vessel which reminded her of the Revenge.

As soon as the anchor was dropped, Kate wished to go on shore, but her uncle would not hear of that. He must know something definite before he trusted Kate or himself in such a lawless town as Belize. The captain, who was going ashore, could make inquiries, and Kate must wait.

In a little room at the back of a large, low storehouse, not far from the pier, sat Stede Bonnet and his faithful friend and servitor, Ben Greenway. The storehouse was crowded with goods of almost every imaginable description, and even the room back of it contained an overflow of bales, boxes, and barrels. At a small table near a window sat the Scotchman and Bonnet, the latter reading from some roughly written lists descriptions and quantities of goods, the value of each item being estimated by the canny Scotchman, who set down the figures upon another list. Presently Bonnet put down his papers and heaved a heavy sigh, which sigh seemed to harmonize very well with his general appearance. He carried no longer upon him the countenance of the bold officer who, in uniform and flowing feather, trod the quarter-deck of the Revenge, but bore the expression of a man who knew adversity, yet was not able to humble himself under it. He was bent and borne down, although not yet broken. Had he been broken he could better have accommodated himself to his present case. His clothes were those of the common class of civilian, and there was that about him which indicated that he cared no more for neatness or good looks.

"Ben Greenway," he said, "this is too much! Now have I reached the depth in my sorrow at which all my strength leaves me. I cannot read these lists."

The Scotchman looked up. "Is there no' light enow!" he asked.

"Light!" said Bonnet; "there is no light anywhere; all is murkiness and gloom. The goods which you have been lately estimating are all my own, taken from my own ship by that arch traitor and chief devil, Blackbeard. I have read the names of them to you and I have remembered many of them and I have not weakened, but now comes a task which is too great for me. These things which follow were all intended for my daughter Kate. Silks and satins and cloth of gold, ribbons and fine linen, laces and ornaments, all these I selected for my dear daughter, and by day and by night I have thought of her apparelled in fine raiment, more richly dressed than any lady in Barbadoes. My daughter, my beautiful, my proud Kate! And now what has it all come to? All these are gone, basely stolen from me by that Blackbeard."

Ben Greenway looked up. "Wha stole from ye," he said, "what ye had already stolen from its rightful owners. An' think ye," he continued, "that your honest daughter Kate would deign to array hersel' in stolen goods, no matter how rich they might happen to be! An' think ye she could hold up her head if the good people o' Bridgetown could point at her an' say, 'Look at the thief's daughter; how fine she is!' An' think ye that Mr. Martin Newcombe would tak' into his house an' hame a wife wha hadna come honestly by her clothes! I tell ye, Master Bonnet, that ye should exalt your soul in thankfulness that ye are no longer a dishonest mon, an' that whatever raiment your daughter may now wear, no' a sleeve or button o' it was purloined an' stolen by her father."

"Ben Greenway," exclaimed Bonnet, striking his hand upon the table, "you will drive me so mad that I cannot read writing! These things are bad enough, and you need not make them worse."

"Bless Heaven," said the Scotchman, "your conscience is wakin', an' the time may come, if it is kept workin', when ye will forget your plunder an' your blude, your wicked vanity, your cruelty an' your dishonesty, an' mak' yoursel' worthy o' a good daughter an' a quiet hame. An' more than that, I will tak' leave to add, o' the faithful services o' a steadfast friend."

"I cannot forget them, Ben," said Bonnet, speaking without anger. "The more you talk about my sins the more I long to do them all over again; the more you say about my vanity and pride, the more I yearn to wear my uniform and wave my naked sword. Ay, to bring it down with blood upon its blade. I am very wicked, Greenway; you never would admit it and you do not admit it now, but I am wicked, and I could prove it to you if fortune would give me opportunity." And Captain Bonnet sat up very straight in his chair and his eyes flashed as they very often had flashed as he trod the deck of the Revenge.

At this moment there was a knock at the door and the captain of the Belinda came in.

"Good-day, sir!" said that burly seaman. "And this is Captain Bonnet, I am sure, for I have seen him before, though garbed in another fashion, and I come to bring you news. I have just arrived at this port in my sloop, and I bring with me from Kingston your daughter, Mistress Kate Bonnet, her uncle, Mr. Delaplaine, and a good dame named Charter."

Stede Bonnet turned pale as he had never turned pale before.

"My daughter!" he gasped. "My daughter Kate?"

"Yes," said the captain; "she is on my ship, yearning and moaning to see you."

"From Kingston?" murmured Bonnet.

"Yes," said the other, "and on fire to see you since she heard you were here."

"Master Bonnet," exclaimed Ben Greenway, rising, "we must hasten to that vessel; perhaps this good captain will now tak' us there in his boat."

Bonnet fixed his eyes upon the floor. "Ben Greenway," he said, "I cannot. How I have longed to see my daughter, and how, time and

FRANK R. STOCKTON

again and time and again, I have pictured our meeting! I have seen her throw herself into the arms of that noble officer, her father; I have heard her, bathed in filial tears, forgive me everything because of the proud joy with which she looked on me and knew I was her father. Greenway, I cannot go; I have dropped too low, and I am ashamed to meet her."

"Ashamed that ye are honest?" cried the Scotchman. "Ashamed that sin nae longer besets ye, an' that ye are lifted above the thief an' the cutpurse! Master Bonnet, Master Bonnet, in good truth I am ashamed o' ye."

"Very well," said the captain of the Belinda, "I have no time to waste; if you will not go to her, she e'en must come to you. I will send my boat for her and the others, and you shall wait for them here."

"I will not wait!" exclaimed Bonnet. "I don't dare to look into her eyes. Behold these clothes, consider my mean employment. Shall I abash myself before my daughter?"

"Master Bonnet," exclaimed Greenway, hastily stepping to the doorway through which the captain had departed, "ye shallna tie yoursel' to the skirts o' the de'il; ye shallna run awa' an' hide yoursel' from your daughter wha seeks, in tears an' groans, for her unworthy father. Sit down, Master Bonnet, an' wait here until your good daughter comes."

The Belinda's captain had intended to send his boat back to his vessel, but now he determined to take her himself. This was such a strange situation that it might need explanation.

Kate screamed when he made known his errand. "What!" she cried, "my father in the town, and did he not come back with you? Is he sick? Is he wounded? Is he in chains?"

"And my Dickory," cried Dame Charter, "was he not there? Has he not yet returned to the town? It must now be a long time since he went away."

"I know not anything more than I have told you," said the captain. "And if Mr. Delaplaine and the two ladies will get into my boat, I will quickly take you to the town and show you where you may find Captain Bonnet and learn all you wish to know."

"And Dickory," cried Dame Charter, "my son Dickory! Did they give you no news of him?"

"Come along, come along," said the captain, "my men are waiting in the boat. I asked no questions, but in ten minutes you can ask a hundred if you like."

When the little party reached the town it attracted a great deal of attention from the rough roisterers who were strolling about or gambling in shady places. When the captain of the Belinda mentioned, here and there, that these newcomers were the family of Blackbeard's factor, who now had charge of that pirate's interests in the town, no one dared to treat the elderly gentleman, the pretty young lady, or the rotund dame with the slightest disrespect. The name of the great pirate was a safe protection even when he who bore it was leagues and leagues away.

At the door of the storehouse Ben Greenway stood waiting. He would have hurried down to the pier had it not been that he was afraid to leave Bonnet; afraid that this shamefaced ex-pirate would have hurried away to hide himself from his daughter and his friends. Kate, running forward, grasped the Scotchman by both hands.

"And where is he?" she cried.

"He is in there," said Ben, pointing through the storeroom to the open door at the back. In an instant she was gone.

"And Dickory?" cried Dame Charter. "Oh, Ben Greenway, tell me of my boy."

They went inside and Greenway told everything he knew, which was very much, although it was not enough to comfort the poor mother's heart, who could not readily believe that because Dickory had sailed away with a great and powerful pirate, that eminent man would be sure to bring him back in safety; but as Greenway really believed this, his words made some impression on the good dame's heart. She could see some reason to believe that Blackbeard, having now so much property in the town, might make a short cruise this time, and that any day the Revenge, with her dear son on board, might come sailing into port.

With his face buried in his folded arms, which rested on the table, Stede Bonnet received his daughter. At first she did not recognise him, never having seen him in such mean apparel; but when he raised his head, she knew her father. Closing the door behind her, she folded him in her arms. After a little, leaving the window, they sat together upon a bale of goods, which happened to be a rug from the Orient, of wondrous richness, which Bonnet had reserved for the floor of his daughter's room.

"Never, my dear," he said, "did I dream you would see me in such plight. I blush that you should look at me."

"Blush!" she exclaimed, her own cheeks reddening, "and you an honest man and no longer a freebooter and rover of the sea? My heart swells with pride to think that your life is so changed."

Bonnet sadly shook his head.

"Ah!" he said, "you don't know, you cannot understand what I feel. Kate," he exclaimed with sudden energy, "I was a man among men; a chief over many. I was powerful, I was obeyed on every side. I looked the bold captain that I was; my brave uniform and my sword betokened the rank I held. And, Kate, you can never know the pride and exultation with which I stood upon my quarter-deck and scanned the sea, master of all that might come within my vision. How my heart would swell and my blood run wild when I beheld in the distance a proud ship, her sails all spread, her colours flying, heavily laden, hastening onward to her port. How I would stretch out my arm to that proud ship and say: 'Let down those sails, drop all those flaunting flags, for you are mine; I am greater than your captain or your king! If I give the command, down you go to the bottom with all your people, all your goods, all your banners and emblazonments, down to the bottom, never to be seen again!'"

Kate shuddered and began to cry. "Oh, father!" she exclaimed, "don't say that. Surely you never did such things as that?"

"No," said he, speaking more quietly, "not just like that, but I could have done it all had it pleased me, and it was this sense of power that made my heart beat so proudly. I took no life, Kate, if it could be helped, and when I had stripped a ship of her goods, I put her people upon shore before I burned her."

Kate bowed her head in her hands. "And of all this you are proud, my father, you are proud of it!"

"Indeed am I, daughter," said he; "and had you seen me in my glory you would have been proud of me. Perhaps yet—"

In an instant she had clapped her hand over his mouth. "You shall not say it!" she exclaimed. "I have seized upon you and I shall hold you. No more freebooter's life for you; no more blood, no more fire. I shall take you away with me. Not to Bridgetown, for there is no happiness for either of us there, but to Spanish Town. There, with my uncle, we shall all be happy together. You will forget the sea and its ships; you will again wander over your fields, and I shall be with you. You shall watch the waving crops; you shall ride with me, as you used to ride, to view your vast herds of cattle—those splendid creatures, their great heads uplifted, their nostrils to the breeze."

"Truly, my Kate," said Bonnet, "that was a great sight; there were no cattle finer on the island than were mine."

"And so shall they be again, my father," said Kate, her arms around his neck.

It was then that Ben Greenway knocked upon the door.

Stede Bonnet's mind had been so much excited by what he had been talking about that he saluted his brother-in-law and Dame Charter without once thinking of his clothes. They looked upon him as if he were some unknown foreigner, a person entirely removed from their customary sphere.

"Was this the once respectable Stede Bonnet?" asked Dame Charter to herself. "Did such a man marry my sister!" thought Mr. Delaplaine. They might have been surprised had they met him as a pirate, but his appearance as a pirate's clerk amazed them.

Towards the end of the day Mr. Delaplaine and his party returned to the Belinda, for there was no fit place for them to lodge in the town. Although urged by all, Stede Bonnet would not accompany them. When persuasion had been exhausted, Ben Greenway promised Kate that he would be responsible for her father's appearance the next day, feeling safe in so doing; for, even should Bonnet's shame return, there was no likely way in which he could avoid his friends.

XXV

WISE MR. DELAPLAINE

Early in the next forenoon Kate and her companions prepared to make another visit to the town. Naturally she wanted to be with her father as much as possible and to exert upon him such influences as might make him forget, in a degree, the so-called glories of his pirate life and return with her and her uncle to Spanish Town, where, she believed, this misguided man might yet surrender himself to the rural joys of other days. Nay, more, he and she might hope for still further happiness in a Jamaica home, for Madam Bonnet would not be there.

As she came up from below, impatient to depart, Kate noticed, getting over the side, a gentleman who had just arrived in a small boat. He was tall and good-looking, and very handsomely attired in a rich suit such as was worn at that day by French and Spanish noblemen. A sword with an elaborate hilt was by his side, and on his head a high cocked hat. There was fine lace at his wrists and bosom, and he wore silk stockings, and silver buckles on his shoes.

Kate started at meeting here a stranger, and in such an elaborate attire. She had read of the rich dress of men of rank in Europe, but her eyes had never fallen upon such a costume. The gentleman advanced quickly towards her, holding out his hand. She shrank back. "What did it mean?"

Then in a second she saw her father's face. This fine gentleman, this dignified and graceful man, was indeed Stede Bonnet.

He had been so thoroughly ashamed of his mean attire on the preceding day that he had determined not again to meet his daughter and Mr. Delaplaine in such vulgar guise. So, from the resources of the storehouses he had drawn forth a superb suit of clothes sent westward for the governor of one of the French colonies. He excused himself for taking it from Blackbeard's treasure-house, not only on account of the demands of the emergency, but because he himself had taken it before from a merchantman.

"Father!" cried Kate, "what has happened to you? I never saw such a fine gentleman."

Bonnet smiled with complacency, and removed his cocked hat.

"I always endeavour, my dear," said he, "to dress myself according to my station. Yesterday, not expecting to see you, I was in a sad plight. I would have preferred you to meet me in my naval uniform, but as that is now, to say the least, inconvenient, and as I reside on shore in the capacity of a merchant or business man, I attire myself to suit my present condition. Ah! my good brother-in-law, I am glad to see you. I may remark," he added, graciously shaking hands with Dame Charter, "that I left my faithful Scotchman in our storehouse in the town, it being necessary for some one to attend to our possessions there. Otherwise I should have brought him with me, my good Dame Charter, for I am sure you would have found his company acceptable. He is a faithful man and an honest one, although I am bound to say that if he were less of a Presbyterian and more of a man of the world his conversation might sometimes be more agreeable."

Mr. Delaplaine regarded with much earnestness and no little pleasure his transformed brother-in-law. Hope for the future now filled his heart. If this crack-brained sugar-planter had really recovered from his mania for piracy and had a fancy for legitimate business, his new station might be better for him than any he had yet known. Sugar-planting was all well enough and suitable to any gentleman, provided Madam Bonnet were not taken with it. She would drive any man from the paths of reason unless he possessed an uncommonly strong brain, and he did not believe that such a brain was possessed by his brother-in-law Bonnet. The good Mr. Delaplaine rubbed his hands together in his satisfaction. Such a gentleman as this would be welcome in his counting-house, even if he did but little; his very appearance would reflect credit upon the establishment. Dame Charter kept in the background; she had never been accustomed to associate with the aristocracy, but she did not forget that a cat may look at a king, and her eyes were very good.

"There were always little cracks in his skull," she said to herself. "My husband used to tell me that. Major Bonnet is quick at changing from one thing to another, and it needs sharp wits to follow him."

After a time Major Bonnet proposed a row upon the harbour—he had brought a large boat, with four oarsmen, for this purpose. Mr. Delaplaine objected a little to this, fearing the presence of so many pirate vessels, but Bonnet loftily set aside such puerile objections.

"I am the business representative of the great Blackbeard," he said, "the most powerful pirate in the world. You are safer here than in any other port on the American coast."

When they were out upon the water, moving against the gentle breeze, Bonnet disclosed the object of his excursion. "I am going to take you," said he, "to visit some of the noted pirate ships which are anchored in this harbour. There are vessels here which are quite famous, and commanded by renowned Brethren of the Coast. I think you will all be greatly interested in these, and under my convoy you need fear no danger."

Dame Charter and Kate screamed in their fright, and Mr. Delaplaine turned pale. "Visit pirate ships!" he cried. "Rather I would have supposed that you would keep away from them as far as you could. For myself, I would have them a hundred miles distant if it were possible."

Bonnet laughed loftily. "It will be visits of ceremony that we shall pay, and with all due ceremony shall we be received. Pull out to that vessel!" he said to the oarsmen. Then, turning to the others, he remarked: "That sloop is the Dripping Blade, commanded by Captain Sorby, whose name strikes terror throughout the Spanish Main. Ay! and in other parts of the ocean, I can assure you, for he has sailed northward nearly as far as I have, but he has not yet rivalled me. I know him, having done business with him on shore. He is a most portentous person, as you will soon see."

"Oh, father!" cried Kate, "don't take us there; it will kill us just to look upon such dreadful pirates. I pray you turn the boat!"

"Oh! if Dickory were here," gasped Dame Charter, "he would turn the boat himself; he would never allow me to be taken among those awful wretches."

Mr. Delaplaine said nothing. It was too late to expostulate, but he trembled as he sat.

"I cannot turn back, my dear," said Bonnet, "even if I would, for the great Sorby is now on deck, and looking at us as we approach."

As the boat drew up by the side of the Dripping Blade the renowned Sorby looked down over the side. He was a red-headed man; his long hair and beard dyed yellow in some places by the sun. He was grievous to look upon, and like to create in the mind of an imaginative person the image of a sun-burned devil on a holiday.

"Good-day to you! Good-day, Sir Bonnet," cried the pirate captain; "come on board, come on board, all of you, wife, daughter, father, if such they be! We'll let down ladders and I shall feast you finely."

"Nay, nay, good Captain Sorby," replied Bonnet, with courteous dignity, "my family and I have just stopped to pay you our respects. They have all heard of your great prowess, for I have told them. They may never have a chance again to look upon another of your fame."

"Heaven grant it!" said Dame Charter in her heart. "If I get out of this, I stay upon dry land forever."

"I grieve that my poor ship be not honoured by your ladies," said Sorby, "but I admit that her decks are scarcely fit for the reception of such company. It is but to-day that we have found time to cleanse her deck from the stain and disorder of our last fight, having lately come into harbour. That was a great fight, Sir Bonnet; we lay low and let the fellows board us, but not one of them went back again. Ha! ha! Not one of them went back again, good ladies."

Every pirate face on board that ill-conditioned sloop now glared over her rail, their eyes fixed upon the goodly company in the little boat, their horrid hair and beards stained and matted—it would have been hard to tell by what.

"Oh, father, father!" panted Kate, "please row away. What if they should now jump down upon us?"

"Good-day, good-day, my brave Captain Sorby," said Bonnet, "we must e'en row away; we have other craft to visit, but would first do honour to you and your bold crew."

Captain Sorby lifted high his great bespattered hat, and every grinning demon of the crew waved hat or rag or pail or cutlass and set up a discordant yell in honour of their departing visitors.

"Oh! go not to another, father," pleaded Kate, her pale face in tears; "visit no more of them, I pray you!"

"Ay, truly, keep away from them," said Mr. Delaplaine. "I am no coward, but I vow to you that I shall die of fright if I come close to another of those floating hells."

"And these," said Kate to herself, her eyes fixed out over the sea, "these are his friends, his companions, the wretches of whom he is so proud."

"There are no more vessels like that in port," said Bonnet; "that's the most celebrated sloop. Those we shall now call upon are commanded by men of milder mien; some of them you could not tell from plain merchantmen were you not informed of their illustrious careers."

"If you go near another pirate ship," cried Dame Charter, "I shall jump overboard; I cannot help it."

"Row back to the Belinda, brother-in-law," said Mr. Delaplaine in a strong, hard voice; "your tour of pleasure is not fit for tender-hearted women, nor, I grant it, for gentlemen of my station."

"There are other ships whose captains I know," said Bonnet, "and where you would have been well received; but if your nerves are not strong enough for the courtesies I have to offer, we will return to the Belinda."

When safe again on board their vessel, after the sudden termination of their projected tour of calls on pirates, Kate took her father aside and entered into earnest conversation with him, while Mr. Delaplaine, much ruffled in his temper, although in general of a most mild disposition, said aside to Dame Charter: "He is as mad as a March hare. What other parent on this earth would convey his fair young daughter into the society of these vile wild beasts, which in his eyes are valiant heroes? We must get him back with us, Dame Charter, we must get him back. And if he cannot be constrained by love and goodwill to a decent and a Christian life, we must shut him up. And if his daughter weeps and raves, we must e'en stiffen our determination and shut him up. It shall be my purpose now to hasten the return of the brig. There's room enough for all, and he and the Scotchman must go back with us. The Governor shall deal with him; and, whether it be on my estate or behind strong bars, he shall spend the rest of his days upon the island of Jamaica, and so know the sea no more."

He was very much roused, this good merchant, and when he was roused he was not slow to act.

The captain of the Belinda was very willing to make a profitable voyage back to Jamaica, but his vessel must be well laden before he could do this. Goods enough there were at Belize for that purpose, for Blackbeard's supplies were all for sale, and his chief clerk, Bonnet, had the selling of them. So, all parties being like-minded, the Belinda soon began to take on goods for Kingston.

Stede Bonnet superintended everything. He was a good man of business, and knew how to direct people who might be under him. There was a great stir at the storehouse, and, almost blithely, Ben Greenway worked day and night to make out invoices and to prepare goods for shipment.

Bonnet wore no more the clothes in which his daughter had first seen him after so long and drear a parting. On deck or on shore, in storehouse or on the streets of Belize, he was the fine gentleman with the silk stockings and the tall cocked hat.

One day, a fellow, fresh from his bottle, forgetting the respect which was due to fine clothes and to Blackbeard's factor, called out to Bonnet:

"What now, Sir Nightcap, how call you that thing you have on your head?"

In an instant a sword was whipped from its scabbard and a practised hand sent its blade through the arm of the jester, who presently fell backward. Bonnet wiped his sword upon the fellow's sleeve and, advising him to get up and try to learn some manners, coolly walked away.

After that fine clothes were not much laughed at in Belize, for even the most disrespectful ruffians desired not the thrust of a quick blade nor the ill-will of that most irascible pirate, Blackbeard.

A few days before it was expected that the Belinda would be ready to sail Bonnet came on board, his mind full of an important matter. Calling Mr. Delaplaine and Kate aside, he said: "I have been thinking a great deal lately about my Scotchman, Ben Greenway. In the first place, he is greatly needed here, for many of Blackbeard's goods will remain in the storehouse, and there should be some competent person to take care of them and to sell them should opportunity offer. Besides that, he is a great annoyance to me, and I have long been trying to get rid of him. When I left Bridgetown I had not intended to take him with me, and his presence on board my ship was a mere accident. Since then he has made himself very disagreeable."

"What!" cried Kate, "would you be willing that we should all sail away and leave poor Ben Greenway in this place by himself among these cruel pirates?"

"He'll represent Blackbeard," said Bonnet, "and no one will harm him. And, moreover, this enforced stay may be of the greatest benefit to him. He has a good head for business, and he may establish himself here in a very profitable fashion and go back to Barbadoes, if he so desires, in comfortable circumstances. All we have to do is to slip our anchor and sail away at some moment when he is busy in the town. I will leave ample instructions for him and he shall have money."

"Father, it would be shameful!" said Kate.

Mr. Delaplaine said nothing; he was too angry to speak, but he made up his mind that Ben Greenway should be apprised of Bonnet's intentions of running away from him and that such a wicked design should be thwarted. This brother-in-law of his was a worse man than he had thought him; he was capable of being false even to his best friend. He might be mad as a March hare, but, truly, he was also as sly and crafty as a fox in any month in the year.

Wise Mr. Delaplaine!

The very next morning there came a letter from Stede Bonnet to his daughter Kate, in which he told her that it was absolutely impossible for him to return to the humdrum and stupid life of sugar-planting and cattle-raising. Having tasted the glories of a pirate's career, he could never again be contented with plain country pursuits. So he was off and away, the bounding sea beneath him and the brave Jolly Roger floating over his head. He would not tell his dear daughter where he was gone or what he intended to do, for she would be happier if she did not know. He sent her his warmest love, and desired to be most kindly remembered to her uncle and to Dame Charter. He would make it his business that a correspondence should be maintained between him and his dear Kate, and he hoped from time to time to send her presents which would help her to know how constantly he loved her. He concluded by admitting that what he had said about Ben Greenway was merely a blind to turn their suspicions from his intended departure. If his good brother-in-law, out of kindness to the Scotchman, had brought him to the Belinda and had insisted on keeping him there, it would have made his, Bonnet's, secret departure a great deal easier.

Kate had never fainted in her life, but when she had finished this letter she went down flat on her back.

Leaving his niece to the good offices of Dame Charter, Mr. Delaplaine, breathing hotly, went ashore, accompanied by the captain. When they reached the storehouse they found it locked, with the key in the custody of a shop-keeper near-by. They soon heard what had happened to Blackbeard's business agent. He had gone off in a piratical vessel, which had sailed for somewhere, in the middle of the night; and, moreover, it was believed that the Scotchman who worked for him had gone with him, for he had been seen running towards the water, and afterward taking his place among the oarsmen in a boat which went out to the departing vessel.

"May that unholy vessel be sunk as soon as it reaches the open sea!" was the deadly desire which came from the heart of Mr. Delaplaine. But the wish had not formed itself into words before the good merchant recanted. "I totally forgot that faithful Scotchman," he sighed.

XXVI

Dickory Stretches His Legs

There were jolly times on board the swift ship Revenge as she sped through the straits of Florida on her way up the Atlantic coast. The skies were bright, the wind was fair, and the warm waters of the Gulf Stream helped to carry her bravely on her way. But young Dickory Charter, with the blood-stained letter of Captain Vince tucked away in the lining of his coat, ate so little, tossed about so much in his berth, turned so pale and spoke so seldom, that the bold Captain Blackbeard declared that he should have some medicine.

"I shall not let my fine lieutenant suffer for want of drugs," he cried, "and when I reach Charles Town I shall send ashore a boat and procure some; and if the citizens disturb or interfere with my brave fellows, I'll bombard the town. There will be medicine to take on one side or the other, I swear." And loud and ready were the oaths he swore.

A pirate who carries with him an intended son-in-law is not likely, if he be of Blackbeard's turn of mind, to suffer all his family plans to be ruined for the want of a few drugs.

When Dickory heard what the captain had to say on this subject his heart shrank within him. He had never taken medicine and he had never seen Blackbeard's daughter, but the one seemed to him almost as bad as the other, and the thought of the cool waves beneath him became more attractive than ever before. But that thought was quickly banished, for he had a duty before him, and not until that was performed could he take leave of this world, once so bright to him.

An island with palm-trees slowly rose on the horizon, and off this island it was that, after a good deal of tacking and close-hauling, the Revenge lay to to take in water. Far better water than that which had been brought from Belize.

"Do you want to go ashore in the boat, boy?" said Blackbeard, really mindful of the health of this projected member of his family. "It may help your appetite to use your legs."

Dickory did not care to go anywhere, but he had hardly said so when a revulsion of feeling came upon him, and turning away so that his face might not be noticed, he said he thought the land air might do him good. While the men were at work carrying their pails from the well-known spring to the water-barrels in the boat, Dickory strolled about to view the scenery, for it could never have been expected that a first lieutenant in uniform should help to carry water. At first the scenery did not appear to be very interesting, and Dickory wandered slowly from here to there, then sat down under a tree. Presently he rose and went to another tree, a little farther away from the boat and the men at the spring. Here he quietly took off his shoes and his stockings, and, having nothing else to do, made a little bundle of them, listlessly tying them to his belt; then he rose and walked away somewhat brisker, but not in the direction of the boat. He did not hurry, but even stopped sometimes to look at things, but he still walked a little briskly, and always away from the boat. He had been so used, this child of outdoor life, to going about the world barefooted, that it was no wonder that he walked briskly, being relieved of his encumbering shoes and stockings.

After a time he heard a shout behind him, and turning saw three men of the boat's crew upon a little eminence, calling to him. Then he moved more quickly, always away from the boat, and with his head turned he saw the men running towards him, and their shouts became louder and wilder. Then he set off on a good run, and presently heard a pistol shot. This he knew was to frighten him and make him stop, but he ran the faster and soon turned the corner of a bit of woods. Then he was away at the top of his speed, making for a jungle of foliage not a quarter of a mile before him. Shouts he heard, and more shots, but he caught sight of no pursuers. Urged on even as they were by the fear of returning to the ship without Dickory, they could not expect to match, in their heavy boots, the stag-like speed of this barefooted bounder.

After a time Dickory stopped running, for his path, always straight away, so far as he could judge, from the landing-place, became very difficult. In the forest there were streams, sometimes narrow and sometimes wide, and how deep he knew not, so that now he jumped, now he walked on fallen trees. Sometimes he crossed water and marsh by swinging himself from the limbs of one tree to those of another. This was hard work for a young gentleman in a naval uniform and cocked hat, but it had to be done; and when the hat was knocked off it was picked up again, with its feathers dripping.

Dickory was going somewhere, although he knew not whither, and he had solemn business to perform which he had sworn to do, and therefore he must have fit clothes to wear, not only in which to travel but in which to present himself suitably when he should accomplish his mission. All these things Dickory thought of, and he picked up his cocked hat whenever it dropped. He would have been very hungry had he not bethought himself to fill his pockets with biscuits before he left the vessel. And as to fresh water, there was no lack of that.

XXVII

A Girl Who Laughed

It was towards nightfall of the day on which Dickory had escaped from the pirates at the spring that he found himself on a piece of high ground in an open place in the forest, and here he determined to spend the night. With his dirk he cut a quantity of palmetto leaves and made himself a very comfortable bed, on which he was soon asleep, fearing no pirates.

In the morning he rose early from his green couch, ate the few biscuits which were left in his pockets, and, putting on his shoes and stockings, started forth upon, what might have been supposed to be, an aimless tramp.

But it was not aimless. Dickory had a most wholesome dread of that indomitable apostle of cruelty and wickedness, the pirate Blackbeard. He believed that it would be quite possible for that savage being to tie up his beard in tails, to blacken his face with powder, to hang more pistols from his belt and around his neck, and swear that the Revenge should never leave her anchorage until her first lieutenant had been captured and brought back to her. So he had an aim, and that was to get away as far as possible from the spot where he had landed on the island.

He did not believe that his pursuers, if there were any upon his track, could have travelled in the night, for it had been pitchy black; and, as he now had a good start of them, he thought he might go so far that they would give up the search. Then he hoped to be able to keep himself alive until he was reasonably sure that the Revenge had hoisted anchor and sailed away, when it was his purpose to make his way back to the spring and wait for some other vessel which would take him away.

With his shoes on he travelled more easily, although not so swiftly, and after an hour of very rough walking he heard a sound which made him stop instantly and listen. At first he thought it might be the wind in the trees, but soon his practised ear told him that it was the sound of the surf upon the beach. Without the slightest hesitation, he made his way as quickly as possible towards the sound of the sea.

In less than half an hour he found himself upon a stretch of sand which extended from the forest to the sea, and upon which the waves were throwing themselves in long, crested lines. With a cry of joy he ran out upon the beach, and with outstretched arms he welcomed the sea as if it had been an old and well-tried friend.

But Dickory's gratitude and joy had nothing to found itself upon. The sea might far better have been his enemy than his friend, for if he had thought about it, the sandy beach would have been the road by which a portion of the pirate's men would have marched to cut off his flight, or they would have accomplished the same end in boats.

But Dickory thought of no enemy and his heart was cheered. He pressed on along the beach. The walking was so much better now that he made good progress, and the sun had not reached its zenith when he found himself on the shore of a small stream which came down from some higher land in the interior and here poured itself into the sea. He walked some distance by this stream, in order to get some water which might be free from brackishness, and then, with very little trouble, he crossed it. Before him was a knoll of moderate height, and covered with low foliage. Mounting this, he found that he had an extended view over the interior of the island. In the background there stretched a wide savanna, and at the distance of about half a mile he saw, very near a little cluster of trees, a thin column of smoke. His eyes rounded and he stared and stared. He now perceived, from behind the leaves, the end of a thatched roof.

"People!" Dickory exclaimed, and his heart beat fast with joy. Why his heart should be joyful he could not have told himself except that there was no earthly reason to believe that the persons who were making that fire near that thatched-roof house were pirates. To go to this house, whatever it might be, to take his chances there instead of remaining alone in the wide forest, was our young man's instant determination. But before he started there was something else he thought of. He took off his coat, and with a bunch of leaves he brushed it. Then he arranged the plumes of his hat and brushed some mud from them, gave himself a general shake, and was ready to make a start. All this by a fugitive pursued by savage pirates on a desert island! But Dickory was a young man, and he wore the uniform of a naval officer.

After a brisk walk, which was somewhat longer than he had supposed it would be, Dickory reached the house behind the trees. At a short distance burned the fire whose smoke he had seen. Over the fire hung an iron pot. Oh, blessed pot! A gentle breeze blew from the fire towards Dickory, and from the heavenly odour which was borne upon it he knew that something good to eat was cooking in that pot.

FRANK R. STOCKTON

A man came quickly from behind the house. He was tall, with a beard a little gray, and his scanty attire was of the most nondescript fashion. With amazement upon his face, he spoke to Dickory in English.

"What, sir," he cried, "has a man-of-war touched at this island?"

Dickory could not help smiling, for the man's countenance told him how he had been utterly astounded, and even stupefied, by the sight of a gentleman in naval uniform in the interior of that island, an almost desert region.

"No man-of-war has touched here," said Dickory, "and I don't belong to one. I wear these clothes because I am compelled to do so, having no others. Yesterday afternoon I escaped from some pirates who stopped for water, and since leaving them I have made my way to this spot."

The man stepped forth quickly and stretched out his hand.

"Bless you! Bless you!" he cried. "You are the first human being, other than my family, that I have seen for two years."

A little girl now came from behind the house, and when her eyes fell upon Dickory and his cocked hat she screamed with terror and ran indoors. A woman appeared at the door, evidently the man's wife. She had a pleasant face, but her clothes riveted Dickory's attention. It would be impossible to describe them even if one were gazing upon them. It will be enough to say that they covered her. Her amazement more than equalled that of her husband; she stood and stared, but could not speak.

"From the spring at the end of the island," cried the man, "to this house since yesterday afternoon! I have always supposed that no one could get here from the spring by land. I call that way impassable. You are safe here, sir, I am sure. Pirates would not follow very far through those forests and morasses; they would be afraid they would never get back to their ship. But I will find out for certain if you have reason, sir, to fear pursuit by boat or otherwise."

And then, stepping around to the other end of the house, he called, "Lucilla!"

"You are hungry, sir," said the woman; "presently you shall share our meal, which is almost cooked."

Now the man returned.

"This is not a time for questions, sir," he said, "either from you or from us. You must eat and you must rest, then we can talk. We shall not any of us apologize for our appearance, and you will not expect it when you have heard our story. But I can assure you, sir, that we do not look nearly so strange to you as you appear to us. Never before, sir, did I see in this climate, and on shore, a man attired in such fashion."

Dickory smiled. "I will tell you the tale of it," he said, "when we have eaten; I admit that I am famished."

The man was now called away, and when he returned he said to Dickory: "Fear nothing, sir; your ship is no longer at the anchorage by the spring. She has sailed away, wisely concluding, I suppose, that pursuit of you would be folly, and even madness."

The dinner was an exceedingly plain one, spread upon a rude table under a tree. The little girl, who had overcome her fear of "the soldier" as she considered him, made one of the party.

During the meal Dickory briefly told his story, confining it to a mere statement of his escape from the pirates.

"Blackbeard!" exclaimed the man. "Truly you did well to get away from him, no matter into what forests you plunged or upon what desert island you lost yourself. At any moment he might have turned upon you and cut you to pieces to amuse himself. I have heard the most horrible stories of Blackbeard."

"He treated me very well," said Dickory, "but I know from his own words that he reserved me for a most horrible fate."

"What!" exclaimed the man, "and he told you? He is indeed a demon!"

"Yes," said Dickory, "he said over and over again that he was going to take me to England to marry me to his daughter."

At this the wife could not refrain from a smile. "Matrimony is not generally considered a horrible fate," said she; "perhaps his daughter may be a most comely and estimable young person. Girls do not always resemble their fathers."

"Do not mention it," exclaimed Dickory, with a shudder; "that was one reason that I ran away; I preferred any danger from man or beast to that he was taking me to."

"He is engaged to be married," thought the woman; "it is easy enough to see that."

"Now tell me your story, I pray you," said Dickory. "But first, I would like very much to know how you found out that Blackbeard's ship was not at her anchorage?"

"That's a simple thing," said the man. "Of course you did not observe, for you could not, that from its eastern point where lies the spring, this island stretches in a long curve to the south, reaching northward again about this spot. Consequently, there is a little bay to the east of us,

FRANK R. STOCKTON

across which we can see the anchoring ground of such ships as may stop here for water. Your way around the land curve of the island was a long one, but the distance straight across the bay is but a few miles. Upon a hill not far from here there is a very tall tree, which overtops all the other trees, and to the upper branches of this tree my daughter, who is a great climber, frequently ascends with a small glass, and is thus able to report if there is a vessel at the anchorage."

"What!" exclaimed Dickory, "that little girl?"

"Oh, no!" said the man; "it is my other daughter, who is a grown young woman."

"She is not here now," said the mother. And this piece of unnecessary information was given in tones which might indicate that the young lady had stepped around to visit a neighbour.

"It is important," said the man, "that I should know if vessels have anchored here, for if they be merchantmen I sometimes do business with them."

"Business!" said Dickory. "That sounds extremely odd. Pray tell me how you came to be here."

"My name is Mander," said the other, "and about two years ago I was on my way from England to Barbadoes, where, with my wife and two girls, I expected to settle. We were captured by a pirate ship and marooned upon this island. I will say, to the pirate captain's credit, that he was a good sort of man considering his profession. He sailed across the bay on purpose to find a suitable place to land us, and he left with us some necessary articles, such as axes and tools, kitchen utensils, and a gun with some ammunition. Then he sailed away, leaving us here, and here we have since lived. Under the circumstances, we have no right to complain, for had we been taken by an ordinary pirate it is likely that our bones would now be lying at the bottom of the ocean.

"Here I have worked hard and have made myself a home, such as it is. There are wild cattle upon the distant savannas, and I trap game and birds, cultivate the soil to a certain extent, and if we had clothes I might say we would be in better circumstances than many a respectable family in England. Sometimes when a merchantman anchors here and I have hides or anything else which we can barter for things we need, I row over the bay in a canoe which I have made, and have thus very much bettered our condition. But in no case have I been able to provide my family with suitable clothes."

"Why did you not get some of these merchant ships to carry you away?" asked Dickory.

The man shook his head. "There is no place," he said sadly, "to which I can in reason ask a ship to carry me and my family. We have no money, no property whatever. In any other place I would be far poorer than I am here. My children are not uneducated; my wife and I have done our best for them in that respect, and we have some books with us. So, as you see, it would be rash in me to leave a home which, rude as it is, shelters and supports my family, to go as paupers and strangers to some other land."

The wife heaved a sigh. "But poor Lucilla!" she said. "It is dreadful that she should be forced to grow up here."

"Lucilla?" asked Dickory.

"Yes, sir," she said, "my eldest daughter. But she is not here now."

Dickory thought that it was somewhat odd that he should be again informed of a fact which he knew very well, but he made no remarks upon the subject.

Still wearing his cocked hat—for he had nothing else with which to shield his head from the sun—and with his uniform coat on, for he had not yet an opportunity of ripping from it the letter he carried, and this he would not part from—Dickory roamed about the little settlement. Mander was an industrious and thrifty man. His garden, his buildings, and his surroundings showed that.

Walking past a clump of low bushes, Dickory was startled by a laugh—a hearty laugh—the laugh of a girl. Looking quickly around, he saw, peering above the tops of the bushes, the face of the girl who had laughed.

"It is too funny!" she said, as his eyes fell upon her. "I never saw anything so funny in all my life. A man in regimentals in this weather and upon a desert island. You look as if you had marched faster than your army, and that you had lost it in the forest."

Dickory smiled. "You ought not to laugh at me," he said, "for these clothes are really a great misfortune. If I could change them for something cool I should be more than delighted."

"You might take off your heavy coat," said she; "you need not be on parade here. And instead of that awful hat, I can make you one of long grass. Do you see the one I have on? Isn't that a good hat? I have one nearly finished which I am making for my father; you may have that."

Dickory would most gladly have taken off his coat if, without observation, he could have transferred his sacred letter to some other part of his clothes, but he must wait for that. He accepted instantly, however, the offer of the hat.

"You seem to know all about me," he said; "did you hear me tell my story?"

"Every word of it," said she, "and it is the queerest story I ever heard. Think of a pirate carrying a man away to marry him to his daughter!"

"But why don't you come from behind that bush and talk to me?"

"I can't do it," said she, "I am dressed funnier than you are. Now I am going to make your hat." And in an instant she had departed.

Dickory now strolled on, and when he returned he seated himself in the shade near the house. The letter of Captain Vince was taken from his coat-lining and secured in one of his breeches pockets; his heavy coat and waistcoat lay upon the ground beside him, with the cocked hat placed upon them. As he leaned back against the tree and inhaled the fragrant breeze which came to him from the forest, Dickory was a more cheerful young man than he had been for many, many days. He thought of this himself, and wondered how a man, carrying with him his sentence of lifelong misery, could lean against a tree and take pleasure in anything, be it a hospitable welcome, a sense of freedom from danger, a fragrant breeze, or the face of a pretty girl behind a bush. But these things did please him; he could not help it. And when presently came Mrs. Mander, bringing him a light grass hat fresh from the manufacturer's hands, he took it and put it on with more evident pleasure than the occasion seemed to demand.

"Your daughter is truly an artist," said Dickory.

"She does many things well," said the mother, "because necessity compels her and all of us to learn to work in various ways."

"Can I not thank her?" said Dickory.

"No," the mother answered, "she is not here now."

Dickory had begun to hate that self-evident statement.

"She's looking out for ships; her pride is a little touched that she missed Blackbeard's vessel yesterday."

"Perhaps," said Dickory, with a movement as if he would like to make a step in the direction of some tall tree upon a hill.

"No," said Mrs. Mander, "I cannot ask you to join my daughter. I am compelled to state that her dress is not a suitable one in which to appear before a stranger."

"Excuse me," said Dickory; "and I beg, madam, that you will convey to her my thanks for making me such an excellent hat."

A little later Mander joined Dickory. "I am sorry, sir," said he, "that I am not able to present you to my daughter Lucilla. It is a great grief to us that her attire compels her to deny herself other company than that of her family. I really believe, sir, that it is Lucilla's deprivations on this island which form at present my principal discontent with my situation. But we all enjoy good health, we have enough to eat, and shelter over us, and should not complain."

As soon as he was at liberty to do so, Dickory walked by the hedge of low bushes, and there, above it, was the bright face, with the pretty grass hat.

"I was waiting for you," said she. "I wanted to see how that hat fitted, and I think it does nicely. And I wanted to tell you that I have been looking out for ships, but have not seen one. I don't mean by that that I want you to go away almost as soon as you have come, but of course, if a merchant ship should anchor here, it would be dreadful for you not to know."

"I am not sure," said Dickory gallantly, "that I am in a hurry for a ship. It is truly very pleasant here."

"What makes it pleasant?" said the girl.

Dickory hesitated for a moment. "The breeze from the forest," said he.

She laughed. "It is charming," she said, "but there are so many places where there is just as good a breeze, or perhaps better. How I would like to go to some one of them! To me this island is lonely and doleful. Every time I look over the sea for a ship I hope that one will come that can carry us away."

"Then," said Dickory, "I wish a ship would come to-morrow and take us all away together."

She shook her head. "As my father told you," said she, "we have no place to go to."

Dickory thought a good deal about the sad condition of the family of this worthy marooner. He thought of it even after he had stretched himself for the night upon the bed of palmetto leaves beneath the tree against which he had leaned when he wondered how he could be so cheerful under the shadow of the sad fate which was before him.

XXVIII

Lucilla's Ship

As soon as Dickory had left off his cocked hat and his gold-embroidered coat, the little girl Lena had ceased to be afraid of him, and the next morning she came to him, seated lonely—for this was a busy household—and asked him if he would like to take a walk. So, hand in hand, they wandered away. Presently they entered a path which led through the woods.

"This is the way my sister goes to her lookout tree," said the little girl. "Would you like to see that tree?"

"Oh, yes!" said Dickory, and he spoke the truth.

"She goes up to the very top," said Lena, "to look for ships. I would never do that; I'd rather never see a ship than to climb to the top of such a tree. I'll show it to you in a minute; we're almost there."

At a little distance from the rest of the forest and upon a bluff which overlooked a stretch of lowland, and beyond that the bay, stood a tall tree with spreading branches and heavy foliage.

"Up in the top of that is where she sits," said the child, "and spies out for ships. That's what she's doing now. Don't you see her up there?"

"Your sister in the tree!" exclaimed Dickory. And his first impulse was to retire, for it had been made quite plain to him that he was not expected to present himself to the young lady of the house, should she be on the ground or in the air. But he did not retire. A voice came to him from the tree-top, and as he looked upward he saw the same bright face which had greeted him over the top of the bushes. Below it was a great bunch of heavy leaves.

"So you have come to call on me, have you?" said the lady in the tree. "I am glad to see you, but I'm sorry that I cannot ask you to come upstairs. I am not receiving."

"He could not come up if he wanted to," said Lena; "he couldn't climb a tree like that."

"And he doesn't want to," cried the nymph of the bay-tree. "I have been up here all the morning," said she, "looking for ships, but not one have I seen."

"Isn't that a tiresome occupation?" asked Dickory.

"Not altogether," she said. "The branches up here make a very nice seat, and I nearly always bring a book with me. You will wonder how we get books, but we had a few with us when we were marooned, and since that my father has always asked for books when he has an opportunity of trading off his hides. But I have read them all over and over again, and if it were not for the ships which I expect to come here and anchor, I am afraid I should grow melancholy."

"What sort of ships do you look for?" asked Dickory, who was gazing upward with so much interest that he felt a little pain in the back of his neck, and who could not help thinking of a framed engraving which hung in his mother's little parlour, and which represented some angels composed of nothing but heads and wings. He saw no wings under the head of the charming young creature in the tree, but there was no reason which he could perceive why she should not be an angel marooned upon a West Indian island.

"There are a great many of them," said she, "and they're all alike in one way—they never come. But there's one of them in particular which I look for and look for and look for, and which I believe that some day I shall really see. I have thought about that ship so often and I have dreamed about it so often that I almost know it must come."

"Is it an English ship?" asked Dickory, speaking with some effort, for he found that the girl's voice came down much more readily than his went up.

"I don't know," said she, "but I suppose it must be, for otherwise I should not understand what the people on board should say to me. It is a large ship, strong and able to defend itself against any pirates. It is laden with all sorts of useful and valuable things, and among these are a great many trunks and boxes filled with different kinds of clothes. Also, there's a great deal of money kept in a box by itself, and is in charge of an agent who is bringing it out to my father, supposing him to be now settled in Barbadoes. This money is generally a legacy for my father from a distant relative who has recently died. On this ship there are so many delightful things that I cannot even begin to mention them."

"And where is it going to?" asked Dickory.

"That I don't know exactly. Sometimes I think that it is going to the island of Barbadoes, where we originally intended to settle; but then I imagine that there is some pleasanter place than Barbadoes, and if that's the case the ship is going there."

"There can be no pleasanter place than Barbadoes," cried Dickory. "I come from that island, where I was born; there is no land more lovely in all the West Indies."

"You come from Barbadoes?" cried the girl, "and it really is a pleasant island?"

"Most truly it is," said he, "and the great dream of my life is to get back there." Then he stopped. Was it really the dream of his life to get back there? That would depend upon several things.

"If, then, you tell me the truth, my ship is bound for Barbadoes. And if she should go, would you like to go there with us?"

Dickory hesitated. "Not directly," said he. "I would first touch at Jamaica."

For some moments there was no answer from the tree-top, and then came the question: "Is it a girl who lives there?"

"Yes," said Dickory unguardedly, "but also I have a mother in Jamaica."

"Indeed," said she, "a mother! Well, we might stop there and take the mother with us to Barbadoes. Would the girl want to go too?"

Dickory bent his head. "Alas!" said he, "I do not know."

Then spoke the little Lena. "I would not bother about any particular place to go to," said she. "I'd be so glad to go anywhere that isn't here. But it is not a real ship, you know."

"I don't think I will take you," called down Lucilla. "I don't want too many passengers, especially women I don't know. But I often think there will be a gentleman passenger—one who really wants to go to Barbadoes and nowhere else. Sometimes he is one kind of a gentleman and sometimes another, but he is never a soldier or a sailor, but rather one who loves to stay at home. And now, sir, I think I must take my glass and try to pick out a ship from among the spots on the far distant waves."

"Come on," said Lena, "do you like to fish! Because if you do, I can take you to a good place."

The rest of the day Dickory spent with Mr. Mander and his wife, who were intelligent and pleasant people. They talked of their travels, their misfortunes and their blessings, and Dickory yearned to pour out his soul to them, but he could not do so. His woes did not belong to himself alone; they were not for the ears of strangers. He made up his mind what he would do. Until the morrow he would stay as a visitor with these most hospitable people, then he would ask for work. He would collect firewood, he would hunt, he would fish, he would do anything. And here he would support himself until there came some merchant ship bound southward which would carry him away. If the Mander family were anyway embarrassed or annoyed by his presence here, he would make a camp at a little distance and live there by himself. Perhaps the lady of the tree would kindly send him word if the ship he was looking for should come.

It was about the middle of the afternoon, and Lena had dropped asleep beneath the tree where Dickory and her parents were conversing, when suddenly there rushed upon the little group a most surprising figure. At the first flash of thought Dickory supposed that a boy from the skies had dropped among them, but in an instant he recognised the face he had seen above the bushes. It was Lucilla, the daughter of the house! Upon her head was a little straw hat, and she wore a loose tunic and a pair of sailor's trousers, which had been cut off and were short enough to show that her feet and ankles were bare. Around her waist she had a belt of skins, from which dangled a string of crimson sea-beans. Her eyes were wide open, her face was pale, and she was trembling with excitement.

"What do you think!" she cried, not caring who was there or who might look at her. "There's a ship at the spring, and there's a boat rowing across the bay. A boat with four men in it!"

All started to their feet.

"A boat," cried Mander, "with four men in it? Run, my dear, to the cave; press into its depths as far as you can. There is nothing there to be afraid of, and no matter how frightened you are, press into its most distant depths. You, sir, will remain with me, or would you rather escape? If it is a pirate ship, it may be Blackbeard who has returned."

"Not so," cried Lucilla, "it is a merchant vessel, and they are making straight for the mouth of our stream."

"I will stay here with you," said Dickory, "and stand by you, unless I may help your family seek the cave you speak of."

"No, no," said Mander, "they don't need you, and if you will do so we will go down to the beach and meet these men; that will be better than to have them search for us. They will know that people live here, for my canoe is drawn up on the beach."

"Is this safe?" cried Dickory; "would it not be better for you to go with your family and hide with them? I will meet the men in the boat."

"No, no," said Mander; "if their vessel is no pirate, I do not fear them. But I will not have them here."

Now, after Mander had embraced his family, they hurried away in tears, the girl Lucilla casting not one glance at Dickory. Impressed by the impulse that it was the proper thing to do, Dickory put on his coat and waistcoat and clapped upon his head his high cocked hat. Then he rapidly followed Mander to the beach, which they reached before the boat touched the sand.

When the man in the stern of the boat, which was now almost within hailing distance, saw the two figures run down upon the beach, he spoke to the oarsmen and they all stopped and looked around. The stop was occasioned by the sight of Dickory in his uniform; and this, under the circumstances, was enough to stop any boat's crew. Then they fell to again and pulled ashore. When the boat was beached one of its occupants, a roughly dressed man, sprang ashore and walked cautiously towards Mander; then he gave a great shout.

"Heigho, heigho!" he cried, "and Mander, this is you!"

Then there was great hand-shaking and many words.

"Excuse me, sir," said the man, raising his hat to Dickory, "it is now more than two years since I have seen my friend here, when he was marooned by pirates. We were all on the same merchantman, but the pirate took me along, being short of hands. I got away at last, sir" (all the time addressing Dickory instead of Mander, this being respect to his rank), "and shipping on board that brig, sir, I begged it of the captain that he would drop anchor here and take in water, although I cannot say it was needed, and give me a chance to land and see if my old friend be yet alive. I knew the spot, having well noted it when Mander and his family were marooned."

"And this is Lucilla's ship," said Dickory to himself. But to the sailor he said: "This is a great day for your friend and his family. But you must not lift your hat to me, for I am no officer."

For a long time, at least it seemed so to Dickory, who wanted to run to the cave and tell the good news, they all stood together on the sands and talked and shook hands and laughed and were truly thankful, the men who had come in the boat as much so as those who were found on the island. It was agreed, and there was no discussion on this point, that the Mander family should be carried away in the brig, which was an English vessel bound for Jamaica, but the happy Mander would not ask any of the boat's crew to visit him at his home. Instead, he besought them to return to their vessel and bring back some clothes for women, if any such should be included in her cargo.

"My family," said he, "are not in fit condition to venture themselves among well-clad people. They are, indeed, more like savages than am I myself."

"I doubt," said Mander's friend, "if the ship carries goods of that description, but perhaps the captain might let you have a bale of cotton cloth, although I suppose—" and here he looked a little embarrassed.

"Oh, we can buy it," cried Dickory, taking some pieces of gold from his pocket, being coin with which Blackbeard had furnished him, swearing that his first lieutenant could not feel like a true officer without money in his pocket; "take this and fetch the cloth if nothing better can be had."

"Thank you," cried Mander; "my wife and daughters can soon fashion it into shape."

"And," added Dickory, reflecting a little and remembering the general hues of Lucilla's face, "if there be choice in colours, let the cloth be pink."

When Mander and Dickory reached the house they did not stop, but hurried on towards the cave, both of them together, for each thought only of the great joy they were taking with them.

"Come out! Come out!" shouted Mander, as he ran, and before they reached the cave its shuddering inmates had hurried into the light. When the cries and the tears and the embraces were over, Lucilla first looked at Dickory. She started, her face flushed, and she was about to draw back; then she stopped, and advancing held out her hand.

"It cannot be helped," she said; "anyway, you have seen me before, and I suppose it doesn't matter. I'm a sailor boy, and have to own up to it. I did hope you would think of me as a young lady, but we are all so happy now that that doesn't matter. Oh, father!" she cried, "it can't be; we are not fit to be saved; we must perish here in our wretched rags."

"Not so," cried Dickory, with a bow; "I've already bought you a gown, and I hope it is pink."

As they all hurried away, the tale of the hoped-for clothes was told; and although Mrs. Mander wondered how gowns were to be made while a merchantman waited, she said nothing of her doubts, and they all ran gleefully. Lucilla and Dickory being the fleetest led the others, and Dickory said: "Now that I have seen you thus, I shall be almost sorry if that ship can furnish you with common clothes, what you wear becomes you so."

"Oho!" cried Lucilla, "that's fine flattery, sir; but I am glad you said it, for that speech has made me feel more like a woman than I have felt since I first put on this sailor's toggery."

In the afternoon the boat returned, Mander and Dickory watching on the beach. When it grounded, Davids, Mander's friend, jumped on shore, bearing in his arms a pile of great coarse sacks. These he threw upon the sand and, handing to Dickory the gold pieces he had given him, said: "The captain sends word that he has no time to look over any goods to give or to sell, but he sends these sacks, out of which the women can fashion themselves gowns, and so come aboard. Then the ship shall be searched for stuffs which will suit their purposes and which they can make at their leisure."

It was towards the close of the afternoon that all of the Mander family and Dickory came down to the boat which was waiting for them.

"Do you know," said Dickory, as he and Lucilla stood together on the sand, "that in that gown of gray, with the white sleeves, and the red cord around your waist, you please me better than even you did when you wore your sailor garb?"

"And what matters it, sir, whether I please you or not?"

XXIX

CAPTAIN ICHABOD

K ate Bonnet was indeed in a sad case. She had sailed from Kingston with high hopes and a gay heart, and before she left she had written to Master Martin Newcombe to express her joy that her father had given up his unlawful calling and to say how she was going to sail after him, fold him in her forgiving arms, and bring him back to Jamaica, where she and her uncle would see to it that his past sins were forgiven on account of his irresponsible mind, and where, for the rest of his life, he would tread the paths of peace and probity. In this letter she had not yielded to the earnest entreaty which was really the object and soul of Master Newcombe's epistle. Many kind things she said to so kind a friend, but to his offer to make her the queen of his life she made no answer. She knew she was his very queen, but she would not yet consent to be invested with the royal robes and with the crown.

And when she had reached Belize, how proudly happy she had been! She had seen her father, no longer an outlaw, honest though in mean condition, earning his bread by honourable labour. Then, with a still greater pride, she had seen him clad as a noble gentleman and bearing himself with dignity and high complacence. What a figure he would have made among the fine folks who were her uncle's friends in Kingston and in Spanish Town!

But all this was over now. With his own hand he had told her that once again she was a pirate's daughter. She went below to her cabin, where, with wet cheeks, Dame Charter attended her.

Mr. Delaplaine was angry, intensely angry. Such a shameful, wicked trick had never before been played upon a loving daughter. There were no words in which to express his most justifiable wrath. Again he went to the town to learn more, but there was nothing more to learn except that some people said they had reason to believe that Bonnet had gone to follow Blackbeard. From things they had heard they supposed that the vessel which had sailed away in the night had gone to offer herself as consort to the Revenge; to rob and burn in the company of that notorious ship.

There was no satisfaction in this news for the heart of the good merchant, and when he returned to the brig and sought his niece's

FRANK R. STOCKTON

cabin he had no words with which to cheer her. All he could do was to tell her the little he had learned and to listen to her supplications.

"Oh, uncle," she exclaimed, "we must follow him, we must take him, we must hold him! I care not where he is, even if it be in the company of the dreadful Blackbeard! We must take him, we must hold him, and this time we must carry him away, no matter whether he will or not. I believe there must be some spark of feeling, even in the heart of a bloody pirate, which will make him understand a daughter's love for her father, and he will let me have mine. Oh, uncle! we were very wrong. When he was here with us we should have taken him then; we should have shut him up; we should have sailed with him to Kingston."

All this was very depressing to the soul of Kate's loving uncle, for how was he to sail after her father and take him and hold him and carry him away? He went away to talk to the captain of the Belinda, but that tall seaman shook his head. His vessel was not ready yet to sail, being much delayed by the flight of Bonnet. And, moreover, he vowed that, although he was as bold a seaman as any, he would never consent to set out upon such an errand as the following of Blackbeard. It was terrifying enough to be in the same bay with him, even though he were engaged in business with the pirate, for no one knew what strange freak might at any time suggest itself to the soul of that most bloody roisterer; but as to following him, it was like walking into an alligator's jaws. He would take his passengers back to Kingston, but he could not sail upon any wild cruises, nor could he leave Belize immediately.

But Kate took no notice of all this when her uncle had told it to her. She did not wish to go back to Jamaica; she did not wish to wait at Belize. It was the clamorous longing of her heart to go after her father and to find him wherever he might be, and she did not care to consider anything else.

Dame Charter added also her supplications. Her boy was with Blackbeard, and she wished to follow the pirate's ship. Even if she should never see Major Bonnet—whom she loathed and despised, though never saying so—she would find her Dickory. She, too, believed that there must be some spark of feeling even in a bloody pirate's heart which would make him understand the love of a mother for her son, and he would let her have her boy.

Mr. Delaplaine sat brooding on the deck. The righteous anger kindled by the conduct of his brother-in-law, and his grief for the poor stricken women, sobbing in the cabin, combined together to throw him into the most dolorous state of mind, which was aggravated by the knowledge that he could do nothing except to wait until the Belinda sailed back to Jamaica and to go to Jamaica in her.

As the unhappy merchant sat thus, his face buried in his hands, a small boat came alongside and a passenger mounted to the deck. This person, after asking a few questions, approached Mr. Delaplaine.

"I have come, sir, to see you," he said. "I am Captain Ichabod of the sloop Restless."

Mr. Delaplaine looked up in surprise. "That is a pirate ship," said he.

"Yes," said the other, "I'm a pirate."

The newcomer was a tall young man, with long dark hair and with well-made features and a certain diffidence in his manner which did not befit his calling.

Mr. Delaplaine rose. This was his first private interview with a professional sea-robber, and he did not know exactly how to demean himself; but as his visitor's manner was quiet, and as he came on board alone, it was not to be supposed that his intentions were offensive.

"And you wish to see me, sir?" said he.

"Yes," said Captain Ichabod, "I thought I'd come over and talk to you. I don't know you, bedad, but I know all about you, and I saw you and your family when you came to town to visit that old fox, bedad, that sugar-planter that Captain Blackbeard used to call Sir Nightcap. Not a bad joke, either, bedad. I have heard of a good many dirty, mean things that people in my line of business have done, but, bedad, I never did hear of any captain who was dirty and mean to his own family. Fine people, too, who came out to do the right thing by him, after he had been cleaned out, bedad, by one of his 'Brothers of the Coast.' A rare sort of brother, bedad, don't you say so?"

"You are right, sir," said Mr. Delaplaine, "in what you say of the wild conduct of my brother-in-law Bonnet. It pleases me, sir, to know that you condemn it."

"Condemn! I should say so, bedad," answered Captain Ichabod; "and I came over here to say to you—that is, just to mention, not knowing, of course, what you'd think about it, bedad—that I'm goin' to start on a cruise to-morrow. That is, as soon as I can get in my water and some stores, bedad—water anyway. And if you and your ladies might happen to fancy it, bedad, I'd be glad to take you along. I've heard that you're in a bad case here, the captain of this brig being unable or quite unwilling to take you where you want to go."

"But where are you going, sir?" in great surprise.

"Anywhere," said Captain Ichabod, "anywhere you'd like to go. I'm starting out on a cruise, and a cruise with me means anywhere. And my opinion is, sir, that if you want to come up with that crack-brained sugar-planter, you'd better follow Blackbeard; and the best place to find him will be on the Carolina coast; that's his favourite hunting-ground, bedad, and I expect the sugar-planter is with him by this time."

"But will not that be dangerous, sir?" asked Mr. Delaplaine.

"Oh, no," said the other. "I know Blackbeard, and we have played many a game together. You and your family need not have anything to do with it. I'll board the Revenge, and you may wager, bedad, that I'll bring Sir Nightcap back to you by the ear."

"But there's another," said Delaplaine; "there's a young man belonging to my party—"

"Oh, yes, I know," said the other, "the young fellow Blackbeard took away with him. Clapped a cocked hat on him, bedad! That was a good joke! I will bring him too. One old man, one young man—I'll fetch 'em both. Then I'll take you all where you want to go to. That is, as near as I can get to it, bedad. Now, you tell your ladies about this, and I'll have my sloop cleaned up a bit, and as soon as I can get my water on board I'm ready to hoist anchor."

"But look you, sir," exclaimed Mr. Delaplaine, "this is a very important matter, and cannot be decided so quickly."

"Oh, don't mention it, don't mention it," said Captain Ichabod; "just you tell your ladies all about it, and I'll be ready to sail almost any time to-morrow."

"But, sir—" cried the merchant.

"Very good," said the pirate captain, "you talk it over. I'm going to the town now and I'll row out to you this afternoon and get your instructions."

And with this he got over the side.

Mr. Delaplaine said nothing of this visit, but waited on deck until the captain came on board, and then many were the questions he asked about the pirate Ichabod.

"Well, well!" the captain exclaimed, "that's just like him; he's a rare one. Ichabod is not his name, of course, and I'm told he belongs to a good English family—a younger son, and having taken his inheritance, he invested it in a sloop and turned pirate. He has had some pretty good fortune, I hear, in that line, but it hasn't profited him much, for he is a terrible gambler, and all that he makes by his prizes he loses at cards, so he is nearly always poor. Blackbeard sometimes helps him, so I have heard—which he ought to do, for the old pirate has won bags of money from him—but he is known as a good fellow, and to be trusted. I have heard of his sailing a long way back to Belize to pay a gambling debt he owed, he having captured a merchantman in the meantime."

"Very honourable, indeed," remarked Mr. Delaplaine.

"As pirates go, a white crow," said the other. "Now, sir, if you and your ladies want to go to Blackbeard, and a rare desire is that, I swear, you cannot do better than let Captain Ichabod take you. You will be safe, I am sure of that, and there is every reason to think he will find his man."

When Mr. Delaplaine went below with his extraordinary news, Dame Charter turned pale and screamed.

"Sail in a pirate ship?" she cried. "I've seen the men belonging to one of them, and as to going on board and sailing with them, I'd rather die just where I am."

To the good Dame's astonishment and that of Mr. Delaplaine, Kate spoke up very promptly. "But you cannot die here, Dame Charter; and if you ever want to see your son again you have got to go to him. Which is also the case with me and my father. And, as there is no other way for us to go, I say, let us accept this man's offer if he be what my uncle thinks he is. After all, it might be as safe for us on board his ship as to be on a merchantman and be captured by pirates, which would be likely enough in those regions where we are obliged to go; and so I say let us see the man, and if he don't frighten us too much let us sail with him and get my father and Dickory."

"It would be a terrible danger, a terrible danger," said Mr. Delaplaine.

"But, uncle," urged Kate, "everything is a terrible danger in the search we're upon; let us then choose a danger that we know something about, and which may serve our needs, rather than one of which we're ignorant and which cannot possibly be of any good to us."

It was actually the fact that the little party in the cabin had not finished talking over this most momentous subject before they were informed that Captain Ichabod was on deck. Up they went, Dame Charter ready to faint. But she did not do so. When she saw the visitor she thought it could not be the pirate captain, but some one whom he had sent in his place. He was more soberly dressed than when he

FRANK R. STOCKTON

first came on board, and his manners were even milder. The mind of Kate Bonnet was so worked up by the trouble that had come upon her that she felt very much as she did when she hung over the side of her father's vessel at Bridgetown, ready to drop into the darkness and the water when the signal should sound. She had an object now, as she had had then, and again she must risk everything. On her second look at Captain Ichabod, which embarrassed him very much, she was ready to trust him.

"Dame Charter," she whispered, "we must do it or never see them again."

So, when they had talked about it for a quarter of an hour, it was agreed that they would sail with Captain Ichabod.

When the sloop Restless made ready to sail the next day there was a fine flurry in the harbour. Nothing of the kind had ever before happened there. Two ladies and a most respectable old gentleman sailing away under the skull and cross-bones! That was altogether new in the Caribbean Sea. To those who talked to him about his quixotic expedition, Captain Ichabod swore—and at times, as many men knew, he was a great hand at being in earnest—that if he carried not his passengers through their troubles and to a place of safety, the Restless, and all on board of her, should mount to the skies in a thousand bits. Although this alternative would not have been very comforting to said passengers if they had known of it, it came from Captain Ichabod's heart, and showed what sort of a man he was.

Old Captain Sorby came to the Restless in a boat, and having previously washed one hand, came on board and bade them all good-bye with great earnestness.

"You will catch him," said he to Kate, "and my advice to you is, when you get him, hang him. That's the only way to keep him out of mischief. But as you are his daughter, you may not like to string him up, so I say put irons on him. If you don't he'll be playin' you some other wild trick. He is not fit for a pirate, anyway, and he ought to be taken back to his calves and his chickens."

Kate did not resent this language; she even smiled, a little sadly. She had a great work before her, and she could not mind trifles.

None of the other pirates came on board, for they were afraid of Sorby, and when that great man had made the round of the decks and had given Captain Ichabod some bits of advice, he got down into his boat. The anchor was weighed, the sails hoisted, and, amid shouts and cheers from a dozen small boats containing some of the most terrible and bloody sea-robbers who had ever infested the face of the waters, the Restless sailed away: the only pirate ship which had, perhaps, ever left port followed by blessings and goodwill; goodwill, although the words which expressed it were curses and the men who waved their hats were blasphemers and cut-throats.

Away sailed our gentle and most respectable party, with the Jolly Roger floating boldly high above them. Kate, looking skyward, noticed this and took courage to bewail the fact to Captain Ichabod.

He smiled. "While we're in sight of my Brethren of the Coast," he said, "our skull and bones must wave, but when we're well out at sea we will run up an English flag, if it please you."

XXX

Dame Charter Makes a Friend

C aptain Ichabod was in high feather. He whistled, he sang, and he kept his men cleaning things. All that he could do for the comfort of his passengers he did, even going so far as to drop as many of his "bedads" as possible. Whenever he had an opportunity, and these came frequently, he talked to Mr. Delaplaine, addressing a word or two to Kate if he thought she looked gracious. For the first day or two Dame Charter kept below. She was afraid of the men, and did not even want to look at them if she could help it.

"But the good woman's all wrong," said Captain Ichabod to Mr. Delaplaine; "my men would not hurt her. They're not the most tremendous kind of pirates, anyway, for I could not afford that sort. I have often thought that I could make more profitable voyages if I had a savager lot of men. I'll tell you, sir, we once tried to board a big Spanish galleon, and the beastly foreigners beat us off, bedad, and we had a hard time of it gettin' away. There are three or four good fellows in the crew, tough old rascals who came with the sloop when I bought her, but most of my men are but poor knaves, and not to be afraid of."

This comfort Mr. Delaplaine kept to himself, and on the second day out, the food which was served to them being most wretchedly cooked, Dame Charter ventured into the galley to see if she could do anything in the way of improvement.

"I think you may eat this," she said, when she returned to Kate, "but I don't think that anything on board is fit for you. When I went to the kitchen, I came near dropping dead right in the doorway; that cook, Mistress Kate, is the most terrible creature of all the pirates that ever were born. His eyes are blistering green and his beard is all twisted into points, with the ends stuck fast with blood, which has never been washed off. He roars like a lion, with shining teeth, but he speaks very fair, Mistress Kate; you would be amazed to hear how fair he speaks. He told me, and every word he said set my teeth on edge with its grating, that he wanted to know how I liked the meals cooked; that he would do it right if there were things on board to do it with. Which there are not, Mistress Kate. And when he was beatin' up that batter for me and I asked him if he was not tired workin' so hard, he pulled up his sleeve and showed me his arm, which was like a horse's leg, all covered with hair, and asked me if I thought it was likely he could tear himself with a spoon. I'm sure he would give us better food if he could, for he leaned over and whispered to me, like a gust of wind coming in through the door, that the captain was in a very hard case, having lately lost everything he had at the gaming-table, and therefore had not the money to store the ship as he would have done."

"Oh, don't talk about that, Dame Charter," said Kate; "if we can get enough to eat, no matter what it is, we must be satisfied and think only of our great joy in sailing to my father and to your Dickory."

That afternoon Captain Ichabod found Kate by herself on deck, and he made bold to sit down by her; and before he knew what he was about, he was telling her his whole story. She listened carefully to what he said. He touched but lightly upon his wickednesses, although they were plain enough to any listener of sense, and bemoaned his fearful passion for gaming, which was sure to bring him to misery one day or another.

"When I have staked my vessel and have lost it," said he, "then there will be an end of me."

"But why don't you sell your vessel before you lose it," said Kate, "and become a farmer?"

His eyes brightened. "I never thought of that," said he. "Bedad—excuse me, Miss—some day when I've got a little together and can pay my men I'll sell this sloop and buy a farm, bedad—I beg your pardon, Miss—I'll buy a farm."

Kate smiled, but it was easy to see that Captain Ichabod was in earnest.

The next day Captain Ichabod came to Mr. Delaplaine and took him to one side. "I want to speak to you," he said, "about a bit of business."

"You may have noticed, sir, that we are somewhat short of provisions, and the way of it is this. The night before we sailed, hoping to make a bold stroke at the card-table and thereby fit out my vessel in a manner suitable to the entertainment of a gentleman and ladies, I lost every penny I had. I did hope that our provisions would last us a few days longer, but I am disappointed, sir. That cook of mine, who is a soft-hearted fellow, his neck always ready for the heel of a woman, has thrown overboard even the few stores we had left for you, the good Dame Charter having told him they were not fit to eat. And more, sir, even my men are grumbling. So I thought I would speak to you and explain that it would be necessary for us to overhaul a merchantman and replenish our food supply. It can be done very quietly, sir, and I don't think that even the ladies need be disturbed."

Mr. Delaplaine stared in amazement. "Do you mean to say," he exclaimed, "that you want me to consent to your committing piracy for our benefit?"

"Yes, sir," answered the captain, "that's what I suppose you would call it; but that's my business."

"Now, sir, I wish you to know that I am a Christian and a gentleman," said Mr. Delaplaine.

"That's all very true, bedad," said Captain Ichabod, "but you're also another thing; you're a human being, and you must eat."

"This is terrible," exclaimed the merchant, "that at my time of life I should consent to a felony at sea, and to profit by it. I cannot bear to think of the wickedness and the disgrace of it."

"Most respected sir," said Ichabod, "if the fellows behave themselves properly and don't offer to fight us, then there'll be no wickedness, bedad. I can make a good enough show of men to frighten any ordinary merchant crew so that not a blow need be struck. And that is what I expect to do, sir. I would not have any disturbance before ladies, you may be sure of that, bedad. We bear down upon a vessel; we order her to surrender; we take what we want, and we let her go. Truly, there's no wickedness in that! And as for the disgrace, we can all better bear that than starve."

Mr. Delaplaine looked at the pirate without a word. He could not comprehend how a man with such a frank and honest face could thus avow his dishonest principles. But as he gazed and wondered the thought of a scheme flashed across the mind of the merchant, a thoroughly business-like scheme. This bold young pirate captain might seize upon such supplies as they were in need of, but he, Felix Delaplaine, of Spanish Town, Jamaica, would pay for them. Thus might their necessities be relieved and their consciences kept clean. But he said nothing of this to Ichabod; the pirate might deem such a proceeding unprofessional and interpose some objection. Payment would be the merchant's part of the business, and he would attend to it himself. A look of resignation now came over Mr. Delaplaine's face.

"Captain," said he, "I must yield to your reason; it is absolutely necessary that we shall not starve."

Ichabod's face shone and he held out his hand. "Bedad, sir," he cried, "I honour you as a bold gentleman and a kind one. I will instantly lay my course somewhat to the eastward, and I promise you, sir, it will not be long before we run across some of these merchant fellows. I beg you, sir, speak to your ladies and tell them that there will be no unpleasant commotion; we may draw our swords and make a fierce show, but, bedad, I don't believe there'll be any fighting. We shall want so little—for I would not attempt to take a regular prize with ladies on board—that the fellows will surely deliver what we demand, the quicker to make an end of it."

"If you are perfectly sure," said Mr. Delaplaine, "that you can restrain your men from violence, I would like to be a member of your boarding party; it would be a rare experience for me."

Now Captain Ichabod fairly shouted with delight.

"Bravo! Bravo!" he exclaimed; "I didn't dream, sir, that you were a man of such a noble spirit. You shall go with us, sir. Your presence will aid greatly in making our hoped-for capture a most orderly affair; no one can look upon you, bedad, without knowing that you are a high-minded and honourable man, and would not take a box or case from any one if you did not need it. Now, sir, we shall put about, and by good fortune we may soon sight a merchantman. Even if it be but a coastwise trader, it may serve our purpose."

Mr. Delaplaine, with something of a smile upon his sedate face, hurried to Kate, who was upon the quarter-deck.

"My dear, we are about to introduce a little variety into our dull lives. As soon as we can overhaul a merchantman we shall commit a piracy. But don't turn pale; I have arranged it all."

"You!" exclaimed the wide-eyed Kate.

"Yes," said her uncle, and he told his tale.

"And remember this, my dear," he added; "if we cannot pay, we do not eat. I shall be as relentless as the bloody Blackbeard; if they take not my money, I shall swear to Ichabod that we touch not their goods."

"And are you sure," she said, "that there will be no bloodshed?"

"I vouch for that," said he, "for I shall lead the boarding party."

She took him by both hands. "Why," she said, "it need be no more than laying in goods from a store-house; and I cannot but be glad, dear uncle, for I am so very, very hungry."

Now Dame Charter came running and puffing. "Do you know," she cried, "that there is to be a piracy? The word has just been passed and the cook told me. There is to be no bloodshed, and the other ship will not be burned and the people will not be made to walk a plank. The

FRANK R. STOCKTON

captain has given those orders, and he is very firm, swearing, I am told, much more than is his wont. It is dreadful, it is awful just to think about, but the provisions are gone, and it is absolutely necessary to do something, and it will really be very exciting. The cook tells me he will put me in a good place where I cannot be hurt and where I shall see everything. And, Mistress Kate and Master Delaplaine, I dare say he can take care of you too."

Kate looked at her uncle as if to ask if she might tell the good woman what sort of a piracy this was to be, but he shook his head. It would not do to interfere any more than was necessary with the regular progress of events. The captain came up, excited. "Even now, bedad," he cried, "there are two sails in sight—one far north, and the other to the eastward, beating up this way. This one we shall make for. We have the wind with us, which is a good thing, for the Restless is a bad sailer and has lost many a prize through that fault. And now, Miss," he said, addressing Kate, "I shall have to ask your leave to take down that English flag and run up our Jolly Roger. It will be necessary, for if the fellows fear not our long guns, they may change their course and get away from us."

"That will be right," said Kate; "if we're going to be pirates, we might as well be pirates out and out."

Captain Ichabod glowed with delight. "What a girl this was, and what an uncle!"

It was not long, for the Restless had a fair wind, before the sail to the eastward came fully into sight. She was, in good truth, a merchantman, and not a large one. Dame Charter, very much excited, wondered what she would have on board.

"The cook tells me," said she to Kate, "that sometimes ships from the other side of the ocean carry the most astonishing and beautiful things."

"But we shall not see these things," said Kate, "even if that ship carries them. We shall take but food, and shall not unnecessarily despoil them of that. We may be pirates, but we shall not be wicked."

"It is hard to see the difference," said Dame Charter, with a sigh, "but we must eat. The cook tells me that they have made peaceful prizes before now. This they do when they want some particular thing, such as food or money, and care not for the trouble of stripping the ship, putting all on board to death, and then setting her on fire. The cook never does any boarding himself, so he says, but he stands on the deck here, armed with his great axe, which likes him better than a cutlass, and no matter what happens, he defends his kitchen."

"From his looks," said Kate, "I should imagine him to be the fiercest fighter among them all."

"But that is not so," said Dame Charter; "he tells me that he is of a very peaceable mind and would never engage in any broils or fights if he could help it. Look! look!" she cried, "they're running out their long brass guns; and do you see that other ship, how her sails are fluttering in the wind? And there, that little spot at the top of her mast; that's her flag, and it is coming down! Down, down it comes, and I must run to the cook and ask him what will happen next."

XXXI

Mr. Delaplaine Leads a Boarding Party

Steadily southward sailed the brig Black Swan which bore upon its decks the happy Mander family and our poor friend Dickory, carrying with him his lifelong destiny in the shape of the blood-stained letter from Captain Vince.

The sackcloth draperies of Lucilla, with the red cord lightly tied about them, had given place to a very ordinary gown fashioned by her mother and herself, which added so few charms to her young face and sparkling eyes that Dickory often thought that he wished there were some bushes on deck so that she might stand behind them and let him see only her face, as he had seen it when first he met her. But he saw the pretty face a great deal, for Lucilla was very anxious to know things, and asked many questions about Barbadoes, and also asked if there was any probability that the brig would go straight on to that lovely island without bothering to stop at Jamaica. It was during such talks as this that Dickory forgot, when he did forget, the blood-stained letter that he carried with him always.

Our young friend still wore the naval uniform, although in coming on the brig he had changed it for some rough sailor's clothes. But Lucilla had besought him to be again a brave lieutenant.

They sailed and they sailed, and there was but little wind, and that from the south and against them. But Lucilla did not complain at their slow progress. The slowest vessel in the world was preferable just now to a desert island which never moved.

Davids was at the wheel and Mander stood near him. These old friends had not yet finished talking about what had happened in the days since they had seen each other. Mrs. Mander sat, not far away, still making clothes, and the little Lena was helping her in her childlike way. Lucilla and Dickory were still talking about Barbadoes. There never was a girl who wanted to know so much about an island as that girl wanted to know about Barbadoes.

Suddenly there was a shout from above.

"What's that?" asked Mander.

"A sail," said Davids, peering out over the sea but able to see nothing. Lucilla and Dickory did not cease talking. At that moment Lucilla did not care greatly about sails, there was so much to be said about Barbadoes.

There was a good deal of talking forward, and after a while the captain walked to the quarter-deck. He was a gruff man and his face was troubled.

"I am sorry to say," he growled, "that the ship we have sighted is a pirate; she flies the black flag."

Now there was no more talk about Barbadoes, or what had happened to old friends, and the sewing dropped on the deck. Those poor Manders were chilled to the soul. Were they again to be taken by pirates?

"Captain," cried Mander, "what can we do, can we run away from them?"

"We could not run away from their guns," growled the captain, "and there is nothing to do. They intend to take this brig, and that's the reason they have run up their skull and bones. They are bearing directly down upon us with a fair wind; they will be firing a gun presently, and then I shall lay to and wait for them."

Mander stepped towards Dickory and Lucilla; his voice was husky as he said: "We cannot expect, my dear, that we shall again be captured by forbearing pirates. I shall kill my wife and little daughter rather than they shall fall into the bloody hands of ordinary pirates, and to you, sir, I will commit the care of my Lucilla. If this vessel is delivered over to a horde of savages, I pray you, plunge your dirk into her heart."

"Yes," said Lucilla, clinging to the arm of Dickory, "if those fierce pirates shall attack us, we will die together."

Dickory shook his head. In an awful moment such as this he could hold out no illusions. "No," said he, "I cannot die with you; I have a duty before me, and until it is accomplished I cannot willingly give up my life. I must rather be even a pirate's slave than that. But I will accept your father's charge; should there be need, I will kill you."

"Thank you very much," said Lucilla coolly.

To the surprise of the people on the Black Swan there came no shot from the approaching pirate; but as she still bore down upon them, running before the wind, the captain of the brig lay to and lowered his flag. Submission now was all there was before them. No man on the brig took up arms, nor did the crew form themselves into any show of resistance; that would have but made matters worse.

As the pirate vessel came on, nearer and nearer, a great number of men could be seen stretched along her deck, and some brass cannon were visible trained upon the unfortunate brig.

But, to the surprise of the captain of the Black Swan, and of nearly everybody on board of her, the pirate did not run down upon her to make fast and board. Instead of that, she put about into the wind and lay to less than a quarter of a mile away. Then two boats were lowered and filled with men, who rowed towards the brig.

"They have special reasons for our capture," said the captain to those who were crowding about him; "he may be well laden now with plunder, and comes to us for our gold and silver. Or it may be that he merely wants the brig. If that be so, he can quickly rid himself of us."

That was a cruel speech when women had to hear it, but the captain was a rough fellow.

The boats came on as quietly as if they were about to land at a neighbouring pier. Dickory and Lucilla cautiously peeped over the rail, Dickory without his hat, and Lucilla, hiding herself, all but a part of her face, behind him; the Manders crouched together on the deck, the father with glaring eyes and a knife in his hand. The crew stood, with their hats removed and their chins lowered, waiting for what might happen next.

Up to this time Dickory had shown no signs of fear, although his mind was terribly tossed and disturbed; for, whatever might happen to him, it possibly would be the end of that mission which was now the only object of his life. But he grated his teeth together and awaited his fate.

But now, as the boats came nearer, he began to tremble, and gradually his knees shook under him.

"I would not have believed that he was such a coward as that," thought Lucilla.

The boats neared the ship and were soon made fast; every help was offered by the crew of the brig, and not a sign of resistance was shown. The leader of the pirates mounted to the deck, followed by the greater part of his men.

For a moment Captain Ichabod glanced about him, and then, addressing the captain of the brig, he said: "This is all very well. I am glad to see that you have sense enough to take things as you find them, and not to stir up a fracas and make trouble. I overhauled you that I might lay in a stock of provisions, and some wine and spirits besides, having no desire, if you treat us rightly, to despoil you further. So, we shall have no more words about it, bedad, and if you will set your men to work to get on deck such stores as my quarter-master here may demand of you, we shall get through this business quickly. In the meantime, lower two or three boats, so that your men can row the goods over to my vessel."

The captain of the Black Swan simply bowed his head and turned away to obey orders, while Captain Ichabod stepped a little aft and began to survey the captured vessel. As soon as his back was turned, the captain of the brig was approached by a very respectable elderly gentleman, apparently not engaged either in the mercantile marine or in piratical pursuits, who stopped him and said: "Sir, my name is Felix Delaplaine, merchant, of Spanish Town, Jamaica. I am, against my will, engaged in this piratical attack upon your vessel, but I wish to assure you privately that I will not consent to have you robbed of your property, and that, although some of your provisions may be taken by these pirates, I here promise, as an honourable gentleman, to pay you the full value of all that they seize upon."

The captain of the Black Swan had no opportunity to make an answer to this most extraordinary statement, for at that moment a naval officer, shouting at the top of his voice, came rushing towards the respectable gentleman who had just been making such honourable proposals. Almost at the same moment there was a great shout from Captain Ichabod, who, drawing his cutlass from its sheath, raised the glittering blade and dashed in pursuit of the naval gentleman.

"Hold there! Hold there!" cried the pirate. "Don't you touch him; don't you lay your hand upon him!"

But Ichabod was not quick enough. Dickory, swift as a stag, stretched out both his arms and threw them around the neck of the amazed Mr. Delaplaine.

Now the pirate Ichabod reached the two; his great sword went high in air, and was about to descend upon the naval person, whoever he was, who had made such an unprovoked attack upon his honoured passenger, when his arm was caught by some one from behind. Turning, with a great curse, his eyes fell upon the face of a young girl.

"Oh, don't kill him! Don't kill him!" she cried, "he will hurt nobody; he is only hugging the old gentleman."

Captain Ichabod looked from the girl to the two men, who were actually embracing each other. Dickory's back was towards him, but the face of Mr. Delaplaine fairly glowed with delight.

FRANK R. STOCKTON

"Oho!" said Ichabod, turning to Lucilla, "and what does this mean, bedad?"

"I don't know," she answered, "but the gentleman in the uniform is a good man. Perhaps the other one is his father."

"To my eyes," said Captain Ichabod, "this is a most fearsome mix."

The Mander family, and nearly everybody else on board, crowded about the little group, gazing with all their eyes but asking no questions.

"Captain Ichabod," exclaimed Mr. Delaplaine, holding Dickory by the hand, "this is one of the two persons you were taking us to find. This is Dickory Charter, the son of good Dame Charter, now on your vessel. He went away with Blackbeard, and we were in search of him."

"Oho!" cried Captain Ichabod, "by my life I believe it. That's the young fellow that Blackbeard dressed up in a cocked hat and took away with him."

"I am the same person, sir," said Dickory.

"So far so good," said Captain Ichabod. "I am very glad that I did not bring down my cutlass on you, which I should have done, bedad, had it not been for this young woman."

Now up spoke Mr. Delaplaine. "We have found you, Dickory," he cried, "but what can you tell us of Major Bonnet?"

"Ay, ay," added Captain Ichabod, "there's another one we're after; where's the runaway Sir Nightcap?"

"Alas!" said Dickory, "I do not know. I escaped from Blackbeard, and since that day have heard nothing. I had supposed that Captain Bonnet was in your company, Mr. Delaplaine."

Now the captain of the Black Swan pushed himself forward. "Is it Captain Bonnet, lately of the pirate ship Revenge, that you're talking about?" he asked. "If so, I may tell you something of him. I am lately from Charles Town, and the talk there was that Blackbeard was lying outside the harbour in Stede Bonnet's old vessel, and that Bonnet had lately joined him. I did not venture out of port until I had had certain news that these pirates had sailed northward. They had two or three ships, and the talk was that they were bound to the Virginias, and perhaps still farther north. They were fitted out for a long cruise."

"Gone again!" exclaimed Mr. Delaplaine in a hoarse voice. "Gone again!"

Captain Ichabod's face grew clouded.

"Gone north of Charles Town," he exclaimed, "that's bad, bedad, that's very bad. You are sure he did not sail southward?" he asked of the captain of the brig.

That gruff mariner was in a strange state of mind. He had just been captured by a pirate, and in the next moment had made, what might be a very profitable sale, to a respectable merchant, of the goods the pirate was about to take from him. Moreover, the said pirate seemed to be in the employ of said merchant, and altogether, things seemed to him to be in as fearsome a mix as they had seemed to Captain Ichabod, but he brought his mind down to the question he had been asked.

"No doubt about that," said he; "there were some of his men in the town—for they are afraid of nobody—and they were not backward in talking."

"That upsets things badly," said Captain Ichabod, without unclouding his brow. "With my slow vessel and my empty purse, bedad, I don't see how I am ever goin' to catch Blackbeard if he has gone north. Finding Blackbeard would have been a handful of trumps to me, but the game seems to be up, bedad."

The captain of the brig and Ichabod's quarter-master went away to attend to the transfer of the needed goods to the Restless. Mander, with his wife and little daughter, were standing together gazing with amazement at the strange pirates who had come aboard, while Lucilla stepped up to Dickory, who stood silent, with his eyes on the deck.

"Can you tell me what this means?" said she.

For a moment he did not answer, and then he said: "I don't know everything myself, but I must presently go on board that vessel."

"What!" exclaimed Lucilla, stepping back. "Is she there?"

"Yes," said Dickory.

XXXII

THE DELIVERY OF THE LETTER

The sea was smooth and the wind light, and the transfer of provisions from the Black Swan to the pirate sloop, which two ships now lay as near each other as safety would permit, was accomplished quietly.

During the progress of the transfer Captain Ichabod's boat was rowed back to his ship, and its arrival was watched with great interest by everybody on board that pirate sloop. Kate and Dame Charter, as well as all the men who stood looking over the rail, were amazed to see a naval officer accompanying the captain and Mr. Delaplaine on their return. But that amazement was greatly increased when that officer, as soon as he set foot upon the deck, removed his hat and made directly for Dame Charter, who, with a scream loud enough to frighten the fishes, enfolded him in her arms and straightway fainted. It was like a son coming up out of the sea, sure enough, as she afterward stated. Kate, recognising Dickory, hurried to him with a scream of her own and both hands outstretched, but the young fellow, who seemed greatly distressed at the unconscious condition of his mother, did not greet Mistress Bonnet with the enthusiastic delight which might have been expected under the circumstances. He seemed troubled and embarrassed, which, perhaps, was not surprising, for never before had he seen his mother faint.

Kate was about to offer some assistance, but as the good Dame now showed signs of returning consciousness, she thought it would be better to leave the two together, and in a state of amazement she was hurrying to her uncle when Dickory rose from the side of his mother and stopped her.

"I have a letter for you," he said, in a husky voice.

"A letter?" she cried, "from my father?"

"No," said he, "from Captain Vince." And he handed her the blood-stained missive.

Kate turned pale and stared at him; here was horrible mystery. The thought flashed through the young girl's mind that the wicked captain had killed her father and had written to tell her so.

"Is my father dead?" she gasped.

"Not that I know of," said Dickory.

"Where is he?" she cried.

"I do not know," was the answer.

She stood, holding the letter, while Dickory returned to his mother. Mr. Delaplaine saw her standing thus, pale and shocked, but he did not hasten to her. He had sad things to say to her, for his practical mind told him that it would not be possible to continue the search for her father, he having put himself out of the reach of Captain Ichabod and his inefficient sloop. If Dickory had said anything about her father which had so cast her down, how much harder would it be for him when he had to tell her the whole truth.

BUT KATE DID NOT WAIT for further speech from anybody. She gave a great start, and then rushed down the companion-way to her cabin. There, with her door shut, she opened the letter. This was the letter, written in lead pencil, in an irregular but bold hand, with some letters partly dimmed where the paper had been damp:

> "At the very end of my life I write to you that you have
> escaped the fiercest love that ever a man had for a woman.
> I shall carry this love with me to hell, if it may be, but you
> have escaped it. This escape is a blessing, and now that I
> cannot help it I give it to you. Had I lived, I should have
> shed the blood of every one whom you loved to gain you and
> you would have cursed me. So love me now for dying.
>
> Yours, anywhere and always,
> CHRISTOPHER VINCE

Kate put down the letter and some colour came into her face; she bowed her head in thankful prayer.

"He is dead," she said, "and now he cannot harm my father." That was the only thought she had regarding this hot-brained and infatuated lover. He was dead, her father was safe from him. How he died, how Dickory came to bring the letter, how anything had happened that had happened except the death of Captain Vince, did not at this moment concern her. Not until now had she known how the fear of the vengeful captain of the Badger had constantly been with her.

Over and over again Dickory told his tale to his mother. She interrupted him so much with her embraces that he could not explain things clearly to her, but she did not care, she had him with her. He was with her, and she had fast hold of him, and she would never let him go again. What mattered it what sort of clothes he wore, or where he had escaped from—a family on a desert island or from a pirate crew? She had him, and her happiness knew no bounds. Dickory was perfectly willing to stay with her and to talk to her. He did not care to be with anybody else, not even with Mistress Kate, who had taken so much interest in him all the time he had been away; though, of course, not so much interest as his own dear mother.

Then the good Dame Charter, being greatly recovered and so happy, began to talk of herself. Slipping in a disjointed way over her various experiences, she told her dear boy, in strictest confidence, that she was very much disappointed in the way pirates took ships. She thought it was going to be something very exciting that she would remember to the end of her days, and wake up in the middle of the night and scream when she thought of it, but it was nothing of the kind; not a shot was fired, not a drop of blood shed; there was not even a shout or a yell or a scream for mercy. It was all like going into the pantry to get the flour and the sugar. She was all the time waiting for something to happen, and nothing ever did. Dickory smiled, but it was like watered milk.

"I do not understand such piracy," he said, "but supposed, dear mother, that these pirates had taken that ship in the usual way, I being on board."

At this he was clasped so tightly to his mother's breast that he could say no more.

The boats plied steadily between the two vessels, and on one of the trips Mr. Delaplaine went over to the brig on business, and also glad to escape for a little the dreaded interview which must soon come between himself and his niece.

"Now, sir," said the merchant to the captain of the brig, "you will make a bill against me for the provisions which are being taken to that pirate, but I hope you have reserved a sufficient store of food for your own maintenance until you reach a port, and that of myself and two women who wish to sail with you, craving most earnestly that you will land us in Jamaica or in some place convenient of access to that island."

"Which I can do," said the captain, "for I am bound to Kingston; and as to subsistence, shall have plenty."

On the brig Mr. Delaplaine found Captain Ichabod, who had come over to superintend operations, and who was now talking to the pretty girl who had seized him by the arm when he was about to slay the naval officer.

"I would talk with you, captain," said the merchant, "on a matter of immediate import." And he led the pirate away from the pretty girl.

The matter to be discussed was, indeed, of deep import.

"I am loath to say it, sir," said Mr. Delaplaine, "when I think of the hospitality and most exceptional kindness with which you have treated me and my niece, and for which we shall feel grateful all our lives, but I think you will agree with me that it would be useless for us to pursue the search after that most reprehensible person, my brother-in-law, Bonnet. There can be no doubt, I believe, that he and Blackbeard have left the vicinity of Charles Town, and have gone, we know not where."

"No doubt of that, bedad," said Ichabod, knitting his brows as he spoke; "if Blackbeard had been outside the harbour, this brig would not have been here."

"And, therefore, sir," continued Mr. Delaplaine, "I have judged it to be wise, and indeed necessary, for us to part company with you, sir, and to take passage on this brig, which, by a most fortunate chance, is bound for Kingston. My niece, I know, will be greatly disappointed by this course of events, but we have no choice but to fall in with them."

"I don't like to agree with you," said the captain, "but, bedad, I am bound to do it. I am disappointed myself, sir, but I have been disappointed so often that I suppose I ought to be used to it. If I had caught up with Blackbeard I should have been all right, and after I had settled your affairs—and I know I could have done that—I think I would have joined him. But all I can do now is to hammer along at the business, take prizes in the usual way, and wait for Blackbeard to come south again, and then I'll either sell out or join him."

"It is a great pity, sir," said Mr. Delaplaine, "a great pity—"

"Yes, it is," interrupted Ichabod, "it's a very great pity, sir, a very great pity. If I had known more about ships when I bought the Restless I would have had a faster craft, and by this time I might have been a man of comfortable means. But that sloop over there, bedad, is so slow, that many a time, sir, I have seen a fat merchantman sail away from her and leave us, in spite of our guns, cursing and swearing, miles behind. I am sorry to have you leave me, sir, and with your ladies; but, as you say, here's your chance to get home, and I don't know when I could give you another."

FRANK R. STOCKTON

Mr. Delaplaine replied courteously and gratefully, and by the next boat he went back to the Restless. Captain Ichabod, his brow still clouded by the approaching separation, walked over to Lucilla and continued his conversation with her about the island of Barbadoes, a subject of which he knew very little and she nothing.

When Kate returned to the deck she found Dickory alone, Dame Charter having gone to talk to the cook about the wonderful things which had happened, of which she knew very little and he nothing at all.

"Dickory," said Kate, "I want to talk to you, and that quickly. I have heard nothing of what has happened to you. How did you get possession of the letter you brought me, and what do you know of Captain Vince?"

"I can tell you nothing," he said, without looking at her, "until you tell me what I ought to know about Captain Vince." And as he said this he could not help wondering in his heart that there were no signs of grief about her.

"Ought to know?" she repeated, regarding him earnestly. "Well, you and I have been always good friends, and I will tell you." And then she told him the story of the captain of the Badger; of his love-making and of his commission to sail upon the sea and destroy the pirate ship Revenge, and all on board of her.

"And now," she said, as she concluded, "I think it would be well for you to read this letter." And she handed him the missive he had carried so long and with such pain. He read the bold, uneven lines, and then he turned and looked upon her, his face shining like the morning sky.

"Then you have never loved him?" he gasped.

"Why should I?" said Kate.

In spite of the fact that there were a great many people on board that pirate sloop who might see him; in spite of the fact that there were people in boats plying upon the water who might notice his actions, Dickory fell upon his knees before Kate, and, seizing her hand, he pressed it to his lips.

"Why should I?" said Kate, quietly drawing her hand from him, "for I have a devoted lover already—Master Martin Newcombe, of Barbadoes."

Dickory, repulsed, rose to his feet, but his face did not lose its glow. He had heard so much about Martin Newcombe that he had ceased to mind him.

"To think of it!" he cried, "to think how I stood and watched him fight; how I admired and marvelled at his wonderful strength and skill, his fine figure, and his flashing eye! How my soul went out to him, how I longed that he might kill that scoundrel Blackbeard! And all the time he was your enemy, he was my enemy, he was a viler wretch than even the bloody pirate who killed him. Oh, Kate, Kate! if I had but known."

"Miss Kate, if you please," said the girl. "And it is well, Dickory, you did not know, for then you might have jumped upon him and stuck him in the back, and that would have been dishonourable."

"He thought," said Dickory, not in the least abashed by his reproof, "that the Revenge was commanded by your father, for he sprang upon the deck, shouting for the captain, and when he saw Blackbeard I heard him exclaim in surprise, 'A sugar-planter!'"

"And he would have killed my father?" said Kate, turning pale at the thought.

"Yes," replied Dickory, "he would have killed any man except the great Blackbeard. And to think of it! I stood there watching them, and wishing that vile Englishman the victory. Oh, Kate! you should have seen that wonderful pirate fight. No man could have stood before him." Then, with sparkling eyes and waving arms, he told her of the combat. When he had finished, the souls of these two young people were united in an overpowering admiration, almost reverence, for the prowess and strength of the wicked and bloody pirate who had slain the captain of the Badger.

When Mr. Delaplaine came on board, Kate, who had been waiting, took him aside.

"Uncle," she exclaimed, "I have great news. Captain Vince is dead. At last he came up with the Revenge, but instead of finding my father in command he found Blackbeard, who killed him. Now my father is safe!"

The good man scarcely knew what to say to this bright-faced girl, whose father's safety was all the world to her. If he had heard that his worthless and wicked brother-in-law had been killed, it would have been trouble and sorrow for the present, but it would have been peace for the future. But he was a Christian gentleman and a loving uncle, and he banished this thought from his heart. He listened to Kate as she rapidly went on talking, but he did not hear her; his mind was busy with the news he had to tell her—the news that she must give up her loving search and go back with him to Spanish Town.

"And now, uncle," said Kate, "there's another thing I want to say to you. Since this great grief has been lifted from my soul, since I know that no wrathful and vindictive captain of a man-of-war is scouring the seas, armed with authority to kill my father and savage for his life, I feel that it is not right for me to put other people who are so good to me to sad discomfort and great expense to try to follow my father into regions far away, and to us almost unknown.

"Some day he will come back into this part of the world, and I hope he may return disheartened and weary of his present mode of life, and then I may have a better chance of winning him back to the domestic life he used to love so much. But he is safe, uncle, and that is everything now, and so I came to say to you that I think it would be well for us to relieve this kind Captain Ichabod from the charges and labours he has taken upon himself for our sakes and, if it be possible, engage that ship yonder to take us back to Jamaica; she was sailing in that direction, and her captain might be induced to touch at Kingston. This is what I have been thinking about, dear uncle, and do you not agree with me?"

High rose the spirits of the good Mr. Delaplaine; banished was all the overhanging blackness of his dreaded interview with Kate. The sky was bright, her soul was singing songs of joy and thankfulness, and his soul might join her. He never appreciated better than now the blessings which might be shed upon humanity by the death of a bad man. His mind even gambolled a little in his relief.

"But, Kate," he said, "if we leave that kind Captain Ichabod, and he be not restrained by our presence, then, my dear, he will return to his former evil ways, and his next captures will not be like this one, but like ordinary piracies, sinful in every way."

"Uncle," said Kate, looking up into his face, "it is too much to ask of one young girl to undertake the responsibilities of two pirates; I hope some day to be of benefit to my poor father, but when it comes to Captain Ichabod, kind as he has been, I am afraid I will have to let him go and manage the affairs of his soul for himself."

Her uncle smiled upon her. Now that he was to go back to his home and take this dear girl with him, he was ready to smile at almost anything. That he thought one pirate much better worth saving than the other, and that his choice did not agree with that of his niece, was not for him even to think about at such a happy moment. It was not long after this conversation that the largest boat belonging to the Restless was rowed over to the brig, and in it sat, not only Kate, Dame Charter, and Dickory, but Captain Ichabod, who would accompany his guests to take proper leave of them. The crew of the pirate sloop crowded themselves along her sides, and even mounted into her shrouds, waving their hats and shouting as the boat moved away. The cook was the loudest shouter, and his ragged hat waved highest. And, as Dame Charter shook her handkerchief above her head and gazed back at her savage friend, there was a moisture in her eyes. Up to this moment she never would have believed that she would have grieved to depart from a pirate vessel and to leave behind a pirate cook.

Lucilla watched carefully the newcomers as they ascended to the deck of the Black Swan. "That is the girl," she said to herself, "and I am not surprised."

A little later she remarked to Captain Ichabod, who sat by her: "Are they mother and daughter, those two?"

"Oh, no," said he. "Mistress Bonnet is too fine a lady and too beautiful to be daughter to that old woman, who is her attendant and the mother of the young fellow in the cocked hat."

"Too fine and beautiful!" repeated Lucilla.

"I greatly grieve to leave you all," continued the young pirate captain, "although some of you I have known so short a time. It will be very lonely when I sail away with none to speak to save the bloody dogs I command, who may yet throttle me. And it is to Barbadoes you go to settle with your family?"

"That is our destination," said Lucilla, "but I know not if we shall find the money to settle there; we were taken by pirates and lost everything."

Now the captain of the brig came up to Ichabod and informed him that the goods he demanded had been delivered on board his vessel, and that the brig was ready to sail. It was the time for leave-taking, but Ichabod was tardy. Presently he approached Kate, and drew her to one side.

"Dear lady," he said, and his voice was hesitating, while a slight flush of embarrassment appeared on his face, "you may have thought, dear lady," he repeated, "you may have thought that so fair a being as yourself should have attracted during the days we have sailed together—may have attracted, bedad, I mean—the declared admiration even of a fellow like myself, we being so much together; but I had heard your story, fair lady, and of the courtship paid you by Captain Vince of the corvette Badger—whose family I knew in England—and, acknowledging his superior claims, I constantly refrained, though not without great effort (I must say that much for myself, fair lady), from—from—"

"Addressing me, I suppose you mean," said Kate. "What you say, kind captain, redounds to your honour, and I thank you for your noble consideration, but I feel bound to tell you that there was never anything between me and Captain Vince, and he is now dead."

The young pirate stepped back suddenly and opened wide his eyes. "What!" he exclaimed, "and all the time you were—"

"Not free," she interrupted with a smile, "for I have a lover on the island of Barbadoes."

"Barbadoes," repeated Captain Ichabod, and he bade Kate a most courteous farewell.

All the good-byes had been said and good wishes had been wished, when, just as he was about to descend to his boat, Captain Ichabod turned to Lucilla. "And it is truly to Barbadoes you go?" he asked.

"Yes," said she, "I think we shall certainly do that."

Now his face flushed. "And do you care for that fellow in the cocked hat?"

Here was a cruel situation for poor Lucilla. She must lie or lose two men. She might lose them anyway, but she would not do it of her own free will, and so she lied.

"Not a whit!" said Lucilla.

The eyes of Ichabod brightened as he went down the side of the brig.

XXXIII

BLACKBEARD GIVES GREENWAY SOME DIFFICULT WORK

The great pirate Blackbeard, inactive and taking his ease, was seated on the quarter-deck of his fine vessel, on which he had lately done some sharp work off the harbour of Charles Town. He was now commanding a small fleet. Besides the ship on which he sailed, he had two other vessels, well manned and well laden with supplies from his recent captures. Satisfied with conquest, he was sailing northward to one of his favourite resorts on the North Carolina coast.

To this conquering hero now came Ben Greenway, the Scotchman, touching his hat.

"And what do you want?" cried the burly pirate. "Haven't they given you your prize-money yet, or isn't it enough?"

"Prize-money!" exclaimed Greenway. "I hae none o' it, nor will I hae any. What money I hae—an' it is but little—came to me fairly."

"Oho!" cried Blackbeard, "and you have money then, have you? Is it enough to make it worth my while to take it?"

"Ye can count it an' see, whenever ye like," said Ben. "But it isna money that I came to talk to ye about. I came to ask ye, at the first convenient season, to put me on board that ship out there, that I may be in my rightful place by the side o' Master Bonnet."

"And what good are you to him, or he to you," asked the pirate, with a fine long oath, "that I should put myself to that much trouble?"

"I have the responsibeelity o' his soul on my hands," said Ben, "an' since we left Charles Town I hae not seen him, he bein' on ane ship an' I on anither."

"And very well that is too," said Blackbeard, "for I like each of you better separate. And now look ye, me kirk bird, you have not done very well with your 'responsibeelities' so far, and you might as well make up your mind to stop trying to convert that sneak of a Nightcap and take up the business of converting me. I'm in great need of it, I can tell you."

"You!" cried Ben.

"I tell you, yes," shouted Blackbeard, "it is I, myself, that I am talking about. I want to be converted from the evil of my ways, and I have made

FRANK R. STOCKTON

up my mind that you shall do it. You are a good and a pious man, and it is not often that I get hold of one of that kind; or, if I do, I slice off his head before I discover his quality."

"I fear me," said the truthful Scotchman, "that the job is beyond my abeelity."

"Not a bit of it, not a bit of it," shouted the pirate. "I am fifty times easier to work upon than that Nightcap man of yours, and a hundred times better worth the trouble. I put no trust in that downfaced farmer. When he shouts loudest for the black flag he is most likely to go into priestly orders, and the better is he reformed the quicker is he to rob and murder. He is of the kind the devil wants, but it is of no use for any one to show him the way there, he is well able to find it for himself. But it is different with me, you canny Scotchman, it is different with me. I am an open-handed and an open-mouthed scoundrel, and I never pretended to be anything else. When you begin reforming me you will find your work half done."

The Scotchman shook his head. "I fear me—" he said.

"No, you don't fear yourself," cried Blackbeard, "and I won't have it; I don't want any of that lazy piety on board my vessel. If you don't reform me, and do it rightly, I'll slice off both your ears."

At this moment a man came aft, carrying a great tankard of mixed drink. Blackbeard took it and held it in his hand.

"Now then, you balking chaplain," he cried, "here's a chance for you to begin. What would you have me do? Drain off this great mug and go slashing among my crew, or hurl it, mug and all—"

"Nay, nay," cried Greenway, "but rather give half o' it to me; then will it no' disturb your brain, an' mine will be comforted."

"Heigho!" cried Blackbeard. "Truly you are a better chaplain than I thought you. Drain half this mug and then, by all the powers of heaven and hell, you shall convert me. Now, look ye," said the pirate, when the mug was empty, "and hear what a brave repentance I have already begun. I am tired, my gay gardener, of all these piracies; I have had enough of them. Even now, my spoils and prizes are greater than I can manage, and why should I strive to make them more? I told you of my young lieutenant, who ran away and who gave his carcass to the birds of prey rather than sail with me and marry my strapping daughter. I liked that fellow, Greenway, and if he had known what was well for him there might be some reason for me to keep on piling up goods and money, but there's cursed little reason for it now. I have merchandise of value at Belize and much more of it in these ships, besides money from Charles Town which ought to last an honest gentleman for the rest of his days."

"Ay," said Ben, "but an honest gentleman is sparing of his expenditures."

"And you think I am not that kind of a man, do you?" shouted the pirate. "But let me tell you this. I am sailing now for Topsail Inlet, on the North Carolina coast, and I am going to run in there, disperse this fleet, sell my goods, and—"

"Be hanged?" interpolated Greenway in surprise.

"Not a bit of it, you croaking crow!" roared the pirate. "Not a bit of it. Don't you know, you dull-head, that our good King George has issued a proclamation to the Brethren of the Coast to come in and behave themselves like honest citizens and receive their pardon? I have done that once, and so I know all about it; but I backslid, showing that my conversion was badly done."

"It must hae been a poor hand that did the job for ye," said Greenway, "for truly the conversion washed off in the first rain."

The pirate laughed a great laugh. "The fact is," he said, "I did the work myself, and knowing nothing about it made a bad botch of it, but this time it will be different. I am going to give the matter into your hands, and I shall expect you to do it well. If I become not an honest gentleman this time you shall pay for it, first with your ears and then with your head."

"An' ye're goin' to keep me by ye?" said Greenway, with an expression not of the best.

"Truly so," said Blackbeard. "I shall make you my clerk as long as I am a pirate, for I have much writing and figuring work to be done, and after that you shall be my chaplain. And whether or not your work will be easier than it is now, it is not for me to say."

The Scotchman was about to make an exclamation which might not have been complimentary, but he restrained himself.

"An' Master Bonnet?" he asked. "If ye go out o' piracy he may go too, and take the oath."

"Of course he may," cried the pirate, "and of course he shall; I will see to that myself. Then I will give him back his ship, for I don't want it, and let him become an honest merchant."

"Give him back his ship!" exclaimed Greenway, his countenance downcast. "That will be puttin' into his hands the means o' beginnin' again a life o' sin. I pray ye, don't do that."

Blackbeard leaned back and laughed. "I swear that I thought it would be one of the very first steps in conversion for me to give back to the fellow the ship which is his own and which I have taken from him. But fear not, my noble pirate's clerk; he is not the man that I am; he is a vile coward, and when he has taken the oath he will be afraid to break it. Moreover—"

"And if, with that ship," said Greenway, his eyes beginning to sparkle, "he become an honest merchant—"

"I don't trust him," said Blackbeard; "he is a knave and a sharper, and there is no truth in him. But when you have settled up my business, my clerk, and have gotten me well converted, I will send you away with him, and you shall take up again the responsibility of his soul."

The Scotchman clapped his horny hands together. "And once I get him back to Bridgetown, I will burn his cursed ship!"

"Heigho!" cried Blackbeard, "and that will be your way of converting him? You know your business, my royal chaplain, you know it well." And with that he gave Greenway a tremendous slap on the back which would have dashed to the deck an ordinary man, but Ben Greenway was a Scotchman, tough as a yew-tree.

XXXIV

Captain Thomas of the Royal James

When Blackbeard's little fleet anchored in Topsail Inlet, Stede Bonnet, who had not been informed of the intentions of the pirate, was a good deal puzzled. Since joining Blackbeard's fleet in the vessel which came up from Belize, Bonnet had considered himself very shabbily treated, and his reasons for that opinion were not bad. During the engagements off Charles Town his services had not been required and his opinion had not been consulted, Blackbeard having no use for the one and no respect for the other. The pirate captain had taken a fancy to Ben Greenway, while his contempt for the Scotchman's master increased day by day; and it was for this reason that Greenway had been taken on board the flag-ship, while Bonnet remained on one of the smaller vessels.

Bonnet was in a discontented and somewhat sulky mood, but when Blackbeard's full plans were made known to him and he found that he might again resume command of his own vessel, the Revenge, if he chose to do so, his eyes began to sparkle once more.

Ben Greenway soon resumed his former position with Bonnet, for it did not take Blackbeard very long to settle up his affairs, and in a very short time he became tired of the work of conversion; or, to speak more correctly, of the bore of talking about it. Bonnet was glad to have the Scotchman back again, although he never ceased to declare his desire to get rid of this faithful friend and helper; for, when the Revenge again came into his hands, there were many things to be done, and few people to help him do it.

"It will be merchandise an' fair trade this time," said Ben, "an' ye'll find it no' so easy as your piracies, though safer. An' when ye're off to see the Governor an' hae got your pardon, it'll be a happy day, Master Bonnet, for ye an' for your daughter, an' for your brother-in-law an' everybody in Bridgetown wha either knew ye or respected ye."

"No more of that," cried Bonnet. "I did not say I was going to Bridgetown, or that I wanted anybody there to respect me. It is my purpose to fit out the Revenge as a privateer and get a commission to sail in her in the war between Spain and the Allies. This will be much more to my taste, Ben Greenway, than trading in sugar and hides."

Greenway was very grave.

"There is so little difference," said he, "between a privateer an' a pirate that it is a great strain on a common mind to keep them separate; but a commission from the king is better than a commission from the de'il, an' we'll hope there won't be much o' a war after all is said an' done."

There was not much intercourse between Blackbeard and Bonnet at Topsail Inlet. The pirate was on very good terms with the authorities at that place, who for their own sakes cared not much to interfere with him, and Bonnet had his own work in hand and industriously engaged in it. He went to Bath and got his pardon; he procured a clearance for St. Thomas, where he freely announced his intention to take out a commission as privateer, and he fitted out his vessel as best he could. Of men he had not many, but when he left the inlet he sailed down to an island on the coast, where Blackbeard, having had too many men on his return from Charles Town, had marooned a large number of the sailors belonging to his different crews, finding this the easiest way of getting rid of them. Bonnet took these men on board with the avowed intention of taking them to St. Thomas, and then he set sail upon the high seas as free and untrammelled as a fish-hawk sweeping over the surface of a harbour with clearance papers tied to his leg.

Stede Bonnet had changed very much since he last trod the quarterdeck of the Revenge as her captain. He was not so important to look at, and he put on fewer airs of authority, but he issued a great many more commands. In fact, he had learned much about a sailor's life, of navigation and the management of a vessel, and was far better able to command a ship than he had ever been before. He had had a long rest from the position of a pirate captain, and he had not failed to take advantage of the lessons which had been involuntarily given him by the veteran scoundrels who had held him in contempt. He was now, to a great extent, sailing-master as well as captain of the Revenge; but Ben Greenway, who was much given to that sort of thing, undertook to offer Bonnet some advice in regard to his course.

"I am no sailor," said he, "but I ken a chart when I see it, an' it is my opeenion that there is no need o' your sailin' so far to the east before ye turn about southward. There is naething much stickin' out from the coast between here an' St. Thomas."

Bonnet looked at the Scotchman with lofty contempt.

"Perhaps you can tell me," said he, "what there is stickin' out from the coast between here and Ocracoke Inlet, where you yourself told me that Blackbeard had gone with the one sloop he kept for himself?"

"Blackbeard!" shouted the Scotchman, "an' what in the de'il have ye got to do wi' Blackbeard?"

"Do with that infernal dog?" cried Bonnet, "I have everything to do with him before I do aught with anybody or anything besides. He stole from me my possessions, he degraded me from my position, he made me a laughing-stock to my men, and he even made me blush and bow my head with shame before my daughter and my brother-in-law, two people in whose sight I would have stood up grander and bolder than before any others in the world. He took away from me my sword and he gave me instead a wretched pen; he made me nothing where I had been everything. He even ceased to consider me any more than if I had been the dirty deck under his feet. And then, when he had done with my property and could get no more good out of it, he cast it to me in charity as a man would toss a penny to a beggar. Before I sail anywhere else, Ben Greenway," continued Bonnet, "I sail for Ocracoke Inlet, and when I sight Blackbeard's miserable little sloop I shall pour broadside after broadside into her until I sink his wretched craft with his bedizened carcass on board of it."

"But wi' your men stand by ye?" cried Greenway. "Ye're neither a pirate nor a vessel o' war to enter into a business like that."

Bonnet swore one of his greatest oaths. "There is no business nor war for me, Ben Greenway," he cried, "until I have taught that insolent Blackbeard what manner of man I am."

Ben Greenway was very much disheartened. "If Blackbeard should sink the Revenge instead of Master Bonnet sinking him," he said to himself, "and would be kind enough to maroon my old master an' me, it might be the best for everybody after all. Master Bonnet is vera humble-minded an' complacent when bad fortune comes upon him, an' it is my opeenion that on a desert island I could weel manage him for the good o' his soul."

But there were no vessels sunk on that cruise. Blackbeard had gone, nobody knew where, and after a time Bonnet gave up the search for his old enemy and turned his bow southward. Now Ben Greenway's countenance gleamed once more.

"It'll be a glad day at Spanish Town when Mistress Kate shall get my letter."

"And what have you been writing to her?" cried Bonnet.

"I told her," said Ben Greenway, "how at last ye hae come to your right mind, an' how ye are a true servant o' the king, wi' your pardon in your pocket an' your commission waitin' for ye at St. Thomas, an' that, whatever else ye may do at sea, there'll be no more black flag floatin' over your head, nor a see-saw plank wobblin' under the feet o' onybody else. The days o' your piracies are over, an' ye're an honest mon once more."

"You wrote her that?" said Bonnet, with a frown.

"Ay," said Greenway, "an' I left it in the care o' a good mon, whose ship is weel on its way to Kingston by this day."

That afternoon Captain Bonnet called all his men together and addressed them.

He made a very good speech, a better one than that delivered when he first took real command of the Revenge after sailing out of the river at Bridgetown, and it was listened to with respectful and earnest interest. In brief manner he explained to all on board that he had thrown to the winds all idea of merchandising or privateering; that his pardon and his ship's clearance were of no value to him except he should happen to get into some uncomfortable predicament with the law; that he had no idea of sailing towards St. Thomas, but intended to proceed up the coast to burn and steal and rob and slay wherever he might find it convenient to do so; that he had brought the greater part of his crew from the desert island where Blackbeard had left them because he knew that they were stout and reckless fellows, just the sort of men he wanted for the piratical cruise he was about to begin; and that, in order to mislead any government authorities who by land or sea might seek to interfere with him, he had changed the name of the good old Revenge to the Royal James, while its captain, once Stede Bonnet, was now to be known on board and everywhere else as Captain Thomas, with nothing against him. He concluded by saying that all that had been done on that ship from the time she first hoisted the black flag until the present moment was nothing at all compared to the fire and the blood and the booty which should follow in the wake of that gallant vessel, the Royal James, commanded by Captain Thomas.

The men looked at each other, but did not say much. They were all pirates, although few of them had regularly started out on a piratical career, and there was nothing new to them in this sort of piratical dishonour. In the little cruise after Blackbeard their new captain had shown himself to be a good man, ready with his oaths and very certain about what he wanted done. So, whenever Stede Bonnet chose to run up the Jolly Roger, he might do it for all they cared.

Poor Ben Greenway sat apart, his head bowed upon his hands.

"You seem to be in a bad case, old Ben," said Bonnet, gazing down upon him, "but you throw yourself into needless trouble. As soon as I lay hold of some craft which I am willing shall go away with a sound hull, I will put you on board of her and let you go back to the farm. I will keep you no longer among these wicked people, Ben Greenway, and in this wicked place."

Ben shook his head. "I started wi' ye an' I stay wi' ye," said he, "an' I'll follow ye to the vera gates o' hell, but farther than that, Master Bonnet, I willna go; at the gates o' hell I leave ye!"

XXXV

A Chapter of Happenings

For happiness with a flaw in it, it was a very fair happiness which now hung over the Delaplaine home near Spanish Town. Kate Bonnet's father was still a pirate, but there was no Captain Vince in hot pursuit of him, seeking his blood. Kate could sing with the birds and laugh with Dickory whenever she thought of the death of the wicked enemy. This was not, it may be thought, a proper joy for a young maiden's heart, but it came to Kate whether she would or not; the change was so great from the fear which had possessed her before.

The old home life began again, although it was a very quiet life. Dickory went into Mr. Delaplaine's counting-house, but it was hard for the young man to doff the naval uniform which had been bestowed upon him by Blackbeard, for he knew he looked very well in it, and everybody else thought so and told him so; but it could not be helped, and with all convenient speed he discarded his cocked hat and all the rest of it, and clothed himself in the simple garb of a merchant's clerk, although it might be said, that in all the West Indies, at that day, there was no clerk so good-looking as was Dickory. Dame Charter was so thankful that her boy had come safely through all his troubles, so proud of him, and so eminently well satisfied with his present position, that she asked nothing of her particular guardian angel but that Stede Bonnet might stay away. If, after tiring of piracy, that man came back, as his relatives wished him to do, the good dame was sure he would make mischief of some sort, and as like as not in the direction of her Dickory. If this evil family genius should be lost at sea or should disappear from the world in some equally painless and undisgraceful fashion, Dame Charter was sure that she could in a reasonable time quiet the grief of poor Kate; for what right-minded damsel could fail to mingle thankfulness with her sorrow that a kind death should relieve a parent from the sins and disgraces which in life always seemed to open up in front of him.

About this time there came a letter from Barbadoes, which was of great interest to everybody in the household. It was from Master Martin Newcombe, and of course was written to Kate, but she read many portions of it to the others. The first part of the epistle was not read aloud, but it was very pleasant for Kate to read it to herself. This man was a close lover and an ardent one. Whatever had happened to her fortunes, nothing had interfered with his affection; whatever he had said he still bravely stood by, and to whatever she had objected in the way of obstacles he had paid no attention whatever.

In the parts of the letter read to her uncle and the others, Master Newcombe told how, not having heard from them for so long, he had been beginning to be greatly troubled, but the arrival of the Black Swan, which, after touching at Kingston, had continued her course to Barbadoes, had given him new life and hope; and it was his intention, as soon as he could arrange his affairs, to come to Jamaica, and there say by word of mouth and do, in his own person, so much for which a letter was totally inadequate. The thought of seeing Kate again made him tremble as he walked through his fields. This was read inadvertently, and Dickory frowned. Dame Charter frowned too. She had never supposed that Master Newcombe would come to Spanish Town; she had always looked upon him as a very worthy young farmer; so worthy that he would not neglect his interest by travelling about to other islands than his own. She did not know exactly how her son felt about all this, nor did she like to ask him, but Dickory saved her the trouble.

"If that Newcombe comes here," he said, "I am going to fight him."

"What!" cried his mother. "You would not do that. That would be terrible; it would ruin everything."

"Ruin what?" he asked.

His mother answered diplomatically. "It would ruin all your fine opportunities in this family."

Dickory smiled with a certain sarcastic hardness. "I don't mean," said he, "that I am going to hack at him with a sword, because neither he nor I properly know how to use swords, and after the wonderful practice that I have seen, I would not want to prove myself a bungler even if the other man were a worse one. No, mother, I mean to fight with him by all fair means to gain the hand of my dear Kate. I love her, and I am far more worthy of her than he is. He is not a well-disposed man, being rough and inconsiderate in his speech." Dickory had never forgiven the interview by the river bank when he had gone to see Madam Bonnet. "And as to his being a stout lover, he is none of it. Had he been that, he would long ago have crossed the little sea between Barbadoes and here."

"Do you mean, you foolish boy," exclaimed Dame Charter, "to say that you presume to love our Mistress Kate?" And her eyes glowed upon him with all the warmth of a mother's pride, for this was the wish of her heart, and never absent from it.

"Ay, mother," said Dickory, "I shall fight for her; I shall show her that I am worthier than he is and that I love her better. I shall even strive for her if that mad pirate comes back and tries to overset everything."

"Oh, do it before that!" cried Dame Charter, anxiety in every wrinkle. "Do it before that!"

Mr. Delaplaine was a little troubled by the promised visit from Barbadoes. He had heard of Master Newcombe as being a most estimable young man, but the fault about him, in his opinion, was that he resided not in Jamaica. For a long time the good merchant had lived his own life, with no one to love him, and he now had with him his sister's child, whom he had come to look upon as a daughter, and he did not wish to give her up. It was true that it might be possible, under favourable pressure, to induce young Newcombe to come to Jamaica and settle there, but this was all very vague. Had he had his own way, he would have driven from Kate every thought of love or marriage until the time when his new clerk, Dickory Charter, had become a young merchant of good standing, worthy of such a wife. Then he might have been willing to give Kate to Dickory, and Dickory would have given her to him, and they might have all been happy. That is, if that hare-brained Bonnet did not come home.

The Delaplaine family did not go much into society at that time, for people had known about the pirate and his ship, the Revenge, and the pursuit upon which Captain Vince of the royal corvette Badger had been sent. They had all heard, too, of the death of Captain Vince, and some of them were not quite certain whether he had been killed by the pirate Bonnet or another desperado equally dangerous. Knowing all this, although if they had not known it they would scarcely have found it out from the speech of their neighbours, the Delaplaines kept much to themselves. And they were happy, and the keynote of their happiness was struck by Kate, whose thankful heart could never forget the death of Captain Vince.

Mr. Delaplaine made his proper visit to Spanish Town, to carry his thanks and to tell the Governor how things had happened to him; and the Governor still showed his interest in Mistress Kate Bonnet, and expressed his regret that she had not come with her uncle, which was a very natural wish indeed for a governor of good taste.

This is a chapter of happenings, and the next happening was a letter from that good man, Ben Greenway, and it told the most wonderful, splendid, and glorious news that had ever been told under the bright sun of the beautiful West Indies. It told that Captain Stede Bonnet was no longer a pirate, and that Kate was no longer a pirate's daughter. These happy people did not join hands and dance and sing over the great news, but Kate's joy was so great that she might have done all these things without knowing it, so thankful was she that once again she had a father. This rapture so far outshone her relief at the news of the death of Captain Vince that she almost forgot that that wicked man was safe and dead. Kate was in such a state of wild delight that she insisted that her uncle should make another visit to the Governor's house and take her with him, that she herself might carry the Governor the good news; and the Governor said such heart-warming things when he heard it that Kate kissed him in very joy. But as Dickory was not of the party, this incident was not entered as part of the proceedings.

Now society, both in Spanish Town and Kingston, opened its arms and insisted that the fair star of Barbadoes should enter them, and there were parties and dances and dinners, and it might have been supposed that everybody had been a father or a mother to a prodigal son, so genial and joyful were the festivities—Kate high above all others.

At some of these social functions Dickory Charter was present, but it is doubtful whether he was happier when he saw Kate surrounded by gay admirers or when he was at home imagining what was going on about her.

There was but one cloud in the midst of all this sunshine, and that was that Mr. Delaplaine, Dame Charter, and her son Dickory could not forget that it was now in the line of events that Stede Bonnet would soon be with them, and beyond that all was chaos.

And over the seas sailed the good ship the Royal James, Captain Thomas in command.

XXXVI

The Tide Decides

It was now September, and the weather was beautiful on the North Carolina coast. Captain Thomas (late Bonnet) of the Royal James (late Revenge) had always enjoyed cool nights and invigorating morning air, and therefore it was that he said to his faithful servitor, Ben Greenway, when first he stepped out upon the deck as his vessel lay comfortably anchored in a little cove in the Cape Fear River, that he did not remember ever having been in a more pleasant harbour. This well-tried pirate captain—Stede Bonnet, as we shall call him, notwithstanding his assumption of another name—was in a genial mood as he drank in the morning air.

From his point of view he had a right to be genial; he had a right to be pleased with the scenery and the air; he had a right to swear at the Scotchman, and to ask him why he did not put on a merrier visage on such a sparkling morning, for since he had first started out as Captain Thomas of the Royal James he had been a most successful pirate. He had sailed up the Virginia coast; he had burned, he had sunk, he had robbed, he had slain; he had gone up the Delaware Bay, and the people in ships and the people on the coasts trembled even when they heard that his black flag had been sighted.

No man could now say that the former captain of the Revenge was not an accomplished and seasoned desperado. Even the great Blackbeard would not have cared to give him nicknames, nor dared to play his blithesome tricks upon him; he was now no more Captain Nightcap to any man. His crew of hairy ruffians had learned to understand that he knew what he wanted, and, more than that, he knew how to order it done. They listened to his great oaths and they respected him. This powerful pirate now commanded a small fleet, for in the cove where lay his flag-ship also lay two good-sized sloops, manned by their own crews, which he had captured in Delaware Bay and had brought down with him to this quiet spot, a few miles up the Cape Fear River, where now he was repairing his own ship, which had had a hard time of it since she had again come into his hands.

For many a long day the sound of the hammer and the saw had mingled with the song of the birds, and Captain Bonnet felt that in a day or two he might again sail out upon the sea, conveying his two prizes to some convenient mart, while he, with his good ship, freshened and restored, would go in search of more victories, more booty, and more blood.

"Greenway, I tell you," said Bonnet, continuing his remarks, "you are too glum; you've got the only long face in all this, my fleet. Even those poor fellows who man my prizes are not so solemn, although they know not, when I have done with them, whether I shall maroon them to quietly starve or shall sink them in their own vessels."

"But I hae no such reason to be cheerful," said Ben. "I hae bound mysel' to stand by ye till ye hae gone to the de'il, an' I hae no chance o' freein' mysel' from my responsibeelities by perishin' on land or in the sea."

"If anything could make me glum, Ben Greenway, it would be you," said the other; "but I am getting used to you, and some of these days when I have captured a ship laden with Scotch liquors and Scotch plaids I believe that you will turn pirate yourself for the sake of your share of the prizes."

"Which is likely to be on the same mornin' that ye turn to be an honest mon," said Ben; "but I am no' in the way o' expectin' miracles."

On went the pounding and the sawing and the hammering and the swearing and the singing of birds, although the latter were a little farther away than they had been, and in the course of the day the pirate captain, erect, scrutinizing, and blasphemous, went over his ship, superintending the repairs. In a day or two everything would be finished, and then he and his two prizes could up sail and away. It was a beautiful harbour in which he lay, but he was getting tired of it.

There were great prospects before our pirate captain. Perhaps he might have the grand good fortune to fall in with that low-born devil, Blackbeard, who, when last he had been heard from, commanded but a small vessel, fearing no attack upon this coast. What a proud and glorious moment it would be when a broadside and another and another should be poured in upon his little craft from the long guns of the Royal James.

Bonnet was still standing, reflecting, with bright eyes, upon this dazzling future, and wondering what would be the best way of letting the dastardly Blackbeard know whose guns they were which had sunk

FRANK R. STOCKTON

his ship, when a boat was seen coming around the headland. This was one of his own boats, which had been posted as a sentinel, and which now brought the news that two vessels were coming in at the mouth of the river, but that as the distance was great and the night was coming on they could not decide what manner of craft they were.

This information made everybody jump, on board the Royal James, and the noise of the sawing and the hammering ceased as completely as had the songs of the birds. In a few minutes that quick and able mariner, Bonnet, had sent three armed boats down the river to reconnoitre. If the vessels entering the river were merchantmen, they should not be allowed to get away; but if they were enemies, although it was difficult to understand how enemies could make their appearance in these quiet waters, they must be attended to, either by fight or flight.

When the three boats came back, and it was late before they appeared, every man upon the Royal James was crowded along her side to hear the news, and even the people on the prizes knew that something had happened, and stood upon every point of vantage, hoping that in some way they could find out what it was.

The news brought by the boats was to the effect that two vessels, not sailing as merchantmen and well armed and manned, were now ashore on sand-bars, not very far above the mouth of the river. Now Bonnet swore bravely. If the work upon his vessels had been finished he would up anchor and away and sail past these two grounded ships, whatever they were and whatever they came for. He would sail past them and take with him his two prizes; he would glide out to sea with the tide, and he would laugh at them as he left them behind. But the Royal James was not ready to sail.

The tide was now low; five hours afterward, when it should be high, those two ships, whatever they were, would float again, and the Royal James, whatever her course of action should be, would be cut off from the mouth of the river. This was a greater risk than even a pirate as bold as Bonnet would wish to run, and so there was no sleep that night on the Royal James. The blows of the hammers and the sounds of the saws made a greater noise than they had ever done before, so that the night birds were frightened and flew shrieking away. Every man worked with all the energy that was in him, for each hairy rascal had reason to believe that if the vessel they were on did not get out of the river before the two armed strangers should be afloat there might be hard times ahead for them. Even Ben Greenway was aroused. "The de'il shall not get him any sooner than can be helped," he said to himself, and he hammered and sawed with the rest of them.

On his stout and well-armed sloop the Henry, Mr. William Rhett, of Charles Town, South Carolina, paced anxiously all night. Frequently from the sand-bar on which his vessel was grounded he called over to his other sloop, also fast grounded, giving orders and asking questions. On both vessels everybody was at work, getting ready for action when the tide should rise.

Some weeks before the wails and complaints of a tortured sea-coast had come down from the Jersey shores to South Carolina, asking for help at the only place along that coast whence help could come. A pirate named Thomas was working his way southward, spreading terror before him and leaving misery behind. These appeals touched the hearts of the people of Charles Town, already sore from the injuries and insults inflicted upon them by Blackbeard in those days when Bonnet sat silently on the pirate ship, doing nothing and learning much.

There was no hesitancy; for their own sake and for the sake of their commerce, this new pirate must not come to Charles Town harbour, and an expedition of two vessels, heavily armed and well manned and commanded by Mr. William Rhett, was sent northward up the coast to look for the pirate named Thomas and to destroy him and his ship. Mr. Rhett was not a military man, nor did he belong to the navy. He was a citizen capable of commanding soldiers, and as such he went forth to destroy the pirate Thomas.

Mr. Rhett met people enough along the coast who told him where he might find the pirate, but he found no one to tell him how to navigate the dangerous waters of the Cape Fear River, and so it was that soon after entering that fine stream he and his consort found themselves aground.

Mr. Rhett was quite sure that he had discovered the lair of the big game he was looking for. Just before dark, three boats, well filled with men, had appeared from up the river, and they had looked so formidable that everything had been made ready to resist an attack from them. They retired, but every now and then during the night, when there was quiet for a few minutes, there would come down the river on the wind the sound of distant hammering and the noise of saws.

It was after midnight before the Henry and the Sea Nymph floated free, but they anchored where they were and waited for the morning.

Whether they would sail up the river after the pirate or whether he would come down to them, daylight would show.

Mr. Rhett's vessels had been at anchor for five hours, and every man on board of them were watching and waiting, when daylight appeared and showed them a tall ship, under full sail, rounding the distant headland up the river. Now up came their anchors and their sails were set. The pirate was coming!

Whatever the Royal James intended to do, Mr. Rhett had but one plan, and that was to meet the enemy as soon as possible and fight him. So up sailed the Henry and up sailed the Sea Nymph, and they pressed ahead so steadily to meet the Royal James that the latter vessel, in carrying out what was now her obvious intention of getting out to sea, was forced shoreward, where she speedily ran upon a bar. Then, from the vessels of Charles Town there came great shouts of triumph, which ceased when first the Henry and then the Sea Nymph ran upon other bars and remained stationary.

Here was an unusual condition—three ships of war all aground and about to begin a battle, a battle which would probably last for five hours if one or more of the stationary vessels were not destroyed before that time. It was soon found, however, that there would only be two parties to the fight, for the Sea Nymph was too far away to use her guns. The Royal James had an advantage over her opponents, since, when she slightly careened, her decks were slanted away from the enemy, while the latter's were presented to her fire.

At it they went, hot and heavy. Bonnet and his men now knew that they were engaged with commissioned war vessels, and they fought for their lives. Mr. Rhett knew that he was fighting Thomas, the dreaded pirate of the coast, and he felt that he must destroy him before his vessel should float again. The cannon roared, muskets blazed away, and the combatants were near enough even to use pistols upon each other. Men died, blood flowed, and the fight grew fiercer and fiercer.

Bonnet roared like an incarnate devil; he swore at his men, he swore at the enemy, he swore at his bad fortune, for had he not missed the channel the game would have been in his own hands.

So on they fought, and the tide kept steadily rising. The five hours must pass at last, and the vessel which first floated would win the day.

The five hours did pass, and the Henry floated, and Bonnet swore louder and more fiercely than before. He roared to his men to fire and to fight, no matter whether they were still aground or not, and with many oaths he vowed that if any one of them showed but a sign of weakening he would cut him down upon the spot. But the hairy scoundrels who made up the crew of the Royal James had no idea of lying there with their ship on its side, while two other ships—for the Sea Nymph was now afloat—should sail around them, rake their decks, and shatter them to pieces. So the crew consulted together, despite their captain's roars and oaths, and many of them counselled surrender. Their vessel was much farther inshore than the two others, and no matter what happened afterward they preferred to live longer than fifteen or twenty minutes.

But Bonnet quailed not before fate, before the enemy, or before his crew; if he heard another word of surrender he would fire the magazine and blow the ship to the sky with every man in it. Raising his cutlass in air, he was about to bring it down upon one of the cowards he berated, when suddenly he was seized by two powerful hands, which pinned his arms behind him. With a scream of rage, he turned his head and found that he was in the grasp of Ben Greenway.

"Let go your sword, Master Bonnet," said Ben; "it is o' no use to ye now, for ye canna get awa' from me. I'm nae older than ye are, though I look it, an' I've got the harder muscles. Ye may be makin' your way steadily an' surely to the gates o' hell an' it mayna be possible that I can prevent ye, but I'm not goin' to let ye tumble in by accident so long as I've got two arms left to me."

Pale, haggard, and writhing, Stede Bonnet was disarmed, and the Jolly Roger came down.

XXXVII

Bonnet and Greenway Part Company

It was three days after this memorable combat—for the vessels engaged in it needed considerable repairs—when Mr. Rhett of Charles Town sailed down the Cape Fear River with his five vessels—the two with which he had entered it, the pirate Royal James, and the two prizes of the latter, which had waited quietly up the river to see how matters were going to turn out.

On the Henry sailed the pirate Thomas, now discovered to be the notorious Stede Bonnet, and a very quiet and respectful man he was. As has been seen before, Bonnet was a man able to adapt himself to circumstances. There never was a more demure counting-house clerk than was Bonnet at Belize; there never was an humbler dependent than the almost unnoticed Bonnet after he had joined Blackbeard's fleet before Charles Town, and there never was a more deferential and respectful prisoner than Stede Bonnet on board the Henry. It was really touching to see how this cursing and raging pirate deported himself as a meek and uncomplaining gentleman.

There was no prison-house in Charles Town, but Stede Bonnet's wicked crew, including Ben Greenway—for his captors were not making any distinctions in regard to common men taken on a pirate ship—were clapped into the watch-house—and a crowded and uncomfortable place it was—and put under a heavy and military guard. The authorities were, however, making distinctions where gentlemen of family and owners of landed estates were concerned, no matter if they did happen to be taken on a pirate ship, and Major Bonnet of Barbadoes was lodged in the provost marshal's house, in comfortable quarters, with only two sentinels outside to make him understand he was a prisoner.

The capture of this celebrated pirate created a sensation in Charles Town, and many of the citizens were not slow to pay the unfortunate prisoner the attentions due to his former position in society. He was very well satisfied with his treatment in Charles Town, which city he had never before had the pleasure of visiting.

The attentions paid to Ben Greenway were not pleasing; sometimes he was shoved into one corner and sometimes into another. He frequently had enough to eat and drink, but very often this was not the case. Bonnet never inquired after him. If he thought of him at all, he hoped that he had been killed in the fight, for if that were the case he would be rid of his eternal preachments.

Greenway made known the state of his own case whenever he had a chance to do so, but his complaints received no attention, and he might have remained with the crew of the Royal James as long as they were shut up in the watch-house had not some of the hairy cut-throats themselves taken pity upon him and assured the guards that this man was not one of them, and that they knew from what they had heard him say and seen him do that there was no more determined enemy of piracy in all the Western continent. So it happened, that after some weeks of confinement Greenway was let out of the watch-house and allowed to find quarters for himself.

The first day the Scotchman was free he went to the provost-marshal's house and petitioned an interview with his old master, Bonnet.

"Heigho!" cried the latter, who was comfortably seated in a chair reading a letter. "And where do you come from, Ben Greenway? I had thought you were dead and buried in the Cape Fear River."

"Ye did not think I was dead," replied Ben, "when I seized ye an' held ye an' kept ye from buryin' yoursel' in that same river."

Bonnet waved his hand. "No more of that," said he; "I was unfortunate, but that is over now and things have turned out better than any man could have expected."

"Better!" exclaimed Ben. "I vow I know not what that means."

Bonnet laughed. He was looking very well; he was shaved, and wore a neat suit of clothes.

"Ben Greenway," said he, "you are now looking upon a man of high distinction. At this moment I am the greatest pirate on the face of the earth. Yes, Greenway, the greatest pirate on the face of the earth. I have a letter here, which was received by the provost-marshal and which he gave me to read, which tells that Blackbeard, the first pirate of his age, is dead. Therefore, Ben Greenway, I take his place, and there is no living pirate greater than I am."

"An' ye pride yoursel' on that, an' at this moment?" asked Ben, truly amazed.

"That do I," said Bonnet. "And think of it, Ben Greenway, that presumptuous, overbearing Blackbeard was killed, and his head brought away sticking up on the bow of a vessel. What a rare sight that must have been, Ben! Think of his long beard, all tied up with ribbons, stuck up on the bow of a ship!"

"An' ye are now the head de'il on earth?" said Ben.

"You can put it that way, if you like," said Bonnet, "but I am not so looked upon in this town. I am an honoured person. I doubt very much if any prisoner in this country was ever treated with the distinction that is shown me, but I don't wonder at it; I have the reputation of two great pirates joined in one—the pirate Bonnet, of the dreaded ship Revenge, and the terrible Thomas of the Royal James. My man, there are people in this town who have been to me and who have said that a man so famous should not even be imprisoned. I have good reason to believe that it will not be long before pardon papers are made out for me, and that I may go my way."

"An' your men?" asked Greenway. "Will they go free or will they be hung like common pirates?"

Bonnet frowned impatiently. "I don't want to hear anything about the men," he said; "of course they will be hung. What could be done with them if they were not hung? But it is entirely different with me. I am a most respectable person, and, now that I am willing to resign my piratical career, having won in it all the glory that can come to one man, that respectability must be considered."

"Weel, weel," said the Scotchman; "an' when it comes that respectabeelity is better for a man's soul an' body than righteousness, then I am no fit counsellor for ye, Master Bonnet," and he took his leave.

The next morning, when Ben Greenway left his lodging he found the town in an uproar. The pirate Bonnet had bribed his sentinels and, with some others, had escaped. Ben stood still and stamped his foot. Such infamy, such perfidy to the authorities who had treated him so well, the Scotchman could not at first imagine, but when the truth became plain to him, his face glowed, his eye burned; this vile conduct of his old master was a triumph to Ben's principles. Wickedness was wickedness, and could not be washed away by respectability.

The days passed on; Bonnet was recaptured, more securely imprisoned, put upon trial, found guilty, and, in spite of the efforts of the advocates of respectability, was condemned to be hung on the same spot where nearly all the members of his pirate crew had been executed.

During all this time Ben Greenway kept away from his old master; he had borne ill-treatment of every kind, but the deception practised upon him when, at his latest interview, Bonnet talked to him of his respectability, having already planned an escape and return to his evil ways, was too much for the honest Scotchman. He had done with this man, faithless to friend and foe, to his own blood, and even to his own bad reputation.

But not quite done. It was but half an hour before the time fixed for the pirate's execution that Ben Greenway gained access to him.

"What!" cried Bonnet, raising his head from his hands. "You here? I thought I had done with you!"

"Ay, I am here," said Ben Greenway. "I hae stood by ye in good fortune an' in bad fortune, an' I hae never left ye, no matter what happened; an' I told ye I would follow ye to the gates o' hell, but I could go no farther. I hae kept my word an' here I stop. Fareweel!"

"The only comfortable thing about this business," said Bonnet, "is to know that at last I am rid of that fellow!"

XXXVIII

AGAIN DICKORY WAS THERE

There were indeed gay times in Spanish Town, and with the two loads lifted from her heart, Kate helped very much to promote the gaiety. If this young lady had wished to make a good colonial match, she had opportunities enough for so doing, but she was not in that frame of mind, and encouraged no suitor.

But, bright as she was, she was not so bright as on that great and glorious day when she received Ben Greenway's letter, telling her that her father was no longer a pirate. There were several reasons for this gradually growing twilight of her happiness, and one was that no letter came from her father. To be sure, there were many reasons why no letter should come. There were no regular mails in these colonies which could be depended upon, and, besides, the new career of her father, sailing as a privateer under the king's flag, would probably make it very difficult for him to send a letter to Jamaica by any regular or irregular method. Moreover, her father was a miserable correspondent, and always had been. Thus she comforted herself and was content, though not very well content, to wait.

Then there was another thing which troubled her, when she thought of it. That good man and steady lover, Martin Newcombe, had written that he was coming to Spanish Town, and she knew very well what he was coming for and what he would say, but she did not know what she would say to him; and the thought of this troubled her. In a letter she might put off the answer for which he had been so long and patiently waiting, but when she met him face to face there could be no more delay; she must tell him yes or no, and she was not ready to do this.

There was so much to think of, so many plans to be considered in regard to going back to Barbadoes or staying in Jamaica, that really she could not make up her mind, at least not until she had seen her father. She would be so sorry if Mr. Newcombe came to Spanish Town before her father should arrive, or at least before she should hear from him.

Then there was another thing which added to the twilight of these cheerful days, and this Kate could scarcely understand, because she could see no reason why it should affect her. The Governor, whom they frequently met in the course of the pleasant social functions of the town, looked troubled, and was not the genial gentleman he used to be. Of course he had a right to his own private perplexities and annoyances, but it grieved Kate to see the change in him. He had always been so cordial and so cheerful; he was now just as kind as ever, perhaps a little more so, in his manner, but he was not cheerful.

Kate mentioned to her uncle the changed demeanour of the Governor, but he could give no explanation; he had heard of no political troubles, but supposed that family matters might easily have saddened the good man.

He himself was not very cheerful, for day after day brought nearer the time when that uncertain Stede Bonnet might arrive in Jamaica, and what would happen after that no man could tell. One thing he greatly feared, and that was, that his dear niece, Kate, might be taken away from him. Dame Charter was not so very cheerful either. Only in one way did she believe in Stede Bonnet, and that was, that after some fashion or another he would come between her and her bright dreams for her dear Dickory.

And so there were some people in Spanish Town who were not as happy as they had been.

Still there were dinners and little parties, and society made itself very pleasant; and in the midst of them all a ship came in from Barbadoes, bringing a letter from Martin Newcombe.

A strange thing about this letter was that it was addressed to Mr. Delaplaine and not to Miss Kate Bonnet. This, of course, proved the letter must be on business; and, although he was with his little family when he opened his letter, he thought it well to glance at it before reading it aloud. The first few lines showed him that it was indeed a business letter, for it told of the death of Madam Bonnet, and how the writer, Martin Newcombe, as a neighbour and friend of the family, had been called in to take temporary charge of her effects, and, having done so, he hastened to inform Mr. Delaplaine of his proceedings and to ask advice. This letter he now read aloud, and Kate and the others were greatly interested therein, although they cautiously forbore the expression of any opinion which might rise in their minds regarding this turn of affairs.

Having finished these business details, Mr. Delaplaine went on and read aloud, and in the succeeding portion of the letter Mr. Newcombe begged Mr. Delaplaine to believe that it was the hardest duty of his whole life to write what he was now obliged to write, but that he knew he must do it, and therefore would not hesitate. At this the reader looked at his niece and stopped.

"Go on," cried Kate, her face a little flushed, "go on!"

The face of Mr. Delaplaine was pale, and for a moment he hesitated, then, with a sudden jerk, he nerved himself to the effort and read on; he had seen enough to make him understand that the duty before him was to read on.

BRIEFLY AND TERSELY, BUT WITH tears in the very ink, so sad were the words, the writer assured Mr. Delaplaine that his love for his niece had been, and was, the overpowering impulse of his life; that to win this love he had dared everything, he had hoped for everything, he had been willing to pass by and overlook everything, but that now, and it tore his heart to write it, his evil fortune had been too much for him; he could do anything for the sake of his love that a man with respect for himself could do, but there was one thing at which he must stop, at which he must bow his head and submit to his fate—he could not marry the daughter of an executed felon.

Thus came to that little family group the news of the pirate Bonnet's death. There was more of the letter, but Mr. Delaplaine did not read it.

Kate did not scream, nor moan, nor faint, but she sat up straight in her chair and gazed, with a wild intentness, at her uncle. No one spoke. At such a moment condolence or sympathy would have been a cruel mockery. They were all as pale as chalk. In his heart, Mr. Delaplaine said: "I see it all; the Governor must have known, and he loved her so he could not break her heart."

In the midst of the silence, in the midst of the chalky whiteness of their faces, in the midst of the blackness which was settling down upon them, Kate Bonnet still sat upright, a coldness creeping through every part of her. Suddenly she turned her head, and in a voice of wild entreaty she called out: "Oh, Dickory, why don't you come to me!"

In an instant Dickory was there, and, cold and lifeless, Kate Bonnet was in his arms.

XXXIX

The Blessings Which Come From the Death of the Wicked

It was three weeks after Martin Newcombe's letter came before Ben Greenway arrived in Spanish Town. He had had a hard time to get there, having but little money and no friends to help him; but he had a strong heart and an earnest, and so he was bound to get there at last; and, although Kate saw no visitors, she saw him. She was not dressed in mourning; she could not wear black for herself.

She greeted the Scotchman with earnestness; he was a friend out of the old past, but she gave him no chance to speak first.

"Ben," she exclaimed, "have you a message for me?"

"No message," he replied, "but I hae somethin' on my heart I wish to say to ye. I hae toiled an' laboured an' hae striven wi' mony obstacles to get to ye an' to say it."

She looked at him, with her brows knit, wondering if she should allow him to speak; then, with the words scarcely audible between her tightly closed lips, she said: "Ben, what is it?"

"It is this, an' no more nor less," replied the Scotchman; "he was never fit to be your father, an' it is not fit now for ye to remember him as your father. I was faithful to him to the vera last, but there was no truth in him. It is an abomination an' a wickedness for ye to remember him as your father!"

Kate spoke no word, nor did she shed a tear.

"It was my heart's desire ye should know it," said the Scotchman, "an' I came mony a weary league to tell ye so."

"Ben," said she, "I think I have known it for a long time, but I would not suffer myself to believe it; but now, having heard your words, I am sure of it."

"Uncle," said she an hour afterward, "I have no father, and I never had one."

With tears in his eyes he folded her to his breast, and peace began to rise in his soul. No greater blessing can come to really good people than the absolute disappearance of the wicked.

And the wickedness which had so long shadowed and stained the life of Kate Bonnet was now removed from it. It was hard to get away from the shadow and to wipe off the stain, but she was a brave girl and she did it.

In this work of her life—a work which if not accomplished would make that life not worth the living—Kate was much helped by Dickory; and he helped her by not saying a word about it or ever allowing himself, when in her presence, to remember that there had been a shadow or a stain. And if he thought of it at all when by himself, his only feeling was one of thankfulness that what had happened had given her to him.

Even the Governor brightened. He had striven hard to keep from Kate the news which had come to him from Charles Town, suppressing it in the hopes that it might reach her more gradually and with less terrible effect than if he told it, but now that he knew that she knew it the blessings which are shed abroad by the disappearance of the wicked affected him also, and he brightened. There were no functions for Kate, but she brightened, striving with all her soul to have this so, for her own sake as well as that of others. As for Mr. Delaplaine, Dame Charter, and Dickory, they brightened without any trouble at all, the disappearance of the wicked having such a direct and forcible effect upon them.

Dickory Charter, who matured in a fashion which made everybody forget that Kate Bonnet was eleven months his senior, entered into business with Mr. Delaplaine, and Jamaica became the home of this happy family, whose welfare was founded, as on a rock, upon the disappearance of the wicked.

Here, then, was a brave girl who had loved her father with a love which was more than that of a daughter, which was the love of a mother, of a wife; who had loved him in prosperity and in times of sorrow and of shame; who had rejoiced like an angel whenever he turned his footsteps into the right way, and who had mourned like an angel whenever he went wrong. She had longed to throw her arms around her father's neck, to hold him to her, and thus keep off the hangman's noose. Her courage and affection never waned until those arms were rudely thrust aside and their devoted owner dastardly repulsed.

True to herself and to him, she loved her father so long as there was anything parental in him which she might love; and, true to herself, when he had left her nothing she might love, she bowed her head and suffered him, as he passed out of his life, to pass out of her own.

XL

Captain Ichabod Puts the Case

In the river at Bridgetown lay the good brig King and Queen, just arrived from Jamaica. On her deck was an impatient young gentleman, leaning over the rail and watching the approach of a boat, with two men rowing and a passenger in the stern.

This impatient young man was Dickory Charter, that morning arrived at Bridgetown and not yet having been on shore. He came for the purpose of settling some business affairs, partly on account of Miss Kate Bonnet and partly for his mother.

As the boat came nearer, Dickory recognised one of the men who were rowing and hailed him.

"Heigho! Tom Hilyer," he cried, "I am right glad to see you on this river again. I want a boat to go to my mother's house; know you of one at liberty?"

The man ceased rowing for a moment and then addressed the passenger in the stern, who, having heard what he had to say, nodded briefly.

"Well, well, Dick Charter!" cried out the man, "and have you come back as governor of the colony? You look fine enough, anyway. But if you want a boat to go to your mother's old home, you can have a seat in this one; we're going there, and our passenger does not object."

"Pull up here," cried Dickory, and in a moment he had dropped into the bow of the boat, which then proceeded on its way.

The man in the stern was fairly young, handsome, sunburned, and well dressed in a suit of black. When Dickory thanked him for allowing him to share his boat the passenger in the stern nodded his head with a jerk and an air which indicated that he took the incident as a matter of course, not to be further mentioned or considered.

The men who rowed the boat were good oarsmen, but they were not thoroughly acquainted with the cove, especially at low tide, and presently they ran upon a sand-bar. Then uprose the passenger in the stern and began to swear with an ease and facility which betokened long practice. Dickory did not swear, but he knit his brows and berated himself for not having taken the direction of the course into his own hands, he who knew the river and the cove so well. The tide was rising but Dickory was too impatient to sit still and wait until it should be high enough to float the boat. That was his old home, that little house at the head of the cove, and he wanted to get there, he wanted to see it. Part of the business which brought him to Barbadoes concerned that little house. With a sudden movement he made a dive at his shoes and stockings and speedily had them lying at the bottom of the boat. Then he stepped overboard and waded towards the shore. In some of the deeper places he wetted the bottom of his breeches, but he did not mind that. The passenger in the stern sat down, but he continued to swear.

Presently Dickory was on the dry sand, and running up to that cottage door. A little back from the front of the house and in the shade there was a bench, and on this bench there sat a girl, reading. She lifted her head in surprise as Dickory approached, for his bare feet had made no noise, then she stood up quickly, blushing.

"You!" she exclaimed.

"Yes," cried Dickory; "and you look just the same as when you first put your head above the bushes and talked to me."

"Except that I am more suitably clothed," she said.

And she was entirely right, for her present dress was feminine, and extremely becoming.

Dickory did not wish to say anything more on this subject, and so he remarked: "I have just arrived at the town, and I came directly here."

Lucilla blushed again.

"This is my old home," added Dickory.

"But you knew we were here?" she asked, with a hesitating look of inquiry.

"Oh, yes," said he, "I knew that the house had been let to your father."

Now she changed colour twice—first red, then white. "Are you," she said, "I mean. . . the other, is she—"

"I left her in Jamaica," said Dickory, "but I am going to marry her."

For a moment the rim of her hat got between the sun and her face, and one could not decide very well whether her countenance was red or white.

"I am very glad to find you here," said Dickory, "and may I see your father and mother?"

"Yes," said she, "but they are both in the field with my young sister. But who is this man walking up the shore? And is that the boat you came in?"

"It is," said Dickory. "We stuck fast, but I was in such a hurry that I waded ashore. I don't know the man; he had hired the boat, and kindly took me in, I was in such haste to get here."

For a moment Lucilla bent her eyes on the ground. "In such haste to get here!" she said to herself; then she raised her head and exclaimed: "Oh, I know that man; he is the pirate captain who captured the Belinda, which afterward brought us here." And with both hands outstretched, she ran to meet him.

The face of Captain Ichabod glowed with irrepressible delight; one might have thought he was about to embrace the young woman, notwithstanding the presence of Dickory and the two boatmen, but he did everything he could do before witnesses to express his joy.

Dickory now stepped up to Captain Ichabod. "Oh, now I know you," cried he, and he held out his hand. "You were very kind indeed to my friends, and they have spoken much about you. This is my old home; this is the house where I was born."

"Yes, yes, indeed," said Captain Ichabod, "a very good house, bedad, a very good house." But hesitating a little and addressing Lucilla: "You don't live here alone, do you?"

The girl laughed.

"Oh, no," she cried. "My father and mother will be here presently; in fact, I see them coming."

"That's very well," said Ichabod, "very well indeed. It's quite right that they should live with you. I remember them now; they were on the ship with you."

"Oh, yes," said Lucilla, still laughing.

"Quite right, quite right," said Ichabod; "that was very right."

"I will go meet your father and mother and the dear little Lena; I remember them so well," said Dickory. He started to run off in spite of his bare feet, but he had gone but a little way when Lucilla stopped him. She looked up at him, and this time her face was white.

"Are you sure," said she, "that everything is settled between you and that other girl?"

"Very sure," said Dickory, looking kindly upon her and remembering how pretty she had looked when he first saw her face over the bushes.

She did not say anything, but turned and walked back to Captain Ichabod. She found that tall gentleman somewhat agitated; he seemed to have a great deal on his mind which he wished to say, feeling, at the same time, that he ought to say everything first.

FRANK R. STOCKTON

"That's your father and mother," said he, "stopping to talk to the young man who was born here?"

"Yes," she answered, "and they will be with us presently."

"Very good, very good, that's quite right," said Captain Ichabod hurriedly; "but before they come, I want to say—that is, I would like you to know—that I have sold my ship. I am not a pirate any longer, I am a sugar-planter, bedad. Beg your pardon! That is, I intend to be one. You remember that you once talked to me about sugar-planting in Barbadoes, and so I am here. I want to find a good sugar plantation, to buy it, and live on it; I heard that you were stopping on this side of the river, and so I came here."

"But there is no sugar plantation here," said Lucilla, very demurely.

"Oh, no," said Ichabod, "oh, no, of course not; but you are here, and I wanted to find you; a sugar plantation would be of no use without you."

She looked at him, still very demurely. "I don't quite understand you," she said. She turned her head a little and saw that her family and Dickory were slowly moving towards the house. She knew that with diffident persons no time should be lost, for, if interrupted, it often happened that they did not begin again.

"Then I suppose," she said, her face turned up towards him, but her eyes cast down, "that you are going to say that you would like to marry me?"

"Of course, of course," exclaimed Ichabod; "I thought you knew that that is what I came here for, bedad."

"Very well, then," said Lucilla, turning her eyes to the face of the man she had dreamed of in many happy nights. "No, no," she added quickly, "you must not kiss me; they are all coming, and there are the two boatmen."

He did not kiss her, but later he made up for the omission.

The moment Mrs. Mander saw Captain Ichabod and her daughter standing together she knew exactly what had happened; she had noticed things on board the Belinda. She hurried up to Lucilla and drew her aside.

"My dear," she whispered, with a frightened face, "you cannot marry a pirate; you never, never can!"

"Dear mother," said Lucilla, "he is not a pirate; he has sold his ship and is going to be a sugar-planter."

Now they all came up and heard these words of Lucilla.

"Yes, indeed," said Captain Ichabod, "you may not suppose it, but your daughter and I are about to marry, and will plant sugar together. Now, I want to buy a plantation. Where is that young man who was born here, bedad?"

Dickory advanced, laughing. Here was a fine opportunity, a miraculous opportunity, of disposing of the Bonnet estate, which was part of the business which had brought him here. So he told the beaming captain that he knew of a fine plantation up the river, which he thought would suit him.

"Very good," said Captain Ichabod. "I have a boat here; let us go and look at the place, and if it suits us I will buy it, bedad."

So with Mrs. Mander and her husband beside her, and with Lucilla and the captain by her, the boat was rowed up the river, with Dickory and young Lena in the bow.

When the boat reached the Bonnet estate it was run up on the shore near the shady spot where Kate Bonnet had once caught a fish. Then they all stepped out upon the little beach, even the oarsmen made the boat fast and joined the party, who started to walk up to the house. Suddenly Captain Ichabod stopped and said to Mr. Mander: "I don't think I care to walk up that hill, you know; and if you and your good wife will look over that house and cast your eyes about the place, I will buy it, if you say so: you know a good deal more about such things than I do, bedad. I suppose, of course, that will suit you?" he said to Lucilla.

It suited Lucilla exactly. They sat in the shade in the very place where Kate had sat when she saw Master Newcombe crossing the bridge.

A small boat came down the river, rowed by a young man. As he passed the old Bonnet property he carelessly cast his eyes shoreward, but his heart took no interest in what he saw there. What did it matter to him if two lovers sat there in the shade, close to the river's brink? His sad soul now took no interest in lovers. He had just been up the river to arrange for the sale of his plantation to one of his neighbours. He had decided to leave the island of Barbadoes and to return to England.

The house suited Captain Ichabod exactly, when Mrs. Mander told him about it, and Lucilla agreed with him because she was always accustomed to trust her mother in such things.

So they all got into the boat and rowed back to Dickory's old home, and on the way Captain Ichabod told Dickory that when they returned together to the town he would pay him for the plantation, having brought specie sufficient for the purpose.

It was a gay party in the boat as they rowed down the river; it was a gay party at the house when they reached it, and they would have all taken supper together had the Manders been prepared for such hospitality; but they were poor, having taken the place upon a short lease and having had but few returns so far. But they were all going to live at the old Bonnet place, and happiness shone over everything. It was twilight, and the two young men were about to walk down to the boat, one of them promising to come again early in the morning, when Lucilla approached Dickory.

"Where are you going to live with that girl?" she asked in a low voice.

"In Jamaica," said he.

"I am glad of it," she replied, quite frankly.

THEY WERE WELL CONTENT, THOSE Jamaica people, when Ben Greenway came to live with them. It had been proposed at one time that he should go to his old Bridgetown home and take charge of the place as he used to, but the good Scotchman demurred to this.

"I hae served ane master before he became a pirate," he said, "an' I don't want to try anither after he has finished bein' ane. If I serve ony mon, let him be one wha has been righteous, wha is righteous now, an' wha will continue in righteousness."

"Then serve Mr. Delaplaine," said Dickory.

THE MANDERS SOON REMOVED TO the little house where Dickory was born. The mansion of their daughter and her husband was a hospitable place and a lively, but the life there was so wayward, erratic, and eccentric that it did not suit their sober lives and the education of their young daughter. So they dwelt contentedly in the cottage at the head of the cove, and there was much rowing up and down the river.

IT WAS UPON A FINE morning that the ex-pirate Ichabod thus addressed a citizen of the town:

"Yes, sir, I know well who once lived in the house I own. I knew the man myself; I knew him at Belize. He was a dastardly knave, and would have played false to the sun, the moon, and the stars had they shown him an opportunity, bedad. But I also knew his daughter; she sailed on my ship for many days, and her presence blessed the very boards she trod on. She is a most noble lady; and if you will not admit, sir, that her sweet spirit and pure soul have not banished from this earth every taint of wickedness left here by her father, then, sir, bedad, stand where you are and draw!"

THE END

A Note About the Author

Frank R. Stockton (1834–1902) was an American novelist and short story writer who became popular during the late nineteenth century. Born in Philadelphia to religious parents, writing wasn't viewed as a respectable or sustainable career. Despite objections, Stockton worked as a wood engraver before joining a local newspaper. He also worked at several magazines including *Hearth and Home*. Stockton became known for his children's stories such as *Ting-a-Ling Tales* (1870) and *The Floating Prince* (1881). His most famous title, *The Lady, or the Tiger?*, is often the lead entry in his short story collections.

A Note from the Publisher

Spanning many genres, from non-fiction essays to literature classics to children's books and lyric poetry, Mint Edition books showcase the master works of our time in a modern new package. The text is freshly typeset, is clean and easy to read, and features a new note about the author in each volume. Many books also include exclusive new introductory material. Every book boasts a striking new cover, which makes it as appropriate for collecting as it is for gift giving. Mint Edition books are only printed when a reader orders them, so natural resources are not wasted. We're proud that our books are never manufactured in excess and exist only in the exact quantity they need to be read and enjoyed.

bookfinity™

Discover more of your favorite classics with Bookfinity™.

- Track your reading with custom book lists.
- Get great book recommendations for your personalized Reader Type.
- Add reviews for your favorite books.
- AND MUCH MORE!

Visit **bookfinity.com** and take the fun Reader Type quiz to get started.

Enjoy our classic and modern companion pairings!

Classic & Modern

Printed in the USA
CPSIA information can be obtained
at www.ICGtesting.com
JSHW022322140824
68134JS00019B/1241

9 781513 277578